Carol Shields Constance Rooke

Alice

Whalley

Janice Kulyk Keefer

Paul

Jane Rule

Judith Thompson

Kristjana

Sandra Birdsell Marian Bradford Fraser

John Steffler AJ Diamond

Alice Munro Guy Vanderhaeghe

WRITING HOME
A PEN Canada Anthology

Edited by

CONSTANCE ROOKE

M&S

Canadian Cataloguing in Publication Data

Main entry under title:
Writing home

ISBN 0-7710-6961-8

1. Canadian prose literature (English) – 20th century.* 2. Authors, Canadian
(English) – Homes and haunts – Canada.* 3. Home – Literary collections.
I. Rooke, Constance, 1942 – . II. International P.E.N. Canadian Centre.

PS8367.H6W74 1997 C818'.540808'0355 C97-930560-8
PR9197.28.H6W74 1997

Typesetting by M&S, Toronto

The publishers acknowledge the support of the Canada Council and the Ontario
Arts Council for their publishing program.

All written material is the property of its respective contributor. Photographs,
unless otherwise credited, are the property of the authors.

No written material or photographs may be reproduced without permission.

Printed and bound in Canada

McClelland & Stewart Inc.
The Canadian Publishers
481 University Avenue
Toronto, Ontario
M5G 2E9

1 2 3 4 5 01 00 99 98 97

Contents

Introduction

by

Constance Rooke, Editor

The title came first. We called the last book *Writing Away*, and when it was determined that it should have a sequel, it became hard to resist one called *Writing Home*.

Writing Away was a travel anthology in which thirty-four of Canada's most celebrated authors wrote about places that were (usually) far away; our first thought, not surprisingly, was that *Writing Home* should be a kind of travel book in which our contributors would take on their Canadian (or other) home places. But the idea of *home* was so beguiling, so insistent as a subject in itself, that the invitation became more open. They could write anything at all about "home," anything from an account of a childhood place to a meditation on the meaning of home. Houses or land, our country or some small piece of it, family or friends or community – anything having to do with home. Just home, please, whatever that conjures up for you.

The attraction of *Writing Away* as a title had partly to do with the idea of "away" as a direction in which writing points. But if that is one pole for the energy of writing, surely home is its other. We yearn both ways. "Away" and "home" are the destinations of writing, the places we get to inside ourselves through writing and also through reading. It's more than a matter of representation: Saskatoon alive on the page when we're reading or writing in Paris, or the other way around. It's the energy of desire, wherever we may happen to sit, the getting there, wherever it seems our spirits are meant to be. Places, whether home or away, are largely metaphors for that; and writing is the trip, the getting closer – and closer – through words.

The words "writing away" and "writing home" have a special relevance to writers in prison, those conscientious objectors to some part of the world as it is, who are the people this book is intended to benefit. These men and women didn't like something they saw. Or they had their own, quite different ideas about home, and spoke to that. They wrote in ways that governments of the day thought inappropriate, unhelpful, a danger to the public good or their own sway. And so these writers were seized. Some are being tortured; others are being killed, or at risk of being killed. All are hidden away, deprived of home and freedom.

PEN is an international organization of writers, editors, and publishers whose self-appointed task it is to remember them and struggle for their release. We write to these prisoners, and also to their keepers, to exert pressure, to say that the world is watching. We say to our fellow writers, the ones consigned to prison, that the writing community at large has not forgotten them. PEN doesn't judge the value of any particular imagining of home; it asserts the right to imagine, the right to see – and write – by one's own lights. We assert the right of "writing home" according to the dictates not of dictators, but of one's own heart and mind.

The Canadian chapter of PEN is one of the most active in the world. We write hard to bring our brothers and sisters home, to set them free. And we need money to do this, money (for example) to barrage the jail-masters with thousands of letters, and phone calls, and faxes. Purchasers of *Writing Home* will have the satisfaction of knowing that all proceeds from the sale of this book will go to support PEN Canada's vital work on behalf of free speech and writers around the world. As with *Writing Away*, all contributions to this book have been donated by their authors. And once again, Avie Bennett and the other remarkable people of McClelland & Stewart have chosen to maximize the return to PEN by donating the company's labour. (*Writing Away* has to date earned more than $150,000 for PEN.)

In *Writing Home*, readers will find a number of recurrent motifs and concerns, ranging from vital links between writing and home, to the spectre of Quebec's separation, to the Cottage (or Cabin) as our ur-Canadian home. Readers are escorted to dense urban neighbourhoods, deep woods, and villages; they see a constellation made up of particular people (like lights) creating for one author a far-flung map of home. Rooted childhoods and rootless ones are laid out; homes are built, imagined, lost, or belatedly discovered.

Repeatedly, as if the security associated with the idea of "home" necessarily summons up its opposite, we find expressions of vulnerability. This may take a political or a geological or a metaphysical shape. There are also celebrations of home, and riffs on the idea of home. Houses feature prominently, often in ways that suggest the connection of the house with the persona, a constructed shell surrounding the furniture of the self. Or the house may be connected with the body. Outside this body, beyond its walls, is nature, into which, at last, we will dissolve. And for a number of the authors assembled here, the landscape itself is home.

A few last words. Only one of the pieces in *Writing Home* has appeared in print before – and even that one, by Rohinton Mistry, has been altered for the occasion. (It was, in the editor's view, too apposite – and too lovely – to exclude.) Some of the invited contributors found they had to withdraw, and some pieces turned out to be shorter than anticipated; for this reason, I have ventured something of my own. I regret the absence of francophone Quebeckers, and that only one of the Native Canadians I approached was able, in the end, to contribute. I wish also to thank fervently on PEN's behalf all of the contributors who gave so generously of their time and talents: Esta Spalding, who (once again) helped all along the way; my wonderful secretary at the University of Guelph, Julia Beswick; and the great people of McClelland & Stewart: Avie Bennett, for being willing and eager to do it again; Ellen Seligman, who saw *Writing Home* through the press with her usual panache; Sharon Bailey, Peter Buck, Tania Charzewski, Rudy Mezzetta, Sharmila Mohammed, Kong Njo, Krystyna Ross, Heather Sangster, and the numerous others in the sales, promotion, and distribution departments, whose efforts are greatly appreciated.

No Port Now

In the ancient struggle of breath against death, one more sleep given.
We took an offer on the house.
In the sum of the parts
where are the parts?
Silently (there) leaves and windows wait.
Our empty clothesline cuts the sloping night.
And making their lament for a lost apparel of celestial light
angles and detritus call out as they flow past our still latched gate.

– *Anne Carson*

Approximate Homes

~

1. Down Home

Down home, they would say, although what they meant was north on the map. I used to wonder – why was home always down? Nobody ever said *up home*. But now I know: home is down the way memory is down, and hidden springs of water. Derelict cities, abandoned bones, lost keys.

Home is buried. You have to dig for it.

2. The Home for Incurable Children

In one of my phases of being a child, which took place in Toronto at the end of the forties, there was a building called The Home for Incurable Children.

We make fun of our predecessors for their euphemisms, but in fact these were mostly for sex. In other matters they were blunt in their labelling to the point of crudeness. Thus we once had The Provincial Lunatic Asylum: no beating about the bush there. And orphans were put into orphanages. Everything in its place.

The Home for Incurable Children was made of brownish-red brick, and was grim. There was the sign with its name in big black letters, right on the lawn. There on the lawn, too, in summer, were the incurable children, dressed usually in white, sitting usually in chairs, wan and set apart – a warning to us other children. If we became for some reason incurable, would we too be put in there? And where were the mummies and daddies?

These children, we were told in sad adult voices, would never grow up. We did not confuse this state with what we knew about Peter Pan. In fact, The Home for Incurable Children made growing up seem a more desirable thing than perhaps it was, and we became very anxious to do it.

Once I'd managed to escape from childhood as far as high school, The Home for Incurable Children still obsessed me. It was the name: I could see it contained a swarm of meanings. Did "incurable children" mean those who could not be cured of being children? Was it childhood itself that was the disease? And "home" – why call it a home, when everyone knew it wasn't a real home at all, but, like "homes for the elderly," the exact opposite? If such places really were homes, what a sinister and quicksand twist it gave the word!

A home wasn't where the heart was, but where it wasn't. It was where you were stuck when nobody wanted you. *Home* was the name for longing.

3. *A House Is Not a Home*

It was little girls who taught me the game called "playing house." It was never called "playing home." The real-estate ads always say "home," not "house," but little girls are the reverse. For them, the house comes first.

My brother was no good at this game. His idea of the thing was a sand house, or better still a fortress, which we would then drop rocks on. Occasionally he would go so far as to play Baby to my doting Mother, but only in order to scream and demand things. I quickly saw that with him I was better off as part of a bombing squadron.

The little girls however knew houses backwards and forwards. The cupboards will be here, this will be the table, these are the beds; here is where we do the ironing, this is the stove, over there can be the sink. Such talk would go on for some time. Then, finally, everything would be in order; and then what?

It was the *and then what* I had trouble with. The other little girls would solve the problem by serving a meal or having someone fall ill, but these were not enough for me; because after the meal must come the washing of the dishes, and then another meal, and after the illness must come a cure; and after the cure, then another meal or another illness, and then what?

Playing house, so comforting for other little girls, caused a great deal more anxiety for me than it was worth. Faced with those dolly teacups, those plates made of leaves, that cutlery of twigs, those relentless cupboards, tables, and beds, in endless variations and proliferations but always essentially the same – how much more desirable it seemed to reduce them to rubble with a few well-placed sticks of dynamite.

At least it would be an end. At least, then, you would know.

4. Home Free

Long ago, before television and the fears of their parents had drawn them indoors, children used to stay out after supper. In the late-spring evenings, humid and dense and smelling of lilacs and mowed lawns, they would play in groups and gangs and mobs, in the streets and in and out of their yards, and in vacant lots and on beaches – long, intricate, exciting, tedious, and inexplicable games.

Here is one we played. It was called "Kick the Can." You needed a can – a tomato juice can, big size, was about right. It had to be large enough to make a clanging noise when kicked. A home space would be marked out, drawn with a stick in the dirt; the can would be placed on its frontier. An It was chosen, who had to guard both home space and can. The other children would run tantalizingly near; if tagged they were caught, and imprisoned in the home, where they had to stay, held by invisible walls, sneering and jumping up and down and licking the blood from their scraped elbows. But if a free child could run close enough to kick the can, there would be a general escape.

When almost all had been caught and were locked into home, the It could go further afield in search of prey; but if the last remaining free one could sneak into the home space untagged, and yell *Home free!*, the power of the It was shattered and all enchantments broken, and the game was over.

The home space – how odd it was! A precious thing, to be guarded; also a dungeon. You didn't want to be kept in it against your will, yet it was bliss to enter it when forbidden, sliding in, skidding in, throwing yourself in, and shrieking at the top of your lungs: *Home free!* What a relief, what a triumph! And what a triumph also to kick the tomato juice can, so that everyone could run away from home. Well, it was more or less how we felt about our real homes: ours to claim when we wanted them, ours to be trapped in, ours to escape from.

I may have got the rules wrong though; I may have mixed them up with some other game. It was quite a long time ago now.

5. *The Consumers' Gas "Miss Future Homemaker Contest"*

The fifties was the age of contests: contests for teenaged girls. I once met someone who had been Miss Wool, and who'd had to wear an itchy wardrobe and carry around a live lamb, which peed on her. A friend of mine was once Miss Vodka, which was more dangerous as it involved a clutch of middle-aged men who'd been testing the product. She leapt from a moving convertible, and quit.

The Consumers' Gas "Miss Future Homemaker Contest" was less hazardous. It was held during the Home Show. You had to iron a shirt with a gas iron, cook a dinner on a gas stove, and do a third thing involving gas, which I have repressed. Myself and my partner – was it you, Sally? – were chosen as the entrants from our high school Home Economics class. In this class we were learning to be homemakers, or else – like our teacher, who was a Miss and whose hobby was skiing – we were learning to teach other girls to be them.

By the year of the contest we were quite advanced. We'd progressed from sewing aprons to sewing whole outfits, with box pleats and interfacing and dressmaker buttonholes; we'd gone from applesauce to balanced meals with each food group represented. I do not jeer at such knowledge. I shudder to think how many young girls now are hurled into life without it, and are forced to read magazines. The making of a choux paste is a skill I retain, though seldom use. They were not called choux then, however, but cream puffs. As I said, it was the fifties.

For the Miss Future Homemaker Contest, Sally and I dressed neatly and wore aprons; homemakers were supposed to be very clean and efficient. The menu for the dinner was pre-set: meat loaf, frozen peas, baked potatoes. There was a time limit – how fast you could get the shirt wrinkle-free and slide the meat loaf out of the oven. (This aspect of it I found hilarious. The husband marches in from the office, left right left right. Off with the old wrinkly shirt, on with the newly pressed one, and Hup! over to the table. Whomp! goes the meat loaf onto his plate! Blop! goes the baked potato! Pitter-patter go the peas! And now, for the third thing involving gas. . . .)

Sally and I were speedy, but we didn't win, although we each received a charm bracelet with little golden bells on it. Perhaps the judges detected my lack of sincerity; but did they really think that I thought that this rushing about in aprons with gas appliances had anything to do with real life? Not mine, that was for sure; I wasn't going to end up making any homes! Not me.

I did make some, though. Several of them. I once knitted a whole bedspread, if you can believe it. I once put up two dozen jars of mustard pickle. I once baked bread.

6. Home Land

I don't have a home town, but I have a home land. A chunk of pink granite sticking out of the ground, a kettle bog, a horizon line of ragged black spruce: ah! there you are! Home!

I'm most at home in an airplane, a thousand feet up, skimming over the taiga at one remove. Lake, lake, lake, swamp, sprinkle of low hills, twist of river; ice creeping out from the shores. It has to be big, though; rocky, sparse, a place you could find yourself lost in easy as pie, and walk around in circles and die of exposure. Me too, you understand; when it comes to home, I'm no expert.

Out the window, way down there: desolation, instant panic, slow starvation. With a view like that you can feel comfortable.

7. No Home Town

Between 1936 and 1948 my parents moved twenty times. Sometimes between two fixed points – to a city in the late fall, to the forest in the early spring; sometimes it was from one city to another. My mother and father were from Nova Scotia, and that was *home* to them. But it wasn't where I was. So where was I?

Here and there, but never both at once. Home was not a place but a trajectory; it was the dotted line that marked our trail. It would appear out of boxes and suitcases, be packed away, appear again in a different form, in a different room, after a long and uncomfortable journey, hundreds of miles in the back of a car stuffed full of bundles and packages, then on the bottom of a canoe with the rain dribbling down your neck or on a sleigh drawn by horses over the creaking ice. You couldn't count on home. You couldn't count on it to stay put.

What has become of them, those provisional homes – the second-floor apartment in Ottawa with its long dark hallways, and the French Canadian and the English Canadian who lived below, and were always squabbling, and were married to each other? Or the drafty mansion in Sault Ste. Marie, which was falling apart and stood in a field of cabbages, with the hole in the ceiling through which we dropped crayons onto the stove to melt in puddles of smelly colour? Or the one house that was torn down, or the other one that burned down; or the tent whose roof you weren't supposed to touch for fear of leaks? That tent had no floor, and the mice always got in; they knew a good home when they saw it.

We're almost home now, they would say, in the middle of the rainstorm or the middle of the night, whichever was darker, and that was always the best part of home: the moment before

Margaret Atwood outside a motel
on her eighth birthday

lamplight. Home was something that was constantly being approached but could never be reached, because we'd left it days ago, we'd locked the door and hidden the key, and it was already behind us. It's not only that you can't go home again, you can never get there in the first place.

Here we are – home at last! they would say; though home had no location, only a direction: *homeward*. And yet we went on – we go on – believing we are there.

Why I Live Where I Live

~

I live in the Red River Valley. I grew up in a small prairie town, moved on, and lived in several others. You know the type: one grain elevator, railroad tracks, abandoned train station, general store, and a curling rink with eight sheets of artificial ice. The kind of place about which people say that if you blink when you drive by, you'll miss it. Now I live in Winnipeg, and I suppose some may say the same comment applies. But these are just tourists skimming across the valley in their boats or trolling with empty hooks. Valley, they say. Where are the hills?

True, one must travel far to find them – but they're here. Comforting little brown humps on the shoreline. Why do I continue to live here in Winnipeg in the Red River Valley? It's God in a CBC T-shirt, calling to make me think.

I've contemplated moving to Vancouver, where they tell me that the difference between Vancouver and Toronto is that in Toronto people dress up in bizarre costumes and pretend they're crazy, while in Vancouver they really are crazy. I don't mind the crazy people in Vancouver. They're like wildflowers on the side of a mountain, pretty to look at from a distance but never meant to be picked and taken home. But I find when I'm in Vancouver that

Emerging author (rear, left) surrounded by four of
her ten siblings, Manitoba, 1948

after three days I no longer see the mountains. All I want to do is
find a quiet place, huddle down in the sand, and stare at the
ocean. And the same thing happens to me when I'm on the east
coast. Why do I live here?

I ask a friend. Grasshoppers and crickets sing from either side
of the dirt road. It's not quite a full moon but bright enough for
long shadows. Perfect night to play Dracula. It's my turn to wear
the cape. The question eats at me, interferes with the game. On
the horizon Winnipeg shimmers pink and still. You live here, he
says, because you're short. You're close to the ground and if a big
wind should come along you'd be safe. And yet you feel tall. Naw,
that's not it, my daughter says.

It's Sunday, and the question rankles as I make my weekly trip
through the forest where thick dark trees wrestle the granite

boulders for soil. I push the speed limit to get to the lake before all the others, and finally I find my spot, huddle down into the sand, and stare out across the water. I think: Why do I live here? The answer comes to me. It's because when I live in the Red River Valley, I'm living at the bottom of a lake.

When you live at the bottom of a lake you get cracks in your basement walls, especially in River Heights, where they can afford cracks and underpinning and new basements. I like the cracks. The wind whistles through them, loosens the lids on my peach preserves, makes the syrup ferment, and the mice get tipsy. In the potato bin, sprouts grow on wrinkled skin, translucent, cool sprouts. They climb up the basement walls, push their way through air vents and up the windows in my kitchen. I don't have to bother about hanging curtains.

And time is different here. The days piled on top of lake sediments shift after a good storm so that yesterday slips out from beneath today. Or even last Friday with all its voices will bob up from the bottom and it's possible to lose track of tomorrow. You can just say to hell with tomorrow and go out and play Dracula.

When you live here at the bottom of a lake you can't pin your ancestors down with granite monuments. They slide out of their graves. They work themselves across the underground on their backs using their heels as leverage, they inch their way back into town until they rest beneath the network of dusty roads, and they lie there on their backs and read stories to you from old newspapers.

Now, this is something tourists can never discover as they roar across the valley in their powerboats, churning up the water with their blink-and-you'll-miss-it view of my place. Sometimes a brave one will leap from the boat, come down, and move in next door. I've seen it happen. They become weak and listless, like flies trapped inside a house at the end of summer. And you'll see them

Delena Mozer

walking along the highway in scuba gear muttering to themselves or rowing across the lake in search of a hill. I'll admit, sometimes it's nice to surface, to take off the cape and put on my respectable prairie jacket and boots and do a walking tour of Halifax, sniff a wild mountain flower in Vancouver, get a stiff neck looking up at all those skyscrapers in Toronto, or a three-day party headache in Montreal. But inevitably my eyes grow tired, glazed, and like a sleepwalker I awake to find myself crouched down beside an ocean, a lake, a river, and I know it's time to get back there – to get down in the basement and breathe the wind in the cracks of my walls where, nestled up against the foundation of my house, is the pelvic bone of an ancestor.

WAYSON CHOY

The Ten Thousand Things

~

for Jacob and Alice Zilber, and for Kitty Wilson-Pote

"I SAW YOUR MOTHER LAST WEEK."

The stranger's voice on the phone surprised me. She spoke firmly, clearly, with the accents of Vancouver's Old Chinatown: "I saw your *mah-ma* on the streetcar."

Not possible. Mother died nineteen years ago.

Nineteen years ago I had sat on a St. Paul's hospital bed beside her skeletal frame, while the last cells of her lungs clogged up. She lay gasping for breath: the result of decades of smoking. I stroked her forehead, and with my other hand I clasped her thin motionless fingers. Around two in the morning, half asleep and weary, I closed my eyes to catnap. Suddenly, the last striving for breath shook her thin body. I snapped awake, conscious again of the smell of acetone, of death burning away her body. The silence deepened; the room chilled. The mother I had known all my life was gone.

Nineteen years later, in response to a lively radio interview about my first novel, a woman left a mysterious message, URGENT WAYSON CHOY CALL THIS NUMBER.

Back at my hotel room, message in hand, I dialled the number and heard an older woman's voice tell me she had seen my mother on the streetcar. She insisted.

"You must be mistaken," I said, confident that this woman, her voice charged with nervous energy, would recognize her error and sign off.

"No, no, not your mother," the voice persisted. "I mean your *real* mother."

"My first crazy," I remember thinking. *The Jade Peony* had been launched just two days before at the Vancouver Writers' Festival, and already I had a crazy. "Watch out for the crazies!" my agent had, half-whimsically, warned me. The crazies had declared open season upon another of her clients, a young woman who had written frankly of sexual matters. I was flattered, hardly believing that my novel about Vancouver's Old Chinatown could provoke such perverse attention. Surely, my caller was simply mistaken.

"I saw your *real* mother," the voice insisted, repeating the word "real" as if it were an incantation.

My *real* mother? I looked down at the polished desk, absently studied the Hotel Vancouver room-service menu. My real mother was dead; I had been there to witness her going. I had come home that same morning nineteen years ago and seen her flowered apron carefully draped over the kitchen chair, folded precisely, as it had been every day of my life. I remember taking the apron, quickly hiding it from my father's eyes as he, in his pyjamas, shuffled on his cane into the kitchen. Seeing the apron missing from the chair, he asked, "She's –?" but could not finish the question. He stood staring at the back of the chair. He leaned his frail eighty-plus years against me. Speechless, I led him back to his bed.

The voice on the hotel phone chattered on, spilling out details and relationships, talking of Pender *Gai* and noting how my brand-new book talked of the "secrets of Chinatown." I suddenly caught my family name pronounced distinctively and correctly, *Tuey*. Then my grandfather's, my mother's, and my father's formal Chinese names, rarely heard, sang into my consciousness over the earpiece.

"Yes, yes," the voice went on, "those are your family names?"

"Yes, they are," I answered, "but who are you?"

"Call me Hazel," she said.

Months later, Hazel turned up to be interviewed; we had tea, some dumplings, and bowls of *jook*. In 1939, when she herself was in her teens, Hazel had taken care of a baby named *Way Sun*. Her family home had been a kind of short-term foster home for in-transit Chinatown children. It was 1939, the year of the Royal Visit, and Hazel's own mother had desperately wanted to see the King and Queen parade down Hastings and Granville streets.

"That's why I remember your name," Hazel said. She proved to be a friendly, talkative woman in her late sixties, wisps of grey hair floating about her. "Unusual name, *Way Sun*. Your new mother worried that you wouldn't have a birth certificate."

"But I have one," I insisted.

"That was because *my* mother was a midwife," Hazel said. "My mother told the government clerk you born at home." She sipped from her teacup and laughed. "What do they know? What do they care?" Her eyes sparkled with memory. "Those old days! Here was a China baby, just a few weeks old! They maybe think, things done differently in Chinatown! Anyway, nobody care about one more China baby! Everybody worry about the war."

A few months before Hazel and I met, I had cornered my two aunts, to whom I had dedicated my book. Was I adopted, I wanted to know, as Hazel had told me? My two aunts looked at each other. In an interview with me, the reporter from *Maclean's* magazine had noted that "a caller" had left me perplexed about my birth. Surely Aunt Freda and Aunt Mary knew the truth.

I had written a novel about the secrets of Chinatown, and in the kaleidoscope of my life, one single phone call had altered the picture significantly, shifted all the pieces: my life held secrets, too. This real-life drama beginning to unfold, this eerie echo of the life of one of my fictional characters, seemed absurd. Suddenly, nothing of my family, of home, seemed solid and specific. Nothing in my past seemed to be what it had always been.

During the Depression and the War years, the trading and selling of children, especially the giving and taking of male children, were not uncommon practices either of Old China or of the Old Chinatowns of North America. Canada's 1923 Exclusion Act and similar racist laws passed earlier in the United States all forbade the immigration of Chinese women and children. Thus, there were only limited numbers of Chinese families in North America. Chinatowns became social and sexual pressure cookers; bachelor-men dominated the population. Children were being born, wanted and unwanted. Scandals and suicides multiplied. Family joys were balanced by family suffering.

In the hothouse climate of Vancouver's Chinatown in the 1920s, '30s, and mid-'40s, children were born and kept mainly within their own families, or family tongs; however, a secret few were sold, traded, or given away to fill a childless couple's empty nest, or to balance a family that lacked a first-born son to carry on their kinship name; family pride and Confucian tradition demanded a son to inherit the family artefacts. And so, I must have been sold, traded, or given away to balance my adoptive parents' empty nest. I was to be the only child, a son, heir to the family name and worldly goods.

My adopted parents had both died, believing that I would never discover that they were not my birth parents, that my memory of home had been fraudulent in a sense, lovingly fraudulent. Now the truth was trickling out. The ground shifted under me. Was it true? Was I adopted?

At the airport restaurant where we spoke, my two aunts looked sheepishly at each other, and then, eyes full of loving concern, they turned to look at me. I said nothing. At last, Freda confessed, "Yes, yes, you are adopted." Mary quickly added, "So what? To me, you're just as much a part of our family."

"You're even better than that!" Freda laughed. "You were chosen. We just got born into the damn family!"

I didn't laugh. Hearing them confirm Hazel's claim made me pause: all those years that I had taken "home" for granted. . . . A long drawn-out sigh escaped from me: I had become an orphan three weeks before my fifty-seventh birthday. I glanced at the date registered on my watch.

"Tomorrow is April Fool's Day," I finally said, voice maudlin. Then, barely able to contain ourselves, we all three burst out laughing.

"Life has no beginning . . . nor ending." The man whom I thought was my father had said this to me three days before he died. "Good things go on being good," he said, sighing that long sigh that I had learned from him. "Bad things go on being bad."

Unlike the woman whom I had thought was my mother, the man whom I'd taken for my father was not afraid to talk of other mysteries and losses, of life past, and even of his own eventual dying that summer's end at St. Paul's Hospital.

In this hospital, throughout the '30s, the nuns had lobbied the city fathers and the health authorities to admit the people of Chinatown into its ill-lit, mildewed basement. In this hospital, the Chinese and other undesirables – "Resident Aliens" – were to be nursed back to health or to die there, at least in the care of God's holy servants. *His* father died there, in the basement; and in September of 1982, the man I had known as *my* father ended his life, at eighty-five, of a stomach cancer he accepted as the last indignity.

He stayed, not in the basement, but in a sixth-floor bed that looked over the West End, in a newly built wing of St. Paul's, in a room that was flooded with morning light, free of dampness and mildew. His eyes had grown too cloudy to see anything but light. I rubbed his back with mineral oil, his skin like a baby's. He barely smiled. He had been happy to greet my friend Marie, who had flown in from Toronto to be with both of us. That last evening, with Marie's gentle encouragement, he accepted from me a spoonful of fruit salad. He took into his dry mouth a seedless grape, but would not swallow.

The next morning at eight o'clock, when he died, a torrential rainstorm lashed the city. Marie, so beloved of my father, touched my father's stiff hands and brought them together. As his only son, I kissed his still-warm forehead and marvelled at life and death.

I did not know then that he was not my *real* father; I only knew that this old man – whose outward frailty betrayed the tough spirit within – was the man I had loved as my father all my life. There was no other.

Since hearing from Hazel, I have thought often of the Chinese phrase "the ten thousand things," whose number symbolically suggests how countless are the ways of living and dying, how much of love and life cannot be fathomed. And I have thought of the Cantonese opera.

"My Aunt Helena says that your father was a member of one of the opera companies," Hazel told me, much later, in her young-again, excited voice.

On my behalf, Hazel had been earnestly digging up as much information from the Elders as she could. She had already learned that the person she thought was my *real* mother, the old woman she saw on the streetcar, was not my real mother after all. She, it turns out, had died decades ago. And, yes, the man who fathered me was a member of one of the opera companies. Alas, there was no more information; at least, no more was revealed by the Elders. Not even Mrs. Lee, a best friend of my adoptive parents, would admit she knew anything. So much you can know, and no more.

For the past two years, long before Hazel's first telephone call sent her seismic quake through my world, I had been, ironically, researching the Cantonese Opera, especially the touring Chinese opera companies that had thrived all through the '30s and '40s from Canton to Hong Kong, from San Francisco to Seattle to Vancouver, the semi-professional companies that formed "the Bamboo Circuit." My second novel, the one I'm writing now, is centred around the Vancouver opera companies of Old Chinatown.

Since childhood, I had been enthralled with the high drama and acrobatics of Chinese opera. The woman who was known to me as my mother had taken me to see the operas and then, afterwards, to visit Shanghai Alley and the smoky backstage of the opera company. There, among jewelled headpieces, gleaming costumes, and prop curtains, she played mah-jong with members of the troop, while I was being spoiled by sweetmeats or left alone to play with costumed opera dolls with fierce warrior faces. Alone, I became a prince and a warrior, my parents the Emperor and Empress. All the adventures of the world were possible, and I the hero of them all. Finally, I remember the laughter and sing-song voices, the *clack-click* of the bamboo and ivory game tiles, lulling me to sleep.

Even today I recall, as a child, dreaming of the fabled opera costumes, how they swirled to glittering life, how I flew acrobatically through the air between spinning red banners and clouds of yellow silk and heard the roar and clanging of drums and cymbals. And how I fought off demons and ghosts to great applause. Were those dreams in my blood?

"The way things were in those old days," Hazel said, pushing back a strand of her salt-and-pepper hair, "best to let the old stories rest. Your father belonged to the opera company, that's what my Aunt Helena says."

For the past two summers, I had pored over the tinted cast and production photos of the opera companies in Vancouver. For intense seconds, without realizing it, I must have caught a smile, a glimpse of a hairline as familiar as my own; I must have seen eyes looking back through the photographer's plates, eyes like my own: I might have seen, staring back at me, the man who surely was my father. I cannot help myself: I imagine the man who fathered me, dressed in imperial splendour, sword in hand; he is flying above me, majestic and detached. If I were seventeen, and not fifty-seven, would I weep to know that this man abandoned me?

"Best to let the stories rest," Hazel repeated.

And so I do. I let the stories rest, though not quite. My writer's mind races on, unstoppable. I had always thought of my family, my home, in such a solid, no-nonsense, no-mystery manner, how could I possibly think that the untold stories would never be told?

I think of myself as the child I was, playing with the fierce-faced dolls among the backstage wooden swords and stretched drums of the opera company. I see myself, five years old, being watched and wondered at by a tall figure behind me, a figure who

The Vancouver Chinatown
photograph that verified Toy and
Lily Choy as the parents of three-
month-old Wayson Choy, 1939

slips away if I turn my head towards him. Was that the man who
fathered me? And perhaps a woman – the birth mother – raises
her hand at the mah-jong table and smiles at me, briefly noting
how blessed my life now seems. How lucky I am, to share the
fate of the man and woman I came to know as Mother and
Father, decent and good people, who, all my life, loved me as
their own.

I marvel that the ten thousand things should raise questions I
never thought to ask, should weave abiding mystery into my life.
How did most of us come to think of parents and family and home,
as if there were no mysteries, really? How did most of us contrive
for decades to speak neither of the unknown nor of the knowable?
And how, with the blessing of a community that knew when to

keep silent and when – at last – to speak up, I am come home again, like a child, opened up again to dreams and possibility.

At home, I turn on my computer to begin tapping out the second novel; in the middle of a sentence – like this one, in fact – I laugh aloud. I had been writing fiction about life in Chinatown; Chinatown, all these years, had been writing me.

The Oven Bird

~

I have no home. The place where I was born, where I lived with my family, was taken away from me when the Japanese army invaded and conquered Hong Kong in December 1941. With that historical event, we lost our house on Broome Road, above the Happy Valley Race Track, the house where I was born, the house with the roof terrace where my brother and I played with the baby chicks and rabbits dyed red for New Year's, which always fell around my birthday in February.

In losing my home, I have always known instinctively that nothing is truly permanent, that loss can be a state of being, but that there is a liberation in knowing that you can't go home again. Not to a home with white clapboard and green shutters and a lawn and a dog called Skippy on a street where everyone knows you in a town where your parents went to high school. So I've become addicted to making nests and atmospheres wherever I am – obsessed with the right colours for the light in Georgian Bay, the perfect drop of cotton curtains in French windows, the perennial cycle of the garden in downtown Toronto. It must be exactly right, the light of the rooms I live in, the texture framing windows, the splendour of flowers cultivated, because they are all

I've ever had of "home," which I carry as an idea, a fossil within me. When I travel, however briefly, to a new place, I peruse the real-estate ads, try to figure out the neighbourhoods from my rental car map, and, as I go about the city – Regina, San Francisco, Santiago – I fantasize about living in this house ("original Victorian restored with loving care, 3 BR, 2 fireplaces . . .") or that apartment. Even in places like North Africa, I imagine whether I would want to live in the *medina* or in the hilly suburbs in a white villa with purple bougainvillaea spilling over the walls. And as I walk in a strange city centre, I furnish this possible habitation with a rug, a chair – everything from that place, just as though I had suddenly been dropped there with only the clothes on my back, starting again. I look at the prices and, usually having some idea of what people earn from my guidebook or from the research of the program I'm shooting, I figure out what I could afford if I were working there. Every place is potentially where I might have to live, where fate might drop me down and say, "Live here, I dare you!"

But there is another aspect to the idea of home as well. Robert Frost said home was the place where, when you had to go there, they had to take you in. So if that's the case, Canada is my only home because it took us in, refugees, with no place to go but here, with one suitcase each, to whom Canada meant some business connections for my father and Neilson's chocolate for us children. Canada took us in when we were the casualties of someone else's victory, the victims of our own loss.

The home I was born to was the fruit of my young father's success – a house with terraces and a garden, close to the racecourse where he kept his own horses and rode them in flat races and steeplechases as a gentleman jockey. A house with an amah for each of the children, a cook, two maids, and a chauffeur. We were not extraordinarily rich, just Hong Kong pre-war middle class. My mother never entered the kitchen – the menus were discussed with the cook every morning, perhaps in the garden, where, the morning after the invasion, my mother saw Japanese soldiers in camouflage leap like large frogs through the shrubs.

My father, as a member of the Hong Kong volunteer militia, rushed off with his motorcycle when news came that the Japanese had invaded the New Territories, the mainland part of Hong Kong. They had been at a ball at the Repulse Bay Hotel; they loved dancing and there seems to have been a lot of it – dancing and beach parties and evenings of poker. I see them swaying to "The Lambeth Walk" or "The Lullaby of Broadway" as the hideous news comes. They rush home across the island in their Opel sedan and an hour later my father takes off on his BSA bike.

As the Japanese began to bomb the city, we fled the house on Broome Road, my mother, my brother, and I. We went first to my grandmother's, then we all fled together from basement to friends' houses, hiding, trying to keep safe. We ate from tins of Jacob's Cream Crackers. I am told I loved the sounds of the bombs and giggled and clapped while my mother clutched us. As a child, she had endured typhoons in Java and witnessed a tidal wave that left a freighter thrown across Des Voeux Road. She survived in icy numbed silence. I can feel her thin arms covering my head.

In these shelters, as we moved from place to place, the fighting went on around us. We did not know where my father was. He could have been dead. Or, as a Chinese fighting for the British, he might have been captured and suffered worse than death. My grandmother prayed in the darkness as the bombs fell; devoutly Anglican, she whispered the *Magnificat* and the *Nunc Dimittis* in Chinese. As we left one basement, after a heavy spell of bombing, we saw the body of a man spread-eagled against the outside wall, his head turned without a neck, both eyes visible to one side of his flattened face. In another basement where we had been for several days, drunken Japanese soldiers broke in, looking for women. My mother was hidden in a closet with my brother; I played on the floor and my grandmother convinced them that we were alone there and that I was a homeless orphan she had taken in.

Somewhere above us, the war went on – for two and a half weeks. This is a long time when you have fled your home and your belongings and are moving by night as a tiny group of women and children, and bombs are falling all around you. When the British and Canadians surrendered and the occupation was a reality, my father found us. He had escaped as soon as he knew that the Japanese had won. He had been to Broome Road and had seen the remains of my mother's grand piano on which she played Chopin nocturnes chopped up and partially used as firewood, the linen sheets and embroidered Swatow tablecloths soiled as toilet paper. He had salvaged a few things: photographs of himself riding into the winner's circle, some 8-mm film of us taken with his Bell and Howell camera, my bronzed first boots with one sole ripped off where looters thought money might be hidden. My brother asked about our dog, Snow White, the silvery Russian Borzoi my father had brought back from a business trip to Manchuria; she had been with us for the first few days of the war, but then we could no longer feed her. When she came to us one day with human entrails hanging from her mouth, we left her behind.

Now we were homeless but occupied. Every ritual of humiliation had to be undergone. The population was ordered out to the streets on Boxing Day to witness the Victory Parade of the conquerors. My mother tied my brother and me to her waist with ropes; we were herded out onto the street in the North Point area. The Japanese army paraded by, as we were made to kneel in the streets, the officers on horseback carrying, between their hands on the stirrups, little lacquered boxes containing the ashes of their dead comrades.

Several days later, the streets became a kind of flea market where the population's belongings which had been looted were sold on the street. The black-market survivors' economy was already in operation, but my mother and father had no currency to buy back their wedding silver, their two sets of china – Minton for European services, *famille rose* for Chinese – or the Tienstin rugs woven specially for the drawing room.

Of course, I do not "remember" all this consciously; I was two and a half years old. But I was absorbed by it; it is the placenta of my rebirth. The visceral knowledge of being uprooted is part of my every heartbeat; it is there in the silence when I can almost hear my blood flow. It leaps toward the people I see in the news with the open unseeing eyes fleeing bombs in Sarajevo or floods in Bangladesh. Frost's poem about home being the place where they have to take you in is about a tramp – an archetypally home-less person. But all the homeless are alike. They don't have a home until somebody offers to take them in. I look at someone wearing a number or lining up to get a visa, and I see myself. It was Canada that let us in, at a time when Orientals weren't allowed to immigrate to Canada. But we waited on a dock in the blazing sun with one suitcase apiece and, somehow, someone Canadian let us in. One Canadian said, "What are these people doing here? They're Chinese; we can't take them." But another Canadian turned on him and said, "Don't be a horse's ass. We're taking them." And so Canada became the place we had to go to.

And once we got here, there were people who made us feel welcome in the cold, white, snowy Ottawa of 1942 – mostly French Canadians like the Marcottes and the Proulxs and the Saint-Denis, a Jewish pharmacist's family, the Molots, and all our public-school teachers. The gift of a cast-iron frying pan, some cooking lessons, picnics together, going by streetcar to Rockcliffe Park or Britannia Beach. So that even if home was gone forever, the idea of being "at home" became possible. And Canada, the whole country, its spaces, its rocks, its trees, its unbearable beauty, its disheartening sullenness and ridiculous self-indulgence, is where I am most at home. It was here that I was taken in and here that I learned, like Frost's oven bird, "what to make of a diminished thing."

JACK DIAMOND

Tree House

~

Tom was the first gardener of my childhood. A Zulu with a beard
and lively eyes, but too dark really, too tall and angular for a Zulu,
he could conjure snakes out of our garden at will. His method
next was to place the flat of a spade on the snake, with just its
head showing, and to dangle a jute sack in front of his prey, then
lift the spade. The snake would make a lunge for the bag, and the
trap would shut.

Periodically, whenever Tom needed the extra money, he would
present one of these snake bags to my mother. She would take it
from his hands, and immediately convey me and Tom's jute sack –
invisible contents writhing – out to Fitzsimmons Snake Park,
where they paid the handsome sum of two shillings a foot for
snakes. So that's where our snakes would live then. On our return
home, she would hand the money over and Tom would acknowledge her complicity with a small nod. Once, just before he disappeared from our lives, Tom caught a fourteen-foot black mamba
in the grenadilla bush. It was too big for the bag, and Tom had his
picture in the paper holding the mamba.

The grenadilla bush was where we had played house, before
Tom caught the mamba. After that, I needed a new place – and

because Tom was gone without a word, we needed a new gardener. Peter came: a safe man, dull and plodding, except that he
had lost one eye – I never found out how. I remember best his feet,
the flattest feet I ever saw, the soles cracked at the edges.

I could not have asked Tom to help me carry the raft I found
near the banana plantation, but I could ask Peter. I had no idea
who had left the raft there, or why it had been built. It was made
of planks nailed to a wattle pole frame, about five feet by seven.
Peter helped me carry it – I must have been nine or ten at the
time – to our house. He walked ahead of me, I carried the rear,
and we struggled on (I struggled on) for the mile or more
that separated the plantation from our garden, with the raft I
had to have.

With ropes, Peter helped me hoist the platform up into a large
pine tree, whose branches (I saw) were perfect: first to make flush
horizontal brackets for supporting my house, and second to make
the stairs I would need to climb up there. The rest I did alone.
Fixing short posts along the perimeter, I could then weave sticks,
basket-like, around three sides of my house. When I lay down in
my tree house, the first house of my own making, I was invisible
to anyone on the ground or to anyone in the house that before
this one had been my house.

The complete satisfaction I felt at this accomplishment has
stayed with me. I can still feel the pleasant burning sensation in
my palms – physical labour, the first I can remember – and the
exaltation that came because I had imagined and created this
place. I had been inspired, filled up with the idea of something
new in the world. This old raft, this pallet, had become because of
my hands and my decision something wonderful: a secure and
secret place. I had organized its construction, had thought of
woven walls. Such a quantum leap this seemed over my previous

efforts: blankets arranged over upturned chairs, corrugated card-board nailed to banana trees.

It was a breakthrough, opening another world for me. But it did not last. It was not, after all, secure. My house was discovered by my father, who thought it was dangerous and had Peter throw it to the ground. So simply. The shock of that act of destruction – and my rage – has also stayed with me. It was the moment at which I first realized my parents were not infallible; they were, like other people, capable of making mistakes, of being foolish, misguided, even mean.

I persuaded my parents to let me rebuild the house, but it was never the same.

~

In 1954, the journey from Capetown to Southampton on the Union–Castle line took two weeks. This voyage gave me a sense of the great physical distance between South Africa and England, but for me, culturally, the distance was not great.

A classmate, who had arrived in London a month ahead of me and so could be presumed to know the ropes, met me at Waterloo station on a Saturday afternoon in November. Fog-shrouded London. We had lunch in a pub and went straight to the Albert Hall to hear a performance of Handel's *Messiah*. I think Sir Thomas Beecham was the conductor. The lamps on the stairs up to the gods were still gas lamps. London was at the end of an era, not much changed from pre-World War I days. I had never before left southern Africa, but this was all familiar to me. From nursery rhymes, from the set books at school, I knew English and Commonwealth literature and history; under Africa's sun, I had read of English fog and English glory. I was a part of the British

Commonwealth. In travelling to its metropolitan heart, I was in some ways really coming home.

I had read so much of this. Read Dickens, Conan Doyle – and, especially, I had read Lytton Strachey, with his devastating satire of Prince Albert and the Albert Memorial. My great-grandfather had been the chief rabbi of London. This place was therefore, from my mother's stories, also my place. Big Ben was not as real as the Big Ben I had known from pictures and descriptions, but it was mine already. Nothing in London was strange to me, and yet nothing was completely real. This strengthened – rather than diminished – my sense of coming home. It was magic realism, perhaps: my heightened sense not of some mundane reality, but of essence – an atmosphere created by the light, the rain, the soot blackening those places of legend.

Best of all, I had my own flat, in a courtyard in South Kensington. The completeness of London's streets and squares, the continuity of London's urbanity in time and space, and also the containment of my own place, my anonymity in the great city – all of it was right; all of it made me feel sublimely at home. I remember especially a moment that came after I'd been to a concert in the Festival Hall. I was standing on Hungerford foot-bridge, looking out at the Thames, and I felt that I could fly, or conquer the world. Anything was within my powers.

～

I spend long hours now travelling by jet. These are hours in which the eye turns inward, hours in which – sometimes – I can recreate that sublime satisfaction my first tree house gave me. I design imaginary houses for myself in conjured circumstances, or for places I might recently have seen. And these designs make for me a complete world. The possibilities in this exercise can far exceed those of my South African tree house – and so I fill whole note-books with these houses.

The designs vary, of course, with place. These contrasts, and the full expression of each difference in approach, are part of the satisfaction. A thick-walled house, the depth of whose walls establishes great security; thin, framed houses whose lightness and delicacy thrill with their vibrancy; the rooms themselves, with their imagined vistas, cosiness or openness – all can be planned with absolute precision. Their characters can be inferred from the shorthand, or code, of the drawing. Furniture, books, textures – all are imagined, articulated, with a graphic economy.

In a few moments, a world I could inhabit with profound satis-faction is imagined and expressed. How to describe the way in which one's soul is massaged, one's spirit nurtured, by this mirac-ulous creation of place, of home? It is like the satisfaction one feels in the presence of familiar music. There is certainty here: it will unfold in this way – as it should, and must, so it will. But such creation is not like life, for here every aspect can be ordered. At least this fragment of the world can be arranged to one's own sat-isfaction, placed exactly as one pleases. It is the living extension of composition – elements placed in relation to one another, mass, form, texture, light, so that they are *right*.

DAVID DONNELL

Woke Up This Morning, Lord, & I've Got Those Baja California Blues

~

Geography and Lakes

My mother was born in White Plains, New York, and my father was born in Mazatlan. But almost everybody else in my family over the last five generations was born in Ontario. Western Ontario. I have a niece and a nephew in Chicago. My sister lives in Cleveland, Ohio. If you look at it in terms of verticals, Nancy is more midwestern than I am – about two hundred miles farther west. I have friends and favourite places in New York, I have never lived in the South, I have never lived for any significant period of time west of the Mississippi. And Brian Tobin in St. John's, Newfoundland, is obviously more of an easterner than I am. Newfoundland is northeast of the Eastern Seaboard and half an hour ahead of our popular EDT Time Zone.

So there you are, I guess this is home: 654,000 square miles of diversity.

But if Ontario is home, then I think there are two packages of observations I can make about Coming Home. Or working at home, or raging at home, or being in love with home.

One package of observations would have to do with how I interact with the geography and how the geography interacts with me. How much New York State is there in southern Ontario, and how much Michigan? The other package of observations has to do with Capitalism versus culture or, perhaps more simply, Culture versus capitalism. I do have a coast-to-coast, St. John's-to-Nanaimo, east/west imagination, but I also have a large north/south. Los Angeles has become such an overpowering cultural force since the 1960s that there are days when L.A. seems to be in between southern Ontario and Michigan. It isn't, for sure; it's way the hell over and south down there on the far west coast. But the communications industry both articulates and blurs various geographic and cultural realities, and there's a ton of communications industry in southern Ontario, most of it in Greater Toronto.

Of course, the term Greater Toronto should be understood as a normal untampered-with Toronto plus its democratic surrounding areas. Any other understanding of the term Greater Toronto, given the present MegaCity debate, should be seen in a correct Marshall McLuhan "WHO" (suits) is saying "WHAT" (tax levy) perspective, or simply as a Queen's Park confusion or Conservative rhetoric.

So there you are, I guess this is home. Plus Conservatives.

Geography is landscape and ocean, that kind of reality; and also, as intellectual knowledge, geography can be an extraordinary floating intellectual dynamic. You're seventeen, you're in a Grade 13 classroom at Jarvis Collegiate in Toronto, and the teacher pulls down a huge map over the blackboard and begins talking about the subcontinent of India and the Himalayas and the trade routes through the mountains that led thousands of years ago to places in China, Persia, and eastern Europe.

If you give most Ontarioans, my spelling, an 8 1/2 x 11 sheet of white paper and a pen and ask them to draw the western border of Ontario, or the northern border, or the southern border, just one simple, semi-detailed line in two minutes, they will probably express not so much confusion as a rather odd, when you stop to think of it, sort of annoyance.

They should be able to draw the western border, but they can't. They should be slightly confused by the question and its implications, but they're not confused. They're not confused because they don't really stop to think about the content of the question.

So home is a place where most people, Michigan or New York high school students included, can't draw the southern boundary of Ontario on an 8 1/2 x 11 sheet of white paper.

And they don't see any reason why they should. Why is it important, who cares? What is important is, Are the Jays going to beat the Athletics? Or, Is Darryl Wasyk's film *H*, shot in Toronto in a rented basement apartment somewhere around Lansdowne and Bloor for approximately $84,750, one of the great films of the 1990s?

No, the Jays are still in a post-victory slump mode, they're just playing reasonably good season baseball, they're not dangerous, they're not putting out pitchers like John Kruk, they're not going to win another World Series for at *least* two years. Plus, there's a sale discussion going on with the Jays. So it may be possible for a home-town baseball team to be sold, even after winning two World Series, even after those incredible games against Philadelphia.

Home is a place where people talk about sports, read newspapers, have illusions about capitalism, perhaps; or perhaps in some cases they have illusions about socialism. Most people I talk to in stores or on a train or in a friend's living room, in Ontario, Michigan, or New York State, seem to believe in decent liberal values, and they seem to believe that Government is doing its best, and that its best is limited in terms of its capacity for dealing with large numbers of people; and a lot of those people believe, I would say, that most people in Government are in it for what they can get.

The novels we've been reading since 1946 have changed a lot. Our reading habits have changed. The technical format of how we read has changed. I came downstairs at the age of six on Christmas Day in St. Marys and there was a gorgeous copy of *The Pathfinder* by James Fenimore Cooper, with colour tip-in plates and a great dustjacket, sitting under the Christmas tree for me. Very nice, you say, Was it a big literary influence? No, I don't think so, but it's an example of reading the classics. I read a lot of classics when I was a child. My father was a classics specialist, Greek and Roman, so there's almost a pun going on here. And my mother was very beautiful and I thought they would both live forever.

I read a lot of the Great Novels between the ages of seventeen and twenty-one, including the Russians, of course. Everything you read changes the kind of person you are, to some degree. You take more people into your world. You perceive the world as being THE WORLD. You come to perceive moral decisions as being dramatic, which, I suppose, was something my father had already taught me. A moral decision is significant, like landscape.

Does everything you read change your sense of geography? Well, to some degree, perhaps, if you have friends in Michigan and you read enough New York novels.

Garnet Harry has been hosting "Real Time" on CBC over the summer. He was saying last week that he's driven through forty Union States but that he has never been east of Edmonton. He hosts out of Vancouver, so I don't know why he gave Edmonton as an example instead of Calgary, which is a livelier city and more American, anyway. His question to the audience was, Where

37

should he stop on his first drive east, all the way to Halifax? And what was interesting about this large, participatory, largely under-thirties audience was that they phoned in almost nothing but *quite* interesting Saskatchewan, *northern* Ontario, and New Brunswick examples, towns where "Garn" should stop at to see the world's largest aluminum mosquito, in Saskatchewan; or Blind River, Ontario, where Neil Young's hearse broke down in 1965 when he was just starting his career; or the world's largest potato, outside Fredericton. I often think of New Brunswick, where my friend David Adams Richards lives, as being mining and lumber country, but actually there's a lot of farming – potatoes, for example, are famous – and fishing, fishing is a vital activity. And, right as rain, another of the examples was the world's largest lobster outside of a small coastal town on the east side of New Brunswick, the Gulf side.

Geography, geography. Geography is all over the place.

But we live here, the Michigan border is right across from Windsor, where Wyndham Lewis spent some of the war years (terrible right-wing pedant, but *The Apes of God* is an extraordinary novel; I don't know anything much at all about the rest of his work). Windsor is actually south of Detroit, they're both river cities, and they're both classic auto cities.

I think one of the problems of geography as it's taught in Ontario schools is the way in which Ontario tries to put an English slant on its own interpretation of places as different as Halifax and Thunder Bay, or Calgary and Vancouver.

And here in Toronto, a bit north of St. Marys and Galt, the rich are buying condos (God knows why), restaurants are going out of business, other restaurants are selling at least a hundred orders of chicken and pasta a day, the police are shooting young black men, and the poor are building cardboard shelters south of

Front Street. New York is directly across the lake, and this particular portion of the southern Ontario border is theoretically right
down the middle of the lake: one can almost imagine a line of
buoys, a bright, cheerful, aquatic yellow.

Intellectuals and Regionalism

Jean-Paul Sartre, who was more or less my God when I was about
twenty, has an essay where he talks about a young student who
came to him when he was lecturing at the Sorbonne for a brief
period. Sartre had been asked to lecture at the Sorbonne a number
of times in the late 1950s and he finally accepted. The student is
young and talented and a tad emotional. He wants to know precisely what he should believe. And Sartre tells him a number of
related ideas he should observe, and then tells him that life is a
great teacher, and also that he should read a lot. And then as
Sartre continues this simple anecdote we get a Søren Kierkegaard
plunge-of-life dilemma. The student says, Yes, yes, but all these
cultural and political events are taking place in the newspapers
and the media and are being discussed in my peer group. Do we
support good art because it's good art? Do we support communism?
Do we support the French Communist Party? François Mitterrand
was probably a fairly young middle-aged man at this time. The
student says, I want to know what I should believe right now. And
Sartre throws up his hands more or less gracefully and says, I can't
tell you what to think. I can tell you what my position is. I can talk
to you about ideas, I can criticize your conclusions.

I think you have to say that generally in Ontario, Northrop
Frye didn't play this kind of role. Neither did Marshall McLuhan.
McLuhan was preoccupied with the methodology of communica-
tions and became famous for his work on the influence of daily

technology. It's unfortunate that a lot of students are walking around quoting Werner Heisenberg and saying things like, Yeah, but if you change the context everything is relative, and not studying McLuhan more closely – *The Gutenberg Galaxy* is still an extremely valid book. Obviously George Grant is actually much weaker than either of the above thinkers. So that's a problem, but this is home, and we have three of the five Great Lakes, and they're all wonderful.

Of course, that's regionalism. I think if you're an Ontarioan, you have to accept the enormous region of Ontario as being: Ontario, New York State, Michigan, etc., to some degree. We've read more William Faulkner, Philip Roth, Mary McCarthy, and Ann Beattie since the beginnings of Canadian nationalism than over twenty or twenty-five different U.S. states.

We take the train to Montreal, it's traditional, and Montreal is a tradition in and of itself. It's the only European city in America; New Orleans is interesting and it's on the Gulf and it's hot but you can't compare nohow. Montreal is fairly big and it's on an island in a huge river; I mean, look, that's sort of unique, and it's a totally changed tradition: it's separate, enclosed, and totally French with large immigrant dynamics and a *tolerance* for English. And their sales to the state of Maine for the year 1995 were around $750 million; not huge, but larger than previous years.

We fly to Vancouver, we eat rock-cod fillets with Chinese greens at ridiculously good prices in restaurants without a licence but where you can bring your own bottle. And I'm struck every time I go to Vancouver by how much Vancouver has fulfilled itself as a major coastal city, and, of course, a major Pacific Rim city. Because Pacific Rim city is ultimately what you're talking about if you're talking about west coast. Robertson Davies isn't big on the west coast and the Toronto Maple Leafs aren't big on the west coast. Goodbye beautiful old faded sepia CN and CP Hotels

Empire bulldog or otherwise dream of east/west monolithic unity. It's not even floating around as an abstract balsa-wood model.

And Vancouver has big money, big independent money. The Stock Exchange, once X-rated by consultants (but that only adds a fashionable note of dangerous glamour and allure to an increasingly major reputation), is now an exploding salmon pizza of mining and industrial futures. Seattle, immediately south, has Puget Sound (gorgeous) and a fabulous late-night music scene which has produced groups like Bikini Kill and Nirvana (whose album *Smells Like Teen Spirit* has sold approximately eight million copies worldwide). But it's Vancouver which has the exploding population, the night life, the string quartets and some very well-known punk groups, the multiculturalism, and, of course, big money. All this is sheltered by the Rockies.

So, as I said to a friend a few months ago, Ontario, in its east/west form, is poised between the Rockies and the Ottawa River – with an enormous vista south all the way to Texas.

Personally, I find this kind of cultural and regional experience more interesting than Dan Rather, or CBC reporting on Sergio Marchi's latest announcement about anti-pollution measures in the enormous context of NAFTA.

But this regional consciousness isn't reflected very much in most current fiction, although you can find quite a lot of non-fiction examples, mostly U.S. I have to admit, in which the author is trying to look at the South, or the Southwest, or the Midwest, or the New York/New England general area as a region with certain laws and conventions of its own.

It's difficult to know what a magazine like *Saturday Night* would think of George Grant. Grant was a philosopher and an outstanding professor who influenced several generations of Ontario youth who passed through his classes. But he wasn't an international philosopher. I expect the Existentialists came and went as far as he was concerned when he was a student, or when he first began teaching at the University of Western Ontario. Grant wanted a more tangible focus. Angst and politics and political choices weren't George Grant's forte. Perhaps his forte was goodness.

And so George Grant became more and more attracted to nationalism, because nationalism offered him an opportunity to talk about goodness, and to talk about politics, perhaps, in a specialized sense. And also it offered him an excellent opportunity, considering how slowly copies of even a brilliant volume of philosophy sell at your neighbourhood bookstore, to be descriptive, to talk about goodness and politics in a specialized sense, and to talk about history in a specific frame. Of course, all these dynamics make George Grant's books, like the well-known *Lament for a Nation*, more interesting.

But as a philosopher, George Grant hasn't left us a model as clear and tangible as the media/anthropological model McLuhan leaves us in *The Gutenberg Galaxy* or his later, more pop-sociology, books with Quentin Fiore. We think of McLuhan and we see his tall stiff angular form with those extraordinary stand-up tweed suits, and we also see the pale blue screen of the universal television set which appears in Orwell's *Nineteen Eighty-Four* and also dominates the evening portion of studying for final college exams.

The rival model is just a short walk on the University of Toronto campus to Northrop Frye's Victoria College. Frye has left us so many books, and there are so many new books out there every week, that we don't know what to do with them. O Lord, what will I do with all these books? Of course there are new philosophers of television out there; but generally techno-speak and the whole idea of extrapolating technology to the heavens (where God will reply) has passed beyond television and planted (if that isn't too botanical a metaphor) itself firmly in the huge, shifting, and morphologically diverse megabillion-dollar area of silicone-chip think and silicone-chip memory and data format-ting. So McLuhan and that tall angular tweed-suited shape with the close-cut grey hair and the broad patient sceptical but good-humoured expression striding across the campus on a sunny day (a bit sunny for tweeds, but I think it was April) on his way from St. Michael's to somewhere or other around St. George and Bloor, is safe. Northrop Frye goes down in twentieth-century North American history as the ULTIMATE literary philosopher of the Bible, and myth, and narrative modes – despite the bright young things with their copies of Jacques Derrida et al., who, after all, may not be around as a trend for that much longer. McLuhan is equally secure, the two big rivals from opposite sides of the campus. The same campus that boasted Étienne Gilson, the major Catholic philosopher of the twentieth century, in the 1950s and '60s.

But if *Saturday Night* were to commission an article on George Grant in 1996, what would they credit him with? Yes, he was one of the distant resource people, intellectually speaking, behind Mel Watkins and James Laxer, founders of the brief Waffle Movement in 1969. And the influence is everywhere. But only, it seems to me, in monetary form. Money is important. We should have more money and less bureaucracy. But what happened to the great criti-cal intellectual discussions we used to have in the 1960s and '70s? Why do we talk about "information" so much? Psychologists tell us that we're talking about information excessively because we're trying to make the distance between ourselves and power seem less extreme. And as far as independence goes, we had far more inde-pendence *before* 1969 than we have now in these torn and bleed-ing post-Mulroney years. *Lament for a Nation* seems to me now to put too much faith and trust in the idea of a perfect Ottawa. Surely Ontario has to look at the question of its autonomy and its internal balances in a somewhat different way.

And *Saturday Night*, what can I say? *Saturday Night* wasn't very kind to Farley Mowat approximately a year ago; but that was a particular feature, and no one has written very much about it. They might be kinder to George Grant. Otherwise, we have to ask the following question: Where do we read philosophers, if they're not reflected in magazine publishing or available in popular trade paperback editions? Do we read them only in university-press editions?

I don't see the point to blocking someone like John Lithgow from participating in a Toronto theatre production, if the "bonus" of the result is going to be that we actually get higher taxes and philosophers are available only in limited and undisplayed university-press editions.

Lake Ontario and the Silicone Chip

Coming home or being at home, writing at home or raging at home, is very simply a much larger and more sophisticated proposition than it was in 1925 when Ernest Hemingway and Morley Callaghan had their famous amateur boxing match in Paris. Scott Fitzgerald was the timekeeper, and he may have had a few drinks. No one wrote the event up for one of the major dailies. Hemingway hadn't yet published *The Sun Also Rises*, and Callaghan certainly hadn't published *That Summer in Paris*. Newspapers were the giant communications industry of the period. Radio was new: *The Sun Also Rises* appeared in 1926 and that just happens to be the year of the first Ottawa broadcast of the CBC. It was 1925, Stravinsky was old hat, but films were still silent, and W. C. Fields was not yet a star.

The geography of what it means to live in Toronto has changed enormously for a variety of reasons, but the geography of what it means to live in California has changed in the same basic ways. The same technological advances – a failing newspaper industry, a psychologically astute publishing industry, far more flamboyant magazines with more film-lab assists than ever before and more computer-assisted design advantages, films that certainly have voices (although a lot of them aren't as interesting to listen to as Sharon Stone's or Nicholas Cage's), and, of course, an enormous and constantly expanding television industry. Ontario has a basic difference with New York or California – there's a consciousness of political guidelines, but the enormous diversity of content on everyday television simply *overflows* the print language of political abstractions, headlines, and subheads put forward by papers like the *Globe and Mail* or the *Toronto Star*.

We've been getting a lot of coverage of the Twenty-Sixth International Olympic Games from Atlanta for the last few days. I'm glad Donovan Bailey did so well, and I'm sorry I missed the rowing events. The red and white of the Canadian flags when Bailey won, setting a new world record, was alluring, flamboyant, and victorious and in some ways regional. There is no dark blue bar, dark blue for the Canadian sky at night, on the Canadian flag for Alberta, and there is no dark blue bar on the flag for Ontario. Which does give Ottawa a peculiar kind of power. But it was great to watch, he's a fabulous runner. I mean, it's nice, it's sort of cool and all that, but I couldn't help feeling that it's significant that an athlete can perform that well, period. That could, I suppose, make the fact of his coming from Oakville seem almost petty. Oakville? How many people in British Columbia – let alone a world viewing audience of hundreds of millions – know where Oakville is? Not many. But I think watching it in Toronto, most of us saw both sides of it, felt an energetic kind of satisfaction that we hadn't actually earned ourselves, but felt that we saw it in context.

We've also been getting large amounts of daily material, on CBC FM, to do with the raising of the K. C. Irving Co.'s *Irving Whale*, a huge oil tanker that went down in the Gulf of the St. Lawrence in 1970. And lots of coverage about historically significant Indian land claims that have been processed recently in British Columbia. But very little serious economic analysis.

What I find interesting, however, on this media question, is how interesting, and I mean this sincerely, it's been for me to be exposed to and to study the general media effect of an auditory version of geographic latitude that does, quite literally, go from shining sea (think of the Gulf of St. Lawrence, think of Cape Breton while you're at it) to the Georgia Strait, Vancouver Island, and the various logging communities and Indian communities north of Vancouver.

It opens up my mind like a very clear glass of cool orange juice first thing in the morning, and then, even if I don't always wind up thinking about Manitoba or Quebec (and no, I generally don't), I do wind up thinking a lot more clearly about Ontario, and this specific region – Michigan, New York to the south, the Northwest Territories to the north – that we belong to and that we have to talk about.

This is my perspective. There are a lot of perspectives out there.

Actually, I think Coming Home is coming home to hot and cold running water and a great bed, and your filing cabinets and your favourite Calabrese bread. Being at home, writing at home, raging at home, being in love with home, is something a bit different.

I don't think you have to wear a Canadian-flag lapel pin to appreciate what a great dancer Peggy Baker is. My family has been in Ontario for five generations plus, since before Confederation.

46

My father and mother would have looked down on a lapel-pin attitude, I think, and even back then they would have probably said that it was a local attitude and a bit narrow-minded. Or to think *Fifth Business* is a fabulous novel about a young man growing up. Or to appreciate what a fantastic dancer Margie Gillis is, or how much film talent there is around Toronto, or to like Susan Aglukark's version of "Amazing Grace."

If you had asked William Faulkner in 1950, Where is here? he would have said, Mississippi. And then he would have said, History. But that's Faulkner. If I were Faulkner I would have a red face and I would write a wonderful book like *Light in August*. But do I want to write *Light in August*? My new book is called *Dancing in the Dark*, afternoon Toronto light, and darkness. And my previous book was *China Blues*. I don't think I have any desire to write *Light in August*. It would be nice to have written it, but that's not a *desire to*. Like everybody in Toronto, I'd like to write *In the Spirit of Crazy Horse* one day, and a great film like *The Piano* the next. There you go, that's life in Ontario.

Interesting bumper sticker on a cherry-red Ford Econoline I noticed some months ago, last summer. I think it said, "Thank God I was born in Ontario, and thanks to Texas for introducing me to Jesus." Interesting, lots of good high attitude. A bit wild.

I don't think Aldous Huxley, the great English author of *Eyeless in Gaza* and *Brave New World*, spent very much time in Texas. Although he did become an expert in comparative religions, which would have interested Northrop Frye. But Huxley said a long time ago, sometime in the early '60s, I think, that he had wanted England to become economically nationalistic but culturally internationalist, but of course what had happened was the complete opposite. There's probably a major lesson for all of us in that simple statement. Well, I think it's more than a statement, I think it has the makings of an axiom.

I don't think that Canada has lost very much independence from Washington since the 1960s. Anyone reading the *Globe and Mail* over the last fifteen or sixteen years can't help noticing the degree to which the Provinces have taken power *back* from Ottawa. So that's different. On the other hand, in Toronto (the fifth-largest city in North America after New York, L.A., etc., and the largest urban metropolis in the second-largest state or province in North America) it seems that we have *given* up some power to Ottawa and also to Queen's Park. So when I hear people talking about Canada having lost independence to Washington since the 1960s, or to Quebec, I think, No, something extraordinarily different has happened.

Think of Canadian nationalism as a large blackboard divided into two different halves. Naturally, you're going to put a slogan at the top of each half. And for me, the slogans are:

A: Canadian nationalism is a defensive and protective formulation. And B: Canadian nationalism is a creative concept. If you've read this far, you'll know that I think it's a creative concept.

Why did I call this essay "Woke Up This Morning, Lord, & I've Got Those Baja California Blues"? Simply because Baja California seems so remote and simple, there are only about two small towns there, more or less resort-based, with some whale watching perhaps, and it seems like the perfect opposite to Toronto or Vancouver in the 1990s.

I think we've given enormous amounts of power to Ottawa, to the extent that a lot of us feel our federal vote is almost insignificant, but that our provincial vote is more significant. More like an exercise of states' rights, but is it? Ontario is geographically larger than various combinations of four or five U.S. states.

On the other hand, we've moved forward, almost deliriously, into several years of enormous triumphs. Achievements at the

Cannes Film Festival, like David Cronenberg's *Crash*, or achievements in international technology to do with space or data engineering. The multiculturalism of Toronto and Vancouver is enormous. The idea of Canada as an English/French partnership is, at this stage, an absurd and confusing idea, especially for new Canadians.

Format. We shouldn't exaggerate the degree to which technology has made the word *Format* more interesting than it's ever been before in history. And it's picked up a lot of associations. (I don't know what Marshall McLuhan would say at this point.) From George Lucas to Bill Gates, they love information, they love ice cream, and they love the word format. It isn't a millennial word. Philosophy may or may not be a millennial word. I don't know. I think format was a big word in '96, and I think it's going to be a big word in 2001. Think of the astronaut outside the spaceship in Stanley Kubrick's *2001*. We're on a spaceship that seems to extend on some days from St. John's, Newfoundland, to Los Angeles or Willie Nelson's Texas; and on other days this enormous ship seems to extend from eastern Ontario to Vancouver or Seattle. So format is important for everybody.

The fact that I would like to go to Baja California, for the month of January at least, doesn't mean that I have an incorrect position on Trade Discussions. It just means that Baja sounds so wonderfully simple, close to the Pacific, how close can you get, and wow, all that butter-soft yellow sunshine plus a few tapes of Maria Callas et al.

But whether Canada is at this time too economically international, or too culturally national – that really depends on who you talk to, or on what day you ask the question. I don't think Canada's independence from Washington is as economically simple as Ottawa likes to suggest, and I don't see, in the daily news blurbs of the last six or seven years, the same melodramatic significance applied to the more up-front and immediate question of who controls the power to make our cultural decisions.

In other words, I think Canada has become a spaceship, and I think the most important question for the person experiencing us and our culture at this moment is what format or sequence of books, films, tangible experiences, and discrete political events you look at us in, and what philosophy you hold in the first place. What, in other words, is the ideal combinational view that suggests what we have in common? What does Brian Tobin have in common with Hugh Hood? What does Alice Munro have in common with Harold Cardenal?

I think the most important question for us is a package of questions not to do with Canadian nationalism as such but to do with how we settle questions among ourselves, within these different contexts of opinion and points of view we've built up over the past twenty-five or thirty years since Trudeau became Prime Minister in 1968 – simply, who controls Arts Funding, who controls the CBC, the Canada Council, and the communications industry as a whole. Why are Canadian writers, professors, curators, and readers, since we're obviously the experts on various questions of language and communication, excluded from these discussions about what happens to *our* arts institutions? And O yes, why do I want to go to Baja California, for the month of January at least? Not because it's warm, but because it sounds so simple.

Solid Ground: The Walking Tour

~

We do the walk.

Likely the tour will wend through time and space, along paths and over streams, through copse and field, so bring along a good pair of boots and talaria grafted onto your ankles. Picking up a trail map at the gate, we're off.

Point of Interest #1: Greenwood

Hard against Main Road in Hudson, Quebec, Greenwood is a ramble of yellow house, shifted and sagging. Old timbers talk of another time. A post office in the days before mail, a meeting-place before church or civic centre, a store before groceries, the house was the first European settlement on this shore. Her lawn and gardens bank to the Ottawa River, known at this widening as the Lake of Two Mountains. The view has welcomed canoe traffic in one century, paddlewheels in the next, sailing regattas in our time.

Old homes have tales and Greenwood treats her historians kindly. A French and Iroquois party in the late 1720s razed Dover, Massachusetts, and carried back to Oka as part of their spoils sixteen-year-old Sarah Hanson. Her lot was not to be a slave or chattel. The Mohawks had discovered a lucrative enterprise – kidnap a daughter of the rich, then wait for her dad to ride north to barter for her freedom. Sarah Hanson's father arrived, but here the story swerves. She declined to return. She had discovered a new place to be, in the Canadian frontier, by the banks of the Ottawa.

In 1732 Sarah Hanson crossed the river from Oka, married, built the house that would later be named Greenwood, and faced the tribe responsible for her abduction. Her husband was Jean-Baptiste Sabourin. A French and English couple built a home in Quebec, their only neighbours Mohawk raiders.

Point of Interest #17: The Clark Farm

Out my back door and through the woodlot we go. If the bank ever repossesses my house, they don't get this bit, which is owned lock, stock, and swampwater. (In Hudson, water collects on the high ridges, not in the valleys.) Soon we connect to the trails of the Clark Farm, pass through a hardwood grove and enter an abandoned crab-apple orchard. A paradise for bees in spring and chickadees year round. The mosquitoes keep us moving.

This section of the farm is no longer worked, left to nature's will and sustenance. More than a century ago, the Lake District in England was besieged by famine, prompting emigration to Canada. At that time, if an Englishman requested land in Quebec, a Catholic priest looked him in the eye and suggested Ontario. The French, however, did not want this place, distance to the nearest parish being too great. So the land by the lake was bequeathed to the people from the lakes, a gentle symmetry.

Other settlers arrived over time. Rigaud, nearby, now French, was Irish. Pointe Fortune, upriver, Scottish, now French. Only

Hudson has withstood the pressures and politics of the region to remain largely English. My separatist neighbours shake their heads, laugh nervously, as we discuss referendum results. They were decidedly outvoted in our poll. We assure one another that we are not fanatics, but in Quebec, when we are not busy deceiving one another, we deceive ourselves.

On a clear day, breezes grazing on the tall summer grasses, we scare up the birds as we walk, and a clutch of boys fellating one another in a hollow. No place is idyllic, or wholly reverential. Hard won by muscle and will, the farm is given to indolence today, and to the benefit of those who walk, and wonder, who muse and continue to brave political shifts and shenanigans and take to the clear air among the chickadees and swooping pileated woodpeckers.

There are those who want to harvest this land. Build massive homes. There are those who conserve space. A walk in the woods has become political.

Point of Interest #29: Des Boswell's Lean-to

It's true, Desi's a point of interest, and the centre of small-town squalls. Of the city folk travelling out on a summer Saturday to visit Finnigan's Market, a few take the slight detour to scan my neighbour's place. Leave it to an English settlement to sponsor eccentricity. A couple of years ago, Desmond Boswell dwelled in a shack. Dilapidated, tumble-down, tar-paper – he lived in the collapse of a cottage never intended for winter, the windows plastic wrap, the roof shingled by tarpaulins. Walls leaned inward, outward, anywhere but straight. Fronting the house bloomed the most elaborate collection of trash this side of the dump, a mine Desi frequently plunders. His across-the-road neighbour is a mythology in her own right, in her nineties now, a former

Principal of the High School for Girls who wants the eyesore torn down and cleaned up.

The Town defends Desi's right to strut naked amid his collection of debris. But there is the small matter of unpaid back taxes, and his habit of defecating in the creek. Wouldn't you know? Another town deadbeat wins the lottery and in the nick of time pays off his friend's debt. If only television could be this serendipitous.

The Principal will get her way, however, for a brief time.

The shack is bulldozed. Friends, during the coldest winter in living memory, talk Des into travelling west to live with a daughter, an experiment that lasts two weeks. He returns to find his beloved lot wiped clean, only fenceposts left behind. So Desi creates a lean-to out of the fenceposts, begins his junk collection anew, and lives there now, winter and summer, a fearsome spirit defiantly poor in the midst of affluence, courageously warm in the middle of an arctic chill. Something of a model citizen.

Point of Interest #30: The Spy House

A.d.S.G.'s back in town, so we must be in trouble. He's bought a house a couple of doors up from Desi's lean-to. A. is also a collector. At Finnigan's he delves for the body parts of mannequins, which he puts together with masks collected from around the world. He's a free spirit in his own right, but art is not his primary profession.

"Intelligence Analyst," he says. His business card concurs.

"Spy," I clarify, hating euphemisms.

The pin in his lapel is the Buffalo Head insignia of the RCMP. A.d.S.G. retired when our spy service went civilian. Now he works for European think tanks. In advance of each referendum he returns to Canada from who knows where, buys and renovates a house in Hudson, and provides clients with an analysis of the news.

The Parizeau crowd, he reports at the height of the last fray, will stop at nothing.

Point of Interest #104: Pavarotti's

This is where the wings on your ankles come in handy, to fly down to Old Montreal for lunch. The crowd is jovial, loud, the food delectable. To be polite and introduce the others at table: Sylvain Lelièvre, singer and, latterly, novelist, Jean-Claude Germain, poet, playwright, literary entrepreneur, and Serge Chapleau, political cartoonist. The discussion is ebullient, wide-ranging, the wine flows – café life is one of the great reasons to live here.

Serge begins a traveller's tale. The anecdotal adventures of Quebeckers visiting Victoria, B.C., have become as ubiquitous as Newfie jokes in our culture. Roughly translated, Serge relates, "This woman, she asks me if I speak French." A few at table believe that that's enough, we're already laughing, Serge needn't say more. But he has more to tell. I fear the worst. In his gentle-manly manner he informs the lady that, yes, amazingly, he speaks French, it's but one of his talents. She wants to know, every day? Yes, every day, Serge says. In the streets, in the restaurants, you speak French? Yes. At home? *Yes, lady, he speaks French at home, now will you give it up? Don't you realize that some of us back home will have to listen to the anecdote later? Mercy, woman, please.* The lady asks if he speaks French at work. Serge replies that yes, he speaks French at work. He does a summary for her. "I speak French every day, all day, at work, at play, at home. I watch tele-vision in French and read the newspapers, including the one that

I work for, in French." Finally, the lady gets to the question that agitates her the most. "Why?"

Serge gets on a plane and heads back home.

A good story, well told.

We go on to discuss Bowser & Blue.

Point of Interest #109: Dominion Square

The day I'm thinking of, days before the referendum, we were here by the tens of thousands. I love my town, my city, my province. I'm a tad fanatical about my country. That day I learned I wasn't alone. We're practically a cottage-industry.

The Sun Life Building oversaw the celebration. When the English were granted farmland around Hudson, the Church had no means of distributing property among *les autres*. So the priests contracted with Sun Life to do the job. For the early homesteaders, Sun Life Assurance became the equivalent of the Catholic Church. Francophones put their faith in redemption after a life of devotion; anglophones in redeeming policies after a life of premiums. You had to do one or the other if you wanted to plough fields.

Following the speeches on the Square, we moved north, up Peel, dispersing along Ste. Catherine, de Maisonneuve, Sherbrooke, searching for some form of closure, alliance, resolve. A sluggish Sargasso Sea of Anxiety.

Point of Interest #117: The Whitlock Golf & Country Club

Picture this. Four retired Air Canada pilots are lining up their putts on the fifteenth green of The Whitlock, one of the more exclusive clubs in Quebec. They are interrupted by the hectic clamour of a double-propeller military helicopter. The chopper lands on the green, right over the cup. Soldiers leap out in battle fatigues and painted faces, rifles poised, bayonets fixed. They demand that the foursome drop their clubs. They do so. An officer demands to see ID.

"On the fifteenth green?" one asks. "My wallet's in the clubhouse."

The remark provokes menace among their captors.

Back in the days when Montreal was still a centre of travel, hundreds of pilots lived in Hudson. About the only fly-boys left now are retirees. A golfer, an ex-pilot who got his start during World War II, speaks up. "Let me talk to your navigator. If you're looking for the Oka crisis," he points out, "it's on the *other* side of the lake."

The army retreats, to fight again, elsewhere.

Only in Quebec can golf be seen as seditious.

Here, it's hard to know what side of the lake anybody's on, and when we do, when it's obvious, it's hard to know *why?*

Point of Interest #139: The Church of St. Andrew & St. Paul

In a land where water pools on the highlands and disappears in the valleys, where golf is subversive, where neighbours cast a ballot for their choice of country as though voting on their favourite sour cream apple-crumb pie at the fair, an English, Presbyterian church in downtown Montreal thrives, contrary to all things English in the city, and contrary to all things religious in the rest of the land.

Daniel's in attendance with his daughter, seated in his customary pew. He chooses to worship here, among the English, among the remnants of the English élite. This is a busy time for him, as he must soon decide if he'll make a run for the leadership of the Bloc Québécois. In a land of contradictions, the former chief aide to Lucien Bouchard, perhaps his successor, prefers to worship God in English.

Y'gotta love this place, y'know?

Point of Interest #144: Chateau du Lac

The Shat, as it's known, is an aged hotel in Hudson where no one's booked a room in fifty years, save an American sculptor who arrives each summer. As a watering-hole it's great, wood floors and ceilings, pool tables in the back, and the place can rock on a Saturday night even if the clientele is more apt to creak. Okay, that's not fair, some of us creak, others are young, curious about the dementia of their elder citizens.

It's a good drinking bar, and on the first night we come Ray Bonneville is singing his urban-track blues. His new CD, *Solid Ground*, is all of that – solid, affirming. To sit in a small-town, old-world bar, attuned to music of this quality, is a rare privilege in the nineties.

The dancing's fun for those who dance, a hoot for the spectators.

I have trouble getting a drink. My table's been served, but I wasn't around. A lone waitress has been abandoned to serve the entire room, and she neglects my on-the-fly request twice. She's cute, in an under-twenty, bare-midriff sort of way, and has won the attention of my tablemate. He exerts what he feels are the greater (read: more youthful) powers of attraction to mention that I am miffed by the lack of spontaneous service, and would she please bring the poor old man a drink? She does, and refuses to accept payment. That I am the recipient of this offering dulls the night for my younger pal, and our wives chuckle.

Do we call this the politics of male sexual competitiveness, or the politics of aging? One week later we are back again, ensconced at our table. The joint is packed. Bowser & Blue are playing tonight. Their rock-a-silly satire runs the gamut of Quebec politics, male aging, native affairs, rectal colon surgeons. In our corner, I am served free drinks by a waitress with a bare midriff. My friend, the short-story writer Scott Lawrence, has taken to smoking six cigarettes at a time, and ripping into shreds whatever paper he can cull from his pockets. "My heart," he mumbles, while our wives berate him. I will allow him to stew for another twenty hours before mentioning that the whole thing was a set-up, an elaborate, beautifully executed practical joke.

I await, warily, his revenge.

Bowser & Blue sing about anxiety and angst, and we laugh. They sing about aging, and we laugh. They joke about a fading Eros. "At our age, when a woman says yes, that's great. If she says no, that's okay too." They sing about the quirkiness of a body politic that can easily strip away the livelihoods of many in the room and devalue their homes and propel their friends and families down the 401 to Toronto, or beyond, and perhaps half those in the room, although they have held on, and held on, and held on, will follow.

We spill out into the night. Starlight that you don't see in the city. Starlight that Sarah Hanson knew, over 260 years ago, carving out a homesite farther along the shore. Lights twinkle across the lake. Mohawk lights. Monastery lights where the monks are up late making cheese. Or perhaps they're also dancing. I'd like to think so. English and French and native circle this mere widening of a river channel, before the Ottawa spills through the rapids at Ste. Anne into the St. Lawrence. It's a place we perpetually admire, and can't believe exists so close to a city. It's not an easy time, but no time ever was, and our anxiety is pitched against a history of change and movement and renewal and the perpetual reforging of the common ground, the solid ground. The waters lap against the shore. It's still a place where we can laugh and play the trickster in the midst of our concerns, frustrations and failures, indolence and industry. Home for now. Home for now. Which is, we freely confess to one another, all that any home can expect to be.

TIMOTHY FINDLEY

Of Trunks and Burning Barns

Though I wasn't "born in a trunk," I lived in one for fifteen years. This was when I was an actor, 1947–1962. There were moments back then when I felt like a ventriloquist's dummy, packed away between engagements, speaking only the words allotted to me by the playwright.

There's a lot of invisibility and a lot of silence in an actor's life – from the moment he leaves the stage to the moment he goes back on. God, it was a lonely time. But wonderful. I wouldn't have missed it for the world. It gave me access to the fund of necessary solitudes a writer requires in order to function – solitudes peopled with all those interior companions who inhabit your work, but not your life.

The trunk I lived in had been my father's during the Second World War. Neatly stencilled on the lid – black on Air Force blue – was FLO A.G. FINDLEY – C2425. I was younger then, of course, and stronger, and used to carry the trunk on my back. I can still feel the metal bump of it against my bum, and the burns from the leather handle. A flat trunk, with one removable tray. I had no suitcase, only a shopping bag, from time to time – often filled with laundry, plus the irresistible paperbacks, mostly Penguins, bought in market stalls. This was in England: Liverpool, Manchester, Newcastle, Leeds. Also Brighton. Also Oxford. Also Cambridge, Bournemouth, and Norwich. Always to Scotland – Glasgow, Aberdeen, and Edinburgh. Sometimes to Dublin, whose streets were in my genes; where I could find my way unerringly back home, drunk and riotous through the dark.

Home.

For an actor, home is mostly *digs.* The word, I think, is Australian – short for *diggings.* No one in the theatre ever talks of *lodgings, bed-and-board,* or *quarters.* These are all civilian references. And a non-civilian breed of women has been in charge of theatrical digs since well before the turn of the century. In all my time in the theatre, I never once had a landlord.

In Dublin, I arrived with my trunk on a rain-wet afternoon, impossibly romantic in the misted views of row houses, each one more dilapidated than the next, all of them redolent of stories waiting to be told. I rang the bell and waited, standing on the Georgian doorstep, watching myself being watched from a dozen windows – all lace-curtained – each with a single inquisitive face beside the single hand that had pulled the curtain aside. *Who is it this time? Male or female, young or old?*

The door in front of me opened.

"Yes?"

"It's me," I said. "Timothy Findley. With *The Prisoner* company."

The Prisoner was the play being toured – with Alec Guinness and Wilfrid Lawson. I had a small but wonderful role, playing the inquisitor's all but silent secretary in Bridget Boland's account of Cardinal Mindszenty's ordeal at the hands of Hungarian communists. A Catholic play, just right for Dublin.

"Ah, yes. The lad," said a woman barely seen in the shadows. "Enter and be welcome."

As my eyes adjusted to the light, I saw that she was middle-aged – a beauty still who, in her youth, must have set the world on fire. She wore a ratty mink coat and an ankle-length silk nightie. Her feet were bare. "Go later to your room," she said. "Now, come with me."

In the kitchen, the table had been set for one. "Sit," she said. "That's you." Her name was Mrs. Higgins. "And I don't mind just plain Missus, if it suits you." A bottle of Jameson's was produced. Cigarettes were lighted. Mrs. Higgins, clutching at her mink, sat opposite – each of us with a glass – and before she went to the stove to prepare my supper, she told a tabloid version of the Troubles – all of its greatest moments in vivid detail, all of its people conjured, all of its martyrs named. Her father, Donnell, who had fallen then, was resurrected between us there in the twilight. Tears and intensity. Laughter with a twist of rue. All of Ireland was in her voice – or so it seemed to me. I was enchanted.

After I had eaten, I unpacked my *home* – postcards and photographs set on the bureau, flashlight and crucifix on the bedside table, books beside the chair. The crucifix was the last surviving remnant of my grandmother's Irish Catholicism, and still it sits beside my bed, protecting me – I like to think – from all the crashing airplanes and sinking ships in my dreams, if not my life.

Few of my digs were as splendid as those overseen by Mrs. Higgins, whose splendour was all in her presence, not in material opulence. The sheets were worn, the food was spare – but a person could survive by means of Mrs. Higgins alone, who had the gift of survival in her being and the gift of life in her words. Other landladies thrived – or so it seemed – on the expectation that you could live on a diet of words such as *no* and *never*.

I depended for survival on the continuity lifted from my trunk. No matter where I was, if I could see my parents and my brother in their cheap brass frames, my postcard Cézannes, Monets, and

Modiglianis sitting on the bureau, and my orange Penguin Waughs and Fitzgeralds, I was safely at home.

One of my Modiglianis was a female nude.

"Oh, you can't have that there, Mister Findley! Anyone might see it!"

This was Manchester.

In Birmingham, the landlady bought a half-dozen eggs for my daily breakfast – each one just a bit more off than the one before. When I pointed out that they were rotten, she apologized profusely. "Isn't that strange," she would say. "And I bought them only yesterday." Next morning's egg went down the toilet. On the Saturday, fearing I might not be able to bear what lay beneath the shell, I carried the egg inside a handkerchief and dropped it down the nearest sewer.

"MISTER FINDLEY!" This was in London. "MISTER FINDLEY! I KNOW WHAT YOU'RE DOING IN THERE! AND I WARN YOU, STOP AT ONCE!"

Think what you will, my sin was nothing more than running a bath beyond the prescribed three minutes. Given the fact that all hot water was delivered from a gas contraption called a *geyser*, three minutes' worth was barely one inch deep. *Madam* – I forget her name – would stand outside the bathroom door with a watch, and listen.

Others were intolerant of light. Their houses were equipped with automatic switches, inevitably timed to leave you in the dark just halfway up the stairs. Some had rules about personal acquaintances. NO ONE OF THE OPPOSITE SEX TO BE ENTERTAINED PAST TEN. Clearly, these women had never heard of homosexuality. *Have all the men you like, Mister Findley, but if I ever find a woman. . . .* Mrs. Brown of Leeds expressed this with great authority: "I know you actors!" she said. "Don't you think I don't!

The minute my back is turned, you're into one another like knives!" An interesting analogy.

A life in *rooms* is a life under siege. Every eye is upon you. And when you leave to go to work, the sense that every eye is upon your belongings is palpable. Steeped in honourable traditions – *we never snoop, we never peek* – theatrical landladies nonetheless know everything there is to know about their guests. *Went to Lawton's, did you? Quite agree – they have the best underwear in town.* . . . Still, as the years go by, you become their own. They play into your lives the way that trees play into gardens. All the right protective shade is offered; all the right fruit is produced.

You travel often in the company of other productions – plays and operas, ballets and orchestras – every single performer carrying *home* in a bag. *You again!* the landlady will say. *And here's your favourite marmalade! You again! And no doubt all your socks need mending.* . . . This is what greeted you, setting down your suitcase or your trunk. *You again! And I have that chicken stew you like on the stove!*

It's a profession: making a home of one-part actor, one-part landlady. Something about it makes you think of animals. *Nesting.* Bill Whitehead, my companion, says: *you could nest anywhere, Tiff.* And yes, I could. I've had the practice.

As I write, robin's nests are tucked on the corners of our porch. Every bit of grass and mud so carefully selected, every laying in and every tamping down exquisitely precise: not just any old straw, not just any spill of wetted earth, but, bit by bit, exactly what was required. A Monet, a Cézanne, a robin's nest, a crucifix. This and this and this and this.

What is home?

It is where we are.

Not just anywhere – but where we survive. And, if we're lucky, where we will die. This is the circle described by *home*. Name one who does not hope that life will end *at home*. Where else? *Down in the woods* – my second choice. *In a hospice* – my third. But first and foremost: *at home*.

Home.

No one ever comes home. Everyone goes home. Where are you going?

Home.

I have an unbearably persistent sequence of images in my head. Sounds and pictures that will not go away. They depict an April night more than twenty years ago when a barn down the road caught fire. Everyone went hell-bent for leather, but to no avail. All the beasts, with their young, were inside. I wish I didn't have to write this, but it tells us something about the meaning of *home*. They would not come out, no matter what was done. In the morning, all were dead.

There are theories explaining why this happens – telling us why the beasts will not come out and why they trample one another, despite the flames, to get inside. That *animals know a fire is borne upon the wind* is one theory. They go towards the flames because beyond the flames is a place already burnt. This well may be. But also, there is the thought that *home* is all there is of safety. Even on fire.

As it is with barns and houses, so it is with countries. Now, my country is on fire – threatening to be razed, brought down, and nothing left of it but a shell, a shape that will bear the tragic image of who we were. Lost, because we played with matches. Lost in the turmoil of the Troubles, just as so much of Ireland has been lost. The home where once we sat together, sharing with one another, laughing together, trying for survival and continuity with one another – that house is smouldering already. Smouldering – and the wind is rising.

Our governments are withdrawing from us, leaving us as refugees are left, abandoned. Homeless. The very young and the greatly old, the sick and the needy have been the first to suffer. This is always so in desperate times. A person might imagine, here, that our governments have declared war on the people. The stringencies are all the same – loss of place and loss of hope; loss of security, loss of dignity. The roof that once was safely set above our heads has been blown away. Gone. Our home is not what it was, not what we intended, not what we created and shared. The arsonists have come, and – God knows why – we seem to be powerless to prevent their fires.

Home is the centre of our lives. Only a fool – a determined, not a true, pessimist – would tell you otherwise. *Home* is not just people. *Home* is what people dream: a bed, a window, food, a blanket. Something, anything, kindly to remember. For horses, the smell of hay and other horses. For cows, the mother-smell of milk. For us, for humankind, a photograph of someone loved, the taste of marmalade, curry, wild rice, the scent of snow. In a trunk or in a suitcase, in a mind or in a memory, something carried everywhere. The permanence of nowhere, nowhere made somewhere, because you have it in your hand. I am here – and, with me, who I am.

We are home – in the rain and on fire, in ruins and in standing walls. No one leaves home. We carry it. It has a leather handle and it burns your hands and bumps against your bum. For me, it has an Irish voice. It says: *Go later to your room. Now come with me.*

And stay.

MARIAN BOTSFORD FRASER

Hearth

~

On summer nights on my street the doors and windows are open, and there is brilliantly backlit stained glass in all the Victorian houses and a tinkle of keyboard music from a balcony at the end of the street – a young musician? Rose of Sharon in the gardens and white plastic or wicker chairs on the porches. The houses are achingly close.

Street smells wrap the senses, bearing down in the sultry evening air. There is an occasional light breeze, a silent race of wispy clouds against a purple sky. Stephen's evening cigar from two doors down overrides residual garlic and fish, and the nicotiana from the pot on the stoop, sweet and heavy, is an incense for the Mozart *Requiem*. I sit on the little sloping second-floor balcony of the house, watching the street, listening to the Solti version, very fat, and rich like a dark chocolate cake, recorded at St. Stephen's, the cathedral in the heart of Vienna.

Every time I sit out here, I imagine both sides of the street with completely identical houses, facing one another peak for peak, porch for porch, person for person staring each other down across the narrow street as if gazing into a mirror. But no: over there would have been, until after my house was built in 1890, the gardens of a great house named Foxley Grove, built by a judge. The houses now there are later, Edwardian, chunky and squat by comparison even though they are three-storey with porches. There are four of the distinctive sharp peaks to the south of mine across the street, two doubles; there are seventeen such peaks on my side, some doubles, some singles like mine. The streetscape is mingled Mediterranean and Victorian.

The twenty-one houses that are all the same are thin, cheap, three-storey brick villas with very sharp Gothic gables at the front, and with the tiniest verandahs perched over most of the deeply recessed, arched front porches. The brickwork is modestly decorative, the tall front bay windows all have stained-glass panels over them, and all the houses have two chimneys. But there is minimal decorative woodwork. The triangle of wood in the peaks of the houses is plain bargeboard, and there is little fancy fretwork or spindlework, except inside the houses.

Few houses are still plain brick. They have been painted white and bright blue and pink-red and grey, and the rough-cut granite facings on windows are also mostly painted. Some have had their tiny balconies blown out into full-scale second-storey decks held up on doric columns.

Thin and cheap are relative, historical terms, comparing these modest, middle-class villas to their grander contemporaries in other, more opulent, areas of the city, like the Annex. Now they almost look like hovels from the back lane, a row of plain, almost crude backs. Or asymmetrical cardboard boxes, the houses a child might make. The back façades are unadorned, the original windows small, the roofs just abrupt, angled lines against the sky. Unused kitchen chimneys are wobbly and twisted or they have been removed. Ivy covers some back walls; others are naked, with peeling paint, broken and chipped brick above the singular add-ons or garages that distinguish or in most cases disgrace each house, add-ons containing the spillings-out of complicated modern families.

And the bricks are small and soft, many of them now crumbling. They leave a rusty powder in the three-foot gap between houses to be swept up every spring. When the entire street was dug up this summer to be repaved, Stephen from two doors down collected the bricks from the foundation of the old street to make a patio. The bricks lining the road, he said, were far superior to the bricks used to build the houses.

From the balcony (it's like a miniature box in a Victorian theatre), my view of the street is filtered through the magnolia tree in the front garden. In my third year here, it was finally exuberant and glorious this spring with hundreds of simultaneous large flowers thick against one another and the branches. Stephen says it may have been damaged by the chemical blasting of the brick of the house next door, the year before I arrived. The forty-eight hours of the magnolia came and went on Victoria Day weekend, with bursting pink blooms, a faint, sweet scent, and then a cascade of pale, waxy petals as big as saucers to the sidewalk, to be swept up in fast-browning clumps and thrown into the storm sewer, or stashed in the garbage can.

The front gardens on either side of mine are stuffed with shrubs and bulbs and perennials. We share hedges; George next door has electric hedge cutters and he does all the trimming along the fronts of three houses. It takes about ten minutes. The Portuguese grandmother two houses up has her impatiens laid out in battalions, white, red, white, pink; she hoses everything down like a hospital ward almost nightly in summer. The magnificent house belonging to Gary, six houses down, is invisible under ivy, Virginia creeper, and a hedge now about ten feet tall. All of these houses are identical in structure, but their appearances are completely individual.

Ever since I moved here, I have longed to see the inside of Gary's house, because it is, I am told, exactly as it was when it was built. And full, full, full of wonderful old junk. And, moreover, the house in which Alexander Muir, composer of "The Maple Leaf For Ever" and schoolteacher to Bea Lillie and maybe Mary Pickford, once lived and probably died. Every time I walk past, I try to peer past the foliage into the interior, but it is hopeless. Even the bricks piled up on Gary's front lawn seem to grow like weeds.

Gary is the silent good neighbour. Sometimes when I go away, I forget to cancel the paper, and when I come back several days later, they are piled neatly on one side of my porch. I ask several people – George next door, Fern the cat lady, the postman – do you do this? No, they say. I learn later that it is Gary, keeping an eye out for me, and we have never spoken except over the shrubbery. Gary is also responsible for distributing Historical Society plaques; I got mine from him last winter, but I haven't put it up yet. Perhaps this week.

From my perch I watch the cats; this is a street of cats and very few dogs. There is a constant flow of fur across the street, under cars, in and out of gardens, under fences, up trees, down porch steps. One splotchy black and white one has scuttled across the road, yowled at an invisible comrade, and disappeared; now the tortoise-shell walks, looking for action. A barrel-shaped calico flops down in the middle of the sidewalk to be stroked by a child with a skipping rope in one hand. A ragged old orange tom marks my hedge as his own, again. I have been adopted by several cats who stroll into my house when the door is open, check it out, stroll out again, never in haste.

Fern across the street has usually eight cats, sometimes more or less, but officially fewer because there is rumoured to be a bylaw about cats. Fern has white hair and a young face and she is often to be seen scooping up strays off the corner and whisking them off to be neutered. Lost cats always find their way to her front porch; there is usually a notice on one or more of the telephone poles on the street about a cat that has been found, call Fern. The cats seem to know one another better than the humans do, but I suspect Fern knows more than most of us.

The dramas behind the doors seldom spill onto the street. We don't know one another intimately, especially those of us who are newcomers. Sometimes the man up the street is brought home by the police in the middle of the night, drunk in a rolling, good-natured way, bantering with the cop. The ambulance comes for the woman across the street who has a stroke. The police take away the son of the woman in the last house before the corner (or was he a tenant? – Fern would know); he looks deranged or simple. Would we know all this if we shared the same language? In some cases, we only deduce an ethnic origin by comparing front-door decorations at Christmas. The WASP houses hang fresh balsam or grapevine wreaths and there appears to be an unstated code: no lights. The Portuguese houses are outlined with twinkling lights and plastic greenery. The remainder are silent, and mysterious to me.

On a summer night people stroll, or sit on their porches, or pick off petunia heads, or water the path. The languages are a symphony, floating up, mingling with Solti's dramatic rendering of the *Requiem*. Flat, plaintive Ontario about the crazy weather we've bin havin this year eh. Teenagers muttering what-the-fuck-man to their friends and shouting back in Portuguese to their mothers. Chinese and Vietnamese voices are a current, a short-wave signal edged in static, voices lowered in flirtation, raised in argument, or is it the other way around?

Cars pass intermittently. To drivers, the street is irresistible as a small ski slope – an S-curve, a slight downward slope, another curve, all unencumbered by speed bumps or much traffic, except delivery vans now and then. Hot rods low to the ground, black or red, tinted windows and neon stripes, pulsing with bass roar through, especially in summer. The Sanctus from St. Stephen's Cathedral is briefly obliterated.

St. Stephen's is a big, heavy, stalwart Viennese church. Its local counterpart is the large, plain, red-brick Portuguese Catholic church down the street and around the corner at Dovercourt and Argyle, both labelled as "Rua Acores" and streets as far from the Azores as one could possibly be. The Portuguese church is always in mid-festival: most recently, Nossa Senhora dos Anjos, the mother of all angels, and the Iglesia Santa Cruz (surely Presbyterian in its origins and demeanour, but all reference to this has been deleted from the façade) is bristling with multicoloured lights outlining flower pots and chandeliers and a large cross and interspersed with Canadian and Portuguese flags.

The church blazes thus for a week in midsummer. This seems to be a deeply atavistic festival, one that, like Easter, cannot be ignored. Men of all ages, on wobbly bikes and in mufflerless cars, can be seen to cross themselves three times in mid-intersection as they pass the church. On Sunday there will be a parade, a brass band, men in white shirts, women in black dresses attending, and Josef's café will sell four hundred coffees and not a lot of barbe-cued corn.

There are little parades up my street at Easter, and little parades down Dovercourt often, people holding silver icons high, and then that same day there will be puffy, lopsided golden cakes, stuffed with eggs still in their shells, in the windows of the bakeries on Dundas. One of the parades down my street in late summer features accordions and children in red sashes and a small, decorated cow bringing up the rear.

Every Sunday, small old women in black, smothered in black mantillas, are slowly escorted to church by their sons, whose devotional sincerity is written in the glittering crosses on their open-shirted, black-haired chests. I have attended a mass at St. Stephen's in Vienna (me, a lapsed Protestant – can there be anything less religious?), but I have never dared venture into this church in my neighbourhood.

Just across Ossington, three blocks from my house, is the biggest, blackest most Baptist church imaginable. In 1887 it was the St. Barnabas Church, Anglican and austere. Now it is The House of the Lord, no less, with services advertised on a bright yellow board. Choral concerts rock late into the night some summer Saturdays – busloads of choirs brought in from Chicago and Detroit, white starched bibs and abundant red or blue gowns, and rich mezzo and bass voices rolling out into the street, embellished with diapason flourishes from the organ and clapping and hollering from the crowded pews. On Sundays, this church is bursting with families, little boys beaming in white shirts and ties, their older brothers in blazers and sisters in high heels and all the elegantly dressed mamas in organza hats and matching shoes and bright suits and flowery dresses. Come on in, said one of them, one morning earlier this summer as I was walking past; she was radiant, all in peach, holding her granddaughter's white-gloved hand. Come join us, she said, so I did. . . .

The *Requiem* ends with resounding echoes, and then, after a pause, the deep, ponderous bells of St. Stephen's invite exodus to the cafés on the tiny streets that twist around the church square. My street is briefly silent, the street lights bright and the stars distanced.

I walk down to Josef's café, past Stephen's neat pile of old bricks, the solid and serene Queen Anne house on the curve, the garages held together with tarpaper, the renovated apartment building. Right on the corner is a house for which I always slow down in order to discover a new detail.

It is like an abandoned ship, huge, robust with porches and pillars and balconies. My friend Nino walks past this house and sees it as a perfect example of nostalgia for ancient, formal, public architecture that infects the domestic architecture of Mediterranean communities in Canada. The scalloped wooden apron under the roof is painted a bright Chinese green. The fence is a procession of white, bulbous pillars joined by tall brick columns. Rich rococo flourishes of white and terra cotta plaster encrust every possible surface. A mere bay window sill drips with an extended lacy plaster fringe. Urns abound.

The house has many household gods on its exterior. (Here, too, the interior is unimaginable.) There is a cherub huddled into its wings folded around its small shoulders like a cape, ankles crossed, perched on a window sill looking miserable and cold. But the next time I see that this cherub is supported by a second, smaller one shouldering a vertical outpouring of vines and leaves. The stairway to the small side door has frothing tongues of plaster flowing from the lip of each step, and thick panels of plaster squares featuring large carved flowers framing the entrance, and large empty urns supported on bench-like extensions, would-be lions. A roaring North Wind face (or perhaps the face of God) has been worked into the peak; cherubs hover around the edges of the arch; slim pillars covered with leafwork flank the archway. How many medallions: thirteen last count, all perky cherubini, and then I notice an extra-large one on the back of the house, between two windows, another North Wind/Godhead with howling mouth and flowing beard and hair, another hapless Atlas cherub bent under the weight.

In the back garden, there is a grand fountain, a young woman bearing a pitcher standing in a curved shell supported by two sturdy life-sized cherubs clutching bunches of grapes. No water.

An old woman, portly, in rusty black, is often tending the garden, which is filled with tall flowering shrubs and annuals. Her middle-aged bachelor son tends the plaster decorations that also seem to grow. On summer evenings, he will be out there, working silently and alone, with ladders and a big bucket of plaster and scalpels and knives and some new, plain concrete surface awaiting decoration. But tonight the house and garden are silent and dark, the cherub turned even more morose by shadows.

As I round the corner I hit a wall of Led Zeppelin; an overmuscled man in a ripped T-shirt hurls beer bottles into the back seat of his Camaro and pulls out, peeling rubber. On Dovercourt, the slight gradient encourages rollerblading, and everyone does it: young and old, beautiful Chinese girls and wobbly little black boys. And middle-aged white guys with their guts flopping over low-belted jeans who rollerblade like the hockey players they once were, serenely even uphill, with a case of empties under their arm on the way to the beer store.

Josef's café is kitty-corner from the Portuguese church and it has become, suddenly, a focal point for the neighbourhood, like a summer romance. Queen Street verité art on the walls. A small piano, an old copper cash register, and a fig tree that has so far borne one fig. Josef's menu is small: bold bustling sandwiches, excellent coffee, and solid, well-crafted cakes, truly cakes, nothing else to be said of them, weighted with fruit, moist with emollients, heavy and rich. Austrian or Hungarian cakes, made by his mother-in-law.

Josef is Dutch by origin. One day earlier in the summer I brought a huge bouquet of dark yellow daisies to the café. Do you know what it means to give flowers to a Dutchman? he asked. No, I don't, I said. He just grinned and kissed my cheek. Josef's assistant is little Richard, a young Aussie with china blue eyes who calls me ma'am. On Thursday nights this summer, Greg comes in to make exuberant sushi, and Josef serves sake which we order as "warm water." Soft red candles sputter on the little tables.

Tonight, as usual, the place is filled with skinny women in short, tight black, smoking, always smoking, with bad shoes on bad feet, and bright barrettes and uncertain skin and purple nails and plummy lips. They share a kind of summer openness, a languid sensuality, sloping up and down Dovercourt where every woman in a short skirt or shorts rides the cusp of whoredom to the low-slung cars and their slow-thinking drivers cruising by the café on their way to or from the infamous hooker corner of Queen and Dovercourt.

Outside the café there are wrought-iron chairs with red taffeta seats, and a bike attached to a buggy from Expo 86 tethered to the lamppost. And more women stroll up and sit down, one with professional calves above high-heeled sandals under a slit red rayon skirt, and several beautiful black women humming under their breaths, black eyes out there, and oldish, thin, balding white men smoking with them, chatting, we are all a neighbourhood somehow. The young men are shaven, tattooed, and thin as rakes; they ride up on bicycles and swap courier tales. Many dogs are wrapped around the legs of the little tables; many, many cigarettes are smoked. And small children stare at the dogs and wander in and out, out and in, and reach up to the counter for a free strawberry from the big glass bowl.

I walk home late, alone.

On the darkened porches, old Portuguese women and men sit, side by side on white plastic chairs facing straight out to the street, murmuring to one another, and they nod regally as I walk past. We never speak.

I skirt past a young woman crouching on the sidewalk before a scattering of stones in which is set a cluster of glowing joss sticks, beside the iron picket fence.

My house too is darkened. I light a candle on the mantel over the fireplace. When I bought the house, the hearth was a blank wall, the original opening sealed over.

Fifteen years ago, we bought our first Canadian house, an old, narrow frame house on Vancouver's east side, a house that resembles this one in age, size, interior layout, and marginal (meaning affordable) place in the housing market. The first thing we did there was open up the original fireplace and build a hearth, an arrangement of thick, stone tiles on which was engraved a large Cheshire-like cat. It was an excellent hearth.

It was the first thing I did here too. When the wall was broken open, I found the opening stuffed with 1950s newspapers. From a junk store down on Queen I bought an art nouveau cast-iron insert that fit the opening as if it had always been there, and is identical to the one in the house next door which has always been there. I had black-and-white tiles put around the insert and into the floor.

A friend gave me the mantel as a housewarming present. The mantel is late Victorian, mahogany, with its side pillars ornately carved up top with fully detailed sunflowers and leaves, then the bottom vertical sides finished in what seems to be a birch veneer that is worn in places but still beautiful. Under the mantel shelf, five black-and-white ceramic tiles with a floral motif have been set. My neighbour George believes this fireplace surround was probably built by a famous milling company in Owen Sound.

Tonight, when I look closely at the carved flowers, I realize that the same flowers form the centre of the plaster panels around the side porch of the huge mausoleum house on the corner.

The mantel had belonged to my friend's great-uncle, an eccentric gentleman bachelor who had taken it from the family house (in Owen Sound) before it was sold when the father died, and who for years had it fitted out with an electric log fire and lights and side shelves, and mounted on wheels so that he could pull it from room to room.

This hearth was a gift of love, from a man I love dearly as a friend, although his own hearth and heart are elsewhere. I realize, as I sit here this summer evening, that it is exactly three years that I have been in this house, and that, yes, I am at home.

Time to get a cat. Maybe two.

ALISON GORDON

One Home of the Heart, One of the Imagination

~

By rough count, I had lived in twenty-four places in six different countries by the time I celebrated my twenty-fifth birthday. Like ivy, I learned to get by with very shallow roots.

But all that moving, all the changing of schools and friends, didn't mean that I had no permanent home. I had one, although I only realized it much later on in my life.

On the map of Lake of the Woods, in the northwest corner of Ontario, it's called Gordon Island. To Gordons, it's Birkencraig, named by my great-grandfather, who still had the Gaelic. It's a purely descriptive name: the thirty-acre island is a rocky crag, and it has been more or less covered in birches for as long as I have known it.

When I think of the island, I imagine myself paddling a canoe around it after supper, as the sun is beginning to set. I try to paddle as my father taught me, the way he had been taught by his father, the man who bought the island in 1906.

The Reverend Charles W. Gordon, writing as Ralph Connor, sold books in the millions around the turn of the century, ripping yarns of the Canadian frontier, full of muscular Christians and their hardy, compassionate women, and he used his royalties to

Alison and her brother, Charlie, with their mother,
Ruth Gordon, c. 1949

provide a summer home to which his wife, Helen, and their children – the eldest a boy, the next six all girls – could retreat from Winnipeg summers.

He built a large main cottage with five bedrooms, a huge living room dominated by a fireplace, a verandah that stretches around two-thirds of the building – half of it screened, including the large dining room – and a curious two-storey octagonal tower off to one side. The bottom of the tower was a bedroom, but the top, surrounded on all sides by screened windows through which he had a panoramic view of the lake, was where he wrote, a room of his own away from the noise and confusion of his growing family and their many friends.

I never knew my grandfather, but feel as if I did, because the Birkencraig he created for his family is the same one I enjoy today.

The main cottage is still the centre of island life. Over the years, sleeping cabins have been added here and there around the island,

Author with fish . . .
and attitude, c. 1953

but all the meals are still taken together on the verandah. A propane two-ring hotplate is good enough to make tea, but the old woodstove is still where the real cooking gets done. We've moved from kerosene lamps to Colemans, but we've kept electricity at bay.

We still play the same peculiar game of rummy that my father's generation did, a progressive five-round card game which involves a great deal of shouting. When my grandmother was alive, we never played it on Sunday, but we do now, even though it makes some of us feel guilty.

Even the no-drinking tradition has been recently relaxed, with the occasional bottle of wine with a special meal, and some family members enjoy a cocktail in their own quarters without creating a scandal. But there are some standards that will never disappear. There is still porridge every morning.

Birkencraig has strange powers. Because of the traditions and the memories, to set foot on the island is to lose completely the identities we enjoy in the rest of the world. We are defined by our relationships to each other and to the place we share. In a strange way, we also become ageless. Dignified cousins who hold positions of great respect in real life are likely to be found here wearing silly hats and playing stupid tricks on each other. It's as if we are all eleven years old.

Our favourite stunt is known as The Water Trick, which was first played by our distinguished reverend grandfather. It's often played on an unsuspecting visitor, preferably a young man or woman hoping to become part of the family. Here's how it goes.

The dining-room table is covered by an oilcloth. On weekends there can be as many as twenty people around it at once, carrying on a dozen conversations simultaneously. In the confusion, it is easy to surprise the victim. The instigator takes the oilcloth hanging down in front of her and holds it up, making it into a trough. A discreet nudge alerts the next in line, who continues the trough. This goes on until the trough ends over the victim's lap. Then, taking a glass of water, the instigator pours.

Consternation! Alarm! The victim leaps to his feet! The rest of the group howls until tears run down their faces! And somewhere my grandfather laughs, too.

More than anything else, more even than the laughter, what makes Birkencraig my home is the island itself. My roots are in the landscape, in the shape of a rock or the reeds at the water's edge, the clouds reflected in the cold water, the feel of pine needles underfoot on the beach path.

When I paddle around the island in the evening, there are memories in each rock face or sandy cove along the way. Here, just at this corner, I caught that big bass. There, I taught my cousin to smoke. Picnic Rock, where we went for cucumber and bacon sandwiches. The beach where I learned to swim. The lagoon, with its resident herons, snapping turtles, and beaver.

There are more memories on the island itself: the Ladies' Path, originally cut by my grandmother and a friend, and cleared lovingly each year; Farquar's Lane, cut by his curate, George Farquar, probably to escape the Gordons for a while each day; and Mrs. Fisher's rock, which my grandmother's friend (whose first name, if she had one, has never been revealed to me) would sit to peel vegetables in the sun.

There's a point on the island where Ellie and Annie's trees used to stand, Ellie and Annie being distant cousins. The trees are long gone, but my generation knows where they stood, even if we never knew the women for whom they were named.

Now there are new places and new trees in memory of those my generation remembers more clearly. Up the Ladies' Path from the pump-house, the tiny white-pine seedling my brother and I found to plant over my father's ashes on a hill where he liked to sit had become a three-foot-high tree by the time my mother's ashes joined his last summer, and will be standing, and recognized, when his grandchildren are grandparents.

There are changes, of course, necessary adaptations to modern realities. We stopped burning garbage in the incinerator years ago, about the time we stopped taking all the tin cans out in the rowboat and sinking them in the lake. Now each trip to town involves bags of garbage.

Everyone takes turns with meals now, and they are not quite so formal as they were when my grandmother and aunts spent most of their time in the kitchen. There hasn't been a great blueberry pie since my Aunt Ashie died.

We even have a propane barbecue, and a few years ago, a nanosecond in the collective memories of the cousins of the fourth

Charles W. Gordon and Helen
Gordon on Picnic Rock, c. 1935

generation, we began to have hamburgers on the back deck on
Saturday nights. Once this summer, it was suggested that we should
do something else instead.

"But we can't!" those of the youngest generation cried. "It's a
tradition!"

This summer, my generation's first grandchild will arrive,
beginning the sixth cycle of family that has made this thirty acres
of rock and birches home for most of a century.

∽

When I created the heroine of my series of mystery novels, I gave
her the home town I never had. Kate Henry grew up in small-
town Saskatchewan. I didn't give it much thought at the time.

There was no great philosophy behind it, but, forced to think about it four books down the road, I realized that through Kate, I was expressing a need of my own.

By an accident of geography, my first passport was an American one. Born in New York City to an American mother and a Canadian father, I was a dual citizen. My father worked for the United Nations for a good part of my growing up, and I quickly learned that everywhere in the world outside of the United States, it was better to be a Canadian.

Ever since renouncing my American citizenship when I turned twenty-one (in what I hoped was dramatic fashion, tied to anti-Vietnam protest), I have been an ardent nationalist. Because I lived outside the country until I went to university, however, I have always secretly felt like an impostor. Kate was my answer. Her roots could be deep in prairie soil. How much more Canadian can you get?

In 1995, I decided that the next Kate Henry book (which would turn out to be *Prairie Hardball*) would include a homecoming. My first problem was to figure out where her home town was.

That summer, aided by suggestions from listeners of CBC Radio, to whom I had turned for advice, I rented a car in Regina and began to drive. I went from Eastend in the southwest of the province to Nipawin in the northeast, exploring dozens of small towns in between.

I hadn't written much about Kate's early life, so I wasn't particularly restricted in my choice. I had made reference in an early book to the sound of a train whistle near her Toronto duplex making her homesick. At the time she fantasized about hopping the train and getting off it by the grain elevator ten blocks from her family home. That hardly restricted me, because most towns had at least one grain elevator and railway tracks, some of them even still in use. I also knew that she had grown up near a major

Downtown Indian Head, 1995

town, either Regina or Saskatoon, where she went for her ballet lessons as a girl.

With a great deal of the province eligible, I had a lot of fun for those three weeks. I drove on highways and gravel grid roads, poked around the local museums, picked up stacks of information from tourist offices, ate in interchangeable Chinese cafés, read small-town papers, and looked for United churches. Kate's father was a minister, you see.

And, finally, that was how I chose the town of Indian Head. I visited it early on my quest, at the suggestion of fellow crime novelist Gail Bowen. She and I drove east from Regina on the Trans-Canada Highway one bright August afternoon. The trip took less than an hour. There were several grain elevators by the railway tracks. Check. Chinese café. Check. Clip & Curl Salon. Check. Local paper. Check. Wide main street (Grand Avenue) with pickup trucks parked diagonally. Check.

More important, it felt right. Unlike many towns I scouted, it didn't look as if it had changed much over the years. There was a new town hall and library, but there was no mall on the outskirts of town or boarded-up storefronts in the tiny "downtown." Businesses were locally owned. It was simply a nice little town.

When we found St. Andrew's United Church, my heart leapt. It was a beautiful solid brick building that anchored the corners of Buxton and Eden streets. The cornerstone bore the date 1907.

The church was locked, but we went into the church hall next door and found the secretary. She was glad to take us through the old church basement (where I could imagine a surly adolescent Kate being forced to do her duty at fowl suppers) into the church itself.

It was wonderful, with dark wooden pews, wainscotting, a balcony, and a great old pipe organ. The entrance was on the corner, and the church was laid out that way, on the diagonal with two side aisles and the balcony curving around above. I could imagine Kate's father (who would look kind of like Tommy Douglas) preaching his sermon from the pulpit.

Going up the stairs, we could see the rope for the church bell hanging down through a hole in the ceiling. I was enchanted. The church secretary gave us bulletins from the most recent service, and Gail and I headed to the hotel for a beer.

A few days later, in some hotel or other, I was reading through the material I had collected on the road and came across that church bulletin from St. Andrew's United. By coincidence, the week before had been the church's anniversary, and the bulletin listed some important events in the church's history, including the fact that the inaugural service, in 1908 had been conducted by a visiting minister, Reverend C. E. Gordon.

My grandfather, the observant reader will recall, was the Reverend C. W. Gordon. Could this be a typo? He was based in

Winnipeg, not far away, and in 1908, he would have been at the height of his fame. Just the kind of guy they would have hoped to snare for such an important occasion.

I returned to Indian Head on a Saturday, but there was no one at the church. I tried the library, and the town history, without success. The librarian phoned the church secretary at home, but there was no reply. I left, question unanswered.

I never did find a better town than Indian Head, though, and when I returned to Toronto, I wrote to the church secretary to ask her to check the troubling initial. By return mail, she confirmed that it had indeed been the grandfather I had never known who conducted the first service.

What else did I need? A giant hand pointing down from the clouds? Kate had found her home.

WAYNE GRADY

The Landmark

~

"A Canadian settler *hates* a tree."
— Anna Brownell Jameson, 1838

"The tallest poppy in the field is always the first to be cut down."
— Australian proverb

I don't know where the idea came from, or who first came up with it. It might have been me. It might have been one of the others. Most likely it was just one of those ideas that appears one day among young people with not much to think about and not much else to do. However it happened, one Saturday morning four of us set out with an axe to chop down the tree. It was Keith's father's axe. It had been hanging in his garage between two nails above the workbench, something that had always been there and then suddenly you see it. Maybe it was seeing the axe that gave us the idea, and we thought of the tree because the tree had always been there, too. Anyway, one Saturday morning in July, four of us started walking downriver from Seven Islands with the idea that we were going to chop down the tree. There was Keith, who was carrying the axe, there was his twin brother, Kevin, there was Ronnie Ormstead, and there was me.

Seven Islands was a small town on the north shore of the St. Lawrence River, a very isolated part of Quebec. Jacques Cartier had named the area Sept-Îles in 1535, we'd been told, because he had counted seven islands in the bay and because there was a place called Sept-Îles near Saint-Malo, his home port in France. But hardly anyone who lived there called it by its French name. It was an English town, actually an American town, maintained by the Iron Ore Company as a depot where ore pellets brought down from Schefferville on company trains were loaded onto company freighters to be taken upriver to places like Cleveland, Ohio. We didn't know much about that at the time, I mean where the ore went, or where it came from. We just lived there. We didn't know precisely what our fathers did. Everything was rust red, from the ore dust. You wiped your hand along a window ledge and your palm came up as though caked in dried blood. We thought it strange that the town had been built on a grid, with all the avenues that ran parallel to the river named alphabetically – Arnaud, Brochu, Cartier. It seemed limiting. All the streets running perpendicular were named numerically – First, Second, Third, up to about Sixteenth in those days. Beyond Sixteenth Street and north of Laurier Avenue, there was just sand and bush.

There were no buildings in Seven Islands higher than two storeys, because of the sand. The original plan for the Hudson's Bay Company store had called for a five-storey building at the corner of Brochu and Second, but when they started digging the foundation they just kept bringing up sand. We'd been told that the whole area around Seven Islands had once been a seabed, that before the last Ice Age the Great Lakes had drained straight into the Atlantic from Lake Superior, and that the Gulf of St. Lawrence had once extended all the way to Quebec City.

Mr. McBurney, our geography teacher, had taken us downtown to watch the excavation for the Hudson's Bay store, by way of proof. The huge backhoe had gone down fifty feet and was still sifting up fine, dry, almost pure white sand with flecks of black feldspar in it. And so they just filled in the hole, poured a kind of floating concrete pad on top of the sand, and built two storeys on it.

After that, no one had ever tried to build anything taller. It was odd to know you were walking on fifty feet of sand. You found yourself testing the sidewalks, noticing cracks, running your eye up the corners of buildings. Retreating glaciers had scraped the land flat, and the receding ocean had buried it in sand. Even the Moisie River, a few miles up the coast, was a slow, twisted, sand-laden gash in the trees; less than a mile from its mouth, it gave a sudden, violent lurch to the east, as if desperate to dump its silt before emptying into the St. Lawrence.

Living in Seven Islands gave you a kind of low perspective. Anything higher than a telephone pole stood out: the radio tower at the airport, the loading cranes down at the shipyards, one or two of the islands in the bay. Inland there were hills, a few rock ridges, but they seemed all but inaccessible to us, as if the grid had caught us. One granite ridge ran north and east of the town, about three or four miles inland, forming a kind of crescent horizon fringed with low evergreen trees. It was the highest point of land we could see. There had been a forest fire in the area a decade or so before, and most of the big trees had burned down, so nothing was more than fifteen years old. It got to you after a while, all that lowness, the newness. It seemed like a judgement, like an inevitability, like nothing in your life was ever going to be higher than two storeys, everything was going to be perpetual renewal.

Except for the tree. About two-thirds of the way along the granite ridge, in a straight line from the end of Sixteenth Street but three or four miles into the bush, one tree stood out from the scrub spruce that flanked it at the top of the ridge. We could see it from anywhere in town. We didn't know whether it was a black spruce or a balsam fir that had somehow survived the fire, and maybe one of the things we wanted to do when we set out with the axe was just find out what kind of tree it was and how long it had been there. It was something that was always in the corner of your eye, like a beacon. Coming out of school or a store, you would look away from town toward the tree to get your bearings – there's the tree, home is this way – without really being conscious of doing so. It was a landmark, an irregularity along an otherwise featureless horizon. People in town noticed it because it was different, and when we cut it down people would notice it because it was gone. Not that we thought of it that way. It wasn't a thing that made any sense to us. It was just an idea we had, to cut it down.

So we took the axe from Keith's father's garage and set off along the shore of the river, intending to walk south to the ridge and then follow it inland to the tree. It felt good, carrying the axe. It felt good to have a purpose, and to have the right tool for that purpose. We walked along Arnaud, following the river, until the town disintegrated into shacks and ruts, and the road merged with the sandy, charcoal-strewn beach. The St. Lawrence there is salt and very wide, nearly forty miles across, more like an ocean than a river. You couldn't see the other side, so that walking along it was like walking on the edge of some vast, eerily calm body of water. There were waves, but small ones, more like whispers, and there was a tide, but it was out, so that the sand was wet and easy to walk on. Here and there deep gulleys had been cut through it where streams or tide water ran out of the bluffs and carved their way into the river, and we had to climb down into them and wade across and then climb back out. But it was sand,

and we could cut footholds in the sides of the gulleys with the axe and climb out easily. We thought about the possibility of the gulleys caving in on us, but it never happened so we stopped thinking about it.

By the time we reached the ridge it was past noon. At the point where the ridge hit the river, the shoreline became a narrow lip of sand at the base of a sharp granite cliff. At high tide, the water would slap right up against the rock. We climbed the ridge and stood for a while at the top, surrounded by spruce and wind, and looked out over the St. Lawrence. We had never seen it before from such a height. We could see what Jacques Cartier had not seen, that there were really only six islands – the seventh was in fact a narrow peninsula on which the town had been built – and on the far horizon we thought we could make out a darker band between the water and the sky that one of us said was the Gaspé Peninsula, and another said no, it was the tip of Anticosti Island. Now I think it was just clouds, a trick of the light, but at the time we felt like settlers, as though we were the first people ever to stand there and really look at what was around us and to consider it as something we could make our own, to see the land at our feet as home.

We turned inland along the top of the ridge and walked toward the tree. We kept our eyes down, taking in the expanse of bush below us. We felt strong, seeing the tops of the trees from above. They seemed dry and brittle, as though we could reach down and snap them off. I think I was carrying the axe at this time. After a while we came to a rock cut, where the railroad line had been blasted through the ridge, and we realized we could have walked along the tracks from town instead of along the river, and we decided to go back that way after we had cut down the tree. We had to climb down one side of the rock cut, cross the tracks, and then climb up the other side, and when we did that we were only a few hundred yards from the tree.

I don't remember who took the first swing. I'd been carrying the axe when we crossed the railroad tracks, because I recall how difficult it was to climb up the rock face carrying an axe, but I might have given it to someone else at the top or I might have kept it. I do know we took turns chopping at the tree. It was huge, at least three feet in diameter and as high again as the ridge, maybe eighty feet. It was a balsam fir, bigger and higher than the second-growth spruce around it, something that had survived disaster and outstripped its neighbours. We didn't even try to climb it, although there were branches so low that we had to duck under them to get a good swing at the trunk.

It took us more than two hours to cut it down. It was hard work, and it was a hot day. We chopped for an hour or so, taking turns, and then stopped to eat lunch and admire the wedge we had made halfway through the tree's rock-hard trunk. We sat at its base, where the ground was covered with chips, and leaned our bare backs against the warm trunk and looked down toward the town. I don't think we talked much. I think we were beginning to feel a bit uneasy about what we were doing, and I think the point at which we had begun to feel uneasy was when we realized how far you had to cut through a tree to make it fall down. We were halfway through it, and it wasn't even shaking when we hit it. I think now about a time, quite a few years before this, when another friend, Terry, and I had killed a squirrel with our BB guns. It had taken more than two packs of BBs, more than a hundred shots, to kill the squirrel. It lay there on the ground, its eyes open and its sides heaving, while we pumped shot after shot into it, trying desperately to kill it. We had both been crying by the time it finally died. I wasn't thinking about that when we were cutting down the tree, but it was the same. You couldn't stop halfway. You had to go on.

We finished our lunch and went back to the tree, taking two or three more turns each. It was nearly four o'clock by the time it began to fall. I think it was Ronnie who noticed it first, but I don't remember who was chopping. The last few strokes seemed to go very quickly; one minute the tree was standing stolidly upright as though we were rodents gnawing at its base, the next minute its tip was gyrating with each blow from the axe, and then it was falling with a tremendous fibrous groan, a wrenching as of muscle and sinew, followed by a kind of sigh as it sank into the lowly spruce around it. Its jagged, yellow trunk swung high over our heads and hung there, held aloft by its own branches, still taller than us.

We stood separately, not looking at each other or up at the tree. I think I turned and looked toward the town, which now seemed smaller and farther away but otherwise unchanged.

No one spoke. No one even thought to count the rings. We picked up the axe and our lunch things and started walking back to town. We worked our way along the ridge to the rock cut, then started climbing down to the railroad tracks. Kevin and I went first while the other two waited above.

I'm not sure how the rock fight started. Maybe someone's foot dislodged a piece of rock that hit someone else, or maybe just seeing the loose rock fall through the air gave us the idea, but the next thing we knew the two of us down on the tracks were throwing rocks at the two still up on the ridge, and they were throwing rocks at us. I think now we were trying to punish ourselves for cutting down the tree. We were trying to hit each other; this was no game. We wanted to hurt. At the same time, we didn't expect to hit anyone. Terry and I hadn't expected to hit the squirrel with the first shot, either, but once we had hit it, we had to keep on hitting it until we'd killed it, and it was like that with the rock fight. We had to keep throwing rocks until we'd hit someone.

I was the one who was hit. I remember looking up at the ridge, the two of them, Keith and Ronnie, silhouetted against the bright sky exactly as, until a few hours ago, the tree had been silhouetted against the distant skyline, and seeing a rock come hurtling toward me out of the sun, and before I could move feeling it – no, hearing it – hit me on the mouth. I heard my jaw crack, and when I put my hand to my mouth it came back with blood on it. I grabbed something, a handkerchief or a T-shirt, pushed it against my mouth, and started running along the tracks toward town. We all did. We could hardly see, there was so much sweat in our eyes, but I don't remember any pain. We ran out of the rock cut and into the sickly sweet smell of spruce and sand. Someone said who's got the axe, and someone else said never mind the axe. We ran for half an hour, straight to my house, and my parents drove me to the hospital. My lip was split right up to the nostril; it took ten stitches. I still have the scar.

RON GRAHAM

A Cabin in the Woods

~

The summer before Quebec's second referendum on independence in October 1995 was a particularly glorious one. Day followed day, week followed week of blue skies and clear nights, with just enough rain to keep the farmers happy and the wells from running dry. Biking along the ridge of Chemin Jordan with its panoramic view south across rolling fields and forests to the hills of Vermont, I sometimes used to wonder if this halcyon summer would be remembered like that of 1914, before the guns of August shattered the peace of Europe. But, literally and figuratively, there were no dark clouds on the horizon.

Everyone looked tanned and relaxed, far from aggrieved or oppressed. Indeed, it was rare to find anyone, anglophone or francophone, who wanted to waste the all-too-fleeting splendour of such a summer arguing the never-ending politics that filled the newspapers. There would be enough grim and blustery days ahead for that. As a result, I was lulled into an optimistic faith that a substantial majority of French-speaking Quebeckers would vote, as they had in 1980, to remain within Canada. There was nothing, not even the polls, to make me suspect that my home and native land might be in real danger of passing away – as ephemeral as a summer idyll.

∾

"I don't feel like myself in Toronto," said my son James, then six years old. "But I feel like myself here."

It surprised me as a rather sophisticated remark from a child, but I knew exactly what he meant. Though I enjoy a happy life ten months a year in a downtown neighbourhood of the city, with a comfortable house, an interesting profession, and many good friends, I never feel so calm or free – so much at home – as I do during the two months we spend at our small, secluded cabin in Quebec. Like Indians fleeing the heat and congestion of the cities on the plain for the pine-scented breezes of the hill stations, we decamp at the end of June in an overladen van of suitcases, bicycles, books, games, rain gear, stuffed animals, specialty foods, and boxes of work-related material – to which we added a dog in the summer of 1995 – and don't return until school starts in September. Even the dog was more himself, rediscovering his atavistic urge to pursue groundhogs and revealing a hitherto unknown passion for swimming.

The cabin is hidden in a forest beside the confluence of two rushing streams at the foot of a valley about a hundred miles east of Montreal. From one of the dark-green Adirondack chairs on the deck, all you can see are the trees and the sky, all you can hear are the birds and the water. After a long walk up the path through the woods, you come out upon an open hillside sown with hay or oats and, farther up, near the eastern ridge, a sizeable pond edged with bulrushes and alive with frogs. Below, on the opposite slope of the valley through which a dirt road follows the

Ball Brook to meet the Niger River a mile north at Way's Mills, sits the Lefebvres' pristine farm, almost Swiss in its neatness and compactness, its fields a changing quilt of subtle colours, its Holsteins moving to and from the barn with gentle bells.

Though we have occasionally hazarded the seven-hour journey on winter highways to spend Christmas week amid its waist-deep, incandescent-white snow, James and his younger sister Emily have sanctified the cabin with the intense sensations of childhood summers, when, as Dylan Thomas remembered, "My wishes raced through the house high hay/And nothing I cared, at my sky blue trades, that time allows/In all his tuneful turning so few and such morning songs/Before the children green and golden/Follow him out of grace." As babies, when they were colicky, the sound of the brooks invariably soothed them to sleep. Learning to walk on the roots and rocks of the woodland paths, they seemed to fly once they were back on the smoothness of city sidewalks. They had their first swims in the cold elixir of the pond; they befriended their first horse, cow, and cat in the Lefebvres' barn; they advanced from napping in the hammock to splashing stones in the stream for entire afternoons to catching bullfrogs and picking wild berries.

Every time we return to Toronto, they have to be recivilized not to wander naked up the street or piss in the local park, and their infinite universe of wilderness and sunlight seems tragically diminished to an enclosed patch of grass in the back yard and the television set in the basement.

Perhaps because of the sunny weather, perhaps because of their age, the summer of 1995 was especially memorable. The primitive tree house, complete with swings, slide, and sandbox, was finally finished, and the new path from the cabin to the pond introduced the children to the deep woods as never before. They found deer tracks, raccoon tracks, the tracks of a moose and a bear! They became curious about the names of birds and wild-flowers, which mushrooms were edible, the different types of trees and ferns. They sighted deer bounding across the meadows and hawks swooping down for mice. One morning we hiked almost a mile uphill along the stream that tumbles beside the cabin into Ball Brook and, at its source, discovered a beaver dam and lodge – to which we returned on a drizzly evening to watch the beavers at work. We each got second-hand bicycles and explored the bucolic trail the village had recently opened along the banks of the Niger, often stopping for a picnic and a swim in one of the pools at the foot of some rapids.

In October, back in Toronto, James sat weeping in the kitchen. It was a few days before the referendum, and, according to the front page of the newspaper spread across the table, the sepa-ratists had an even chance of winning. "Does that mean," he sobbed, "we can't go to the cabin any more?"

~

There is a Chinese adage that every man should do three things during his lifetime: have a son, write a book, and build a house. I have been blessed with all three. The house, this cabin, came first. Though I had more to do with its design than its construc-tion, it is as much an expression of myself as my children and my books.

Before the house had come the land. I had been familiar with the Eastern Townships, as the region is called, since my own boyhood in Montreal. My father was involved with a limestone operation to the east of its biggest city, Sherbrooke, and he would sometimes bring the family for weekend visits to the manager's house and once to the company's annual sugaring-off party. We holidayed for a couple of summers on its largest lake, Lake

Memphremagog, and I was sent to a boarding school in its countryside from ages nine to sixteen. Though I was very much a city
boy, with little enthusiasm for the great outdoors, I unwittingly
fell under the spell of the Townships: the undulation of its landscape, the smell of its seasons, the charm of its towns, the civility
of its people.

It is a unique corner of Canada, indeed of North America – a
hybrid society of American refugees, British settlers, Irish emigrants, and French farmers with an added mix of factory workers,
wealthy cottagers, draft dodgers, back-to-the-landers, and people
from around the world who chanced upon its serenity and beauty
and couldn't leave. Tavern conversations hop back and forth
between English to French in mid-sentence without apparent
rhyme or reason. There are Arnolds who can't speak a word of
English and Tremblays who sport Scottish kilts. They live in
places called Sainte-Marguerite-de-Lingwick and Saint-Isidore-
d'Auckland. Amid their dairy farms and pulp mills, within a mile
or two of the cabin, are several Jews (including a distinguished
poet, a well-known sculptor, a Polish hippie, and a retired
doctor), a pair of McGill medical professors from South Africa, a
painter from British Columbia married to a nurse from the
Philippines, and a Japanese master ceramist.

Though I had left boarding school vowing never again to be
exiled from the intellectual and social excitements of a big city,
friends kept drawing me back to the Townships. And though I
spent two and a half years roaming the planet, from the isles of
Scotland to the oases of Algeria, from the plains of Kenya to the
ranges of Nepal, from the jungles of Sumatra to the islands of
Tonga, it was only to realize that I had to complete the circle and
return home. Home was Canada, of course, but it was also
Quebec. Once, at a film festival in Auckland, New Zealand, I
found myself overwhelmed with sharp pangs of homesickness by

scenes of the Laurentian woods in autumn, and when I finally sighted the hills to the east of the Ottawa River after hitchhiking from Vancouver, I knew there was no place else in the world I'd rather be.

I was changed, however, for I had become accustomed to avoiding cities as much as possible and camping under the stars in pastures, deserts, mountains, and beaches. I no longer saw much romance in the congestion and squalor of Montreal, and I grew sad if I couldn't watch the sun go down. I soon settled into a rather dilapidated nineteenth-century farmhouse near Bishopton, east of Sherbrooke, but it proved a short-lived fantasy. I was hardly prepared for the realities of frozen water-pipes, organic corn, or first novels. After two winters I went off to make a career in journalism, first in Ottawa, then in Toronto. But I couldn't abandon the Eastern Townships altogether, as so many of its young farmers and mill workers had had to do. Before leaving, I decided to buy a piece of land as a kind of pledge that I would be back.

Experience had taught me what to look for. I wanted to be in the vicinity of my friends on Lake Memphremagog and Lake Massawippi, but I didn't want to be near their tourist towns, crowded shorelines, or loud motorboats. I wanted some fields, some woods, and someplace to swim, but I didn't want to be exposed to the transmission lines, skidoo trails, transport trucks, and weekend traffic that blight many a scenic backroad. In truth, I was seeking nothing less than a spiritual refuge.

On a rainy morning in the spring of 1977 an agent showed me two properties. The first was squashed beside an ugly chalet on the edge of Autoroute 55. But the second, a mile from the two small wooden churches that face each other in the picturesque village of Way's Mills, seemed the very realization of my dream. Even with the valley covered in a chilly mist, with no leaves on the deciduous trees and only the flat tones of a Canadian spring, it was a place of sublime beauty and meditative tranquillity. Contained yet diverse, introverted yet uplifting, it made up for what it lacked in sweeping vistas and lakeside romance by its subtlety and seclusion. And, as a consequence of the Anglo exodus and real-estate bust following the unexpected election of a separatist government six months earlier, it was as cheap as dirt.

The original homestead had been in the fields at the top of the dead-end track that climbs the eastern ridge, not far from where the pond now lies, but it had burned to the ground some twenty-five years before, leaving no trace except for a well-hole in the grass and the grove of cherry trees. Near its site, back among the pines, I parked a bright-yellow trailer that had once served as a mobile scientific lab for the Ontario highways department. Just large enough for a bed, a desk, a chair, a woodstove, and three shelves of books, it became my summer "cottage" for the next couple of years. I bathed in the waterfalls along the trail through the woods; I cooked on an open fire as the sun dropped behind the opposite ridge; I read by the light of a kerosene lamp; and I gradually got to know every square foot of my ninety acres, the light of each season, the source of the various streams, the particularities of the fields and forest.

Things might have remained that way for many more years if the Parti Québécois hadn't introduced the Agricultural Land Protection Act, the so-called "Green Law," in 1978. Designed to prevent the destruction of good farm land by weekenders from the city, it severely restricted the subdivision or development of arable zones. In my case, while it helped preserve the peace and beauty of the valley, it compelled anyone who already owned a vacant piece of land to build a house on it within five years or forfeit the automatic right to do so in the future. And so in the summer of 1982, a year before the deadline, on a special site I had

discovered thick in the woods where the two streams meet, protected from the full sun of summer and the north wind of winter,
out of sight or sound of the road but easily serviced by electricity,
phone, and car, I built the one-room log cabin with a cathedral
ceiling, a covered gallery, and a stone fireplace.

I used to joke that I really built it to house the hundreds of
books I had been storing in boxes in half a dozen locations since
my university days. But, in a psychological sense, bringing them
all together, never to move them again, gave me a base from
which I could go forth with a light step and to which I could
return with a joyous heart. Home was not so much where I hung
my hat as where I kept my books. In time, the cabin also became
the repository of my exotic bric-à-brac: pieces of decorated tapa
cloth from Fiji, a monk's palm-frond umbrella from Sri Lanka, a
temple gong from Burma, a tambourine-like hide drum from the
Northwest Territories and a square version from Morocco, rock
fossils from the Sahara and the Himalayas, shells and bits of coral
from the Caribbean and the South Pacific, wooden bowls from
Tibet, a carved mask from Dahomey, a stone Nandi and Shiva
lingam from India, a shard from Greece.

When I was away, whether working in Toronto or travelling
abroad, I drew comfort from the thought that there existed one
speck of the globe awaiting me like Ulysses' dog, permanently
mine. And when I came back, sometimes after many months, I
always passed between the two churches in Way's Mills with a
mixture of trepidation – would it be damaged? would it be there?
– and exhilaration. There were several periods, especially when I
was writing magazine articles and books, when I stayed for most of
the year, exhilarated by the autumn colours on a crisp October
day, snug by the fire during the worst blizzards of February, dozing
in the hammock after a picnic lunch with visitors in July.
Changes came bit by bit: a footbridge replaced the wade across

Ball Brook to get from the drive to the cabin, the pond was excavated in the upper field and fed by a dozen underground springs, a new building went up beside the stream to make a sunny working space and more room for guests.

Suddenly, early in 1989, I thought I was going to lose it all. At the age of forty-one I fell deeply in love and got married. How often had I been told that, as perfect as the cabin was as a bachelor's retreat, I would never find a civilized woman willing to spend any length of time in what was effectively a single room thirty-five feet long by twenty-three feet wide in the middle of the woods ten miles from the nearest grocery store. Moreover, not only was Gillian bound to Toronto by her many close friends and the joint-custody arrangement involving her three-year-old son, Sam, she had grown up in Kingston, Ontario. To her, it was clear, summers meant swimming on the sandbanks of the St. Lawrence River and sailing among the spectacular Thousand Islands. So I resigned myself, as a relatively small price to pay for the great gift of a contented wife, to quit my paradise in Quebec for a house in downtown Toronto and, in due course undoubtedly, a waterside cottage in Prince Edward County.

I had underestimated the power of the Townships' spell and the cabin's magic. Gillian fell completely under their sway within her first visit. Every June she pressed to leave the city as early as possible; every September she wept when we drove away along Chemin Ruisseau Ball. She even mused about living in the cabin year-round, and it took me to remind her about the practicalities of my work and Sam's schooling, the miserably muddy months of November and April, and the various compensations of urban life. As for Sam, whenever we talk about enlarging the kitchen and adding another bedroom, he actually sheds tears. "I don't want you to change anything," he says. "I like it exactly as it is."

When James and Emily came along, of course, we had to make a few modifications. We converted the concrete cellar into three bedrooms and a second bathroom. The deck was expanded to accommodate a bigger picnic table, more chairs, and ball-hockey games; each day began to include a walk to the Lefebvres' barn to watch the cows being milked and give the horse an apple; the pond, now overrun with a rowboat, a plastic alligator and shark, a floating mattress, and some multicoloured noodles, got a new dock and a sandy beach.

For all that, in the eyes of many of my separatist and federalist friends alike, I had betrayed my love for this place by leaving it. I was no longer a citizen of Quebec. I wouldn't be able to vote in the referendum. My emotions, to say nothing of my opinions, were discounted because I had joined the hundreds of thousands who departed the province for political, economic, or personal reasons. It was all very well for me to think of here as home, where I had grown up, where I expected my ashes to be scattered, but I had become little more than a summer tourist who visited more regularly than most and lingered somewhat longer.

~

What made the summer of 1995 so enjoyable, in addition to its fine weather, was its idleness. For the first time in years I didn't have an assignment on my desk. The manuscript of my latest book had gone to the publishers, after many labour-intensive months, the day before we departed for the Townships; I was still emotionally exhausted from my father's death six months earlier; and I vowed to do nothing but read Trollope's Palliser novels. The only exception was a commitment to write a brief memoir for the souvenir album the local municipality was preparing to celebrate its fiftieth anniversary in 1996, which was also the two hundredth anniversary of the arrival of the area's first settler, Joseph Bartlett, who erected a log cabin not far to the south of mine.

The municipality of Barnston-Ouest had been carved out of Barnston, one of the hundred or so townships the British Crown created in 1792 from the hilly and uncultivated "wild lands" of French Canada east of Montreal along the new United States boundary. Its earliest pioneers were in fact New Englanders with names that still grace the map as Baldwin's Mills, Burroughs Falls, Chemin Heath, and Ball Brook. (A family of black settlers, the Tattons, caused the local river to be called the Negro, which later became the Niger.) They weren't exiles loyal to the King and Church of England on the run from the American Revolution; they were Methodists, Baptists, Congregationalists, and Adventists moving north for the free land. In 1810 Ira King opened a tavern at King's Corner, present-day Kingscroft, around the time Daniel Way built his grist, shingle, and saw mills in nearby Wayville, now Way's Mills.

Even though the authorities discouraged American settlers in favour of British immigrants, following the War of 1812 and a bit of republican agitation during the Rebellion of 1837, the local population remained predominantly Yankee by the time Canada was founded in 1867, with only a few Anglicans, a few Brits, a few Irish Catholics, and three French-Canadian land-owners. But that soon changed. The opening of the West lured many young men away; the Massawippi Valley Railway brought in fresh arrivals from the United Kingdom and Ireland after 1870; and a wave of French Canadians poured south from the St. Lawrence River system in search of fertile farms and forestry jobs. In 1888 the Anglicans built their white clapboard church directly across the road from the evangelicals' Union Church in Way's Mills. In 1904 the Roman Catholics established a new parish in Kingscroft, which had already become a French-speaking community.

"Tolerance and generosity of spirit have become the norm," Léon Gérin, the noted French-Canadian academic observed about the region as early as 1887, "and tend more and more to impose themselves as the rule of conduct for those who under-take the leadership of the different groups."

Like most local histories, Barnston West's souvenir album turned out to be heavy on official records, genealogical connec-tions, commercial developments, and studio portraits – the public face of home – with proud pictures of farms, round barns, prize bulls and goats, a 1959 Buick, and Roger Lagueux's backhoe. I learned, for example, that Mrs. Clark in the small blue house this side of the village was one of the three surviving children of Iris Bryan, née Daniels, "best remembered for her cooking and needlecraft and for reading stories to the very young," herself the great-great-granddaughter of the founder Daniel Way and his native wife, Keziah Jaquith. I also discovered that Morton Rosengarten's sculpture studio had been a creamery, beginning as the Wayville Butter and Cheese Manufacturing Society in 1896 and ending as La Coopérative agricole de Way's Mills in 1958.

But among the family recollections of baseball teams, summer socials at the Women's Institute, and Harry and Jessie Emo's general store – written either in English or in French – are hints of private hardships and sorrows amid the inexorable decline in the birthrate and the increase in migration to the cities: the Morrill boys killed in the Great War, Durwood Cunnington's bout with polio, young Charles Keysar losing his right arm to gan-grene infection after falling from a hay-mow onto a pitchfork, the accidental deaths of Laurette Leblond and Simon Provencher, the fire at the Sheard woollen mill, the closing of the Way's Mills Academy. In 1938 Clarence Davis lost his first wife, Ruby, when she died giving birth to their twin girls, Ethel and Evelyn. In 1947 Mabel Whipple had to take charge of the family farm while raising three young children after a wagon rolled over her husband, paralysing him, "and many said that she could handle a crosscut saw better than most men." In 1987 Turner Hunter was found dead, at the age of seventy-eight, "next to his faithful old International W4 tractor – the one he had driven in all those ploughing matches for so many years."

"Although we are now comfortable in our cosy home in Way's Mills, life was not always easy for us," wrote Syd Davis, a descendant of another early pioneer, who does indeed have a cosy bungalow he built himself on what is effectively the village's one and only street. He turned eighty in 1995, and now winters with his wife, Hazel, in Cape Canaveral, Florida.

> I was only fourteen when I quit school to help out. I sawed wood through the winter. The following summer, I laboured for Stanley Jordan for $15.00 a month and board. After that, I worked for Bon Little. He had me build a wall along the river bank in North Hatley. It is still there. I even learned to dynamite the rock we used – all for $10 a month and meals. I then worked for Fred Wheeler for 50 cents a day and my dinner and supper.
>
> In 1933, William Collie's Mill opened, and I became a weaver – at the princely wage of three cents a yard. When Collie sold to Sheard, I stayed – for nine years altogether. But I suffered terrible migraines and the doctor advised me to leave. I quit Sheard's, and Hazel and I went into business. We borrowed $100 to start a feed store in the old barn.
>
> In those days, the farmers would all line up along our street, to take their milk to the Creamery, forty or fifty of them, and we did well, soon paying back the loan. In 1941, we put in groceries,

and in 1951, we had the new store built next door. Despite the closing down of the Creamery and fierce competition, we managed to keep our heads above water until we finally sold the store in 1975.

That was also a landmark year for Alain Bouffard, a young stonecutter in the granite quarry at Beebe, and his new bride, Pauline, a nurse at the hospital in Coaticook. In August they bought the family farm in Kingscroft from Alain's parents – his father died six months later and his mother retired as a nun – and, in October, Pauline's parents sold them theirs on nearby Chemin Corey. "Alain and Pauline, friends from childhood, neighbours, joined in holy matrimony, forged another bond by acquiring their family farms," they wrote, according to my translation.

Young and full of enthusiasm, they decided to rise to the challenge of becoming good farmers. They knew that the land they now owned would be generous to them if they were attentive to it. Pauline quit her job, wanting to assist Alain on the farm, but also wanting to educate their children to the same ideal. Conscious of sailing against the prevailing social winds, they decided to have numerous children, secure in the knowledge that Providence would support them. They appreciate all the assistance their families gave them.

Despite and because of their growing family, the tasks increase and get done. At a very young age, the children accept their responsibilities, often performing them with pleasure. They know the love of work and often it isn't much of a sacrifice to put off certain amusements. How happy they are to skip a few days of school to lighten their father's load! Many of them want to become farmers. The farm has always been diversified, with a woodlot, a sugarbush, and, principally, a milk herd. Two years ago the Holsteins were replaced by Charollais cattle for the production of meat.

Our family is made up of eleven children. They bring us a lot of happiness. The family and country life are for us sources of stability, of dignity, of growth, and of greatness. Everyone feels useful in such an environment. Moreover we have always been convinced that if we take the time to serve God, to follow His laws, He will help us every day. We feel privileged to live in a municipality that offers us peace, marvellous scenery, and good neighbours. We are happy to do our work, above all in the company of our children whom we love so much.

∾

There are some who say, with a bite, that my devotion to the Eastern Townships is really a sentimental nostalgia for a lost childhood when the sun never set on the British Empire, the colonial lords and plutocrats dominated Montreal, and the French Canadians were folkloric peasants who rode sleighs in wintertime and went to Mass on Sundays. What does a log cabin in the woods have to do with the modern suburbs and computerized industries of Quebec on the eve of the twenty-first century? What does a summer among farmers, sculptors, and vacationers have to do with the daily grind of technocrats, textile workers, and the unemployed? Indeed, what does either have to do with the realities of my own life in downtown Toronto?

Yet, I respond with a question of my own: what is a home other than a place of withdrawal from the world, a retreat into privacy, a refuge for the family, a storage house of coded memories and personal mementoes, an ideal in your head and a sanctum in your heart?

It has something to do with a sense of belonging, too. And that's the rub, because there are Quebec separatists who would deny that I belong here, not just in a legal sense but in a historical and psychological sense as well. To them, the Eastern Townships itself is not the "real" Quebec, because it's too English. Despite all their protestations about constructing a liberal and pluralistic nation, they see Quebec as the homeland of the French-speaking descendants of the seventy-five thousand pioneers of New France who were conquered by the British army in 1763. No one else can fully belong – not the native peoples who had occupied this land for thousands of years before the first French explorers arrived, not the anglophone settlers who have farmed these fields and operated these mills for the past two hundred years, not even the French-speaking immigrants who happen to be Jewish or black or Vietnamese. By their languages and colours, by their ethnicities and backgrounds, they are not made to feel included in the nationalists' definition of *Québécois*.

"Being an English Quebecker is like living in a hotel," a friend once told me. "It's comfortable for the moment, but you always know that someday you will have to leave."

I would argue, in fact, that the separatist vision of their Quebec home is even more illusory than mine, more nostalgic, and much less benign. It is rooted in its own utopian escape from the forces of global economics and social change, back to a fairy-tale realm before the Conquest when the people were resolutely isolated and the strangers were beyond the gates. Certainly there are fanatics among the separatists who will not rest, whatever the economic and social costs, until the last word of the English language has been eradicated in Quebec and the last anglophone forced to leave.

Of course, there are moderates on both sides who insist that the fracturing of Canada could take place without undue dislocation or conflict. Common sense and the pocketbook will prevail; ethnic violence and social turmoil cannot happen here; life will carry on. A few days before the referendum, my neighbour Réjean Lefebvre shrugged and said by way of a conclusion, "Oh well, whatever the outcome, nothing's going to be different, eh?" I was surprised that he, the most prudent and practical of men, didn't worry about the consequences to Quebec dairy prices, which are artificially elevated by federal policies, or the conflagration a few hotheads in the anglophone, francophone, and native communities could ignite. Not long ago my mother and sister came out of a restaurant in Old Montreal to find all four of their tires punctured by a spike. "Ontario licence plates," the policeman explained.

Then, on the night of the referendum, after the separatists had lost by a mere percentage point, their leader – ostensibly the premier of all Quebeckers – himself stoked the embers of bigotry by telling his distraught followers that the blame lay solely with "money and the ethnic vote."

The closeness of the thing changed the situation irrevocably. The separatists, instead of abandoning their pipe-dream, hardened their resolve to press on toward it with a kind of vengeance. In the meantime, they wanted the Quebec government to again apply a technical clause to override the freedom of expression supposedly guaranteed by the Canadian Charter of Rights in order to outlaw the use on commercial signs of any language but French. The anglophones and immigrants realized that the improbable had become the more likely. About two out of every three francophones they met in the office or saw on the street had voted Yes to some vague notion of independence; the "language police" were back at work patrolling the streets for an illegal "SNACK BAR" sign or a bit of Hebrew-only on an imported kosher package.

"ANGLOS GO HOME!" read one especially preposterous graffiti, as though we weren't home already.

Many years ago an astrologer in Benares, India, read my chart and pronounced, among other prophecies, "I see a small house in the countryside. In the last stage of your life, when you are sixty, you will retire there to devote the rest of your years to your spiritual development."

"That's awful," joked one of my more ambitious brothers when I told him of it. "I mean, if you know that's where you're going to end up, what's the point of striving for anything? Why not just move there now and get it over with?"

To my mind, however, it seems a wonderful fate. I hope it will be allowed to come to pass.

TERRY GRIGGS

Burning Down the House

~

Home is a word so warm it's on fire. To me at any rate, five years old and watching The Lodge, my first home, burn to the ground, as the saying so aptly goes. Bed on fire, tricycle on fire, all family photographs and mementoes, where our modest history is stashed, gone in a puff of smoke. Like a magic trick, but black magic, bedevilling us as we stood watching (some of us weeping) in the dark, in the cold. It must have happened around Christmas, for I remember being taken afterwards to a neighbouring farm where the tree in the living room was decorated simply with streamers of white toilet paper, one-ply, a light layer of snow. Materialism didn't have such a grip then, and none, at that destitute moment, on us.

Home, the word, must have been annealed for me then, tempered and transformed. Just when I was learning its more conservative and contained definition – safety, security, permanence – it opened up and let in the chill night air. (Not to mention a few nascent fire-breathing notions about passion and purification.) Loss now became part of that definition, disfiguring it, like my brother's melded marble collection we later excavated out of the ashes, but also prefiguring what we all discover eventually anyway.

And liberating it. The idea of home, my understanding of it, slipped out of that burning house like a spirit leaving a body. After, it came to haunt the grass, the rocks, the shoreline, the lake. I am one of those for whom home – *real* home and not one of its many surrogates – is a place, a particular geography. All islands draw me, but my very own is Manitoulin in northern Ontario, where, though surrounded by fathoms of water, the fire can't be put out. No matter where I am and in whatever mood, I'm not lost, you see, because I have this little pilot light burning inside, helping me to navigate, telling me exactly who I am and where I belong.

What is it about islands, anyway? Do they all come with sirens, their northern equivalents equipped with tackle and bait? You can't help but notice the strong homing instinct in islanders of all description. Some are free of it, I suppose, but most have swallowed the hook, and deeply. Honestly, you can feel it tugging at your innards as it plays the line, reels you in. Best not to resist.

You're probably not supposed to admit this, but I loved those Thomas Wolfe novels when I read them years ago, that barely controlled sea of words. Too bad that his fine *You Can't Go Home Again* title has become not only a cliché, but an actual belief and prohibition, a tattoo on the brain. Well, I'd say, break the neck off that baby and take a long dangerous drink. You can go home if you want, walk down Main Street without feeling alienated, too large and knowing for the place, or in danger of being stoned for what you've written about it. (You've learned to duck, haven't you?) I believe it's entirely possible, and fruitful, to jostle along with your younger selves, to enliven the present with the past, and this without becoming a prisoner of nostalgia. Why is it considered better, even necessary, to float displaced like a speck in the eye of the world? Is it a fear that emotional connection will tie us up in blood knots? That we will grow incurious, backward, intellectually homogenized, and, well, homely? Could happen anywhere. You might go home, having divested yourself of this idea that it can't be done, and be absolutely amazed at what you find there. Might be where the treasure's buried, right where your personal signature is located, your X on the map.

Home is portable, of course, and metamorphic. You can build it on the spot out of nothing but affection. Or even on rotten foundations, re-imagined and repaired, if your early home life was stark and troubled. Somehow the very thought of home keeps hope alive – keep those home fires burning, yes, keep 'em stoked, but don't forget the insurance.

I wish the word "homily" meant "aphorism," and then I could say, "Home tips so easily into homily." Like this: Home is where the cat is. Home is the distance between your knife and your fork. Home is the circumference of your hat. Home is the book in your hands. Or your heart.

Home. How splendid, and wondrous, that one word can generate so much heat.

KRISTJANA GUNNARS

Pebbles on the Beach

∼

The high grind of a small Cessna cut the morning stillness. In the first dawn, we awoke to that working boat heading north on the inlet. It was only 6 A.M. and the sound reverberated on the water and echoed uncomfortably from the hillsides on both sides, like a headache. A rhythm to it, a pulse. Then it was gone. But by that time we were already up. The light was beginning and I opened all the blinds. I looked for wild animals outside. They tended to sit around at night, outside the bedroom window where there was shelter. A bobcat, probably, or a lynx. There were cougars too. But we didn't see any that morning. It was hard to tell where they came from or where they went. The deep woods, tangled up into endless knots, tree around tree and branches in other branches, all covered in moss and clothed in ferns below. A jungle you could not walk through.

Pebbles on the endless beach bunched in groups among the trunks of driftwood. Some trunks wandered from a log cache. They had arms of steel hammered into them with huge rusty nails. The steel was bent and curled. The water rustled calmly. Gulls and ravens and ducks played on the water. A bunch of geese flew off in front of us as we wandered along. My boots were not tied tightly. Every step I took, they flopped and I could feel the inside sole moving around. My raincoat was buttoned up and my umbrella was in my hand. But there was no rain. The sky was grey but not overcast. The small beach houses by the road were devoid of life just then. Cottages with wooden seagulls by the door, rocking horses carved and painted, hanging on the outside wall. Shells and stones from the beach decorated the walkways.

J. and I had lunch at Molly's Reach. We found a table by the window, overlooking the marina below. Directly in front was a grey-painted houseboat with a For Sale sign on it. We talked about buying a houseboat and I wondered what it would be like to live in one. Waking up in the morning and feeling the water under the floor. Sitting on the houseboat deck looking out at a hundred boat masts sticking up in the air, swaying to and fro. And the colour blue. That deep, resonant blue they use in marine craft everywhere. And behind them, the open water of the Strait and the mountains of the islands beyond.

We were at the Blue Heron in the evening and I had a rack of lamb and oysters. The matron there, who is quite young and has long, curly red hair, was excited because of the earthquake. It happened when J. and I were sitting in the living room after a lunch of ham on rye with mustard and cheddar. We had an espresso by the fire. We each took a couch to sit in. J. was reading a philosophical article. I started Peter Høeg's *Borderliners*. I immediately recognized the environment he was talking about. The rain was coming down and the wind was blowing. Suddenly a great rumbly rush came over everything and the trees, so tall and sturdy, swayed and bent towards the ground. Those huge pines and cedars leaned over for a minute or two, as though it were an extremely strong wind. But it was not. It was an earth-quake that turned out to measure 3.9 on the Richter scale. We sat by the fire in the evening at the Blue Heron and talked about the earthquake.

In Gibsons we had fish and chips at Molly's Reach. I noticed Truffles had been upgraded to an ice-cream place and the small-town café atmosphere was gone. The sign outside was bright pink and inside it was full of tourists leaning over the ice-cream counter, selecting flavours. So we didn't go there. Perhaps in the winter it will revert to its old atmosphere. We stopped at the Quay Gallery. They were showing oils by an artist whose name I forget. He used mannequins as models. His canvases were dark and unpleasant.

The air in Gibsons is always salty and fresh. The sun strikes hard on the edges of the pier. Wood worn down to its innards and boats leaning against the planks, wet when people walk by. They slip easily in their shoes. The Salty Dog boat store down by the water, run by two young women who live with each other and work with each other. Both are blonde, short-haired, tanned, and they look like each other. I even asked them if they were sisters. But of course they aren't. If you do everything together, you begin to resemble each other. They say this about married people. Those two were at E.'s solstice picnic last year and rowed out the sound to meet a hauling tug that was bring-ing them supplies. Wood, I think. They live in Davis Bay on the water, probably on leased Indian land like E. and E. There the driftwood is piled up after decades of being washed up. The small strip of sand goes on for a long stretch, all the way to Gibsons and around, stopped only by the ferry terminal. Then the beach is rocks after that. Pebbles.

I took J. down to our own beach and we started throwing rocks out into the inlet. J. was trying to throw past the red buoy that ties up someone's boat, but the boat wasn't there. Three tries, and the second stone got as far as the buoy. J. said the stones need to be flat, and then they sail into the air with a momentum of their own. I sat on a log and watched J. throw an arm out of its shoulder socket. There was no one on the beach. There never is. I have only found people down there twice. Playing in the water. Kids jumping. Adults in beach chairs, folding out canvas backs on wooden frames. The people who live in the house at the beach, built on the rock and standing on stilts looking over the water, were home. One fellow was sitting precariously on the railing of the deck, with his back to us.

The crows make a dirty, tortured sound over each other. Three crows landed in the alder at my railing. They began to argue. They were arguing before on another alder down the hill. A high-pitched gawk that went on for the whole time, without pausing. Like a child crying. A child in pain. I had the vague notion I should run down the road and rescue the child that was screaming repeatedly, a low guttural scream. Like a cat tearing another cat to pieces, growling. The muffled sound of anger buried in fur. Then the crows all flew together over to my alder and continued. One of the crows dug into the other with its beak and the screams became gurgly, as if someone were dying. This went on for a long time. The steady screams and calls. Thankfully they all flew off. Out over the water on their broad black wings, still yelling at each other as they sailed off in the direction of the dark mine.

On the trail to Skookumchuck Narrows, we met the tall trees that competed with each other for the sunshine over the canopy of leaves. They had to grow so tall because the sun was up there. Below the ceiling of the forest, there were no branches on the trunks. They were fir, maple, cedar. And on the floor of the forest, a sea of ferns spread itself in small whirlpools everywhere. The green of lime lay around like a prickly carpet. Instead of green leaves, the grey-brown tree trunks had scraggly branches covered with a netting we came to call angel hair. Avocado green angel hair hung like cobwebs from every branch, streaming down in a vision reminiscent of the *Body Snatchers*. The path was smooth as silk, with bark mulch under our feet. The forest was so quiet. Now and then a screeching bird somewhere. Then the still water of Brown Lake with dead stumps of trees sticking precariously out of the purple water. Floating water lilies with yellow flowers in the middle and green stalks going down into the depths below. The sun glinting on the small wavelets that flurried in the breeze.

We stayed on the deck and watched the stars till midnight. The pale magenta haze remained in the air so long, the stars were not visible until very late. Then they all appeared at once, not in bunches but spread all across the sky. Twice we saw a satellite racing across the Big Dipper. In the northwest, the evening light became brown, coral, lemon, turquoise, and dirty grey and pink down by the water. Over the mountains the light was aquamarine in places, even deep green or avocado. We had a conversation about families. Family problems. The dark night closing in was warm and comfortable. Twice bats flitted into view of our deck chairs. One bat was flying into the eaves of the house. Another bat flew darkly over us, very fast. It sounded like a muffled machine. On the window from the inside, white moths of various sizes clung to the window pane and its light. The night life is just as busy as the day life, except at night the creatures are furry and coarse.

The day before, we drove in the Jeep with the top down. We dis-mantled the top of the car in Gibsons, parked in front of Sea Breeze Realty. The sun was beaming, striking hot on everything. People were wandering the streets of lower Gibsons with straw hats and cotton hats and sandals, holding bags, cameras on their shoulders. Walking down to the pier where the boats stood idly, many of the mooring places empty because the boats were out sailing. Wind chimes hung out in the breeze in front of shop windows. Molly's Lane was the only place in shadow. We each took down one side of the car roof, pulled it back, and tied it to the rear. Then we jumped in and wheeled off with the wind flying in our hair, the hair slapping our cheeks harshly. J. was happy, said this was a new experience.

A man of sixty-two went out on the sea in an open aluminum boat to look at cruise ships plying the Georgia Strait on the way to Alaska from Vancouver. They go up the strait two and three at a time, huge milk-white passenger vessels with lights on in the early dusk. It was Saturday evening at 6:45. He did not return. His boat was found floating upside down a mile out from Chaster Park. The family hired a helicopter to search the beaches for a body, but none was found. He is presumed drowned.

At Chaster Park next morning, people were picnicking and sunning themselves. People who lived in the beach huts on Gower Point Road, with the driftwood seagulls and dangling seashell wind chimes. We walked away from the sunbathers and up the beach on the pebbles. It was hard to walk on those rocks.

The stones were too big and our feet kept slipping. We moved a little higher, where the stones were smaller and we could get a firmer foothold. A quarter-mile along, there was a large log of driftwood, cut coarsely by the sea and wind. We sat down on the log facing the sea. The breeze was bright, coming off the sea onto the bushes behind us, where the tiny red berries hung in clusters. I was expecting to see the body float up to the sand below us. Almost any moment now.

Down below the mine, the rusty tins threw themselves around in tune to the changing tides. We sat on the boulder and watched the marine life wiggle back and forth in the pools. Molluscs and sea anemones lay in the pools created on the rocks when the sea washed over. The sea swirls in small whirlwinds, circles forming, frothing, widening, and dissipating like ash on the surface of the water. The changing of the tides. The tide is still flowing out when the new tide comes in. The two meet in whitecaps and surges of foam. Purple and coral starfish lie in bundles on top of each other on the skirts of the coast, waiting for another rush of plant-filled foam. The rocks were baking. Abandoned anemone shells were everywhere like ghost towns. White encasings turned dry in the sun, barnacling the surface of the rock.

Drove J. to the ferry in the Jeep with the sides off. We left the roof on. We turned the corner down to the foot passengers' lane where J. got off and said it was sad to leave. The ferry was just rounding the corner to dock at the slip. Cars were piled into the lanes, obviously two sailings thick. J. got out of the car and took the backpack. And I headed back home, up the hill and into the mountains, where the green hillsides turn blue in the sunny haze.

Bill C-31

~

The walk began before I was a seed.

My mother strung my umbilical cord through my moccasins.

When I was a grasshopper my Grandfather would open a big book. His fingers moved along the path of L's, V's, W's, mouth moving quietly.

Long after my Grandfather died my memory went to sleep. I woke in the mountains lying in the crook of my white husband's arms, cocooned in the warmth of our tepee.

Grandfather took my fingers and guided me through his book. Another old man sat me in the groove of trees, lifted his Pipe, my hands on the stem.

When I returned to the cabin I filled the pockets between the logs with papers, stacked the walls with my books. A man came, braids hanging past his shoulders, and laughed.

Still in my walks, the mountains beneath my feet, I picked feathers as I climbed, the wolves gentle in their following. Soon the mountain too had feet. I swam down her clear water and stood naked beneath her falls.

Nearby wind-burned fences enclosed crosses, their hinged grey arms dangled. I heard the screams of a man dying from a gunshot wound in the early dawn. After the fierce weeping of thunder and mad dash of lightning, the robins danced with the drumming of the little people. I woke as the brilliant ribbon of Northern Lights melted into a sunrise.

Another journey. I was stuck, the weasel untangled my braids, ran down my heart while Grandmother sat at the foot of my bed, her weight shifting as she sang. I walked up the mountain again, loaded with gifts.

Come back, she said. She rubbed my eyes with her sweat and I saw her many faces. Each face sat at the altar with one large eye.

We picked chokecherries, lips stained. Crushed them between the rocks.

In her cabin where my Grandmother waited was a stone boat stacked full of her belongings. Spotted blue enamel plates, over-size spoons, crazy quilt blankets. She invited all of my relatives to her feast.

She sang, her voices echoing through the cabin. As I slept through the songs my hands became rocks too heavy to lift. Ants scurried in and out of the cracks, carrying crumbs, chewing through bits of dirt, digging many holes. Eggs squirmed.

I'm awake now and remove my ring.

When I married him I dragged the cord past the road where my reserve ended.

Eahtaskit, they said.

I put my land elsewhere when I became his wife.

The prairie is full of bones. The bones stand and sing and I feel the weight of them as they guide my fingers on this page.

See the blood.

On my left breast was a hoofprint. It disappeared when I began the walk.

DIANA HARTOG

The Carpenter's Pencil

~

Preferably a few windows are broken. The door stands ajar; it needs only the push of a shoulder to open it farther, the bottom of the door scraping along the sill.

The interior is dank, musty. Leaves have drifted in through the broken windows. The interloper's heart skips a beat; a voice in the head whispers, *You could make this place beautiful, you could live here.*

~

Here in the south of France, any house abandoned for the winter sits tight within iron shutters painted pastel blue or pistachio. On unshuttered windows, vertical iron bars curve in wiggles like doodles by Miró, playful yet serious.

The stone walls of this old farmhouse are an impregnable one foot thick. The door locks with a skeleton key and a loud and satisfactory click.

The rain falls on this tiled roof with an unfamiliar music. Missing are the three random notes that drop along the strip of tin outside my bedroom window. In Canada I lie in bed, staring up at the ceiling before turning out the light, and hear those notes, striking at odd intervals. Without arriving at any final sum, I count the beams in the high ceiling that I built, and marvel – along with the mice, earwigs, silverfish, spiders, ants, and cedar-bugs within the walls – at being warm and dry.

Well do I know this ceiling, these walls. The stairs leading down from the bedroom were cut from a four-inch-thick plank found washed up from the lake. The old wood is polished smooth by age, and by my bare feet. In the third step from the bottom there's a small round hole in the plank, probably drilled by a miner. Miners are always drilling holes into things and spitting out the debris, leaving it around in piles. Leaving this little eyehole which peers up under my nightgown as I ascend. The house knows me well. It knows my habits. It knows that my left foot is the one that gains the landing and swivels as I pull back the maroon velvet curtain to enter the bedroom. The curtain's velvet is worn thin where my fingers have clutched it, night after night. Strangely, this curtain is never here when, lifting in dream from my sleeping body, I float down the stairs and out into the night; picking up speed, gaining altitude.

Chalkline

First, a small metal hook is secured to a nail at one corner of the platform. The Carpenter stands up, and begins to slowly walk backwards, keeping the string taut as it unreels from a bulb filled with chalk. Blue, powdery chalk, clinging to the string, which now stretches eighteen feet long.

The Carpenter kneels down. She pulls the line even tighter and winds it around another nail. The Chalkline now lies flat, corner to corner, and straight. To one side, boards jut out – uneven odds and ends to be sawn off.

A simple string decides what stays, what goes; divides a house from what is not a house; divides "this" from "that" – a task not so simple, and considered arbitrary by some.

The Chalkline is pinched between thumb and forefinger, and lifted – heightening the tension, the taut string quivering with its blue pollen.

Pencil

By Design a Carpenter's Pencil is oval or flattened on two sides, so as not to wander rolling down the length of the two-by-four where it was placed for a moment. Only a knife can sharpen this oddly shaped Pencil; a knife whittling off dull bits of wood and graphite. *I could be wrong.*

When not in use, the Pencil fits snugly behind the ear, where it rides a warm ridge of cartilage. The Carpenter soon forgets the Pencil is there – until she stops to compute. Think hard enough on the math, and the Pencil grows warm, making itself felt. Still thinking, the Carpenter reaches up without thinking, and the Pencil finds itself useful again, scribbling down figures (after first crossing out previous calculations, since a Carpenter's Pencil has no eraser).

The Carpenter grimaces, clenching the Pencil between her teeth as she saws – instead of tucking it up behind the rosy flesh of her ear amongst sweat-dampened hair.

Level

An imaginary line dropped from a perfectly level Level falls straight to the centre of the earth. It's a little like fishing, every Carpenter's line dangling for the same elusive prey. Of course the "exact centre of the earth" is imaginary as well, that's the point.

A point represented up here on the surface by a tiny bubble in the Level.

A window let into the Level allows a glimpse. The bubble floats within a miniature aquarium, in a clear liquid – perhaps water, perhaps saliva from the gods.

To level a new sill is a matter of tiny adjustments, tilting the Level up at one end . . . only slightly . . . very slightly . . . too much! if the bubble darts past and out of sight; or tilting it down, keeping in mind that the bubble isn't the real thing but only a distant cousin thrice-removed from the point.

Here it comes: the bubble slowly drifting back into the picture. It must be coaxed towards the centre, where two vertical bars are etched on the glass; coaxed to drift in between them, and hold still.

The bubble hesitates, drifts back to the left – then right, suddenly skittish; then floats left, slowly . . . swimming right into the trap.

~

Some creatures build shelters from their own substance, exuding the building material, and are often stuck wearing them; so it's best to get a good fit. A house is a second skin. Some builders, finding their house too large, too slack, fill it with objects. Even a shack can feel too large for a hermit, and he lines the walls with ceiling-high stacks of newspapers.

Over time, if one's house is a particularly good fit, it's possible to confuse it with oneself.

Every so often I dream that my house has slid down the hillside. I return home to find it collapsed in an unreadable heap of jutting timbers. Sometimes I'm inside (sleeping of course) when the four supporting pillars buckle at the knee, the bedroom tilting as the floor groans and boards snap. Miraculously unhurt, I wander out in my nightgown, stunned.

Waking from a particularly vivid version, I reach for the lamp – and nearly swoon. There's no lamp, no bedside table, it's really happened! And then I wake to a bedroom whose right angles and level sills bask in moonlight. The following week is spent strengthening both of the lower pillars with buttresses of concrete: three batches of concrete braced against a dream.

Hammer

One hand reaches into the nail pouch while the other draws the Hammer from its holster, giving the handle a little toss, the hand sliding down to the butt to grip firmly. Meanwhile the nail has been positioned and set with a preliminary tap, the Carpenter already reaching into the pouch for the next nail as three sharp whacks from the Hammer sink the first nail. Even two whacks can suffice, given a good aim and a strong arm.

But sometimes the nail bends under pressure. The Carpenter must tap the bent nail upright if possible, then try to drive it true. Otherwise smash it flat – an unsightly blot on one's reputation – or pull it out to be tossed to the dirt with the other nails bent or no good. The Hammer's claw slides up the nail and tilts backwards with a sharp jerk.

Of course the working rhythm is now broken. The blame is not the Hammer's, an expensive Framing Hammer, finely balanced. The fault lies with the nail, mass-produced, weaker than its ancestor, the square nail – each pounded into shape on an anvil, then thrown into a bucket of water to cool and harden, steam rising in a hiss. A nail forged to last centuries.

Today's nail protests, but another sharp jerk pulls it out.

Drawknife

The Drawknife is not a demanding tool. The Carpenter can comfortably sit straddling an old beam that is being skinned to a new life. The beam rests, either end, on a pair of wooden sawhorses – those unsung beasts, spines nicked with old cuts.

Comfortably sit, feet braced to the ground, and contemplate the length of the beam. In its previous life the timber functioned as decking for a narrow one-lane bridge. The bridge spanned a rushing creek high in the mountains. Cars driving the summit crossed over the bridge, tires jouncing between parallel timbers before passing on to the hum of pavement.

Years of wear, along with clumsy digs from the snowplough winter after winter, can't be removed by a Drawknife. A Drawknife only skins off the biggest slivers, the odd patch of road tar, strips of old bark; tidies up, here and there.

A pair of bulbous handles on either side of a wide, smiling blade comfortably dull: this is a Drawknife. Gripping the handles, the Carpenter pulls the blade flatly along the beam, in a rowing motion; pulls, then leans forward, rowing the old beam through a pleasant afternoon.

The beam is to retire. No more logging trucks; no more roadside pebbles pressing into a crack. Retire to the ceiling, an old beam prized for the weathered beauty which passes as wisdom.

Boxwood Rule

The Boxwood Rule hinges on a series of brass joints and the numbers one through thirty-six. These last represent inches, and the Rule unfolds to measure off twelve inches . . . eighteen . . . twenty-four, and, fully extended, the common yard.

The Rule is an elegant device at any length. From thirty-six inches it folds to a compact six. The brass knuckles swing inward with ease, the inches opposing each other in rarely seen combinations upside down. Indeed, if Beauty is Truth, the Boxwood Rule would seem to fold upon itself all human knowledge of any practical value.

Children sense this.

Often the Carpenter reaches for her Boxwood Rule – a beloved tool passed down from grandfather to father to daughter; an authentic antique, made in England, rubbed smooth by its passage from the Old World to the New – to discover it gone.

The Rule is now off somewhere being flexed and unflexed, measuring thin air, measuring the distance between a rock and a hard place.

∾

Returning home from a night out of one's body is sometimes painful. Gravity and force-fields come into play. Ignoring the walls I know so well I find myself suddenly back in my bedroom, hovering above my own sleeping form. This is the tricky part.

A psychic has predicted that I shall soon be selling my house and moving on. (A jellyfish, moving on, propels in its wake a perfect facsimile of itself, pure water, dissolving.)

If I make the mistake, when returning from a long trip, of pausing at the threshold – the room so coldly familiar – I'm shocked at a palpable Absence. *Is this what someone buys?*

I glance down. On the Welcome mat, one of my old comfortable shoes gapes empty, revealing the imprint of the sole of my foot, that most intimate of parts.

Handsaw

A house is more than the sum of its beams and planks and two-by-fours and wires snaking through walls. There comes a workday when a house, even half-finished, becomes a "whole" and is welcomed into the neighbourhood. Clouds pause overhead; a coyote passing on the game trail glances over mid-trot; tall birches crowd the site, their limber trunks swaying as if in mockery of so many straight lines and right angles.

But to get back to work: the Carpenter knees a board, and with thumb as guide, draws the Handsaw's sharp teeth slowly upwards to set the cut. And again . . . slowly . . . lest the blade jump and gouge her thumb. Human reflexes being what they are, there is little danger. A Handsaw is a slow and steady tool, the turtle to the electric power saw's hare.

With a Handsaw, the likelihood of having to grab for one's back-pocket handkerchief in which to enfold a severed digit is nil. Avoided is the surreal dash to the local emergency ward or village clinic, one hand steering, the other bound with an improvised tourniquet. Not forgetting the bloodied handkerchief, holding within its folds the estranged body part, which has now taken on a life of its own and looms in importance, riding on the passenger seat.

By Obstinate Isles

∽

Denn meine Heimat ist das, was ich schreibe

A few days after returning to Canada from the Far East, where I'd spent two years travelling and teaching, I found myself in a Vancouver library copying down the German phrase that appears above. I'd been browsing uncomprehendingly through a German literary magazine left on a table in the periodicals room, and the phrase, plastered in boldface on an otherwise blank back cover, caught my eye. There was no attribution, as if the line were too famous to need one – or was it the motto of the magazine? I knew just enough German to translate it. *So my homeland is what I write.*

The irony of my discovering the line on that visit to the library was not lost on me. I'd gone there to check through the Canadian magazines to which I'd been sending, over the past two years in Asia, manuscripts handwritten on blue airmail paper or sloppily typed on sheets taken from cheap notebooks. I'd used a variety of unreliable return addresses; unsurprisingly, I'd only heard back from a few of the editors. *Sorry. Sorry.* Now, hoping to find some of my work in print, I ransacked issues of the magazines I'd been writing to from Asia. I think I sensed that finding my words in a legitimate public space would make me feel less foreign, disaffiliated – more truly at home. Because in those first days back, Canada did not feel like home. And when I found several poems and a story in recent issues of quarterlies published in British Columbia and New Brunswick, I did feel more landed, more grounded – halfway back. It hardly mattered that the clear unforgiving typefaces of the magazines brought my rough-draft clunkers into cruel focus; my name in large caps above the writing seemed to ratify my presence, my return "home," so that I felt less counterfeit, homeless, and ghostly.

I still keep that phrase up on the wall above my desk – unaccredited, still. I've tried to trace it, but without luck. That's better in the end – better that the words, cut off from authorship, gender, nation, and age, remain themselves, in a sense, homeless.

After settling in Kingston and working for a year and a half as an editor, a freelance writer, and a farcically incompetent waiter, I went to Greece with a view to deepening my tenuous connection to the place. My mother is Greek-Canadian; my grandmother, though she lived most of her life in Canada, always defied the hyphen and remained stubbornly and utterly Greek. Her birthplace, the Peloponnesus, was allegedly dense with distant cousins and old friends avid to welcome me. . . . My wife, Mary Huggard, and I decided to go in late fall when the prices were lower, the tourists scarce. We were not tourists, of course, but travellers. Above all I was a kind of returning son.

Like so many others these days, I trace my roots to very different places – Scotland, Ireland, and England on my father's side, Greece and (more remotely) Turkey on my mother's – and I always have liked the way that such geographical range seems to offer a greater latitude of identification, a sense of having homes, or halfway-homes, in many ports. And so many puerile excuses!

In times of emotional remoteness or unavoidable tight-fistedness, cite the stereotypical Scots; when arriving late for an appointment or forgetting something important, blame the Greeks, too busy enjoying life to bother.

But I could hardly blame, or claim, the Greeks. I'd lost even the childish command of the language I'd had briefly years before. If I was serious about infusing my life and my writing with the hybrid vigour of varied sensibilities and worldviews, I must go back, relearn some Greek, meet my relations, wander the streets of Tripoli and visit the chapel on the outskirts, under the Arcadian range, where *Yiayia* was christened close to a century before.

It was early November and winter was on its way down out of the mountains. Tripoli, my *yiayia*'s home town, was bleak with drizzle and bitter east winds. The same arid landscape that looks so brilliant and lovely in the Greek sun looks especially desolate and futile under rain. The grounds around my *yiayia*'s baptismal chapel were deserted, and as we walked back through the streets of the city the few locals we passed looked hurried, gaunt, and cross.

Some of them, I supposed, must be distant cousins. As for the nearer relations who were putting us up for our stay, they were generous but harried, distracted, struggling to tend the seventy-five-year-old father of the clan on his deathbed – a divan in the family room where we gathered for meals. Sometimes while we ate – with a guilty quietness, a funereal decorum untypical of Greek gatherings – the dying man would moan in his sleep, heartrendingly, and outside the house the wind would give echo while hail ticked at the panes like dust or locusts blowing in over some doomed desert town.

The city was economically depressive, as my cousins put it. Shops along the main street were closing for good and the young people were all looking north, towards Athens or the new Europe, and trickling away in a slow, irreversible stream. I was discouraged by the thanatic ambience of the place and longed to push south, into the Mani, a primitive, pristine fastness little touched by the new Europe, or the new Greece. I might find other relations there, I was told. But, more than that, I hoped to find my way to the heart of something primary and authentic, the old elemental Greece, a spiritual as well as familial home, and the Mani – a desert peninsula of stark and savage simplicity – seemed the place to look. I decided I wanted to go there alone. Spreading a roadmap on the table of a taverna, I chose for my final destination what looked to be at most a hamlet, as far south as you could go, a few miles off the highway and in the shadow of an old Byzantine fort. If there was no regular accommodation there – and surely there would not be – I would camp in the ruins.

It was drizzling when I reached the village after an hour's walk down an unpaved switchback road descending through a moonscape of scattered boulders, lapsed walls, the eerie green palisades of prickly pear. The road's many ruts and potholes brimmed with sludgy water. In the raw air I could see my breath. The German couple I'd hitched a ride with had seemed reluctant to let me out in the rain on such a barren stretch, their newer map showing the Byzantine ruins but no living settlement nearby. But there must be something still, I thought. And there was: a few bungalows, huts, and drying-sheds ramshackling down from the road's dead end to a cove where three ruined skiffs lay beached on the bone-white shingle. A larger boat, red paint blistering, bobbed at anchor a few metres offshore. I passed the tiny church: padlocked doors, windows boarded. All deserted until the next fishing season, or maybe forever.

In the doorway of one of the bungalows an old man stood watching me, the bowl of his pipe cupped pensively in hand. He was squat and sturdy, heavily moustached, with that look of ferocious dignity you still see in old-school Greek men – the farmers, the workers, the fishermen. Nodding, he raised one hand, palm outward, and held it up, priestly. For a moment I wondered. But in Greece the priest does not show himself in canvas trousers and a coarse-knit baggy fisherman's blouse.

In my awkward but improving Greek I greeted the old man and began answering questions. Yes, I was here to visit the ruins, like the summer people. A tourist? No, not exactly. Was I German? Not at all. In fact, I said quickly, I was Greek – at least my mother was Greek, and her people came from the Peloponnesus, from around here. The old man was pleased. Smiling, he exposed long teeth stained rusty like the underside of his white moustache.

The red curtains in the window beside him parted and a woman squinted out irritably. Then two men with matching Zapata moustaches appeared in the doorway to either side of the old man. Brothers, maybe twins. I must come in for coffee, the old man said, it was cold. We would take a coffee together and then he would row me across the bay to the ruins – that was wiser than walking the long way around.

The old man and his middle-aged twin sons, Nikos and Kostas, sat with me at the table that dominated the house's sparse front room. Icons and fishing tackle – nets, small winches, scythe-like gaff-hooks – hung on the walls like nautical ornamentation in a seafood restaurant. But the tackle was not decorative. The season was almost over, the old man explained, but the boys still went out for an hour or two a day, just to feed the family. There are children, then, I said? The two men looked embarrassed. There was a daughter, the old man said gravely, but she is now in Thessaloniki. Since then there have never been any children.

The old man tapped his upended pipe on the side of the table and looked impatiently towards the kitchen, where the woman, Nikos's wife – whose name I was never told and whom I never saw sitting or eating when I was in the house – was making coffee, in the old way, grinding the beans. Her pale stern face was framed in a rectangular throughway in the wall, like the harried face of a cook in a short-order restaurant.

"This one here, my Kostas, must marry still," the old man declared in his hoarse, quavery tenor. Kostas leaned back in his chair and smirked lazily, shrugging.

"And you," the old man said, "have you no children? But you are still young. Have you no wife?"

I explained that my wife was staying with relatives in Tripoli. We had no children, not yet. I was a writer, a *singrafefs* – later this detail would prove important – and my wife and I did not yet make enough money between us to raise children.

The sons nodded solemnly at this admission; the old man looked troubled.

"Your wife works, then?" he said.

"She does."

"*Ach!*" he spat out.

"Like the women in Athens," I said, intending diplomacy. A mistake. The old man rolled his eyes and coughed out a cloud of indignant smoke.

"Like my granddaughter!" He shook his pipe in the smoky air as if it were an Orthodox censer. "Have modern husbands no shame?"

"Ach, *Papa*," Kostas said.

"*Singrafefs ine!*" said Nikos with a kind of aggressive *bonhomie*. "Like Omeros. He was born near our town."

"I've been reading him during this trip," I said, eyeing the old man. "The *Odyssey*."

The old man's face lit up. He puffed hard on his pipe, yanked it from his mouth, and proceeded to recite the first dozen lines of the *Odyssey* – a moment that rhymed beautifully with another a few days before when a shepherd outside Tripoli, finding me hunkered book-in-hand on an outcrop overlooking the town, had asked me what I was reading, and on hearing "Omeros" had quoted a famous passage from the *Iliad*. What a place to be a writer! I'd thought, and thought again now as the old fisherman finished his recitation and slumped back with a sigh, puffing his pipe, eyeing his daughter-in-law in the kitchen. Once more he looked vexed. His own feat had not impressed him. And it was to remain the only real moment of light between us. More and more as he muttered on about the government and the young people and the bad weather and the stupid tourists I felt his tension and unhappiness and thought of the charcoal-burners in Jean Giono's *The Man Who Planted Trees* – those isolated souls in their exposed, decrepit towns, men and women slowly hardened into bitter grotesques by poverty and "the endless conflict of personalities."

Nikos's wife brusquely brought thimble-cups of thick bitter coffee, then retreated to the kitchen.

"There was once a Stephanopoulos in this village," Nikos said. My mother's maiden name. Nikos's voice, like his father's, was high and thin, emerging strangely feminine, or falsetto, from under his heavy moustache. "But he was drowned in a storm. The *meltemi*."

"There were many people here once," the old man said.

"Do you have many tourists in the summer," I asked, "to see the ruins?"

"Few," the old man snapped. "Most of them stay with us. You will stay too."

I looked around the room. Nikos's wife was now in the back of the house and there was a faint sound of sweeping, shifting furniture. The rain made sluggish trails down the window. I acted surprised at the invitation, but in fact I'd been expecting it. "I meant to camp in the ruins," I said. "Are you sure you have room?"

The old man looked miffed. The twins, impassive, sipped their coffee.

"My granddaughter's room is empty. You will stay there. I will row you across to the ruins. And tonight you will eat fresh fish."

I fidgeted for a moment. "I'd like to pay you," I said, then saw by the way the old man's eyes briefly widened that he'd always meant for me to pay, certainly, as the other tourists had paid. By now I was so used to having beds and glasses of ouzo and coffee and roast goatheads, flaming cheeses, sweetmeats, platters of garlic lamb with basil-braised potatoes thrust upon me by friendly Peloponnesians delighted to hear I was Greek (and some of them claiming to have a vague memory of my *yiayia* or *papou*) that I was surprised myself. But not unwilling to pay. They were lords of this deserted village, the family, but not well-to-do; I realized their pleasure at my arrival was largely due to my bearing fresh currency, not common DNA.

Twelve hundred drachmas for the room, the old man and I agreed. The twins were now playing cards at the table, rolling smokes, Nikos's wife in the kitchen but invisible, perhaps seated. "And then twelve hundred more for dinner, and one thousand to cross the bay." But this seemed to me unreasonable. And since my money was running low, and I had bread, cheese, and olives in my pack, and would rather walk awhile, alone with my thoughts, than struggle on in Greek with this moody, unpredictable man, I told him I would skip the dinner, if that was all right, and save him the trouble of taking me across. I didn't want to put them all out.

As I settled my backpack on the worn carpet in the spare room, I knew by the smoky, masculine atmosphere that this was not the granddaughter's room but Kostas's.

On the lonely headland across the bay the Byzantine Greeks had built an outpost: rough walls of stone collected from the parched, thistled fields that sheered off on all sides to the sea, and within the walls a few houses, a church, defensive towers marking the four corners of the post. It had been built shoddily, perhaps in haste. Little remained but the rubbled base of the walls, pyramids of skull-sized stones where the towers had loomed, and the stepping-stone outlines of many-roomed houses. The tiny rooms were floored with thorns and dead grass, like grave-plots long untended.

At the heart of the ruins was the church, whose walls had been far thicker, more carefully made – probably not so much out of piety as with a view to last-ditch defence. They were still more than man-high. There were no windows, only a doorway gaping under a lintel of charred slate.

The chill east wind scudding in off the Aegean made a mournful drone as it gusted under the lintel and piped through fissures in the walls. The remote outpost had been stormed and taken over five hundred years back and all its inhabitants put to the sword. Now red lichens crusted the stones like dried blood. I sheltered against a wall of the church, hunkered down out of the wind and spitting rain; shivering deep inside. In the socket of the doorway, a grey square of churning sea where a fishing boat appeared, pitching silently, and passed on.

By the time I'd hurried back from the ruins I was hot and sweating for the first time in days, and because there was no shower I decided to swim. Nikos and Kostas – back from fishing, the old man kept saying, and with a good catch – clearly thought I was insane. The old man shook his pipe in my face and lectured me ardently. But I refused to see reason. The tropical green of the cove's calm shallows might well be deceptive, I thought, but the sea could not have cooled to unswimmable temperatures so soon. Besides, I told the old man in a jocular tone, I'm Canadian.

For a moment he looked confused.

I was right about the water – it was bracing but not icy. I leapt out refreshed, exhilarated, more alive than in days. Relieved. Back in the ruins I'd felt far away from everything, spectral, on the edge of the earth and of something else that frightened me, and I'd rushed back to the dying village as if it were Athens on a Saturday night, lights blazing, cafés crammed. . . .

As I came inside shivering in a towel, the old man confronted me and urged me again to have some of the fish they'd caught. I explained again that I had food with me, and little money, but I'd be happy to have a little; if we all sat down together and ate and drank with dedication, I thought, things would surely warm up.

"How big are the fish?"

The old man indicated something about the size of a small child.

"Perhaps we can share one," I said.

The old man was aghast. "They are only a thousand each!"

Outrageous.

"Make it six hundred and I'll have one. Please."

"Eight hundred each. Fifteen hundred for two."

I was anxious to get to my clothes. "Seven hundred," I said, teeth chattering. "For one."

"One! One only?"

"I told you, my money is low!"

Now the old man looked frankly incredulous. If I had so little money, his sharp eyes seemed to say, how could I have travelled this far from home? I had to guess what his eyes were saying because he was less and less inclined to speak in the clear, civil, standard Greek he had used with me until then. Staccato cadences in the local dialect – the fish would go to waste, he was saying something more about the fish. They had caught extra for me! But I had told them, I said, that I wouldn't be having any! From the table Nikos and Kostas, snacking, drinking glasses of ouzo and looking windburnt and weary, eyed me from under their fierce brows. I felt watched from behind as well, but when I turned towards the kitchen Nikos's wife was looking down, chopping vegetables or gutting fish.

I saw that I was a disappointment to all of them.

It was the silence that woke me. For the first time in days there was no wind blowing and from the cove only the faintest sound of sea lapping shingle. The sky had cleared. From where I lay I watched the sickle moon rising, or was it setting, over the Aegean and the far headland where the toppled towers and jagged church walls were silhouetted with light.

It was the silence, but it was also the ache in my guts. When the oblong platter had appeared in front of me hours before, there had been two fish there, stuffed with bread and herbs. They were big fish, but not half so big as the old man had shown me. Defeated, wryly amused, I'd eaten both.

When I woke again near dawn the warped, unlockable door had come ajar. Passing through the front room on my way out for a piss I saw Kostas curled fetally in a nest of fishing nets under the table. The moonlight lit his profile, softening his face back to boyhood, and for a moment I felt touched, protective, brushed by the wing of some elusive sorrow.

In the morning I packed my bag and tidied up quickly, with tiptoe quietness, as if the family, audible in the front room, were not already awake. I didn't like the sound of their conversation – not that I could catch what was being said, but the tone of it lacked the typical Greek mealtime animation, the affably tempestuous crest and trough of familial raillery. In Greece, I thought, a calm sea means trouble. I was uneasy about the bill. There was still no wind outside the window, but more cloud.

I slipped out into the front room with an awkward, guilty grin, dragging my pack behind me like a corpse. *Kalimera!* I called out, too loud. And the family did respond, the old man and his sons from the table where they sat smoking and drinking coffee, Nikos's wife from the kitchen.

"You will take a coffee," the old man said with force.

"I will," I said. "Thank you. Then I must get back on the road, I slept later than I meant to."

"You found your room comfortable, then?"

"It was very comfortable. Though I do feel I've put you out. Put Kostas out, I mean."

The old man looked at Kostas, then at me, furrowing thick white brows and reddening till I realized he took my deduction and remark as a piece of unspeakable rudeness – as if I'd admitted to snooping through the other back rooms while the family ate breakfast.

"Sit down," the old man said.

"I should pay you now," I said, still standing, taking the thimble-cup Nikos's wife brought me and drinking with a haste I knew to be rude but felt to be uncontrollable. The coffee, thick and boiling, burned like hot tar on its way down. "How much is the coffee? I want to pay for the coffee I've drunk as well. Yesterday's, today's."

The old man's face had clenched into a look of perpetual vexation and reproach. Kostas seemed to be repeating what I'd just said, but in a high mumble, as if incredulous. Then it came to me that he was mocking my Greek.

"The coffee, yes, of course," the old man said. "Three hundred each for the coffees. Fifteen hundred for the fish and twenty-four hundred for the room. As agreed."

Three hundred for a coffee was ludicrous, but I was prepared to let it go. The price of the room was another matter. *There must be some mistake.*

"We agreed to twelve hundred, I think."

The old man raised his terrible brows and tilted his head back theatrically. "But we agreed to twenty-four hundred! Twenty-four hundred drachmas! Is that not so, Nikos?"

Nikos nodded fiercely, eyes fixed on the table.

"Kostas?"

"Of course," he said quietly. His back was turned to me. Then he twisted round in his chair and glowered: "Twenty-four hundred drachmas for the room!"

"We agreed to twelve hundred," I said. "Twelve hundred drachmas." I tried to keep my voice even, but felt my throat tightening, squeezing my voice thinner, higher. I set down my empty cup, the grounds spattery and obscene. "You heard us agree to twelve hundred, didn't you, *Kiria?*" I looked towards the short-order slot, but Nikos's wife would not look up. I went over and looked directly into the tiny cluttered kitchen. "You heard us, *Kiria* – please tell them!"

Defiantly unhearing, she glared down at hidden hands, still working. When I turned back towards the table the old man and his sons were on their feet. I dug for my wallet and counted out thirty-three hundred drachmas.

"Here. What we agreed on."

"You are mistaken."

"It was twelve hundred and you all know it!"

"Your Greek is very poor. Perhaps you misunderstood."

"Or he's lying," Nikos said.

"*You're* lying!" I burst out. "You're all lying! We counted it out on our fingers!"

"Poor at Greek, poor at counting," the old man said out of the side of his mouth. He was puffing shrewdly on his pipe. Kostas, in profile, stood behind him, studying the scythe-like gaff-hooks on the wall.

"It comes to forty-five hundred in all," the old man said. "Not a drachma less."

"Liar!" Nikos said.

And then I did hear myself lie, lie baldly and with an abrupt inspiration. I still have no idea how I made them understand what I said next. But they understood. "All right," I said, digging back into my wallet for the extra cash. "But you remember I told you yesterday that I was a writer. . . ."

"Yes, yes, a *singrafefs*," the old man said impatiently, hand stuck out, while Nikos and Kostas squinted at me.

"I forgot to tell you the kind of books I write. I write travel books. Books for the summer people, the tourists. American, Canadian, German tourists. That's why I had to see the ruins. Here's the extra money you wanted. I hope it's worth it. I'll be telling my readers how I was treated here."

For a moment after I finished, the old man's eyes widened, mouth slack, pipe drooping, then he yanked the pipe free and shook it in the air between us as if warding off a demon. "*As to diavolo vrai! As to diavolo!*" He took a step towards me and swiped the money from my hand, skimming off the extra bills I'd added and shoving them back at me.

"Now get out! Leave us! Leave us before we throw you out!"

Kostas was eyeing his father wildly as if hoping for violent instructions. Without looking further at him or any of them I grabbed my pack with one hand and lugged it, in a pathetic show of strength, towards the door.

"*Fige amessos!* Go!"

"With pleasure," I said roughly, pulling on my pack and hurrying down the front steps. I started up the dirt road towards the highway. Anger numbed my legs and fuelled them at the same time and I was clear of the village in seconds. I kept listening for the crunch of boots in the dirt behind me, running feet, but there were only my own steps and the tidal rush of blood pulsing in ears and temples. At the first hook in the road I looked back down at the village: the old man, a twin son peering over either shoulder, stood in the doorway watching me. Nikos's wife could be seen, or sensed, behind the window where the red curtains were parted. None of them moved. Like wax figures in a museum tableau: citizens of the old-time Greek village.

At the second hook in the road I looked again. Now only the old man was visible, pipe-smoke clouded around his head like breath. Enough of my anger was gone, vented by exertion, that I could feel shame at my silly imposture – but I still didn't regret withholding the money. The point was . . . the point was, in the end, not just the principle of the thing but something more irrational, sentimental. I began to sense as much, if not to see it. I rounded the third hook in the road and no one was visible below. The village looked deserted, disintegrating, in a state between that of the towns to the north and the Byzantine ruins still visible, barely, on that headland across the bay.

It wasn't just the principle. It was hurt surprise. I hadn't thought they could do this to me. I was not a *tourista*, after all, I was family.

Liar.

When I think back to my retreat up the dirt road to the highway through those bristling, incurious hills, I always see myself from a distance, like a stranger on a road across a valley. Cold rain is falling. The figure is bent under a cumbersome pack, walking stiff and fast with what could be cold, or anger, eyes fixed on the road like an obsession, his breath in white puffs. Caught in a cloud of his own making. He could be anywhere.

GREG HOLLINGSHEAD

Defence of Floating

for Ronald Burwash

At the lake, c. 1990

If home is where I go when I am asked in the relaxation exercise to imagine myself in that place where I feel safest and happiest and most at peace, then it is a ten-by-three-metre platform of weathered-grey and rotting two-by-six spruce boards nailed to a pair of cedar timbers each a metre in diameter and floating (with the help of as many sawed-off chunks of foam pallet as I have had the weight and strength to force underneath) on a Shield lake three metres in depth for most of the length of this dock, which is held perpendicular to the shore by steel cord attached from the foot of one cedar timber to a white cedar and from the foot of the other to a white birch. Here, at night in spring, summer, or fall, under the stars, or the moon and stars, or in the pitch dark, it makes little difference, though windless is best, with no one aside from my family in a five-kilometre radius, shining the beam of a six-volt lantern down into the water, I pace and muse, sometimes for hours, and I have come home.

The other day I was pleased to learn that dry land was not created by evaporation of the primeval sea but vomited up out of the Earth's mantle through a fault in the basalt crust. The substance of the continents is not revealed seabed but of an entirely different nature, a recycled and ever-recycling mixture of weathered and disintegrated granitic materials. The seabed – tougher, denser than granite, fifty times younger, and relatively unsedimented because it is constantly passing under itself and so being more drastically renewed – is basaltic. Granite is a light rock, lighter than basalt, coarse-grained, a real floater. It lies like thick scum high on heavy basaltic plates, which themselves are afloat upon – when they are not sinking back down into – the flowing upper mantle of the Earth.

When I step off my dock onto the rock, I am stepping onto another floater. I am pleased to know this because for as long as I can remember it has been obvious to me that floating is the essence of life.

I have two houses, 3,400 kilometres apart, a prairie bungalow and a cabin on the Canadian Shield. Each is a good distance above sea level, the Shield cabin at 430 metres, the prairie bungalow higher, at 670. Where the prairies are was once the bottom of a shallow sea, but the prairies are not always either low or flat. My cabin on the Shield sits on a jumble of till and boulders of granitic gneiss. Twelve thousand years ago these rocks were approximately three kilometres under ice, in fact four times over the past million years they have been under ice, and three times in the past two billion years they have been as far as twenty to thirty kilometres under rock. The Canadian Shield at the point where I live on it is the roots of the third of three successive mountain ranges that have pushed up on that spot, the first a little more than two and a half billion years ago, the last just over a billion years ago, all now eroded away to a half-billion-hectare saucer of rock no higher than 1,500 metres around its visible rim. "Visible rim" because, like most of North America, the prairies where I live are on the Shield, only separated from it by two vertical kilometres of clay and silt and other sediment, much of it the remains of those three mountain ranges.

In the prairies I float two kilometres above the pink granite of the Shield, somewhere high in the midst of what, nearly two billion years ago, was also a mountain range, which eroded away long before the sea rolled in from the west (no Rockies yet to stop it), long before the accumulation of those two kilometres of sediment. On the Shield I stand on rock that at least three times in three billion years has been buried and – thanks to the rock above it having eroded away and so not only exposed it but removed a great weight – three times has floated to the surface.

Christ advised us to sink our house in rock because a house in sand will be swept away, but this is a metaphor for faith. Here in the physical world everything will be swept away and has been many, many times. Faith is one answer. Another is to do what you can to avoid being buried too soon on this planet of landslides, earthquakes, volcanoes, meteorites, hurricanes, tornadoes, and floods. I think our lives must be as brief as they are relative to geological time because, like insects, we need all the chances we can get to adapt to cataclysmic change.

My own experience is with floods; they are what terrify me like nothing in nature, and for me it is always a nightmare of flood-water that is rising in the darkness beyond the perimeter of *home*.

The house I grew up in was a yellow-brick storey-and-a-half built on a marshy outwash near the edge of a broad river valley a few hours' drive south of the Shield. This river, which by August was invariably a trickle among bleached rocks, only eleven thousand years ago was a raging sluice of glacial meltwater coursing south into the vastness of Lake Iroquois, now receded to Lake Ontario. When I was a child I would push through the beach-sand grass of the back field and stand at the edge of a clay bluff and stare down at the narrow brown meander of that river twenty metres below and marvel that it could ever have covered a valley floor at least a kilometre across, because it had, again and again over thousands and thousands of years. Even in my own lifetime it had. The October I was seven a hurricane came through, and the next morning my father brought me to this place and I saw it: the valley floor a uniform expanse, the buildings of the farm that yesterday had stood on its banks now islands in a brown sea. And later he took me into the sludge at the bottom of the main street to see where the old concrete bridge had been washed out and the river a headlong surge only just returned inside its banks, flowing past at tremendous speed, carrying with it the destruction of the valley: uprooted trees, drowned animals, sections of building. What shocked me – and it went with the outrage, the insolence of the height the water had risen in defiance of the most familiar features of our village – was the force of the moving water, the force of it but also its terrible opacity. This was not water as in a tumbler or bathtub but water the colour of clay, more liquid earth than water as I had ever thought of water. This was water gone hellish, water capable of displacing, of reducing to its own state of muck and disorder even space sanctioned by adult consciousness and adult industry.

Our house sat too high above it to be flooded by the river, but our house was flooded more often than the river left its banks, because every year or two in the spring or when the rains came hard, the sump pump would break down or fail to keep pace with the rising water, and I would sit on the basement landing and watch it well and spread silently – oh the terror of that silence – across the basement floor and creep up the steps below my feet and up the concrete walls and pass into the recreation room with its paperboard panelling and its raised floor and warped tiles and its stink of permanent damp, and climb the furnace, dousing the coals, and my fear was that it would never stop. When I was very young it did not occur to me that it could not possibly flood more than the basement, and I would imagine it filling our house to my bedroom ceiling, and the fact that this was my parents' house would make no difference to it. And I would sit on the cellar steps and under the light of a bare bulb from the ceiling I would watch the water engulf and gently lift the objects in the basement that could float – wood, inflated toys, plastic things – and bury the rest under its glass black surface, and I knew that in the world there are the things that float and there are the things that do not.

It makes no sense to build basements in country like this, to sink houses into the moving frost-heaved sea of the earth, which can only create disaster below, cracking and crumbling foundations, leaking into them, filling that pointless subterranean space with damp and cold and miasmal gases. Really this is land that demands flotation. Its first nations understood that, why can't we? What is this need to sink foundations that can only be violated? Surely this is old root-cellar thinking, or something perverse in us, or a Bible metaphor lapsed to literalism. It is certainly not appropriate in a country whose land mass is nearly half Shield. If you have no basement it is not going to flood. My prairie bungalow has a basement – actually my office is down in it, all my work is a dredging operation – and though the foundations are solid, and though it is on high well-drained ground (on the edge of a river valley), and though I have had weeping tiles put in because I am neurotic about this, when it rains a lot there is dampness in the lower floors and walls, and in the past, before the weeping tiles, there have been occasions of standing water. On the Shield my cabin sits on rock and it can rain for days and there is no fear, because the rain flows off the roof to the rock and over and among and through the rock and down into the lake. There is nowhere for it to go but into the lake, which is rainwater in a bowl of rock. When the lake level rises, as it does in the spring, it will pour south before it floods the cabin. Pour south off the Shield as it has here for more than two billion years.

And so I float.

I know that this is about survival, a compulsion given shape, like most, by early experience. This is what I do, how I reckon, against the terror. And I realize that beyond death the terror is the terror of the unknowable, the unarticulatable other. It is, as I say, as much the darkness of the flood, the obscuration as surely as the sweep of it, that for me holds the terror. And fascination. My main fantasy as a child was unearthing – or discovering at the bottom of the sea – a treasure chest of puppets; was unearthing multi-tiered highway cloverleafs buried like Pompeii, and what could be made of what was found at this level, and this level, and this? And as an adult it is pleasing to me to know that I am floating at the roots of vanished mountains when I am not floating two kilometres above the Shield, somewhere high in the mountain range that once stood here, floating as high above the Shield as above the bottom of what, a billion and a half years later, after those mountains eroded away, was the sea. You stand on prairie and you think, Yes, of course this must have been the sea. But on the prairie you also feel you have been half lifted up into the sky, and you have been, and the land itself is now the swelling main. And at night at my cabin on the Shield I pace my rotting, foam-bolstered ten-metre floater for hours into the night, telling myself stories, and I shine the beam of my six-volt lantern along the muck and rock bottom three metres down and I watch the nighttime follies of crayfish fighting over wisps of offal, and I watch the minnows and the snapping turtles and trout and pearly clamshells and catfish and leeches and water snakes and tadpoles and all the submerged inhabitants of that world, unearthed by my light. And this is home. Down there with them, the living and the dead. Floating here.

Tener Morriña

~

We'd had too many homes, too quickly, ever to be able to say where home was. Over the ten years since we'd quit our parents' roofs to make a life together we'd settled down in no less than nine different places: an apartment on – where else – Toronto's Brunswick Avenue; a Regency bedsit in seedy Sillwood Place, in England's boisterously seedy Brighton; a twee granny flat attached to a stockbroker's mansion in Ditchling, a village in the Sussex Downs; the upper floor of a Ditchling cottage owned by an endearingly grumpy gent who warned us (getting his colonies mixed up) not to bring the outback into his back garden; another Regency flat in Brighton, this time in posh Montpelier Place, over whose cream-coloured walls our two-year-old grandly scribbled his name, again and again; the ground floor of a stately, once-tranquil Dijon villa, now fronting one of the busiest roads in all of Burgundy; a skinny, red-brick special in Ottawa's Sandy Hill; a clapboard mansion in Nova Scotia, in the pine woods at Fort Point, where Champlain was supposed to have made one of his own stabs at home-making; another, less luxurious clapboard house at Pointe-de-l'Église on Nova Scotia's French Shore.

Of all these flats and houses we'd only owned one, and that for less than a year, in Sandy Hill. We'd moved as and where our work had taken us: we were university students and then teachers, following the intricate, capricious routes created by scholarships and job markets. Along the way we had two children and perhaps it was for them, all along, that we'd embraced each new set of walls, each neighbourhood or surrounding view of hills or sea as home, and not as temporary shelter. Why else would we have embarked on that most tenacious or wishful task of homemaking: planting gardens, each one a further quantum leap from the coleus plants on our windowsills at Brunswick Avenue. (Our landlord's garden there was crammed with cabbages swathed in ancient copies of the *Globe and Mail*; he was always on patrol, guarding against rapacious squirrels or tenants or possibly dispossessed archivists. Though he never seemed to harvest anything, and the newspapers made their own, sad snow when the bad weather set in after October.)

Homes in Ontario and Nova Scotia; in England and France: the painfulness of leaving some of these places, and the pains we took simply to stick it out in others. The elusive nature of belonging: belonging not as some god-given effect of being born into a place, a language, a culture, but the constant effort of making ourselves fit, only to end up like Alice in the shrinking house, with the white rabbit scurrying forever elsewhere. Sometimes it seemed that only by writing a place into fiction could I shake the feeling I was haunting someone else's home. "Writing home" in another sense of those words, for what more compact, unassailable home could you find than a book, as all those who've lost themselves in the pages of one will know?

Long after we'd left it, I wrote back to our house in Dijon, turning it into the main character of a story called "Accidents." It was a curiously doubled house, one side of it fronting roaring traffic while another did a *belle au bois dormant* act along the sleepy rue Jules-Violle (Jules Violle being one of those innumerable academicians whose sole purpose in life seems to lie in providing names for dull French streets). This double-face seemed an allegory for its two different sets of occupants: the brash Canadian couple with their young son, and Madame S., the ancient lady who'd retreated to the top-floor apartment with her villainous cat and long-suffering maid. Madame had once owned the house, working as a partner with her architect husband, taking over the business when he'd suffered a severe head wound during the Somme offensive, surrendering the house to Nazi bureaucrats some thirty-five years later, reclaiming it after the war, and finally selling it to a certain monsieur who let her remain in the attic on grace and favour terms. Our own part of the house had been modernized and redecorated: chocolate-box covers hung on picture hooks, iceberg-coloured tiles in the cavernous bathroom (easily the largest room in the house). The bathroom could be reached only by parading through the main bedroom, which was graced by a blackened-oak bed and purple satin duvet cover, the whole effect not a little like that of Napoleon's Tomb. Whereas Madame's apartment brimmed with skittish little tables and elegant sideboards, Sèvres serving dishes, over-varnished but still enchanting still lives, landscapes, even a crucifixion hung over a tallboy on top of which the cat would perch, since it was the only place she was out of reach of Madame's long ivory cane.

Yet it wasn't the disparity between the crowded splendour of the top-floor apartment and the kitsch decor of the *rez-de-chaussée* that troubled me. It was the presence of death in the house, death-in-waiting. Crippled, barely able to shift from her bed to her chair, Madame would call from her window to the garden below, where our small son might be pushing Tonka trucks through the gravel or trying to coax the jaded cat out of the rosemary bush. *Je vais mourir*, Madame would moan in a piercing voice: I've nothing left, no one but Death to call on me. Which was our cue to climb upstairs, past the coffin niche cut into the wall, to Madame's apartment, where her maid would serve coffee and *chocolat chaud*, and our son would build castles out of ancient ivory and ebony dominoes while Madame showed me her albums. Brittle photos of herself, svelte, dark-haired, lounging in the same voluptuous garden where I now hung out the wash or fought the weeds. She died a few months after we left that house, and despite all the photographs we took of leafy garden and sun-steeped kitchen, 37 rue Jules-Violle has contracted into one thing only: that utterly functional hollow in the hallway wall, permitting coffins to be carried down the steep and twisting stairs.

And that other unaccommodating house, the one on Nova Scotia's French Shore: not part of a village, despite the enormous down-home Gothic church from which Pointe-de-l'Église, or Church Point as the Anglos call it, takes its name, but one of a straggle of buildings along a highway where eighteen-wheelers thunder. The house we never succeeded in making our own, though it was there we brought our newborn second son, and there we'd lived the longest. A square, unlovely house, its boards painted rust and that grating white that shouts of searchlights and the carbolic glare of hospital wards. We began our time there in high spirits, painting the kitchen and playroom fever-bright; stalwartly roto-tilling an acre of the field out back, until it became clear that each shattered chunk of Japanese knotweed begat a dozen more to spring triumphant through the weedy arms of what few onions and potatoes could keep struggling up. Little by little our attempts at transformation stopped – what was the point? we asked ourselves at last. We would soon write our way out of Church Point to a place that could boast more than a bank, a post office, a general store whose most exotic item was frozen peas. Yet somehow four years passed and we stayed put, feeling more and more as though some grim God were making us pay Him back for all the light and joy of our former days.

At what point did we realize we had to go, or go under? I know exactly: early one winter morning when I'd gone to the basement to feed the insatiable, unreliable, wood-burning furnace. I'd forgotten to shut the cellar door, and our three-year-old son, wanting to help, had tiptoed down behind me. Hoisting a log into the furnace, I heard a noise behind me: Christopher, tugging at a log from the centre of the woodpile. How I pulled him safe from the avalanche that followed I have no idea. It wasn't anything like the scare we'd had in another house, when, after an afternoon at the park, I'd walked into the small and narrow kitchen, baby in arms, to find that all the cupboards had slipped from their bolts and crashed to the floor. As I shovelled out smashed glass and crockery and dented presswood, I kept telling myself, "Thank God this didn't happen when you were in here with the baby." Yet I never doubted that the shelves had held off from their descent on our account, that the house was, somehow, looking after us, as you'd expect in any place that was your very home. But this near-disaster with the woodpile was different: *get out,* the house was telling us; *get out before I force you out.* It took me the whole morning to stop shaking. By noon I'd decided: we couldn't wait any longer for another job in a better place to sail onto our horizon: we were moving, now, as far away as we could manage. Three days later we'd bought a noble barn of a house an hour's drive away in what seemed, after the Church Point

captivity, a metropolis: it had a bookstore, a restaurant, a theatre/
cinema and – a decisive point – sidewalks instead of a ditch for
walking. Annapolis Royal, and as good as Jerusalem the Golden.

What is at work when the place where you live refuses to be
home? Whose fault is it, that of the house, the city or landscape
in which it finds itself, or that of the people who cannot take, but
have to leave it? We'd tried so hard to make *la Pointe* our home; to
learn its language, not just *acadien* but the speech of spruce grove
and cranberry bog, of endless wind and water. The priests sent out
to save souls here a hundred years before had called it *notre Sibérie*.
Nor had it been viewed more kindly by some of the *coopérants* –
young Frenchmen avoiding a year's compulsory military service
by spending two years in an ex-colonial hardship post where some
kind of French was still spoken. One of them, a native of
Normandy (a region not normally known for the mildness of its
climate), had holed up for two years in a cabin by the shore,
emerging only to teach his classes at the tiny local university.
Another, one starry August night, had stepped off the train from
Halifax into the open field which served as station; had miraculously avoided turning onto a concession road going intricately,
endlessly nowhere but taken the right road, to the university; had
abandoned his luggage there and proceeded to commit the gaffe
of asking for the whereabouts of the nearest café. He was given a
ride to the Fish and Game Club, where, as legend has it, he
downed a dozen beers, stood up from his table, proclaimed, "See
Church Point and then die!" and collapsed, rarely to be revived
during the next two years.

All of this went into my first novel, *Constellations*, which was
denounced by several high-school valetudinarians and excori-
ated by a reviewer in the *Petit Courier de la Nouvelle-Écosse* for its
"betrayal" of the region. I couldn't have written any thing or way

else than I did in that novel, although it was my great attempt
to make myself at home in *la Pointe*. I tried to put down, not just
the unavoidable strangeness of the place, and the sensation of
ethnic claustrophobia, all too familiar to someone who'd grown
up in Toronto's Ukrainian community, but also the discoveries
which so delighted me: wildflowers named "shooting stars" that
you had to crouch to see; sandhills fringed with marram grass,
somehow holding their own against wind that blew snow into
Sahara-like dunes and whipped freezing spray like shattered
glass into your face in summer. The spare, bare bones of the
place, the sheer tenacity of the people, the clarity I mistook for
simple daylight, or a quality of air, but which I now see had more
to do with the moral, even the metaphysical, than with the
business of the weatherman.

The 20/20 vision of the escapee. When we lived there, why
hadn't we had the wit or heart or the good fortune – since so
much of being-at-home in strange places depends on serendipity
– to see what was there for us? Not that we could ever have felt
towards *la Pointe* as did the Acadians, for whom the reality of
home was bitterly entangled with that of history. Victims of the
imperialist wars of the late eighteenth century, exiled by the
British to the Thirteen Colonies, they'd trekked back home to
find New Englanders settled in Grand Pré, on land the Acadians
themselves had made lush by the ingenious system of dykes and
sluice gates they'd created there a century before. And so they'd
had to take the consolation prize the Nova Scotia government
was offering them: the province's harsh and rocky western shore.
In so doing, they turned themselves from farming into fishing
people. Such a translation we could never attempt, lacking the
Acadians' loyalty to a language, an ancestral history and tradition, a sense of place without which they would have ceased to
know or want to know themselves. And yet we might have stayed

there and learned what we could from our very failure to make ourselves at home.

"We are not reliably at home in our interpreted world," Rilke reminds us: the choreography of desire depends upon a longing to return to that paradisal home, however mythical, from which we've been displaced – the mother's body, according to Roland Barthes, Eden's garden as earlier theorists have pronounced: you can take your pick of *fons and origo*. Not only can we never go home again, but any new home we are able to make for ourselves, through labour or through love, we're bound to lose. And sooner or later that home into which each one of us is born, the body, will evict us all. Had we stayed in that place where we were least suited to live; had we, like friends of ours "from away," bought a piece of land hugging the sea, and built a house, our own house, painted azure or vermilion – any shade but rust-brown-and-white; had we wrestled to the ground and up again the angel of unbelonging, would we have learned by heart this wisdom of radical homelessness? Rilke again: a poem called "Autumn Day," a poem built on images of twilit rooms and fading music, to house an utterance I have always found terrifying, and thus true:

he who has no home now
will never have one.

∼

As for me and my house, we have moved on, of course. For a while we thought we'd settled down for good in Annapolis Royal. We bought an 1860s house of Georgian design, right across from Fort Anne with its wonderfully steep, absurdly emerald hills. Fifteen rooms, a self-contained apartment that we rented out to fill the belly of the oil, not wood-burning furnace; furnishings that "came

with the house" – everything from the former owner's false eye-
lashes to a Venetian credenza to a pre-electric vacuum cleaner
that worked on the principle of a friction toy: if pushed frantically
over a length of carpet, the rotor fan attached to the wheels
might pick up something less than a handful of dust. Four years
later we were packing up again, this time for Eden Mills, Ontario,
promising the kids we'd never move again (rashest of oaths, given
our record); swearing that this time we'd find a place quiet
enough to keep a dog – that is, to keep a dog from being run over.
Packing up our books and bric-à-brac I began, for the first time in
all our moves, to panic. Is there a point at which it becomes
impossible to put down roots, to make good friends, to fall in love
with a landscape? To find endearing instead of hateful the
hundred quirks and foibles of any strange house, especially an old
one? How long would it take us to stop longing for the sea, the
streets, the friends, the very rooms we'd be abandoning; to stop
making useless comparisons: the new house is fine, but it's not – it
can't – it doesn't really feel like home. . . .

We've been in our new-old house for six years now, and though
it feels odd to have lived so long in one place, it would be
unthinkable, we tell ourselves, to have to move anywhere else, to
forsake the friendships we've made, the fields through which we
walk our dog each morning, the river onto which we escape with
our skates or canoe. And yet I write this not in my study overlooking the road that winds through Eden Mills, but before a
window innocent of any glass, and lined with grapevines and
chains of beads. The window gives onto a narrow street which is
gloriously, maddeningly full of life – housewives hurling gossip to
one another, firewood-laden mules clicking their hooves against
the pavement; full-throated canine theatre, always to do with sex
or food or territory; vans that stop to honk or let their drivers
cry their wares: jugs of olive oil, bananas and apples, bread (three

different vendors three different times a day), cylinders of butane gas for cooking and heating water, fresh fish from the ocean half a dozen miles away, and sometimes – thankfully not very often – the two-in-the-morning bottle collection, which sounds like the rolling of vast barrels filled with a year's worth of wine bottles down the steeply inclined street. I tell myself I'll learn the art of shutting out the noise I do not wish or need to hear, just as I'll become adept at sensing sounds I could listen to forever – like the *cante jondo* sung by middle-aged men in the Blue Night Pub, *El Pub de Noche Azul*: wild deep Andalusian song. Though I suspect that what I'll end up hearing by the time we leave this small mountain village south of Granada is dogsex and vanblurts and *duende* all mixed up together.

We are happy here; we could even say we're beginning to feel at home. We've rearranged the furniture of our rented house, organized the books we shipped over at hideous expense, drunk more than a few bottles of wine. It's the end of September and 80 degrees on the rooftop terrace from which we look out at the Sierra Nevada; here pomegranates and custard pears fall as casually from the trees as crab-apples do at home; the Alhambra palace and Generalife gardens are half an hour's drive north, and if anything humanly made or ordered can be a candidate for the earthly paradise, it must be those rosebanks and sprays of jasmine flowers that stare out at you from their dark leaves like the whites of a hundred eyes; latticework and groves of pillars carved as though the chisel were in love with the stone, so that light seems to pulse from within. And yet in the midst of all of this, we are learning how to say homesick in Spanish: *tener morriña*. Yesterday, the brightest and bluest-skied of Sundays, we dragged about our house, unable to read or write or even chat to one another; lacking the energy to do so much as poke our heads outside. Suddenly it came clear to us that we were sick for a home that had nothing to do with walls and furniture, and certainly nothing to do with weather, but with the friends and family we'd left behind, the faces in the photos tacked onto the wall over our makeshift, azure-painted desks at which, now that the holiday of settling-in is over, we must start to work.

Or was it more than sentimentally induced, this burst of homesickness? Could it have simply been the familiar we were pining for, the ability to take what we see around us purely for granted, as we would at home? In this place where we are as exotic to our neighbours as their olive groves and green-husked almonds are to us, we can't help but feel jumpy, even a little blue, thinking how dispensable we are to this village and the lives of people who know us only as *los Canadeses*. For we're discovering that we are, at least in part, what others know us as: given our halting Spanish, this is something close to village idiots, brought in from abroad. Rich idiots, too, since we must appear to eat and drink and keep a roof over our heads without doing anything at all resembling labour. We know that Andalucia, despite its oranges and olives, is the Newfoundland of Spain: unemployment is more than 20 per cent here, and many of the men beating almonds down from the trees or keeping the complex irrigation systems going are working for absentee landlords in Madrid, and working for a pittance. It is a status symbol, here, to have plastic beads or streamers curtaining your open door: the poor use burlap bags, stitched carefully together.

We'll feel it often this year away: a momentary panic at being so far from what is, after all and at long last, home. We can't help thinking of the last time we spent such a long time out of Canada. That was seven years ago, in Sussex, when we survived ten months in an appallingly ill-built, ill-heated '60s box: moss growing in the bathroom, Niagaras to be sponged off each window every morning. (Nil ambience, but close to good schools – oh, how one's priorities in housing change once school-age children hit the scene.) Our return to England, exactly ten years after we'd left for good, showed us how quickly a place that once had felt like – had become – home can change. Ten years of a political regime that had destroyed or damaged so much of what we'd come to love or admire about England – all this had turned us back into the foreigners we'd been the day we first arrived in Brighton, checking out that seafront bedsit in Sillwood Place. Returning to Canada after our stay in Spain, will we also feel like foreigners, and just as unhappy ones? For this is what we can't help recognizing at this distance: home is a collective, not just a private place. Contrary to Maggie Thatcher's declaration that "there is no such thing as society, only individuals," we know that "home" is the society of which we can't help being a part, and which we help to shape or to deform.

We've been gone for six weeks, and have read no news of Canada in the various papers we've picked up in France or Spain. But we know what we've left behind: governments that seem intent on rooting out every institution and program designed to work for the public good and to sustain, across an entire continent, that spirit of place that has to do with culture rather than nature – with what we make of ourselves, together. Will we find ourselves, come next September, not home again, but in a stranger's house, one whose windows will cast back to us reflections we no longer want to recognize? We who have the privilege of speculating about such things as "radical homelessness" since we're not, at least yet, among those lacking a material roof over their heads. And perhaps, though it's taken me all this time to discover it, this non-imagined, doggedly unliterary fact of homelessness is the most urgent, the most necessary context in which to think of "writing home" at all.

YANN MARTEL

Philadelphia Green Blue – Musings on the Meaning of Home

~

(i)

The settled and the nomadic live very different lives. So the settled, in his habits, throws his net not so far but his catch is heavy: his apartment and its goods and chattels, his favourite haunts and streets, the buildings and parks of his beloved city. The nomadic throws her net much farther – over new rooms and new cities, across plains and atop mountains – but her catch is light, little more than what she can carry on her back. Yet the result is the same: each is content.

This is because the settled and the nomadic approach place, understand home, in similar ways.

There is one time, one place, where this apparent paradox does not exist. Let's start there.

The fetus is both settled and nomadic. It can travel without leaving home. Only when it is born does the problem of home begin to pose itself.

At first, home is a body, the mother's body. Her sweet skin is refrigerator, furnace, bedroom, and living room all in one. Her face is a window onto the world. Her eyes are a bookshelf crowded

171

with books. Her hands are doors, open and closed. Her voice is a sound system.

In time the toddler decides it wants a bigger home. So the home expands, somewhat uncritically, in that manner typical of the very young: anything will do as plate or plaything, no matter how dirty, anything will do as bedroom, the floor here or there, anything will do as anything, no matter how incongruous. But the gravitational centre of this home is still the mother. Home is a circumscribed space around her body. Father's body is a secondary home, the cottage in the country.

The toddler is perhaps toying with destroying the home when it closes its eyes and plays with the idea – oh how scary – that its mother is gone. This is the beginning of nomadism: the closing of the eyes and the imagining of a different reality. But the toddler always opens its eyes and is delighted to see its mother, to be settled. Any other reality would bring on shrieks and cries.

It is when the toddler discovers the material world, realizes that this reality is independent of its mother, even of itself, and therefore that it can – must – be explored, that the question becomes vital to the toddler, because it is one of identity: will he settle or will she travel?

In answering this question, the question of what is home begins to be answered too.

(ii)

Even before my parents joined Canada's Department of External Affairs (as it was called at the time, before the new, slightly xenophobic Foreign Affairs), even before they embarked on their poshly nomadic careers, they were on the move. A doctoral scholarship awarded to my father by the University of Salamanca was their ticket out of a province of Quebec that at the time was a deep, dark bottom of a Roman Catholic well. Spain in 1963 was a worse place than Quebec, a deep, dark bottom of a *fascist* Roman Catholic well, but it was exotic and Miguel de Unamuno, the subject of my father's thesis, was a noted antifascist. So they left for Spain, never to return to Quebec.

I tagged along, as a fetus.

Moving from Spain to Alaska, where my father would teach at the University of Alaska for two years, was climatically brutal, but I was swaddled and unaware. Indissociable from the idea of home is the notion of warmth; a cold home is an intolerable oxymoron. My parents kept me warm. I recall no difference between Spain and Alaska.

Nor do I recall the celebrated temperateness of coastal British Columbia, where my father did a one-year stint at the University of Victoria.

Of Ottawa – the next place – I have vague memories of home. I remember the range, over whose coils of red heat I laboured with the sweaty zest of Vulcan, boiling eggs till they cracked and carrots till they were mush, and melting plastic soldiers in a frying pan once. And I remember a brick-and-plank bookshelf because that's where I found the cat, dead, its head hidden in the shadow of the lowest shelf, its body in the open. I clearly remember thinking that this layout was not haphazard; just as Artaud was found dead clinging onto one of his boots – a last grasp at the familiar – so our cat had chosen to die in this position, its head, seat of consciousness, in a dark, cosy place. There, in the homiest part of home, it could give up life with a modicum of desperate peace.

If exile, living in a foreign place, is bad enough for the settled, imagine *dying* in a foreign place. Death brings us home, the desire to be home.

But my memories of Ottawa as home are nonetheless vague. They do not come together to form a consistent weave of comfort. Home, then, was still my parents.

It is to Costa Rica, more precisely to our house in San José, that I can trace the first change in my idea of home.

(iii)

Traditionally, men are tied to land. It is usually a man, not Scarlett O'Hara, who grasps a handful of soil and says, hoarsely, "Tara!", giving himself by this utterance a name. Thus Leonardo da Vinci, the Prince of Wales, Viscount Bennett of Mickleham and of Calgary and Hopewell. A man without land is a man without a name. Witness poor, mocked John Lackland.

Traditionally, women are tied to men. Thus Jacqueline Kennedy Onassis, née Bouvier.

The woman, who has to leave home, learns how to build a new one, while the man, who stays put, does not. A woman carries the notion of home both with her and within her, since she can be a home herself, to new life.

The woman is the archetypal nomad, while the man is the archetypal settled.

(iv)

Our house in Costa Rica was the world to me. Within its two storeys, enclosed garden, and interior fountain I lived my life fully. Of course there were trips beyond – to school; to play in the street; with my parents – but these had an extramural quality, indefinably abnormal. It was within the bounds of the house that I existed naturally.

The garden was the jungles of the Congo, the sky above my parcel of NASA's playground. The interior fountain – a kitsch horror to my parents – was Atlantis and the Atlantic, the islands of the Pacific and the river Kwai. On certain floors, Lego civilizations succeeded themselves in numbers greater than Schliemann found at Troy. Every room, every closet, every cubbyhole was Herodotean in its permutations: I never stepped into the same space twice. What was once the burial chamber in the Pyramid of Cheops after having been the rim of Krakatoa subsequent to its incarnation as the main vault at Fort Knox was now an examination room in which Mary Ann was in need of a diagnosis.

If fancy could be turned into bubble gum, my parents would have found their house with the windows and doors busted out and the rounded walls straining to contain an expanding mass of sweet pink.

This, overlaid onto rooms whose functions I knew and which reflected aspects of my physical being: there was the sleeping room, the eating room, the cooking room, the playing room, the cleaning and natural needs room, my parents' room – home is a place that is comfortable, of course.

So that was home to me, aged four to seven: no longer a body, but a place, a house. Yet home was also the world, for the world was at home. I was still both settled and nomadic.

I was not aware – yet – of the number and weight of dichotomies that I was living. For example, that my Canadian home was in a foreign land. That I spoke French at home while learning the ways of the world at school in English. To name only two dichotomies.

(v)

I was a boy before I knew it. I slowly grew into the role that society, in tandem with my sex, allotted me. Which means I grew used to the notion of power. All my dreams and ambitions as a boy empowered me. I would grow to be hairy and muscular, that was one dream. I would lead an adventurous life, that was another (and who is more powerful: the desert, the moon, the mountain, the cyclops – or the solitary figure of the camel-riding British soldier, the American astronaut, the New Zealand beekeeper, the wily Greek wayfarer who defeats each one?). I would be well educated, with academic endorsements from MIT, Harvard, and Oxford to prove it, for knowledge is power. Lastly, my beard a distinguished grizzle, I would exercise power in a direct way, as Prime Minister of Canada.

Like a Strasberg method actor, I learned my role as a boy, as a future man, by living it. By study and observation I gathered the expressions I should use, the lines I should deliver, the scenes in which I should star. My acting coaches were legion, from the neighbour who with a stick picked up a big snake that was undulating on the street and twirled it in such a way that the snake could not fall off the stick until he deftly flicked it down the sewer – he was d'Artagnan to me – to Eckhardt's father, Eckhardt being a German friend whose family had come to Costa Rica right after the Second World War (suspicious, isn't it?), a Buddha of a bald man whose permanently impassive expression and rumble of an accent filled me with terror – the Devil! the Devil! (but what charisma) – to all the famous men who hung in the portrait gallery of history that was television, books, magazines, newspapers, and the conversation of adults.

Meanwhile, at home, my meals were cooked for me, my clothes were washed, my bed was made, my flights of imagination were entertained, my happiness was assured, by women.

(vi)

San José, Paris, Ottawa, Madrid, Port Hope, Peterborough, Montréal; different postings, different dwellings, different schools; an evolving different me – home changed. It was still a place, but my relation to it changed. In one way, even when it was physically bigger, home became a smaller place, a too small place, for the world had departed it. The world was now in a more obvious, less imaginary place: beyond. What was left of home was the too-close-for-comfort comfortable place where I lived with my parents. I was a difficult teenager.

Like many North Americans who make the trek from adolescence to adulthood and from high school to university, I found that as my lodgings got smaller, my beds got bigger. The moist dark horizontal world of the sexual was the one place where home expanded.

My university career was a disaster. I obtained my little three-year Bachelor of Arts degree by the skin of my teeth. There would be no Harvard or Oxford for me.

Upon graduation I stood at the threshold of life panting and confused. I had no idea about anything. No idea who I was, what I needed, where I was heading.

So I travelled, hoping to find myself in motion.

(vii)

I came to women late. I don't mean passing Checkpoint Charlie – unfortunately I was sleeping with women long before I began learning from them. But it was through this close contact that I realized eventually how much of my deep weariness with myself was linked to my maleness. That's where it came from, this talent for authoritarianism, this ability to know nothing and defend it with hidebound conviction, this easy recourse to wrath, this pen-chant for nihilism and destruction.

Very deliberately I went about exploring femaleness. I don't mean the contact between maleness and femaleness. I mean femaleness all by itself.

I started on a literal level, with what defines a woman: her menstrual cycle. Till then an otherly abstraction – oh to have had a dear sister or an earth-goddess-like mother – menstruation was to be made real.

I read. I asked questions. I touched. I was met with embarrass-ment, eye-rolling, sighs, the occasional smile of delight. I smelled earthy iron on the tips of my fingers and thought of Prometheus.

My interest was neither prurient nor intellectual. It just did me good to know about and consider this otherly phenomenon. It relieved a parchedness in my being. It came like a red Nile across a desert.

(viii)

I left Canada at age twenty-one determined never to come back. On my bed at my parents' house I spread out all the things I needed for my survival, which ranged from a large aerosol can of mentholated shaving cream to my unfinished first novel. It all fit into my medium-size blue backpack.

My vaccinations would keep me immortal, my guidebooks knowledgeable, my confusion moving.

Home was no longer a place. Or if it was, it was an elusive place: elsewhere. I was neither settled, since I was now on the move, free, nor nomadic, since I didn't move in peace.

I departed, seeking discomfort and foreignness. I sought it in Portugal and Syria, Greece and India, Peru and Ireland, Mexico and Turkey, Czechoslovakia and Indonesia, Norway and Iran.

(ix)

It was women I found. For though I saw a thousand and one wonders during my travels, from aqueducts to ziggurats, from Andean ruins to Zoroastrian temples, a full rich compilation of male masonry, what impressed itself most deeply on my mind was this neglected half of humanity, whether met for a second – a glimpse from an Indian train, say, captured in my memory like a photo – or intimately.

It was a defining moment of irony: I was angry at Ruth and ignoring her, pretending to be absorbed in my book. She spoke, but I looked all the more fixedly at the same line of print, ordering my eyes not to move. She walked out of our room, the signal that my sulkiness had triumphed. I began to read. Then it struck me, accompanied by a sickening dip in my emotions, the irony of it: the book I was reading was Mahatma Gandhi's autobiography. Why did it take a man – along with another one, Martin Luther King – to make respectable in our century a notion of non-violence that women have been practising patiently and anonymously for thousands of years? I lay frozen on the bed for a few seconds. Then I jumped up and ran out into the sunny dry Greek landscape to find Ruth. With every step I wished to leave my former self behind.

(x)

In time I became a better nomad, with a stronger equanimity. I move through places – whether foreign or local – the way a blind person's fingers glide over dots of Braille: lightly, ephemerally, significantly. I try to retain of places only their sense impression, their meaning.

It's all in the way you mix imagination and place.

(xi)

"Where are you from, again?" I asked Ruth.

That's how we got close: I was plying her feet and ankles with my fingers, and the significance of it had moved beyond the soothing. I was so engrossed in the moment that I had become confused, had forgotten the trimmings of her identity. Our gazes met.

She sat up on the bed. We kissed, a little out of breath. She was from Philadelphia, I remembered.

She looked out.

"I'm from here," she replied. And smiled, her green eyes turning back to me.

The blue Aegean sparkled in the afternoon sun.

(xii)

Home is a feeling of pregnancy with place. The settled and the nomadic will tell you this.

DON McKAY

An Old House Beside the Military Base

~

"Maybe it is a good idea for us to keep a few dreams of a
house that we shall live in later, always later, so much later,
in fact, that we shall not have time to achieve it."
– Gaston Bachelard, *The Poetics of Space*

It spoke directly from the nooks of imagination, easily bypassing
everything we'd ever learnt. As though the solitudes lived in by
the writing mind, usually represented chastely by a particular
cushion and chair, had grown from perches into nests. An elfin,
irresistible doorway led to a low loft over the kitchen where the
windows came nearly to the floor. On the third storey, Captain
Weston had built a lookout so he could watch the river traffic in
his retirement – a den and weather-eye with just enough room for
a desk and chair. "Womb with a view," I joked; later an extra-
strong explosion cracked a pane. Out back, the drive shed had
been turned into a workshop by one owner, into a pottery by
another, then back into a workshop. Now it had a solid bench
and a potbellied stove, affable as an uncle. We learnt that the
ground-floor bathroom had once been the village post office,
when the village had been a village with two general stores and a

blacksmith. Foolishly, we browsed between shy spaces, imagining a lamp, a corner table, a rug, and shelves, shelves, shelves. We were several metamorphoses away from real estate, with its problematic of plumbing, taxes, resale value, and, in this case, simulated warfare. Later we came to realize that spaces like these cannot not listen; they are inner ears whose power lies in their complete susceptibility to tremor.

Is language the house of being, as Heidegger says? Or is the house of being simply a house – the one that haunts you from the future, with its porch, its secret spaces, its path dawdling off into the birches? The one you dwell toward and mustn't catch; the one where you will always, unshaken, play the fool.

ROHINTON MISTRY

From Plus-Fours to Minus-Fours: A Fable

~

"From Plus-Fours to Minus-Fours" was originally part of a convocation address at the University of Ottawa in spring 1996, part of an effort to employ two songs from *Mary Poppins* and *The Sound of Music* to inspire the graduating class, keeping in mind the times we live in.

Whether or not one is fond of these musicals, one has to concede that they would not be what they are without the two songs in question: "Let's Go Fly a Kite" and "Climb Every Mountain." Without Maria in the Alps, and the Mother Abbess egging her on to climb them, urging her to "follow every rainbow till you find your dream," *The Sound of Music* would never get off the ground. And if the career-fixated Mr. Banks did not go to the park to fly a kite, "up to the highest height," with Mrs. Banks and their children, Jane and Michael, *Mary Poppins* could not come to a satisfactory conclusion, wherein we witness the full restoration of the father unto the bosom of his family.

As it is with these musicals, so it is with homelands: they are not complete without kites and mountains. The kites and mountains may be metaphoric, hyperbolic, or paradoxic, but their presence is essential. It is a well-known fact that when people choose freely and wisely, they elect to have a society which includes kites and mountains.

~

Once upon a time, not so very long ago, in a land that was not at all far away, there lived a people who were considered the most fortunate by the rest of the world. And there was good reason for this: theirs was a land that was blessed in every way. And, what was more important, theirs was a society that lived by the principles of tolerance and good will and compassion for its members. Now not all of the citizens were bursting with tolerance and good will and compassion all of the time, but the important thing was: they did their best to *believe* in these values, they believed they were worth striving after.

The people of this fortunate land had two passions: kite-flying and mountain-climbing. Some practised one, some the other; many practised both. The most accomplished among them flew their kites from the mountain tops, and it was a truly awe-inspiring sight. The kite-flyers and mountain-climbers had their various teams, the team uniforms were fashioned in fabrics of red and white, and they took great pleasure in friendly competitions and games. But they never forgot their credo of tolerance and good will and compassion.

Thus, they were always urging the less agile among them to climb the mountains, and assisting those who had not yet mastered the laws of aerodynamics and glue and paper to fly their kites. Special agencies had even been set up to bring to fruition this vision of a just society. And so the disabled, the feeble, those too poor to buy their mountain-climbing gear or their kite-flying equipment, and, most importantly, their elegant red-and-white uniforms, were all looked after and encouraged to participate fully.

The wise king of this fortunate land, himself an enthusiast of kites and mountains like his predecessors, gazed upon his kingdom and saw that it was good. He watched his people singing and laughing and playing together, and his eyes moistened with happiness.

Now it came to pass that there arose in the land a shortage of cloth. No one could explain exactly why the shortage arose, especially in such a prosperous land, but it had something to do with people who called themselves international fabric-traders, who speculated in the commodity and created artificial deficits. The king did his best to ensure that his people would not suffer. He lowered tariffs, raised taxes, tried to impose rules and regulations on the traders, but in the end the fabricated deficits defeated him. He had to take the unprecedented step of establishing limits on people's wardrobes.

Most people accepted this modest restriction. They understood that it was fair, equitable, and necessary for the common good. But there were some who protested, especially when their cherished red-and-white team uniforms were unavailable. The dissent spread, and, as is inevitable in these situations, brought forth in their midst a challenger who promised he could restore prosperity to the land if he became king.

"Waste in the king's bureaucracy is the reason for this shortage," he said. "I will cut out the waste. I will downsize and restructure and consolidate. I will be lean and mean for a while, but soon you will reap the rewards, trust me."

This is what he said in public. In private, he sang a different song: "Oh-uh-oh yes, I'm the great pretender."

In view of his healthy girth, the need for leanness was self-evident, but why meanness? Alas, no one sought to question him on this point, and then he was already ensconced on the throne of the realm.

The new measures now went into effect. The first proclamation stated that no more fabric would be issued from the royal textile warehouses for uniforms for kite-flyers and mountain-climbers. The new king had no interest in these two groups – he himself was a golfer. Meanwhile, red, white *and* blue fabric continued to be made available for golf-shirts and golf-slacks and plus-fours.

The unfairness of it all was not lost on the people. When they complained, the new king said: "Golf is the activity of the nineties. It's a now kind of thing, a global thing. It will bring prosperity to the land, and soon there'll be fabric enough for everyone. It's the theory of trickle-down textiles."

Time passed, but balls – stray golf balls – were all that trickled down the courses. Sometimes they flew at great speed, injuring innocent bystanders. In retaliation, groups of kite-flyers and mountain-climbers began attacking the golfers, tearing their clothes off, altering their plus-fours to minus-fours. It became necessary for the king to station his imperial guard on every fairway and green. With their black face visors, body armour, and weapons, the guards looked as though they had stepped out of a video game rife with unspeakable violence.

The shortage of fabric in the land did not abate. The king went on television and explained that further austerity measures were needed before things could get better. "We have no choice but to issue a downsizing decree," he said. "We are not mean-spirited or heartless, as some of our enemies suggest. We do not enjoy causing pain. But we have to fulfil our promises." Between sentences, the king's lips kept disappearing; he continued: "We will start by saving on skirts and trousers. People's legs will be downsized. Less fabric will then be required to clothe them. Instead of the ankle bone connecting to the leg bone, the leg bone connecting to the knee bone, the knee bone to the thigh bone, and the thigh bone to the hip bone, we will connect the ankle bone directly to the hip bone. Then everyone can wear very short pants and very short skirts. The savings will be immense."

The first cuts began to take effect, and the cries of the people rent the once-tranquil air of the land. The kite-flyers and mountain-climbers pleaded that such drastic measures were not necessary, there were surely better ways to deal with the problem.

"We can't be distracted by special-interest groups," said the king.

"But sire, we will no longer be able to fly our kites and climb the beautiful mountains," said the people.

"Nonsense," said the king, unable to control what seemed to be a tiny smirk. "Of course you will. It will be a greater challenge, that's all. Your downsized legs will have to work harder, that's all. My daddy taught me that if I worked hard, I would be able to fly kites and climb mountains as much as I wanted."

As the cutbacks continued, the king noticed that things were not proceeding fast enough. He inquired into the delays. "We do not have enough operating theatres and hospital beds," explained the surgeons in charge of downsizing legs.

"Is that all?" said the king. He met with his advisers. A new decree went forth: the butchers and meat-packers and all the abattoirs in the land were to pitch in. "Same difference," said the king. "They all work with flesh and bone, and use the same tools. We have too much specialization for our own good." He wiped his sweat-beaded upper lip and continued. "While we are at it, let us restructure education. From now on, metal workshop teachers will also teach English – they can recite a sonnet, for example, while giving a welding demonstration. And the English teachers will be retrained as caddies – they'll be more useful on our golf courses."

Misery and despair settled like a fog upon the land. And the people saw that once again the golfers were left unscathed. In fact, the golfers seemed to *grow* in size. The amputated leg bones and thigh bones were being grafted onto the golfers, making them taller and stronger than ever before. Now they were able to stride faster down the fairways, sinking holes-in-one with regularity, completing their eighteen holes in no time.

The kite-flyers and mountain-climbers, their numbers greatly dwindled, crawled to the king in their very short pants and very short skirts and tried to explain that it was not just a luxury or a hobby of which they were being deprived. "All of society suffers, your highness, downsizing diminishes us all, including your majesty and the members of your royal court."

"And how's that?" asked the king, standing tall.

"Kite-flying and mountain-climbing are necessary for our spiritual well-being," said the people. "Kites let you soar as though you had your own set of wings. With your feet on the ground you're a bird in flight, with your fist holding tight to the string of your kite."

"Rhyming rubbish and figurative flim-flam," said the king dismissively.

"But, sire, from the mountain top you can see forever, it's like having a glimpse of the paradise that we could share on earth. Kites and mountains – they help us to dream. And you are taking away our dreams, your majesty. Without dreams, people perish. Come with us, fly a kite with us, hike up to the mountain top with us. Even a small, teensy-weensy mountain will enrich you."

"Socialist claptrap and metaphorical mumbo-jumbo cannot shake my belief in common sense," declared the king, his lips disappearing completely as he spoke.

And like the king's lips, the art of kite-flying and mountain-climbing also disappeared from people's lives with the passing of time. But it lived on in their hearts and minds, and in their imagination. It helped them to endure, it kept hope alive, for they continued to secretly sing their two songs while waiting for deliverance, their two sacred anthems: "Let's go fly a kite, up to the highest height," and "Climb ev'ry mountain, ford ev'ry stream."

At this point, it is normal practice for the fabulist to present the moral of the fable. Alas, I have none to share with you. The end of the fable is not yet written. That task falls upon us collectively. That is our responsibility, for all our tomorrows.

ALICE MUNRO

Changing Places

∿

We sailed from the harbour of Leith on the 4th June into the Leith Roads. There we lay the 5th, 6th, 7th and 8th getting the ship cleared out till the afternoon of the 9th when we set sail the 10th. We were passed the corner of Fifeshire all well nothing occurred worth mentioning till the 13th in the morning we were awakened with the cry of "John o'Groat's House" but we had a fine sail across the Pentland Firth having both wind and tide with us and no way dangerous as was reported but it came on such a breeze of wind in the afternoon from the Northward that set the ship a trembling and almost every passenger in the ship was spueing but I never got sick nor none of our family that I remember of, 14th was a calm day and we got all well again but could take little meat and that night we lost sight of Scotland. The 15th there was a child the name of Ormiston died and its body was thrown overboard sewed up in a piece of canvas with a large coal at its feet. 16th was a very windy day from the S.W. the sea was running very high and the ship got her gib-boom broken on account of the violence of the wind. This day our sister Agnes was taken into the cabin but she was not better till the 18th when she was delivered of a daughter. Nothing occurred till the 22nd this was the roughest day we had experienced. The gib-boom was broken a second time nothing happened worth while. Agnes was mending in an ordinary way till the 29th we saw a great shoal of porpoises and the 30th was a very rough sea the wind blowing from the west we went rather backwards than forwards.

We saw nothing but water the 14th June till the 5th July when we saw a ship homeward bound but she was not nigh us. We came on the Fishing Banks on the 12th on the 17th we saw land and it was a joyful sight to us. It was part of Newfoundland. We sailed between Newfoundland and St. John's Island and having a fair wind both the 18th and 19th we found ourselves in the River on the morning of the 20th and within sight of the mainland of North America. I think every passenger was out of bed at 4 o'clock gazing at the land it being wholly covered with wood and quite a new sight to us. It was part of Nova Scotia and a beautiful hilly country. We saw several whales this day such creatures as I never saw in my life but we were becalmed the 21 and 22 but we had rather more wind the 23 but in the afternoon we were all alarmed by a squall of wind accompanied by thunder and lightening which was very terrible and we had one of our mainsails torn to rags by the wind. This squall lasted about 8 or 10 minutes and the 24th we had a fair wind which set us a good way up the River where it became more strait so that we saw land on both sides of the River. But we becalmed again till the 31 and we had a breeze only two hours. Several boats came alongside us with fish, rum, live sheep; tobacco which they sold very high to the passengers. The 1st of August we had a slight breeze and on the morning of the 2nd we passed by the Isle of Orleans and about eight in the morning we were in sight of Quebec in as good health I think as when we left Scotland. Blessed be God for his mercies to us all. We are to sail for Montreal tomorrow in a steamboat.

My brother Walter in the former part of this has written a large journal which I intend to sum up in a small ledger. We have had a very prosperous voyage being wonderfully preserved in health. . . . There is a great number of people landed here this season but wages is good. I can neither advise nor discourage people from coming here as yet. The land is very extensive and very thin peopled. I think we have seen as much land as might serve all the people in Britain uncultivated and all covered with wood. We will write you again as soon as settled. God bless you.

This letter, posted from Quebec on August 3, 1818, was addressed to William Laidlaw, Wolfhope, Parish of Ettrick, County of Selkirk, Scotland. The person who signed it was his father, James Laidlaw, but it was obviously written by his brothers Walter and Andrew. Nineteen-year-old Walter writes with a quick appreciation of himself and his adventure, Andrew more cautiously and circumspectly and with a hint of dry amused reproach. These different ways of responding to experience seem to me not reconciled in my family to this day.

Agnes was Andrew's wife. They had a little boy, James, not quite two years old. There was also, in the party that crossed the Atlantic, Walter's and Andrew's older sister Mary, and the father of course, and the baby born early in the voyage. They may have all been well when they landed, but little James was dead before the end of the month. The baby Isabella had six children and lived to be an old woman. On her tombstone is written *Born at Sea*.

This family had lived in the Scottish Borders and particularly in the Ettrick Valley – called in old days the Ettrick Forest – for centuries. The "law" in Laidlaw is Anglo-Saxon for hill. So it seems they may have come north in some big pre-feudal migration, reached a part of Scotland that was maybe not Scotland then but Northumbria, settled down, and stayed put. I have found the name on court rolls for the fifteenth century – Laidlaws brought up more than once for "theftuously removing" wood from Ettrick Forest when it belonged to the Kings of Scotland. A common crime, it seems, and not too serious – they got off with a fine. So did the Laidlaw who murdered another Laidlaw – murder may not have been so serious either, unless the person killed was of political importance.

James was born in 1763. For about twenty years before he left the country, he seems to have been obsessed with the notion of America – that is, with North America. His cousin James Hogg says that James Laidlaw "talked and read about America until he grew perfectly unhappy, and when approaching his sixtieth year actually set out to find a temporary home and a grave in the new world." When Laidlaw first began to hear tell of America, Hogg adds, "He would not believe that Fife was not in it, or that he could not see it from the top of Castle hill in Edinburgh." He had by his own account tried in 1816 to get a free passage for himself and his five sons – there was some promise of two hundred acres each – but he could not sell his sheep for ready cash because of the depression following the end of the Napoleonic Wars, and so he did not get away. In 1818 there was no longer any offer of free passage, and the land available was down to a hundred acres, but he was going anyway. Only two of his sons were going with him. One son, James, was out there already, teaching school in Nova Scotia though he could not possibly have had more than a village education in Scotland, and the other two, William and Robert, had, as Hogg says, "formed attachments at home and refused to accompany him."

1819. They are living in York (Toronto). James writes his own
letter this time, to another uncooperative son, Robert. This is the
letter which fell into the hands of James Hogg and ended up in
the pages of *Blackwoods Magazine*, preceded by Hogg's description
of the writer as "a singular and highly amusing character cherish-
ing every antiquated and exploded notion in science, religion,
and politics. . . . Nothing excited his indignation more than the
theory of the earth wheeling around on its axis and journeying
around the sun. He had many strong logical arguments against it,
and nailed them all with Scripture. . . ."

> I write you this to let you know that we are still alive which is
> a great mercy . . . as there is no land ready misered we were
> obliged to take a House for the summer and an acare of a
> garden. We had to stay in it till we got a crop of the Garden.
> We are mostly all Scottsmen and has got a Township to be
> together or what is called a parish in Scotland. There is a great
> many people settling hear. Goverment bought a Large Tract of
> Cuntry from the Indians last year. . . . We have eighteen
> months to do our settling deuties in where we have to clear five
> acers each and put up a House and then we get our Deed for
> ever to our Selvs and hirs. Robert, I will not advise you to
> Come hear as I am afraid you will not Like this place; so you
> may take your own will when you did not Come along with us.
> I do not Expect Ever to See you hear; I am very glad that you
> have got a place for you and your wife. May the good will of
> him that Dwelt in the Bush rest on you and hir. If I had
> thought that you ould have deserted us I should not have
> comed hear; it was my ame to get you all near me made me
> Come to America but mans thoughts are Vanity for I have
> Scattered you far wider but I Cannot help it now. Them that I
> have hear is far more contented than I am; indeed I can do very

Little for the support of a Family for the work is very heavy it is
not a place for old men Lik me altho it is a fine country. Robert
if this comes to you as i Expect it will you may take it over to
Wolfhope and Let William see it. . . .

James goes on to say they have good health except that both
Andrew and Walter have had the ague. But they have "wrought
all this Summer with people in the town for Six Shillings a-day."
From their garden they have sold "100 duson of cowcombres and
thirty Bushels of potatoes and had peas 10 foot High and beans 12
foot."

There is Every kind of grain and Hundreds of people Coming
from the old cuntry to eat of it Twelve stone of it is 27
Shillings. . . . The money here with Merchants and people of
tread is as plenty as Ever I saw it in any Town in Scotland.
There is a market here every day for Beef and Mutton and
people comes with Butter and Cheese and Eggs and potatoes,
onions and Carrots, melons and Skuashins and pumpkins –
with many things unknown in Scotland. The people hear
speaks very good English there is many of our Scots words they
cannot understand what we are Saying and they Live far more
independent than King George for if they have been any time
hear and got a few acers Cleared they have plenty to Live on.
. . . There is a road goes straight North from york for fifty miles
and the Farm Houses almost all Two Story High. Some have as
good as 12 Cows and 4 or 5 Horses for they pay no taxes but
Just a perfict trifell and rids in ther gigs or Chire Like Lords. We
like this place far better than the States we have got Sermon
three times Every Saboth. They are the Baptists that we hear
there is no Presbetaren minister in this Town yet bit there is
a Large English Chapel and Methodist Chapel but I do not

think the Methodists is very Sound in their Doctrine. They Save all infants and Saposes a man may be Justified to day and fall from it to-morrow. And the English minister reads all that he says unless it be his Clark Craying always at the end of Every peorid, Good Lord dliver us. if Tom Hogg could Come over and hear the Methidists one day it ould set him Craking about it for one Year for the minister prays as Loud as ever he Can and the people is all doun on there knees all Craying, Amen so that you Can Scarce hear what the priest is Saying and I have Seen Some of them Jumping up as if they ould have gone to Heaven Souls and Body – but there Body was a filthy Clog to them for they always fell down again always crying O Jesus O Jesus, Just as he had been there to pull them up through the loft. They have there field meetings where they preach day and night for a week where Some thousands attends and Some will be asleep and Some falling down under Convictions and others Eating and Drinking. now Robert write to us how you are all and if you think William will Come hear or not we have as much land as will serve us all but neither you nor him will Like America at the first as every-thing is New Here and people has Every thing to learn. . . . I shall say no more but wish that the god of Jacob may be your god and may he be your gide for Ever and Ever is the Sincer prayer of your Loving Father till Death.

Then he warns them, "Pay your Letters to the Sea, or they will not Come to us."

It does not seem that William paid his letters to the sea, or that there was any correspondence at all between him and his father, or his brothers, for many years. There may have been some rift or he may have been simply a modern sort of man, busy getting on, rational and independent and wary – with good reason – of his father's manipulations. No letter of his to anybody survives, but he did write one to Mary Scott, a girl in Ettrick (William had by this time gone to work in the Highlands, for a sheep-farmer). I have her answer – he must have been the one who preserved it.

Dear William,
I recived your letter and was glad to hear that you are got better of your ilnes I am verry well at present hoping this will find you in the same I recived your letter a bout ten days ago Walter Amos gave it to my father I was thair but I think he does not know me I wrot you in my last letter that Mr. Laing had got A wif but she has not had a days helth sinc Robert Turnbull is a bridgromn he is getting a wif with to hundred pounds if you had been hear you would have had a chance for A weding John Reid of Delorigh is wed Baldy Irvin of Fedlings daughter was proclaimed to a serving man but they have stoped it becaus he is poor and perhaps he is not a Cameroning. Walter Sheel is comed from America to see his freends and he was at your fathers a twelve munth Ago and they were doing verry well your Father says he would not change with any farm in Ettrick. Your brother James was going to be wed your father he says is as chery as ever he says all the people knows him. . . . You said in your letter that you expected to hear of my weding it is not but what I might but have never thought A bout it yet or sertnly I would have wrot you and given you A invitation I supos I will be lik the old Almaniks that no person will by you wrot about me comming to you which i think something hard to answer I will not say that I will not come but perhaps I think that is a jok in your letter you say you have plenty of tim for seeing the lasis you may come some moonlight night and see me which I think you would perfed before any you say you would think it painful to come and live in Etterick again I think you would

feel more paiun in leving the hiland thain me if ever you came
back to the soth i would lik to see you married or not I wish you
weel what ever way it be and A better wif thain ever I could
have been I think you will think me trublsom by answering
your letter so soon you may write whain you pleas if you intend
writing Any mor your friends is all well for any that I know my
brother and sister has thair compliments to you no more but
remains, Mary Scott.

By Cameroning she must mean a Cameronian.

This letter was written in January of 1825 and within the year
William and Mary were married.

Two years later James – old James – is writing to the *Colonial
Advocate* – William Lyon Mackenzie's paper, whose presses the
Tory young bloods of York had at one time thrown into the lake –
and he does not sound so "chery," though there isn't any doubt
that after the letter was printed all the people would know him.

I have taken upon me to write a few lines to let you know that
the Scotts bodies that lives heare is all doing tolarabley well for
the things of this world but I am afraid that few of them thinks
any thing of what will come of there soul when Death there
days doth end for they have found a thing they call whiskey
and a great many of them dabbales and drinks at it till they
make themselves worse than an ox or an ass for they differ
among themselves and men that meets good friends is like
before they part to cut one anothers throts. Burns speaks of the
barley bru sementing the qurall but the ray bru hear is almost
sure to make a qurall for since the Bodys is turned Lairds everyone is for being Master and they never consider that there
neighbour is as far up in the world as themselves, but America

is a good cuntry for a poor man if he is able to work but it is full of rougs that is not what I like for they will cheat you if they can if I had known it to be what it is it should never have seen me but times being bad in Scotland after the war and old shepheards like me being not much thought of when we get old I thought of coming to America . . . so I came to york and went through all there offices according to acts of Parlement I sopose aye the other dollar to pay but they ould give us only a hundred acers each and that was to be dran by ballot if it was good land we were the better of and if bad we bid glad with it if there map said it was capable of cultivation. I believe the criblers in york ould take the last shilling that a poor man has before they ould do anything for him in the way of getting land in one of there offices they were crying it is five and sixpence it is five and sixpence and only marking two or three words but I will pas them for they are an avericious set. I am really feard that the deil will get most of them if they do not bethink themseves in time I sopose that they never read the tenth commandment or they ould not covet their nighboures money the folkes hear is for getting a liberery and we have got Mr. Leslees catalogue of books for 1825 the nixt catalogue he prints he would do well to let people know the price of books but he is got into the yankee fashion but whin a man sees a book and knows the price he knows wither he can purchas it or not I never saw a catalogue of books in Scotland but the price was marked at the tail of it now sir be so good as not to put me in your newspepers as I will stand a chance of getting the Lake to keep me where they put your types. If you let theys fellos away wothout punishment you should be whipped with a road of links it ould be well done to take them and dip them twise or thrise a day in the lake in the cold whether it auld cool them and let them find that douking in the Lake is no joke.

Now Mr. Mcanzie I ould not have taken this liberty I hope that you will not take it ill I am afraid that you ould not read it as I am a very bad writer but I was never at school a quarter of a year in my life Now Sir I could tell you bits of stories but I am afraid you ould put me in your Colonial Advocate I do not like to be in prent I wrot once a bit of a letter to my son Robert in Scotland and my friend Jas. Hogg the Poeit put it in Blackwoods Magazine and had me through all North America before I new that my letter was gone home. Hogg poor man has spent most of his life in coining lies and if I read the Bible right I think it says that all liares is to have there xxx in the lake that burns with fire and brimstone but they find it a laquarative trade for I believe that Hogg and Walter Scott has got mor money for lieingg than old Boston and the Erskins got for all the sermons ever they wrote but the greatest blessings in this world is set by far more light people is fonder of any book than the Bible altho is it the greatest blissing in this world now may the blissing of God rest on you all doers of his name is the sincer prayer of your loving countryman old James Laidlaw.

James was an old drinking companion of Hogg's, so the thing called whiskey was hardly new to him and certainly not something he had avoided himself. Hogg was present on the night in Tibbie Shiels's Inn when James got down on his knees to pray for the salvation of Walter Bryden (Cow Wat). "And if it be true that the object of our petition cheated James Cunningham and Sandy of Bowerhope out of tow to three hunder pouns of lamb-siller, if it be farther true that he left his ain wife and took up with [he named the name] really we have hardly the face to ask any mitigation" . . . and so on. Hogg and another had to hold Cow Wat down.

With that scene in mind you might wonder if the above letter was a fake production. But I don't think so. James was a much older man than when he provided the entertainment at Tibbie Shiels's. And Upper Canada in those years was full of the drinking and brawling that would occupy a rootless male population mauled by the deep black bush and stymied by winter blizzards and ague-ridden summers. He would not be all wrong either about the impudence of the clerks, and their delays and charges. Anna Jameson as well as the outraged William Lyon Mackenzie found the colony stagnant and corrupt. James would have had no use for the ruling clique known as the Family Compact. But notions of equality – every man a Laird – don't seem to sit well with him either. He is an old man taking a whack in every direction. And especially at Mackenzie for printing his letter – though it is hard to see why else he wrote and sent it.

Very dear sir, This will let you know that you have done me a very bad trick in printing my bit simpel letter that I sent you You are shurely very scarce of news I thought you had more honour in you than expose an old body like me when I told you not to put me in your paper but i will trust no more to you for the folk hear is so ill pleased about their bits of falts being told that they look to me like stink and when they pass by will scarce say good day. I like to live in peace with all my neighbours but you have put an end to it now but it was my foley in writing to such a donent stump that puts all in your ill prented peper that you can get either by hook or by crook I shall say little mor but if ever i come to you I will give you your xxx and would give you my advice to read your bible and it will tell you to do Justice and Love Mercy and Walk Humbly with your God I remain yours Humble svnt. James Laidlaw.

In May of 1831 Andrew wrote to William, who was near Fort Augustus in Inverness-Shire in the Highlands.

Dear Brother,

It is now upwards of five years since we had any letters from you or Robert, we understand he has been in the Highlands for some years but we know not in what place, when Francis Hogg was here two years ago we got all the news about Ettrick he also told us you were married to a daughter of John Scott's. James and Walter are both married, Walter has two children a son and a daughter. You have probably heard of our Fathers death he died on the 13th of February 1829 by a Cancer on his left cheek it began a year before his death he suffered much pain the last half year it cut away a great part of his cheek and Jawbone so some of his teeth fell out he was confined to bed several months but had not much sickness till a few days before his death our sister Mary is still weakly and often troubled with the pains. James has had the ague about a month but is now a good deal better and able to go about again. . . . Our neighbours are mostly Scots people we have a meeting-house built on my land and we have occasional preaching in it from the Presbytery of Upper Canada and from the Associate Synod in the States. . . . I expect you do not intend to come to this country now yet we understand by Francis Hogg that Robert still inclines to come we have looked for you every year since we came and has yet been disappointed my wife has been weakly for three years past we have seven children three boys and four girls write to us frequently and tell Robert to write to us and send us word how our friends are about Etterick I wrote several letters to my Aunts but never got an answer would you try to learn if they ever received any of them and let me know remember me to your wife and all our friends I remain yours dear Brother, Andrew Laidlaw.

Old James's wife had died in 1800, so it is likely the children had all been brought up and cared for by those aunts, probably the three spinster Laidlaw sisters who were buried in one grave and had a combined age of 236 years.

During the three years that she had been "weakly," Andrew's wife, Agnes, had borne her sixth and seventh children. She had twelve in all (counting the boy who died almost as soon as they landed), and she must have recovered her health, because she lived to be eighty-four.

By 1836 William and Mary had four sons. A daughter had died in infancy. And now when everyone had given up urging or expecting them, they decided to come to America. But not to Upper Canada. They sailed for New York – my great-grandfather Thomas was a babe-in-arms – and made their way – without, as far as I know, paying a visit to Halton County – out to the frontier state of Illinois. This was just after the Black Hawk Wars, when some of the Indian farmers had resisted being moved to the west of the Mississippi and had been killed or forced into reservations. The family settled in Will County, about thirty miles from Chicago. The second son, John, wrote down, when he was an old man, everything he could recall about their time there. He was writing to his brother Thomas, who obviously could remember nothing. The eldest son James had at that time been dead for fifty years so John was the only source. He said that his father had a piece of land on shares and he described in detail the building of the house. "Rafters you might call them four pair the seam to me now about 8 inches at the but end and a crook in them about 8 feet up and then the rest formed a rafter pinned at the top and boards or poles on them to hold up the thatch it seems to me about 25 feet long 16 or 18 feet wide and a lean-to of 6 or 8 feet and 7 feet high walls built of prairie sods." This is what the seven-year-old boy observed with the most interest. But he also saw the Indians passing by, and the "Hussurs" who were "going to settle somewhere else in the state." He remembers swimming in the Fox River and getting horse leeches on him and "the beautiful grand Prairie in that direction on the southeast side of the river." When John wrote this in the early years of the twentieth century, he was living in Vancouver. He had seen the Rocky Mountains and the Fraser Valley and the Coast Ranges and the profiles of the Gulf Islands, and the Pacific Ocean, but this is the only time in any letter that he uses the word *beautiful*. The open grasslands with their invitation to the plough, their promise to the settler, had an appeal that no conglomeration of rocks or density of trees could ever match.

He writes of hoeing beside his father and his brother James and often stopping to fix his "galases" (his suspenders) and making poor work, and of the tall Indian corn and the great onions and pumpkins and potatoes from the first ploughing. He tries to remember the names of neighbours. The man who had a bank barn built against a rock was named Mr. Sissons, and a Mr. Taylor lived about half a mile west "in the direction of Father's Grave."

Father's grave. Yes. There was a canal being built at the time on the Des Plaines River – part of a system that would link Lake Michigan with the Illinois River, so eventually linking the St. Lawrence and the Mississippi drainage – and William would get some work on it, probably in the winters when he wasn't farming. He may have worked before on the building of the Caledonian Canal – perhaps that was what took him to the Highlands. When he was at work he would have a source of drinking water other than the one he shared at home with his family, and that might explain why he got cholera and they didn't.

He died on the 5th of January 1839. He was forty years old. On the same day, no doubt in the same sod house, his daughter Jane was born, the first girl in the family since the baby Ellen had died in Inverness.

Mary had her husband buried where nobody could find him today, and her daughter christened, and she wrote to her brothers-in-law, and when the winter was over and the roads were dry either Walter or Andrew came to Illinois with an ox-cart. The route taken would be that of Michigan Highway 12, the old track west from Detroit. Back they came in the heat of early summer through the great oak forests that covered southern Michigan, and sometimes the oxen spying a pond or a creek would veer from the path and wade into the water. They could not be deterred or budged till they had drunk their fill, because that is the way oxen are. Back they came to Upper Canada, to Esquising in Halton County, bound to the family after all, and not to become Yankees as their father must have wished.

I am sure they were treated fairly or even generously, but there was no land for them, and as soon as they were old enough the boys struck out for a new wilderness, for Morris Township in Huron County. When they had a shack built, their mother and young sister came to join them.

Mary Scott Laidlaw is buried in Blyth Union Cemetery. Beside her is buried her daughter Jane, who died at twenty-six (two years before her mother died) having her first baby. Somewhere in the cemetery, in a grave I haven't found, is James the eldest son, moved there from the grave he was put in on the farm, in 1853, after being killed by a falling tree. Just a little while before that, he had made a name for himself by carrying a sugar-kettle, weighing a hundred pounds, all the way from Goderich, on his back. And nearby are two grandchildren of Mary's – a girl of thirteen and a boy a year old – who died in the same year she did, 1868. I had heard all my life, it seemed, the story of the two children and the grandmother who died all at the same time, of cholera, in the hot weather, and how in the haste to bury them, the lace curtains in the house were taken down and used for shrouds. But when I went to verify this I saw that the girl had died in July and the boy in August and their grandmother Mary in October, so the story falls apart.

A husband, a son, a baby daughter and a grown daughter, two grandchildren – this may not be so high a count of losses, for somebody born in 1800 who lived sixty-eight years. And Mary, like old James, was a person who had got her heart's desire.

MICHAEL ONDAATJE

Death at Kataragama

~

For half the day the power blackouts stroke this house into stillness so there is no longer the whir of a fan or the hum of light.
You hear the sound of a pencil being felt for in a drawer in the
dark and then see its thick shadow in candlelight, writing the
remaining words. Paragraphs reduced to one word. A punctuation
mark. Then another word, complete as a thought. The way
someone's name holds terraces of character, contains all of our
adventures with them. I walk in corridors which might perhaps,
I'm not sure, be cooler than the rest of the house. Heat at noon.
Heat in the darkness of night.

There is a woodpecker I am enamoured of I saw this morning
through my binoculars. A red thatch roof to his head more
modest than crimson, deeper than blood. Distance is always
clearer. I no longer see words in focus. As if my own soul is a blunt
tooth. I bend too close to the page to get nearer to what is being
understood, what I write will drift away, I'll only be able to understand the world at arm's length.

Can my soul step into the body of that woodpecker? He may
be too hot in sunlight, it could be a limited life. But if it had been

offered to me this morning, at 9 A.M., I would have gone with him, traded this body for his.

A constant fall of leaf around me in this time of no rain like the continual habit of death. Someone soon will say of me, "His body was lying in Kataragama like a pauper." Our vanity even when we are a corpse. For a blue dead hand that contains no touch or desire in it for another.

There is something else. Not just the woodpecker. Ten water buffalo when I stopped the car. They were being herded back and forth under the sun. It was the sloshing sound of their hooves in the paddy field that I could hear thirty yards away, my car door open for the breeze, the haunting sound I was caught within as if creatures of magnificence were undressing and removing their wings. My head and almost held breath out there for an hour so that later I felt as if I contained that full noon light.

It was water in an earlier life I could not take into my mouth when I was dying. I was soothed then the way a plant would be, brushed with a wet cloth, as I reduced all thought into requests, Take care of this flower. Less light, curtain. As I lay there prone between the long vigil of two friends. Rib bones ache from too much sleep or fever – those that protect the heart and breath in battle, during love beside another. Saliva, breath, fluids, the soul. The place bodies meet is the place of escape.

But this time brutal aloneness. I enter the straight stern legs of the woodpecker braced against the jak fruit as he delves for a meal. Would he feel the change in his nature as my soul enters? Will it grow darker? Or will I enter as I always do into another's nest, in their clothes and with their rules for a particular life.

Or I will leap into knee-deep mud polite with rice. Ten water buffalo. A quick decision. Not goals we have considered all our lives but, in the final moments, sudden choice. This morning it was a woodpecker. A year ago the face of someone on a train. We depart into worlds that have nothing to do with those we love. This woman whose arm I would hold and comfort, that book I wanted to make and shape tight as a stone – I would give everything away for sound of mud and water, hoof, great wings.

P. K. PAGE

Darling Mother, Dearest Helen:
Imagined Letters Home

~

March 10th

Darling Mother,
Here we are without mishap.

The coat you urged me to buy was, of course, exactly right for a first impression. "Neat but not gaudy, the monkey said." Do you remember the next line? "As he painted his tail sky blue." I am sure you taught me that and, like everything else you have taught me. . . .

I do hope you are going to be well. That is perhaps my greatest concern, that you will be ill and I shall be so far away. But, first, you mustn't be ill; and second, if you are I shall come to you at once.

We found to our delight that friends we had made in Australia are posted here. They were at the airport to meet us. So wonderful to see faces we knew. The Embassy staff – those we met – seemed attractive.

You mustn't believe the World Health report that Mexico has the highest incidence of amoebic dysentery in the world next to Egypt. Who on earth was kind enough to tell you that?

I am sure in the cities there is no truth in it. We shall buy bottled water, avoid raw foods, and look after ourselves, I promise you.

It is hard to imagine a place when you haven't seen it. But this is a sophisticated city. More sophisticated than any city in Canada – wide boulevards, fountains, skyscrapers.

My only reservation so far is the Residence itself which is quite monstrous. I can't imagine how to make it look attractive. You would do something, I am sure, and I suppose, with time, I shall too. But what? The entrance leads into an enormous rotunda graced at one end by what can only be described as elephant legs – two gigantic pillars made from grey lava – which flank the open entrance to the dining room, a room, if you please, with no windows! However, we shall probably entertain mainly at night.

I am ashamed to complain about any form of opulence when the poor districts here are more than the heart can bear.

Know that we are well and thinking of you and that a new posting, whether one likes it or not, is after all an adventure.

Our warmest love,

March 10, 1960

Dearest Helen,

Well, we are here. You know how much I dreaded coming. It was quite agonizing saying goodbye to Mother, and turning the key in the last suitcase was like a small surgical act. But now, rather as happens in hospital when you are awaiting an operation, objectivity takes over. There are immediate practical things to attend to, and for me, with my tiresome curiosity, I get sucked in. But I need hardly tell *you* that.

We had a good flight, non-stop from Toronto. Marred only by the pretentious absurdity of the CPA meal which was very hard on readers; the tray always in the way of the book. It was five courses dragged out over hours. Designed to please Canadian tourists, I trust, rather than a preview of what Mexicans expect!

My first overwhelming impression is of blackness and carnations and small brightly dressed Indians – mother, father, and all the little papooses trailing along the wide tree-lined boulevards of a European city. It may well remain stronger and sharper than those that will come later.

The hotel where we are staying is very modern, very Hollywood, and, to my taste, utterly depressing. It is dark and stagey with water falling and large plants growing in its darkness. Night plants? Are there such things? Our room looks out over the rooftops of this low city – flat roofs, bulbous here and there in a rather anatomical way, with cement water-storage tanks. Coming in by air, the city appeared grey. And grey it is, compared with the red tiles of Brazil, which are still bright in my eye, and the heavy smog which greys the sun. I think of Sitwell's "I Live Under a Black Sun." Well, I live under a grey.

But black, black, black is the colour of a Mexican night, and our very first was splintered by the melancholy two-note whistle of police communicating with each other. Towards dawn, little chunks were gobbled out of it. "What's that?" I asked. "It's a turkey," Tom said, waking from sleep. "A turkey! Here? In downtown Mexico? In . . . ?" "It's a turkey *anywhere,*" Tom said and went to sleep again. And it was. It lives on an adjacent roof among the laundry, and I love it.

The Residence is a fifteen-minute drive from the centre of town along a fine boulevard, Paseo de la Reforma. Down its centre, on Sundays, the Don Quixotes ride in large felt sombreros, tilted according to personality – dour, cheerful, fierce.

They wear wide little armless jackets – which give their torsos great breadth – and the most beautiful trousers imaginable, with embroidered or tooled strips running from waist to ankle, which make their legs look long and slender.

On each side of the grassy boulevard, as far as you can see, stretches an avenue flanked by rows of trees. So, coming or going, you drive down a tunnel of green – young and delicate now because it is spring.

Surprisingly, spring is the hot season. Hottest at midday and cooling rapidly towards evening. Mornings are hazy; the thick smog hides the surrounding mountains. By afternoon, you can see the horizon with its sinister-looking volcanoes, their tops like sawed-off shotguns. On brilliant days, Popocatéptl appears, standing guard over the reclining figure of Ixtaccíhuatl, his sleeping bride. Popo, they call him, which in the context of an inflected language sounds like the masculine form of El Papa, the Pope.

Down the Reforma, too, on a Sunday, with all the populace out, are the balloon men looking exactly as if they've descended by parachutes of multicoloured helium-filled balloons – painted or nippled or tufted – unlike any I have ever seen. And *los indios*, scores of them, the men in straw sombreros, the women with pigtails, idling along the lovely boulevard.

No wonder Lawrence was fascinated by their skin colour. Incidentally, I am reading his *Plumed Serpent* again and it is terrifying. He did have absolute pitch, that man.

Guillermo, our driver, is small, immensely dignified, serious. Pure Aztec, he tells us. He has Lawrence's "obsidian eyes"; and his peach-coloured skin, if peeled, would surely reveal a blood orange.

I wish you were here to see it all with me – me *telling* you about it, pointing out the details that I see and you don't because your extraordinary mind is off like a dog following a scent.

Write to me very soon. We both send loving embraces to the whole family,

March 15th

Dearest H,

The house is going to be a headache. It has not had a woman in it for a long time, and it shows it. Also minor redecoration is required for the PM – painting mostly. Why does he have to come so hard on our heels? Before we can speak Spanish or know if there are sheets enough for all!

I feel as if I have a small tribe of Indians running my house. Another small tribe is busy painting it. Its headman, surely brother to Diego Rivera, delights me. The daily meeting between him and Tom, so full of dignity and feeling, nearly breaks my heart. They shake hands – *copiously*. The only word for it.

But let me tell you more about the city, before I become engulfed by domesticity and Dief the Chief (which rhymes with grief – it's funny about rhyme!). *La ciudad* – which means the city – only tourists call it Mexico City – is high – 9,000 feet – and you feel it. You puff and pant as you climb stairs. As to its look, in addition to the grey light, many of the trees are gums, and they are grey too. Its large buildings are just that – large buildings – immense in conception but architecturally disappointing, heavy. I suppose they've been influenced by the colonial churches. Also heavy.

University City, which we drove to see yesterday, is impressive by its sheer size, by the number of murals, and its library – an elongated cube, all four sides of which are completely covered with mosaics made from Mexican stone – the colours running the gamut of earth colours, plus white, grey, and grey blue. The scope of the whole complex is fabulous: Olympic swimming pools, football arenas, jai alai courts. But it is male, perhaps threateningly so.

Beyond the university, on what was once a vast lava field, is a new suburban development for the very rich – Pedregal, a good name, combining as it does the idea of stone with that of regality. Many of its houses and the walls that surround them are made from chunks of lava put together with coloured cement of a dirty pink, blue, or green – a queer effect, the rough, brown-black lava contrasted with soft, powdery pastels. Sometimes the lava chunks are painted to blend with the landscape – a sere, dried-out, and wonderful world of grasses and plants with pods or tangled briars – all greybrownblack. And in their midst, a small bush, stubby-fingered, its finger-tips bursting into clumps of brilliant yellow; or the weird *colorin* trees, their trunks like stylized human forms posturing strangely below a burst of thin, whip-like branches. On them, perched bird-like, are bright artery-red flowers. And on little ponds, hollowed out of the lava, ducks float. Ducks! The houses are low, almost subterranean, walled – a submerged ruin of a city. But chic. Ultra modern. Hermetic.

The old city, the Spanish city, is equally walled. *More* walled. You can see no houses at all. Top Secret.

I shall have to develop a taste for this countryside, for the vegetation is almost totally grey. There are gums with gun-metal leaves; peppertrees which veil themselves in fragile grey-green; organ cactuses, which look as one would expect; and nopals which grow one flat spiny vegetable disc out of the previous one and, from a distance, appear to be crocheted from coarse grey wool. Even the earth itself is grey, and the houses – made from the same earth patted into unbaked bricks – seem to be either unfinished or falling down. A world of rubble. But Pedregal, come to think of it, is not so very different. Rich man's rubble.

This beauty, if beauty it is, is in another scale entirely from the scale I know. Microtonal. Something to be learned.

Today we lunched with Johanna and Walther Hess – just us. Did I tell you they are old friends? Nice to have them here. Johanna and I nearly die laughing watching Tom and Walther together. They knew each other first in an Anglo-Saxon country. Now that Tom has been in Brazil and Walther here, they greet like human beings, with great embraces. I don't know whether *they* know they are funny! Johanna, who has an eye, has made their house beautiful and has picked up some of the marvellous gun-metal pottery made in Oaxaca, some of the copper pots, old blond wood chests, woollen serapes, and Indian saints. I can hardly wait to get out of the city.

The Palacio de Bellas Artes, or national art gallery – imitation classical, domed, doomed,[*] wombed – is offset, outside, by some trim little phallic cactuses. Inside – not content with the classical – art nouveau has been introduced: fans and flutings with zigzag areas of glass and great sharply square pillars of toffee-coloured marble, their edges not softened by sucking. Upstairs – and up stairs it was, as well as down, for the elevators weren't functioning – we saw the Diego Rivera room containing mainly his very early work. Nothing that I thought good. Some immense Siqueiros murals dated 1944 which are violent and horrible. Some softer, large, plum-coloured Tamayos. A room of rather ordinary sculpture and one of early Mexican chromos, which I've not yet developed a taste for. That was all this great domed womb of a room revealed.

I grow suspicious about Mexican art. It may not be as good as I had hoped. Or is it merely a matter of acclimatization? And yet I remember an exhibition of Mexican art in Montreal in the forties – did you ever see it? – which I found astonishing. And I suppose it was. But perhaps it was its political message that so appealed to me, matching, as it did, the most political phase of my own life. I remember a cartoon in the exhibition of a peon with a newspaper blown over his face and an old lady – or so thought I, a youthful know-all – saying, "Incomprehensible. Utterly incomprehensible." But *I* knew what it meant. And I remember the colours of the paintings I saw then as being more vivid. Perhaps they were. Perhaps they have faded. Perhaps they are dirty, and need a wash, housed as they are in this polluted city.

I must end this and get changed for dinner. I wish we could talk. I miss you more than I can say. Write to me – tell me about the children, what you are reading, how things are with Davie. Everything, in fact. Less will not do!

P.S. *Doomed is not there for word-play alone. The building *is* doomed, as is much of downtown Mexico – sinking, in fact. Many buildings appear so off the true that Tom, who has, as you know, a spirit-level built into his pupils, can feel sick just looking at them.

March 20th

Darling Mother,
You would be astonished by my absorption in this house! The painters are still in it. Likewise plumbers who are tearing out the walls of all bathrooms in order to get hot water in the

showers. So nice for the PM to have to have a sponge bath! We have now acquired a full staff which does nothing but clean – first, because the house is badly in need of it; second, because there are workmen in it; and third, because it is the dusty season. "If seven maids with seven mops/should sweep for half a year. . . ."

There have been the usual number of far too many parties. The Dean of the Corps gave a dinner the other night and I sat on his left. He is from Uruguay. Suave, smooth, attractive. As you know, I like Latin American men. They behave as if they are glad you are a woman. I wore – and I tell you this because I know it amuses you – the black lace dress I adore. Tom gave me an approving glance as we left. At dinner the Dean raised his glass, looked me in the eyes, and said what an asset I was to the Corps. Without flattering myself, I do know what he means. Most ambassador's wives are twenty years older than I am. I thanked him and replied that I was afraid I mightn't be as much of an asset as he hoped. This was not the answer he expected. He raised his eyebrows. (I might add that he speaks English. Good English. It is rumoured he is hoping his next post will be the U.K.) "I am not sure that I take diplomatic life as seriously as you would like me to," I said, and added as a softener, "or as seriously as perhaps I should."

To my surprise, instead of a disapproving moue masked by a polite phrase, he said, "Good. Good." And then, nodding his head towards his wife sitting opposite him, he went on, "You see my wife. Thirty years ago she was the most beautiful, joyful girl you could possibly imagine. Now look at her."

I looked. Dyed, painted, almost shellacked, his wife sat at the foot of the table, a travesty of a society woman. A model for Ensor is perhaps the most accurate description. "And," he added sadly, "she has done it all for me."

A touching story. Unexpected to be taken so quickly into his confidence. And you know, I am sure he is right. Diplomatic life might have been possible for a woman raised to do nothing else, but today . . . women want something more. It has all happened between your generation and mine. You would have been content. I no longer am, although I do it. I'm a hybrid. Try to do both. Already the younger wives are rebelling. And I am sympathetic.

Lovely to have your letters – a whole batch arrived at once. They are not for a moment boring. They tell me *exactly* what I want to know . . . the details of everyday. Most important – that you are well.

Your loving daughter,

March 20

Dear H,

So glad to have your two letters. I eat them. You've no idea. A new post is lonely. Tom gets on with his life – it is not so very different from his working life anywhere – an office, a secretary, etc., etc. But for me, I struggle with a new language, have to work in it from day one; struggle with new ways of doing all the old things – feeding us, keeping us clean. However, enough of that! There are better topics.

Today we had an adventure! It being Sunday Tom allowed himself some time off from all the plotting and planning for the PM's visit he is having to fit in between calls and the protocular stuff. And so we set off on the Toluca road, bound for Calixtlahuaca, famous for its rare, circular ruin, said to have been a training centre for Aztec priests in its latter days. Its Aztec days were indeed its latter days. Four different civilizations are displayed here like rings in the bole of a tree. The outer ring is Aztec, the next – built from a glowing rosy stone – is Toltec. About the previous two, nothing is known. Of course I should tell you about these cultures for they must be totally unintelligible to you – but for the time being I don't know enough myself.

But back to the adventure. We had no sooner reached our Calixtlahuacan destination, clearly marked by a sign, when as if synchronized the two of us sprang out of the car, Tom on his side, I on mine, locking the doors as we did so! Key safely in the ignition. There we were, alone in this lovely valley of green corn while inside the car our field glasses, picnic basket, camera, and my handbag were smiling at us. No window was the slightest crack open, and unfortunately there was no coathanger handy. A rock through the windscreen seemed the only way. While we were considering what to do we found ourselves surrounded by people. A villainous-looking fellow in a fine straw hat had a great deal of advice to give us, as had dozens of small girls in long skirts and rebozos, and dozens of small boys, all of whom had materialized as imperceptibly and silently as smoke. (There is a wonderful Spanish verb *esfumar* – *fumar* is to smoke – that perfectly describes this materialization. I wonder if it exists in other languages? Its primary meaning is to smudge with a stump – that little roll used for shading or blending a drawing in charcoal, pastel, etc. A secondary meaning is to appear or disappear in a similar manner – smokily. And this is what *los indios* do.)

No sooner were we surrounded by *los esfumados* than boys in black on motorcycles pelted up, eager to help. They even picked up stones. I assure you we were a centre of very great interest.

Finally, we decided that one of us would have to get to a phone and ask Guillermo to come with another set of keys.

The nearest phone was in Toluca some distance away, but at that moment a bus appeared in the distance, trailing a wake of pearly dust. When it finally drew up beside us, overflowing with livestock and drunken Mexicans, Tom, without consultation, jumped onto its step, waved cheerfully, and was gone. He said later he had ghastly misgivings as they drove off and he saw me standing there, but his immediate instinct had been to protect me from all those drunks.

What I felt, now alone with the guide – for once the excitement was over, the small crowd smoked itself away in the same manner in which it had come – was a need to be protected from the guide himself, who was saying something to me that I didn't understand and becoming more and more aggressive each moment. Was I to be raped within a month of coming to Mexico? I remembered all the awful stories I had heard!

And then, miraculously, a troop of Boy Scouts arrived. Never have Boy Scouts looked so beautiful in my eyes. Luckily they found my attempts at Spanish amusing but unluckily they teased the guide, told me he was *loco*, and set up a kind of opposition to him in which I was implicated. I didn't want to antagonize either side, and, while I smiled and attempted to make placating noises, I was, at the same time, showing the scouts my entire stock of string tricks in an attempt to keep them there. You would be surprised how many string tricks I was able to remember! When my vocabulary and my tricks finally came to an end, the scout leader started organizing his troop to explore the site – which was, after all, what they had come for. Panicked by the thought of them going, I asked him if it was safe for me to be there – a woman alone. It didn't feel safe to me. No, he said, apparently only just realizing I *was* alone, and immediately began another organization whereby half the troop would explore the site, and half stay with me.

A plume of dust in the near distance signalled what could only be a car. And it was. Tom in a cab and delighted with himself! He had found a phone, spoken to Guillermo, and was now all set to enjoy the afternoon. He promptly tipped the guide, who was instantly transformed from a threat into a source of information. What he had been wanting was for me to pay his admission, but my money was in the car.

He told us that Calixtlahuacans speak Spanish and their own language – "narwhal," I thought he said, but I was clearly wrong. It is *narhuatl*. His sample sentence sounded like the clicking of knitting needles and made me think of Van der Post's description of the language of the Bushmen. He also claimed to know Latin, and there and then he bent and picked up a stone and wrote in the dry earth two illegible sentences. He is self-educated and boasts a library of fifty books. He has eight living children, four dead, and none of them knows anything. All stupid, he says angrily.

The ruin overlooks a valley which is irrigated and very beautiful. It grows *maguey* and corn. The corn is green and young. We watched a man with his *pulque* equipment – not unlike bagpipes – suck the *agua miel* from the *maguey* and fill his pigskin. *Pulque* is a kind of milky beer – quite good. In the middle distance the locals are playing football. In the background, too softened by dust to appear sinister, are the inevitable volcanoes. The afternoon light is golden. But the small cruciform building, decorated with rows of stone skulls, robs the gold of its lustre.

We are surrounded by death. I am not sure how I am going to bear it. Seriously. Although they may not be, the other "wives" *seem* impervious. I guess that blackness I sensed when we arrived was real, all right. Thank heaven Tom knows what I am talking about. He feels it too. When the Mexican Goddess of Love gives birth to an heir she bears an obsidian knife, according to Lawrence. You see what I mean.

Later. You will think me a complete idiot when I tell you that I have only just realized on the basis of Spanish that we have a Sun Day and a Mo(o)n Day. Monday is *lunes*. But, of course, *lundi!* How was I so slow?

I must end. Larry Mackenzie and Jack Clyne are in town and we are taking them to dinner, not being yet equipped to dine them chez nous.

Love, as always,

March 27

H, dear H,

Friday is market day at Toluca and last Friday was the first chance I've had to get away, so, as you can imagine, I leaped at it. I could spend my life at markets. Not even buying. Just looking and looking.

It's an easy drive from here. A good highway leads through the Park of the Lions (lions?) across the top of the world – grey, dry, and mountainous. The valleys are patterned in a kind of wild candlewick, by *maguey* whose leaves look as if they are made of metal – stiff, long, and radiating from the base. This spike-leafed plant which grows a couple of feet high provides *pulque*, a kind of milky beer – I think I told you this before – as well as paper, needle, thread, and soap, according to our driver. Farther on we passed a fish hatchery and great, scented pine forests. Then miles of adobe walls bordering the road tell us we are in a village. On such a drive one changes continents and epochs.

Toluca, which is the capital of the State of Mexico, has a population of about 75,000 and on Fridays all 75,000, seemingly, give themselves up entirely to the market. Merchandise covers the sidewalks: Woolworth jewellery, nylon underwear, silk dresses, combs. But in the market proper, stalls with canvas tops are set up and there are the crafts: serapes, rebozos, baskets, pottery, and squares of embroidery of stylized birds in various shades of red and pink. I saw any number of things I would like to buy – these last among them. But they can wait. Bought instead, for immediate use, two straw wastepaper baskets for seven pesos each (about fifty cents!). Indian women in braids sit beside their wares eating tortillas, and their black-eyed babies crawl about among yolk-yellow, newly hatched chicks, pottery, and wooden spoons. As it's a tourist market, most of the Indians speak English, and, not unnaturally, they think you are a gringa, which, here, means an American, so the absurdly low prices are, of course, doubled. (How can you make a basket for fifty cents, let alone twenty-five?)

Yesterday, Saturday, after a full morning of work with the decorator from Ottawa, we did a quick tour of the city. How we both long to get it under our belts, as it were. Went first to the city market – an enormous new construction. Such mounds of fruits of all names and kinds and colours and sizes: watermelon, cantaloupe, papaya, oranges, grapefruit, apples, and then the tropical ones, pineapples, mangos, *mames*, and all the others I can't yet name. Vegetables too. Red radishes as long as your forearm, and very strange-looking root vegetables! A flight of stairs leads down to an arcade lined with basket sellers, which, in its turn, leads to the hall of the fish and meat vendors. And everything laid out as if in a still life. Enormous red snappers – *huachinangos*, there's a word for you! – and cuts of meat I don't even recognize.

It interests me, as you can tell, and I can't resist putting it all down *whether you want it or not*. Where on earth will I put it, if you don't?

From there we went on to the Cathedral on the Plaza de la Constitucion, said to be America's oldest and largest church, built in 1523 on what was once the site of the Aztec temples. And herein lies the story of modern Mexico – the Spanish attempt to desecrate a faith they could not understand. Today, the whole building lists dizzyingly in two directions. Tom felt queasy. The neighbouring Sacrarium, built from blocks of intricately carved rose-coloured lava, is more baroque than the Cathedral, and because it is smaller, seems to tilt less. Both buildings are not without a certain dark beauty, but the truth is it is not Catholic Mexico that interests me.

The National Palace, constructed as a home for Cortés, takes up almost an entire side of the same plaza. Inside, interminable as the Devil's entrails, are murals by Diego Rivera – many of them still only in the cartoon stage but some fifteen or so are completed. I don't much like feature paintings, to use the expression a Russian once used to me. When I asked what he meant, he replied, "What do *you* mean by a feature movie?"

As one would expect, the murals tell the painful story of the Spanish conquest, depicting the site as it was at the time of the conquerors' arrival – a great salt lake stretching in all directions and the Aztec temple rising like something out of faerie. What hatred is expressed in these murals. How evil the face of Cortés. Yet, I suppose in *his* eyes he was only behaving like a good Christian!

Enough or I'll put you to sleep with all this guidebook talk.

PAUL QUARRINGTON

Two Homes

~

(1)

When I was twelve years old, my parents rented a cottage on the shores of Lake Couchiching. The weather for the two weeks was very poor. My mother translated *couchiching*, from the Ojibway, as *lake which the sun only shines on one side of*, because the far coast was always brilliantly lit, while we lived in shadow and struggled on under turbulent black cloud. So, because we could not pursue outdoorsy activities, the family made several excursions by automobile to local tourist attractions.

At this time I read voraciously, which is to say piggishly, cramming stuff into my brain that rendered me pimple-faced and pudgy. I was a great connoisseur of espionage novels, and had determined that I would one day be a spy. There are very few ways for a twelve-year-old boy to apprentice as a spy in southern Ontario. About all I could manage was to sit in the back seat on automobile voyages with my head stuck out the window, allowing the wind to burn my forehead and flap my cheeks, so that some day, when espionage was possible, I would possess the requisite "weather-beaten" features.

One day we visited the Leacock Home, which stands at Brewery Bay on the same Lake Couchiching. It was here that Stephen Leacock, professor of economics at McGill, wrote the books that earned him his reputation as Canada's greatest humorist and also millions of dollars (or the 1920s equivalent thereof). It was an elegant home, and not immodest. If you entered the front door too quickly you were in danger of skittering across the floor and directly out the back, so the house was not all that grand. It had a sitting room with a huge fireplace, and it was here that the Brewery Bay Players, Leacock and family, mounted their little productions. The grounds were large and spacious, although I was not really all that interested in grounds, as you can likely deduce from "large and spacious" – as lame a phrase as you'll ever come across. I was more interested in the bay itself, shallow and weed-choked. Leacock sunk a mattress out in the waters, an old thing popping with springs, thereby supplying an inviting structure for smallmouth bass. Leacock would challenge visitors to a fishing contest, and while they fired plugs blindly, Leacock would aim where he knew the mattress to be. He therefore never lost one of these contests. That story appealed to me as a twelve-year-old, even if Leacock had been cheating, because, well, I didn't think he was cheating, not when I was twelve, not now.

But what I remember best about the Leacock Home is the little alcove in the foyer, the one that contained a stool and a fairly rudimentary telephone machine. The walls of the little booth were dense with scribbled numbers and messages. Apparently Leacock would talk on the phone and when he needed to write something down, he would pluck a writing instrument out of his pocket and simply scratch it onto the wall.

I was deeply impressed.

So much so that, on the drive home, I neglected to stick my head outside the window. I was actually rethinking my career choice. While it may have been true that spies got to kill people (a perk which I valued more highly even than the frequent sexual encounters, although I was canny enough to realize that those would mean a great deal to me someday), writers, I realized, got far more. All this was, to my unformed mind, made manifest by their ability to scrawl on walls. And so I determined to become one.

(2)

We can vault ahead thirty years now. Not just for convenience and/or brevity; we can vault ahead thirty years because that's the way it feels to me, as though it were just the other day that I was wandering around the Leacock Home. So we take the thirty-year vault, and we find me once more in a car, again on summer holiday. This time I am driving. My wife sits beside me; in the back seat are my two daughters, Carson and Flannery. We are driving through the Berkshires, taking a daytrip away from our borrowed cottage because the days are overcast, the sky bloated with raincloud. We are nearing our destination (the second of the two homes mentioned in the title), which lies a mile or two down this road; the reason I haven't started at the home proper is to give myself an opportunity to fill in a little background.

I did manage to become a writer. That's the good news. I am not without my small successes, either, and I've had more fun than most men my age, but the writerly life is fraught with unpaid bills and poor reviews. I am brooding about this as we near the second home (the children are bickering in the back seat, both demanding that their own particular brand of caterwauling be played on the tapedeck), and I suspect that my mood will sour further. Because just up the road – here it is now – is Arrowhead, the home (for a time) of Herman Melville.

I have become a bit of an authority on Melville in connection with another project, so you must now suffer the consequences of my research. It shouldn't really be that much of a trial, because Melville's life and career are truly fascinating. After spending much of his youth and early manhood riding the briny, as a sailor and whaler, Melville settled down at age twenty-six to begin a career as a man of letters. His first book, *Typee*, was based on his experiences at sea. It was a popular success, and Herman (no doubt thinking, *hey, that was easy*) followed up with another salty yarn, *Omoo*, which was another smash. The first remarkable thing about Melville's career is the astonishing productivity. This is hard to believe, especially for me and all of my writing friends, but over the course of six years, Melville produced seven long, dense novels. What my writerly friends and I have no trouble believing is that each book sold more poorly than the preceding. The whale thing, *Moby Dick*, was pretty much a dismal failure, although Melville's friend Nate Hawthorne liked it. Herman then did what many a writer does, he wrote a dark, troubling, and intensely personal book. *Pierre (Or, the Ambiguities)* – I can imagine Melville's publisher pursing his lips at the title, wondering wistfully if he couldn't maybe come up with another catchy zinger, like *Opee* – sold only a handful of copies, and there was the bright young flame all but extinguished. Melville was broke, married, and a father. He struggled on as a magazine journalist, knowing of no other way to make a living apart from returning to sea, and I'm certain that the notion occurred to him, I'm sure he sat up nights staring out his window and feeling the roll of the ocean in his belly.

He'd moved into Arrowhead in 1850. It is a big imposing house, and stands near the crest of a hill. The view is one of endless valleys and hills, rippling and undulating like waves. It is a house for a man who owns the world. But Herman Melville couldn't afford the upkeep, not given the meagre sales of his books, and he was forced to give up Arrowhead. He moved his family into a small apartment in New York City, and he took a job at the Customs Office. He worked there for the next twenty years, occasionally writing poetry late at night, otherwise maintaining complete and utter silence.

The visit to Arrowhead does indeed blacken my spirit. In the gift shop I buy a bumper sticker that says "Call Me Ishmael." I corral the family into the car and drive away in silence.

(3)

Three weeks later, I an sitting in my own kitchen, late at night, my face made sickly luminous by the light of a small computer. I have written about the two homes, because this book is called *Writing Home* and we writers have been told to consider "home" in whatever sense we wish, and this is what I came up with. But I am not entirely sure what point I'm making. I stare at the words on the screen and drink whisky, hoping that it will soon make sense. (This is unrealistic.)

The editor, Connie Rooke, calls me on the telephone. I wrest it from its cradle and sit back down at the kitchen table, mostly to be nearer my whisky. She wants to know where the piece is, because apparently I'd promised to have it in weeks earlier. "I'm almost finished," I assure her. "I just have to figure out what point I'm making."

"When you finish, call me right away."

"Sure."

"Here's my number."

The computer has a little "notebook" feature, a virtual writing pad, but it doesn't occur to me to employ it. Or perhaps it does, fleetingly. But I reach instead for a ballpoint pen that my wife has abandoned beside a crossword puzzle. And as Connie says numbers, I reach over and scribble them onto the wall.

Publishers' Clearing House

~

As a young child I had an obsession with drawing houses. There was nothing especially imaginative about these drawings: they all followed the same basic design of a triangle topping a square, with two mullioned windows and a door on the ground floor positioned with as much symmetry as my four- or five-year-old hand could muster. Sometimes there was a chimney to one side, with a wafting squiggle of green or orange smoke, and sometimes, more exceptionally, two further windows and a further door on the second storey, though it was hard then to get the windows to fit under the roof line. But these additions, it seemed, were not so much embellishments as an attempt to arrive at a sort of Platonic completeness: this was what a house was, all it needed to be whole, to do the job.

My notion of house-ness must have drawn something from our own house, which, sitting foursquare and plain at the entrance to our farm, was about as basic and house-like as a house could be. Yet it could not be said that our house was ever more than just barely adequate to the job required of it, or that any of the fifteen-odd people who passed through it during my childhood – aunts, uncles, cousins, siblings, parents, grandparents – ever considered it anything more than a waystation, what would have to do until some more permanent arrangement could be made. In the case of my aunts, my father's teenaged sisters, that meant making a suitable marriage; in the case of my uncles, for whom cots were set up in whatever corner could be spared, it meant amassing a little nest egg before returning to families in Italy; in the case of my grandfather, it meant exchanging the largest bedroom in the house for somewhat more cramped quarters after he dropped dead one day when he was coming home from the fields. As for the rest of us, we made do, though with always the idea in our heads that our real house was not the one we lived *in* but the one we lived *for*, the not-quite-even-imagined dream home that all our sacrifice and hard work would one day bring into being. In the meantime we were lucky to have a house at all, or so I had gathered from the dire warnings of my parents and from certain notions about mortgaging and repossession that I had picked up from the Saturday cartoons.

Our house had a glassed-in front porch that was quite special in many ways, not least in that it had a crawl space underneath that was very convenient for hiding in in the event that chores needed doing or punishments were being meted out. The porch itself was special perhaps exactly in being superfluous: in a house crammed full with people, with beds in the living room and three-quarter walls built around alcoves to accommodate still more beds, here was a room that no one actually slept in, and which therefore constituted the one feature of our house that could be considered a luxury. We children were often sent into exile there, three or four or seven or eight of us as the case might be, during which time the rest of the house, stripped down to its mere adults, must have seemed as sane and sedate as a Victorian boarding house. In the cool of evening, the porch took on a tangy porch-and-old-furniture smell that it shared with other porches I knew (the ones of those relations who did not actually live with us), as if it was joined with them in a kind of porchy fraternity.

In the future house we lived for, there would also be a front porch; except that this porch would not be the butt-end of the house that our own porch had become, where extraneous objects, old newspapers, furnishings, children, were shoved out like droppings, but rather its elegant, welcoming entranceway. I had seen houses in town of that sort, with elaborate front porticoes or generous verandahs where, I imagined, people who never had mud on their shoes were ushered into rooms with polished floors or spotless wall-to-wall carpeting. Our own household, of course, had not yet evolved to the state of civility that allowed anyone to enter the house from the front; and indeed for those of us who lived there a sort of ritual of decontamination had to be followed out before we could even so much as set foot on the back stairs. This ritual involved a trip down to the basement, where, if you were small, you climbed up into the big porcelain laundry tub to wash your feet under the faucet, or, if you were big, you filled a blue plastic basin for the purpose; and when you had scrubbed your feet clean and towelled them dry you slipped them cosily into the house shoes you had earlier exchanged your outside shoes for at the shoe rack in the furnace room.

The shoe rack was perhaps the place where present reality came up most starkly against future hope. The rack itself was a crude structure cobbled together from spare bits of wood and which in its triumph of function over aesthetics showed the unmistakable handiwork of my father. On its bottom shelves were rows of shoes that could break your heart – ancient, cracked, mud-caked work shoes or old high-topped Keds that had passed from my aunt to my older sister and were now working their way through my older brothers down to me; on the middle shelf were a few lonely pairs of too-small Sunday shoes. But the top shelves were reserved for the house shoes – slippers, they might be called elsewhere, but in our house they were considered full-fledged shoes. These shoes played a major role in our ongoing apprentice-ship for our eventual accession to elegant living, being one of the ways in which my father hoped to breed out of us our fundamen-tal barbarity. Gamins and ragamuffins we might be, steeped in pond sludge and frogs' blood and briars, but then every evening, scrubbed down and scoured, we would waft through the house in our house shoes like little aristocrats-in-waiting. In later years I would be reminded of our house-shoe regime by one of the novels of Italian writer Elio Vittorini: in it, a formerly wealthy family reduced to penury after the war goes through the motions every evening of eating an imaginary chicken using only knives and forks, to make sure the children will be in practice should the family's fortunes rise again.

Much of what went on in our house had this same air of being a sort of training for our more civilized future. Saturday after-noons, for instance, my mother waxed the kitchen floor, which in itself, being old and not even linoleum but asbestos tile, did not merit, in most of our opinions, the attention she lavished on it. But that did not stop us from regarding the activity with a certain measure of reverence. Sometimes one or two of us were seconded from work in the greenhouses or fields to help with the polishing, getting down on hands and knees with our polishing rags and scooting around the floor like water spiders. When we were done, waxy-kneed and smelling of lemon, the floor had a sheen like glass, which it would hold a couple of days before the heavy traffic in our household, house shoes or no, had worn it down to dullness again, though in the interim we would have had a taste of what those houses in town, shiny-floored all, merely took as their daily due. There was always an hour or two after the polishing was complete but the wax was still in its final, fragile stages of hardening when the utmost care had to be taken, when the tiniest water drop or a careless bare or house-shoed foot could wreck utterly the momentary perfection the floor reached then. My mother placed rags at every entrance to the room then, and we would shimmy our way through it careful and hushed as if not to disturb a sleeping child.

Saturday was also bath day, and those dangerous couple of hours before the wax had decisively set often coincided with the first bath shifts of late afternoon. Bath shifts were allotted accord-ing to complex rules that we children worked out amongst our-selves, having often to do with certain code words that had to be uttered over the course of the day. Despite the wax issue, it was still immensely preferable to be on one of the earlier shifts, not only because of the time you thus shaved off work but because of the assurance you then had of a supply of hot water. When we were small, my brothers and I usually shared our bath time, often creating together then a special secret world we called Soapy Land. But when we had become old enough to merit separate baths, competition over shifts grew quite fierce. In our future house, of course, such unseemly battles would be avoided because there would be many bathrooms and because, more importantly, we would be equipped with that essential item of modern living, a shower. A shower, we believed, would make possible a veritable promiscuity of cleanliness, since showers, unlike baths, were prac-tically instantaneous and could be had on the merest whim. We had heard rumours that in certain households it was not uncom-mon to shower daily; though when our oldest sister, entering her mid-teens, got in the habit of bathing every night before bed, we all considered this a form of derangement.

Sleeping arrangements in our house were a matter of some cre-ativity and also of considerable flux. Until I was five and the last of the unmarried aunts left the house, I continued to sleep in the crib in my parents' room (where, judging from the birth of twins nine months or so after my departure, I had apparently functioned as a form of birth control). Thereafter, as babies grew and as uncles came and went, I was part of a shifting arrangement of beds that culminated finally in the demolition of our beloved porch and the construction of two purple-walled bedrooms there, complete with folding-doored closets and sliding windows. This momentous event was a bit of a shock to our systems, not only in its demonstrating the mutability of a structure that we had until then considered, for all its shortcomings, a sort of fixed, organic whole, but also in its suggesting, more ominously, that the grand, total, life-shifting change we had all been anticipating might be usurped by such patchwork half-measures. It was true, of course, that for the first time since we'd lived in our house there was not a single bed in the living room, and that we had been able to arrange there a plastic-covered chesterfield and armchair, a Formica-topped coffee table, a General Electric TV, with an admirable, almost enviable degree of decorum (and this is not even to mention the holographic portrait of Christ on the wall that changed, at a certain angle, to the Last Supper). But there were still those of us – myself – confined to the old ghetto area of the house, with its poor excuse of a three-quarter-walled alcove for a bedroom, and also those of us – my older brothers – who, though beneficiaries of one of the new rooms, were not properly appreciative of same, being unable to tolerate, in said room, each other's presence. This incivility on my brothers' parts, no doubt hormonally based, did much to set back the cause for our eventual dream home, being often cited as evidence by my father that we had not yet been sufficiently domesticated to warrant the investment a new home would entail.

For many years, however, we children planned to do an end run around my father's recalcitrance, faithfully completing the entry form every spring for the Publishers' Clearing House Sweepstakes. This was the contest in which the grand prize was a luxury home of one's choosing – what I thought of as the "clearing house" referred to in the contest's name, imagining that a clearing house was a sort of vast, cleared, open structure that one then divided and gaudied up according to one's tastes; and amongst us children there was a general feeling that this contest had been expressly designed to meet the needs of our own household. It came as somewhat of a surprise to us every year when we did not actually win, since it was unclear to us how there could be other families in the world who coveted a luxury home, or deserved one, as much as we did. Eventually, growing more worldwise, we decided that the "No purchase required" rule of the contest was actually a ruse, and began to place orders from among the wares offered by the Clearing House publishers in the hopes of improving our chances of winning. A slew of magazines started appearing in our mailbox, *Better Homes and Gardens*, *Ladies' Home Journal*, *Popular Electronics*, *Popular Mechanics*, *Teens & Boys*. Our parents didn't show much interest in these magazines – our mother couldn't read a word of English and our father mostly chose not to – until the bills for them began to arrive, at which point we were unmasked as their source and all our hopes for our own private clearing house were dashed. The only upshot of our years of diligence was an apparently lifetime subscription to *Chatelaine*, which continued to arrive long past the time when most of us children had left the house.

Leave the house we eventually did, one by one, without ever seeing our hope of a dream home realized. But when the last of us had gone, leaving behind for the first time the incredible luxury of empty bedrooms and no waiting line at the bathroom, my parents sold the farm, bought a four-acre lot, and built a house whose master bedroom alone had more sleeping area than all the bedrooms combined of the house in which they'd spent the previous twenty-five years. Four bathrooms, two kitchens, living, dining, family, and rec room: a veritable clearing house. I imagine my parents wandering the empty rooms there now in their house shoes agoraphobic with space, huddling perhaps in the closets trying to recapture again that cramped, secure feeling they had always associated with home.

As for our old house, it still stands, looking from the outside not much changed from how we left it, if a bit sprucer. Though inside who knows what changes have been wrought, what happened to those sepia-toned asbestos tiles in the kitchen, to the shoe rack in the furnace room, to the three-quarter wall around the alcove. A two-carred, two-childed family lives there now, and the place – with a few walls torn down, perhaps, and an *en suite* bathroom or two installed – probably fits them like a glove, as if it has finally, with its simple house shape, reached that state of Platonic completeness I hankered for as a child. But though I often drive past the place whenever I visit home, I never ask to go inside. You can't go home again, make no mistake; there are no house shoes made to enter that place, the past.

SHARON RIIS

The Cartography of *Home*

~

Home is where the heart leaps when it wraps around someone. And the heart, beating beyond reason, often finds itself coming home in a most peculiar fashion.

When my children were small I lived in the bush near Lac La Biche, Alberta. At that time I confused the notion of home with place. And felt homeless. Almost everyone I knew there was third or fourth generation. They came from enormous extended families. There was always someone to help them out with their own small children, give them a break, a whole weekend off now and then. And the men and women, having known each other since child-hood, shared the obdurate intimacy of siblings. They often didn't much like one another but if one of them was up against one wall or another they'd rally all the way. Defend to the death. Save.

My own first family was living in Kamloops, a town I'd only visited. Not my home, in no way my home.

I grew up in Longview, Alberta, and fancied for a long time that might be my one true home. But I left before puberty and when I went back, expecting the embrace, I knew no one and my old house was gone. Even the gully where I'd played as a girl had been filled in for suburban development. That the landscape itself should be altered seemed an unholy blow. I was bereft. Homeless after all.

Around this time, in my mid-thirties, I imagined myself one in a constellation of lights across the map of the world. Me and those few towards whom my heart had leapt. I'm not talking about romantic love here but love that settles inside and stays, shifting your self about forever on a cellular level. In 1982 the constellation consisted of old mentors: Warren, treading water on welfare in Sherbrooke, John in Vancouver, old friends like Cece and Keith in Mission, Donna in Edmonton, Henry in Toronto; my Dad in Kamloops, my brother in Ottawa, my mother's friend Tillie in Port Moody, Tillie's son Garry in Kelowna, Howard in Edmonton . . . and on and on. These are the obvious examples. People I was and continue to be wrapped up with. People whose flaws are blatant and who know my own but still. . . . Love in its "infinite variety" connected us. But even then there were others whom I didn't know at all and who certainly didn't know me towards whom my heart leapt nonetheless: a young tired woman called Ida who cleared tables in the cafeteria at Simon Fraser University when I was young. I saw her maybe four times and was introduced to her on one occasion, which is how I got to know her name. Ida. Forever on the map. A White Russian widower, working on my house in the bush, who became my lover for a time. I didn't know him at all (except in the biblical sense) but still. . . . A connection beyond the pale was made. He changed the shape of my shadow. He'd been working on my house day in, day out, and we would talk now and then, with difficulty because of the language problem. And then he was done and he went away. I started to write a short story about him and me. About the wordless unholy energy connecting us. Making it up as I went along, the way one does. And one day he drives up to the end of the gravel road, walks up to me where I'm chopping kindling, and (with no fear of the axe in my hand) takes me in his arms and kisses me, lascivious and grave at the same time. "Your heart was calling to my heart," he says. How can you not give yourself over to someone who has the wherewithal to say *that*? How can you not write a short story, a film script, and thence a novel after the fact. His name is Stephan. Pure light.

Time passes and the constellation grows. Effortless. Jutta in Vienna; Lina in Toronto; Kozina in Lac La Biche; Gilly in London; John in Toronto; Henry in Saskatoon. . . . On and on. If I feel homeless or home*sick* I can call or write or fax or visit. Or simply reflect and consider and dream a little. Tillie, her son Garry, and Lina are all dead now. It makes no difference. Their lights burn bright as they ever did on my map of home.

In July 1991 my dear friends Cece and Keith's son Noah was killed. Two weeks short of his fifteenth birthday. A dreadful time. I flew out to the Fraser Valley to be with them, helpless, hopeless. Useless. How will they live through this? How will any of us live through this? I wondered. And came home to Saskatoon and told my son, fourteen himself, that he could do anything, anything at all, but die. It was a terrible time. But life goes on. By rote, I suppose. I had to fly to Toronto for a script meeting. All my ambition having thinned out to nothing at all. But still. . . . I flew to Toronto and checked into a hotel and slept not at all and didn't care didn't care about *anything*. In the morning I took a cab to my meeting. The driver was an old black man with a grey crew cut. Wide and muscular. I got into the back seat (the way one does in

Toronto), told him where I was going and away we went. A beautiful clear sunny August day, early. The radio was on low. Suddenly the cabbie turned to me and said: "I'm sorry, I can't help it" and turned up the volume full blast to the Righteous Brothers singing "You've Lost That Lovin' Feelin'." After about ten seconds he started to sing along, full out. He didn't have a particularly good voice. He wasn't singing for me; he was singing because he couldn't help but sing; he was singing for himself. Another twenty seconds into the song I was singing too, full out. I don't have a good voice at all but it didn't matter. We sang the song through, at the top of our inadequate lungs, all the way to my meeting. A veritable choir. I gave him a weepy kiss and a big tip. He brought me back to life. And as I write this he is shining like a dime on my heartfelt map. I will love that man forever and I don't even know his name.

A year later after a bout with malignant melanoma I went to Toronto again to work a little voodoo on the Canadian Film Centre residents. The surgeon who had removed his pound of flesh from my right leg, just above the knee, had pretty much convinced me that my time in the here and now was up. I had had tests to see if the cancer had spread to my liver and lymph system but no results before I left Saskatoon. My attitude was cavalier. I believe along with Ivan Illich that death rides on your shoulder your whole life through. When your number's up – I'd even had a half-dozen conversations with death by then. Death riding my shoulder like one of those paintings by Munch. A lovely blonde woman, staring out to sea; a dark, not unfriendly shape, just behind her. Protective. Ready. I worked flat out with those novice writers, directors, and producers for a week. Pumped up on nervous energy and Black Bush. My endless amicable cigarettes. By the end of the week my nerves were shot.

And then it was over. And then I received a fax from my daughter and then husband to say that all the tests were negative. Perhaps my conversations with death worked. I had had lots to say. Perhaps I wore her down. At any rate, I had a free day in Toronto. Cancer free. Free. I drank two pots of coffee and read the Saturday *Globe* cover to cover; I smoked a thin reefer that some lovely friend had given me, and went for a walk. A beautiful sunny July day. I got caught up in a parade down Yonge Street of some of the ugliest people I've ever seen. What kind of parade is this . . . obscenity? Well, it was July 12th, the Orangemen's Parade. So I cut out of all that marching and sidled up some street or other on my way to the World's Biggest Bookstore. A small dapper beggar, handsome, full of life, called out to me: "Hey! Darlin'! Can you spare a quarter for an old man from P.E.I.?!" I looked at him, right into him, and smiled and said, "No." When I came out of the store an hour later, empty-handed (it might be the world's biggest but it's not the best: none of Georges Bataille's pornography for instance; only *one* novel by Denis Johnson), there he was again. The old man from P.E.I. sprang to his feet, arms wide, smiling. . . . "But darlin'," he said, "You don't understand! If you give me a quarter I'll love you for the rest of my life!" Whereupon I gave him a five-dollar bill, saying: "Why didn't you say that before?!" and he kissed me, full of exuberance and real affection. He smelled . . . funky. But rather nice. And he's lighting up my map of home like we're joined at the hip. Whatshisname . . . the old bugger from P.E.I.

I'm thinking now about death and home. Maybe, if I'm lucky, the map will be so suffused with light I'll just sashay right into it. A smile on my face. Arms extended. Real love, as I know it, taking me home. Maybe not. But it's a thought.

SHELAGH ROGERS

Dreamhouse

∾

I have no memory of lying on the floor staring at the buzzing wings of a fan. Nor do I remember the variety of popsicles at Sherman's on Bronson Avenue. In fact, I have no memory at all of the heavy heat of my childhood summers in Ottawa. I have to be told in order to know because I wasn't there. I was up at the cottage. At the lake. At the cabin. The camp, depending on what part of the country you're from.

The cottage was built in the 1940s on a lake in Quebec. I'd tell you which lake except I still go up there a couple of times a year. And it's not my family's. Hasn't been for twenty-eight years.

A real-estate ad for the cottage would have read:

One hour away from the city: cottage property on _____ Lake.
Kitchen with gas and wood stove. Complete Blue Willow set.
Living/dining room built around large fieldstone fireplace.
Screened-in porch with view of lake. Two bedroom cabins.
Another cabin used as workshop. Nearest neighbour half-mile away.

What it would not say:

Loons, kingfishers, the occasional American bittern, water
snakes, wasps, pickerel, rock bass, snapping turtles, cinnamon
ferns, moss, boulders with bibs of lichen, trilliums, bloodroot.
Up the hill in a meadow, pink and white clover, buttercup,
loosestrife, black-eyed susans, snow on the mountain also known
as goutweed, goldenrod. Back down the hill again for white oak,
red pine, sugar maples, poplars.
Land of the Silver Birch, Home of the Beaver.

Summer would begin with kids and cats piling into the wood-panelled station wagon. Supplies were wedged into the back: clothes (minimal), diapers (many), food (enough to see us through two months of no electricity), candies (ditto), booze. The idea was to never run out of booze. This was the early '60s. There were more hours in the day. Cocktail hours. Golden hours wherein children should be neither seen nor heard. Elevenses. We had all the makings for "martins," Gibsons, manhattans. There was bottled beer to be stored in the lake.

The drive there took us out of Ottawa across the river to Hull, through Gatineau, Templeton, Perkins-sur-le-lac, the names an old reel of English and French. We'd arrive after forty minutes of driving on dirt roads slicked down with oil and we'd park under a canopy of trees. The smell of pine could sear your nostrils.

The first job of the summer was to see how far the boathouse had travelled as a result of the tectonic shifting of winter ice. Next came the airing out of the big cabin, the unshuttering of the windows, the plumpfing of cushions. Then, over to the bedroom cabins to sweep away spiders and shake out eiderdowns. My bed was beside a window. In the cool late evening, I'd watch sequins of sunlight dissolving into the lake, shimmering fish dancing with no fishers in sight. Later the frogs would sustain a chant that rumbled low like a Russian Orthodox chorus. That music would close the day as surely as the loons' matins would open it.

My mother, my sister, my brother, and I lived at the cottage for the entire summer. My father came up on Friday nights and stayed weekends. Once, my father came up on a Thursday. I was so excited, I went down the road to pick him some flowers. I wandered into the meadow, then into a forest and got lost. The trees all looked the same. And their monstrous gnarled branches linked hands above me to secure a trap. I screamed. The scream echoed. I screamed again and again. After what seemed like hours, but must have been minutes, an old man in overalls and a plaid shirt came to save me. He took my hand and brought me back to our road. Then he disappeared into the trees. A few days later, I found my bouquet exactly where he had left me. I never saw my Boo Radley again. I would have liked to have said thank you for bringing me home.

The summers at the cottage were happy. My family was there. Our friends came up. We played games of Monopoly, cribbage, and Risk. We swam. We canoed. We sang "My paddle's clean and bright, flashing with silver. Dip, dip, and swing." I fished with my father. We did crafts with my mother. When my parents finished their manhattans, I got to eat the rye-soused cherry. Our cat gave birth to four kittens the same night Neil Armstrong walked on the moon. That was the only night we watched TV up there. I was torn between miracles: one giant step for mankind and the glistening felines that kicked into life at the first prickly brush of their mother's tongue.

We were one kind of family then. We are another kind now.

My parents sold the cottage the summer after the moonwalk. Sold it to my aunt, who sold it to a guy who thinks a forest is where you dump your old car. I dream of reclaiming the place. As

I said, I still go up there. Usually it's in the fall when I can cover my tracks with leaves. Lord, forgive us our trespasses as we forgive those who trespass against us. It is, if not mine, my home. When I dream home, I dream this place.

CONSTANCE ROOKE

Real-Estate Dreams

~

In Victoria, we lived in a house high up on the rocks with a view of the mountains and the sea. I lay in a huge green bathtub before a wall of glass, and thought that the mists swirling outside were Chinese. Remembering the story of my childhood – if you dig far enough, you'll reach China – I thought I had indeed come out the other side. By some lucky *bouleversement*, I had been delivered to the right place. This was a miraculous house, acquired by miracle. And I want to tell its story. But another story comes first. (Then there's a third.)

First House

The first house we bought in Victoria was a tiny place in Oak Bay. I'd read a "for sale by owner" ad in the *Times Colonist* and gone to see it, a house (like the next, miraculous one) that was built on rock. It was owned by an elderly couple who had decided to move into a condominium because the woman had quite recently developed a fear of high winds. She was terrified that the house on which she and her husband had lavished so much care would crumble to smithereens.

That was her word: smithereens. And their name was Smith. You might say it was a terrible sales pitch, except that no one of my age then could possibly have worried about winds assaulting this tiny fortress. There was so much rock. Even the garden had been cemented over, and all of its many bushes and flowers consigned to pots, producing (I thought) a quite eccentric, somehow Mediterranean air. Besides, she was afraid. And her fear was no laughing matter; it was, I felt sure, an expression of the fear of death.

I worried about taking advantage of her. I did say that I was sure the house was not dangerous. ("Oh, not for YOU, dear. I'm just being silly.") But they were determined to sell, and they liked us. This was important. ("We couldn't possibly sell to STRANGERS, dear.") We were the first people to answer their ad, on the first day it had appeared, and so it seemed fated that their house should become ours. We were such a nice young couple. Our baby was such a love. (I felt that we were thieves and impostors, even our angel-faced, two-year-old son, who had immediately hopped onto her lap.) I kept thinking what a nice *old* couple they were. How much I liked *them*. Whether it could possibly be okay to make our home on a foundation of imaginary smithereens.

Perhaps the worst of it was that both of them were so tickled about the fact that we wouldn't have to DO A THING; it had all been done over, every last inch of the place. For example, the fireplace in the living room had been nicely walled up. So much tidier that way. And the panelling, which they'd done a room at a time over the years, was now complete – the fake stuff, patterned to look like oak. We knew that all of this would go. They were so nice, and we really did feel rotten, knowing what changes we would feel compelled to wreak, knowing that because of this we could never invite them to tea if we happened upon them in Oak Bay Village.

As I did, quite often – never inviting them to tea. Even now, when a conversation turns to the subject of guilt, it is this I think of first.

But we could not have been happy with that panelling, and we had owned for years some blue-and-green bird tiles brought back from Mexico that would, and did, look lovely on the fireplace – and once we'd done all of that, there was no turning back. Though jackhammers were regularly discussed, we left the cement garden alone; and I can never decide whether that was because they took walks in the neighbourhood, and would see, or because the garden had sufficient appeal just as it was.

The last thing they said to us as we were closing the deal, and repeated on two occasions when I met them on the street, was that if ever we decided to sell we should be sure to let them know first. Who knew? Her fear of high winds might pass with time, and if it did they would wish to return to their home. I believe I promised.

Years passed, about five of them. There were now bookcases in the bathroom and the dining room, and real cedar planks nailed to the kitchen cupboards. The house was charming, by our lights, but it had begun to be much too small. Our son, Jonathan, was sleeping in a sort of closet off the kitchen, his toys had encroached everywhere, and he was now old enough to make caustic remarks on the size of his room. Leon was writing in a drafty back porch whose floor was not even remotely flat. There was nowhere to put guests, and nowhere for me to set up a study. I think I might have decided earlier to find us another house, but for a reluctance to embark on the inevitable, further betrayal of the people I knew to be the rightful owners of this little house. I knew that I would not call them.

Finding the Second House

I started looking. I spent several months looking, and found only one house that would do. Indeed, I recognized it immediately as the house we were meant to live in. I had become fairly knowledgeable about the Victoria real-estate market, and knew that this house was underpriced at one hundred thousand dollars; I went to the bank again, and heard once more that eighty-five thousand dollars was our utmost ceiling. I looked reality in the face; I accepted the fact that this door (which *seemed* to have my name on it) was closed to me. Although I had been lucky most of my life, it was not to be. Right. I decided not to take Leon to see it, or to go there again myself. I tried not to talk about it. What point was there? I skipped three open houses on successive Sunday afternoons, imagining throngs of people moving through those rooms; horrible, unworthy creatures who had only to pull out a fat chequebook to become buyers. I was flummoxed that this lovely – too cheap! – house still hadn't sold, but determined to stay away. To be strong.

We had at this time a friend who was a real-estate agent, and quite unlike any other real-estate agent I had encountered. Adam was gay, lived on a yacht – and for the whole period of my futile search for a house had been off gallivanting somewhere on his damned boat. He would disappear like that for months at a time. Normally I found this free-spirited; this time I was miffed. But at last he appeared at our door, saying he had heard from his colleagues that I was everywhere, haunting every open house. We were considering a move! How exciting! And of course he knew precisely what I had in mind.

Terrace Avenue. (Bull's-eye.)

How had I missed it? I explained that I had not; I was capable of identifying the house on my own, but we could not afford it.

Adam waved my objection away. He was unstoppable. This would come to pass. He would set up an appointment. All three of us would go with him, so that the vendor could see what an attractive family we were. (Did a goblin not tiptoe across my grave?) I was to follow his lead, and not depart from his instructions by one iota. Dress well. Accept tea. Above all, don't enthuse too much – "You do that" – and leave the negotiating to him. All of this struck me as hilarious. Idiotic. But I was fond of Adam, and desperately eager for an excuse to see the house again.

Perhaps because I had worked so hard to stay away, I turned to jelly as soon as the house came into view. There was the beautiful old English garden, smelling of wallflowers and rich earth; a moss-covered fountain by the path, the nymph pouring water into a shallow basin; tall cedars and massive rock gardens, with a hundred kinds of tiny flowers – mauve, white, yellow, pink, purple, deep blue – all safe in the crevices. And there, open to the glorious spring day, were the old casement windows with leaded panes that I had loved.

It was a pretty house, spacious and full of light; a house without eyesores of any kind, a house whose storybook charm was not cloying. It had been styled a "Tudor cottage" in the multiple-listings book, making it fraudulent by definition in this Canadian place. However, it was old enough not to seem so to a Victorian. In Victoria, we had what were called the "real" Tudor houses, mellow-looking places built more than a generation back, and also the fake Tudors – raw things, contemporary horrors, the houses as well as pubs and "tea shoppes" and fish-and-chips shops and mini-malls that had shot up only yesterday or last week.

This was real. It had a garden gate and holly bushes. I had lived as a child in a house very much like this, a house bestowed on us by my grandmother when finally we left her apartment in Manhattan for Garden City, on Long Island.

It had a room that was called a butler's pantry in the paper, and another called the library. These were rooms I remembered by name from my grandmother's New York apartment, in which there had been an actual butler. It had a powder room off the front hall with black-and-white tiles on the floor, and these were the very tiles I had crawled on in my grandmother's domain. To this day, these tiles are always on the floors of my dreams. In my sleep I wait for them to appear.

The library and the kitchen were in the front of the house and had the leaded windows. In the back, because of the mountains and the sea in the distance, because of the remarkable bamboo garden that had been built in terraces down the hillside, there were "picture" windows.

Adam introduced us to the owner, an elegant woman in her late sixties. She accompanied us as Adam took us through, but left most of the house talk to him. When we reached the master bedroom, she observed that it had no "*en suite*" bath. Some people mind that very much, she said – and I laughed. Then she laughed too, as if relieved that one other inhabitant of our planet had penetrated the absurdity of the *en suite* craze. The principal bathroom was only steps away.

When we entered the living room, the breeze was hurling white silk curtains into the room, and they were like flags, like giddy ballerinas, like Isadora Duncan's scarves.

I was enraptured and did not conceal it.

In truth, all three of us were starry-eyed. Goners. Adam, however, kept making furtive pushing-down gestures at me with the palm of his hand, and once hissed: "Damn it, Connie. Keep a lid on it, can't you?"

When we had seen it all, inside and out, our hostess gave us tea from a Georgian silver tea service. There was hot water in a silver jug, a thing I had not seen in many years. (When we got married, there were mainly fondue pots.) I felt eerie sitting in her beautiful room, for I was experiencing both foresight and *déjà vu*. (The room a palimpsest, and I transported into some middle layer.) Adam began to speak in very businesslike tones, about the age of the furnace, and she listened politely for a moment, then turned to me.

"Well, my dear, I can see you love my house."

"Oh, I do!" said I. "*We* do." And then I told her that I felt we were there under false pretences. The house was more than fairly priced, it was underpriced, but we could not afford it. It had been wrong of us to take up her time.

"What can you afford?" she asked, looking me straight in the eye.

"Eighty-five thousand dollars," I said. Adam was beside himself, in ecstasy, or in horror at the unprofessional nature of this woman-to-woman exchange.

There was a very slight pause.

"Well, that's all right. You can have it. I want you to have it." We moved toward one another and embraced, and she immediately began to offer us other things.

"The andirons perhaps? Have you got any decent fire tools?" She asked this searchingly, as if prepared to distrust my answer.

"Would you like the buffet? I won't have room for that in the Toronto apartment."

I learned that her husband had died recently; she was going east to be near the children. Later, I discovered from Adam that she had somehow managed to turn down three full-price offers because she didn't take to the people. I hadn't known you could do that. I wondered if they had been discomfited by the absence of an *en suite*, if that gave her a quasi-legal or just a moral out.

She even gave us the white silk curtains that had undone me. When the breeze died down, I could see that these curtains were exceptionally long: they fell into pools on the pale grey carpet. I had not known before, or had forgotten, that this is what curtains ideally do. I never saw our "vendor" again after she moved away to Toronto, but I have often thought of her. She appears occasionally in dreams as my mother, though always under her own name.

Selling the First House

Eighty-five thousand dollars. That was all very well, but it depended on selling our house in Oak Bay at a good price. The house had been on the market (for sale by owner) for over a month by that time, with very little action. I had begun to wonder how widespread was our distaste for artificial wood panelling; their house, the home of the people I wasn't calling, had been sold in a day. I could perhaps acknowledge that the rough cedar planks on the kitchen cupboards had been a mistake. (The look of them still appealed to me, but they were impossible to clean. I knew too about the thousand splinters lurking there, awaiting future fingers.)

Because Terrace Avenue had become my measure, this house was revealed as more hippie-like, more "ethnic" and rustic, than I had understood it to be.

But it was still dear, and I was offended by the failure of Victoria's house-hunters to appreciate its merit. How, for example, could anyone in his or her right mind not be mad about the Mexican fireplace? We were. All our friends were. Adam, in any case, was quite confident that he could sell the house for us without difficulty.

"You just need one buyer – people who will appreciate what you have done here. I will find this buyer."

Perhaps two weeks more passed, and still the house had not sold. I was tired of keeping it tidy, tired of racing home from work to discover that our poor house had been spurned yet again. Then one day I came in and found Adam and Leon, as well as two other men I had not seen before, all drinking deeply of champagne. The deed was accomplished. The story of how it had come to pass – by miracle – is one that beggars belief, though I am assured that all of it is true.

It seems that Adam had decided it was time to stop messing around: he would go to see his palm reader and ace-in-the-hole. He explained to her that selling the house of his friends was a matter of life and death. And she replied very simply: "Drive north." Adam understood this to mean a trip up the Malahat Drive in his old MG, and he set out at once. In perfect ignorance of what his next move might be, but trusting his ace, Adam drove on up the Malahat. Just at the highest point, he observed another decrepit MG travelling in the opposite direction – and in it, some friends of his, a young gay couple. Horns were honked madly, and both cars pulled off the road.

Adam's friends were on their way to Victoria, and very excited because they'd just bought their first house.

"You've done what?!" Adam exclaimed. "Tell me you haven't signed the papers!"

Well, of course they hadn't. They were on their way to do so at this very moment. Adam explained their mistake, that it was our house they were meant to buy, and led them to it. It was love at first sight, and the deal was clinched before I got home from work that afternoon.

Terrace Avenue was ours.

An Excursion

Some months after we had moved into the house on Terrace
Avenue, I set out alone for North Carolina where I had some
research to do for a book. It was blistering hot there, and I found
myself in need of something thin to wear. With my old friend
Maria, I went shopping for a simple sundress – and bought, in the
end, after Maria and I had tried it on several times each, darting
out from behind racks of lesser dresses, astonishing one another,
what was certainly the most expensive as well as the most unusual
garment I had ever owned. A very strange and splendid sundress,
with a sort of apron attachment. I wore it every day without fail for
two weeks; I could, because it washed like a handkerchief and
dried in minutes. A man I knew who had never uttered a compliment to a woman in his life said it was the most beautiful dress he
had ever seen. Strangers by the dozen came up to ask about it.
Finally, I said to Maria: "If this dress should burst into flames
tomorrow, it wouldn't matter. I have had the good out of it." We
agreed that this was a most peculiar thing to have escaped my
mouth, no dress of our acquaintance having ever burst into flames.

The next day I flew to Pennsylvania to visit my parents. The
plan was that I would then borrow my mother's car so that I could
also visit my grandmother, who was living (for purposes of her
research) in a museum in Vermont. My father and I had had a terrible argument about politics, as was our custom. I was at the wheel
of Mother's car, just starting to fasten my seatbelt, when he came
out to kiss me good-bye. I was so moved by this gesture that I forgot
the belt. He was determined to part on good terms, and so, oddly,
for the first time ever, he refrained from telling me to buckle up.

Some fifteen miles away, a car on the other side of the high
median rose into the air and began a series of aerial manoeuvres

that seemed designed to make that car converge with mine. Because of my father's forbearance, I was able to hurl myself into the only part of my mother's car, a womb-like space under the glove compartment, that was not pancaked entirely when the other car landed on mine. I say "I" here, but it was my body, ignoring my terror, that saved me.

On the operating table, the nurse who was approaching my bloody sundress with her scissors could discern what an exceptionally pretty dress this was. She was sorrier about having to cut that dress than about having to saw the wedding ring from my finger.

The point of telling this story here, of taking this excursion, is first that it is a part of the deeper design I'm tracing. The precariousness of what we live in. Mothers and grandmothers. My two distant families – the one that made me, the one I have made – and the spaces that join us through time. Danger and that small safe place beneath the glove compartment, from which I was born a second time by magic, essentially for the purpose of rejoining my husband and child. (It must be recorded, these things cannot be helped, that I began life sleeping in a glove drawer, in my grandmother's New York apartment – the delivery of a bassinet having been delayed.) Secondly, my accident produced through legal action a sum of money that would launch us two years later into the renovation of Terrace Avenue.

Renovating the Second House

Why? When it was lovely as it was? This time, I had thought, we really didn't need to DO A THING. There was room enough and beauty enough for reasonable mortals. It was just that one day as we climbed up on the roof-high rocks beside our house, we observed to one another that the view from HERE was to die for. There was so much more of the sea. We became greedy, perhaps – imagined another storey on our house, and having imagined it, could not let this vision go. Besides, we had money from the accident (recompense for the arthritic hands that were prophesied for me) and wanted to spend it on something . . . well, *expansive*.

I had met a contractor recently who was repairing fire damage on the house of some friends who were away on a sabbatical. I was to oversee his work, which seemed fine to me. Seamus complained often that because winter was coming on, no one would employ him. And this was lunatic, in his professional opinion; Victoria's winter climate was never a problem for builders. So we gave him our house.

In late November, Seamus took the roof off. On the next day, it began to rain – and went on raining hard for a month. This was acknowledged widely as the worst spell of rotten weather in decades. Seamus and his men put out "tarps." And as the weeks went by it seemed they did little more up there than to adjust and repair these tarps, a word we came quickly to loathe. The tarps were always falling down or being whipped apart by the fierce winds.

Her hard winds, rerouted. Come at last to a different address. Our second house, it seemed clear, would collapse not from some fault at its rock-solid base, but from above; it would disintegrate not as an emblem of extreme old age or death, but to repay our hubris or sheer stupidity.

Pockmarks appeared on the ceilings. And then more – mushrooms that became holes. Bits of soggy drywall began falling into our plates at dinnertime.

It was now raining steadily *inside* our house. The beautiful wool carpets were sodden, then ruined. Every vessel we had, and dozens more we borrowed or bought – soup pots, plastic garbage bins – had been dragooned to collect the infernal rain, and there was soon nowhere left to step in our galumphing rubber boots. We would stumble and, reaching out to save ourselves, upset yet another pailful of water.

At a few points, boards were laid out on bricks to form walkways. Our living room became the Piazza San Marco.

Our son's bedroom was all right. We hadn't taken off the roof in that part of the house. And for a while, inexplicably, the ceiling in our own bedroom held. When that too began to fail I could sense that hysteria was not far off. (*"Keep a lid on it, Connie – can't you?"*) More rain vessels were acquired, and each night we would move the king-sized bed to a new position in the room. On the night that we were obliged to put rain receptacles on the bed itself, I began to weep.

Had we been doing nothing all this time – just *taking it?* What of Seamus? We realized right away that the trick was to PUT THE NEW ROOF ON. When we could get him to stop mumbling about *tarps*, Seamus would confirm that this was the right approach. The framing had at last been done. Why then, we inquired, did they not get busy on the roof?

Well, it was a simple matter of materials. There weren't any. Of course they were on order. They just hadn't come in yet. Not much he could do without materials, was there? I had begun now also to hate the word *materials*.

In hiring Seamus, we had neglected to secure references. By this time, however, we had collected a good many testimonials on the sly, all livid. We learned that his *modus operandi* was to pay off the building supply companies for his last job with the up-front money from a new one. In our case the up-front money had been ten thousand dollars; the next draw was to be for another ten thousand, after the roof was up. Seamus was jockeying for receipt of the second instalment now.

My husband argued that we should give it to him so he could buy the damned roofing materials and get on with it. While he did not approve of robbing Peter to pay Paul, he could at least feel some scrap of compassion for Seamus as a fellow human being in a tight corner. My perspective differed. I thought we should write off the money we had given him already, fire Seamus's ass, and find someone who would put a roof over our heads. We went round and round on this, but could not reach consensus.

One evening a few days before Christmas, I came home to dis-cover that my husband had purchased six bottles of Irish whiskey as a Christmas present for Seamus. I blew up. After several minutes of muffled, but intense debate – Leon kept pointing vig-orously at our erstwhile ceiling, to remind me who was up there – I managed to get him down to a single bottle. He would budge no further.

He had also, he informed me, invited Seamus and the long-suffering tarp-shifters down for hors-d'oeuvres and Christmas cheer. They would be here momentarily. I looked at the tree we had up, the few forlorn ornaments we had judged to be rustproof, and could almost see his point. Who else could we dispense hos-pitality to in these circumstances? Also, my outrage was directed at Seamus. I had no objection to entertaining the others, whom I tended to regard as fellow victims.

We heard a racket like Santa's reindeer on the ladders and then a knocking at the front door. No Seamus, but the other three were in a very festive mood. To their astonishment, they had received a portion of their back wages. There was wild talk of Christmas turkeys, toys for the children, perfume for their wives. The unmarried one would now be able to kick in something toward his mother's TV. Leon kept beaming at our guests as the eggnog cups were refilled and the sausage rolls handed round.

A horrible idea came into my head.

And so it was. Unable to convince me on the matter of the second draw, my husband had acted unilaterally. I recall two details of our subsequent dispute: my questioning of his right – *after this!* – to call himself a feminist, and his observation that one of us had to win this argument. If we did nothing, I would win. And if so, what about their Christmas?

It could not have been lavish, in any case. Seamus had given each of them three hundred dollars and absconded with the rest. We never saw him again. My initial outrage had turned (mainly) to appreciation of my husband's generosity. Our son's tentative complaints about "the atmosphere around here" became a source of hilarity for us all. And on Christmas Eve we stayed up until three, drinking our customary yuletide champagne and dancing to the Beatles on a wet carpet. At first we had huddled on a small dry patch by the fire, but the lure of Beatle-dancing on Christmas with our nine-year-old became too great.

There was Christmas music too. Leon sang the first two words of "Ave Maria," in a huge voice, then bowed for our applause. (The birth of a family tradition.) Together, we sang "We Three Kings," "Good King Wenceslas," and the one about little Lord Jesus with no roof for his head. We had in fact a particularly tender and homelike Christmas, that year we had no roof over ours.

On Boxing Day, we found another contractor. By New Year's Day, we had a new roof. But a new quandary too, arising from our decision (on Seamus's advice) to forego the expense of an architect, was shortly to consume us. The plan for our "upstairs" was entirely workable, we were told, except for the stairs part: we couldn't CONNECT the new part of the house to the old. Stairs were out of the question. Sorry. Nowhere to put them. Can't be done. Consultants were called in to no avail – and then one day, we came upon a curious listing in the Yellow Pages: just one name, under "staircase specialist."

He said he could do it. For three weeks' worth of eighteen-hour days all this man did was algebra – I suppose that's what it was – on our dining-room table, taking most of his meals there as well, for we had become friends. But he figured it out. His announcement, one evening over chili, led to more guzzling of champagne. It would be a magnificent curving staircase off the front hall, with each stair of a different size and sweep, and there would be a massive overhead intrusion – like a piece of sculpture, really – in the butler's pantry.

From the drawing board to the flesh, his vision sped. The staircase that could never be was a clear architectural triumph; it was beautiful, and it worked. We were connected at last. On the day it was finished, when dozens of photographs of the staircase, and staircase-with-ecstatic-clients, had been taken for his private archives, our specialist friend announced that he had never previously built a staircase of any kind. He had us get out the Yellow Pages and revealed that he was listed as a "specialist" in several other esoteric domains of carpentry as well, none of which he had ever essayed. He had so been looking forward to sharing this joke, he said. He had loved hearing how confident we felt, now that we had him, a real specialist, on the job.

We had gone from con artist to artist *tout simple*, a man who disliked repeating himself. And had been utterly safe in his hands. All was well. The carpets were replaced, the ceilings freshly dry-walled, the addition finished and *accessible*, and we loved every bit of it. But there is one thing more to admit. In our new upper storey, there was this huge, absurdly luxurious bathroom. With my big green tub and more blue-and-green Mexican bird tiles. Although the distance from bed to bath was greater than it had been below stairs, it was, inescapably, *en suite*. We even described it as such, with silent apologies to the woman who gave us Terrace Avenue, in the ad we placed when it was time to move on to Ontario.

Third House, Last House

I said it had to have water. We were looking for an old stone house, what in Ontario is called a "century home." But it also had to have water of some kind: a pond, a lake, or, preferably, a river. (We were, after all, giving up the Pacific Ocean.) These requirements proved a challenge for our real-estate agents. There was nothing of this description on the market at the time, and so they were reduced to knocking on doors. In the village of Eden Mills, they found at last a gay couple who worked in Toronto and were getting tired of the commute.

The house, I was warned, was smack on the street. No front yard at all, and no land on either side, though the area at the back was private. (I had specified privacy too.) It had been a stagecoach hotel, was built in 1867 and made of stone, and it backed on the Eramosa River. The river here was little more than a stream, but this was all they could do in the way of water-cum-elderly stone. Did I want to see it?

I did. When I heard that the owners were gay, like the people who had bought our house in Oak Bay, little bells rang – and I could *sense* a continuing story line.

All of my life, I have had these dreams I call my real-estate dreams. I am shown a house or an apartment. It is always modest outside, entirely unassuming. Inside though, it starts to expand. I open a door and find an extraordinary old library, the size of a ballroom, with fifty- or a hundred-thousand real books, an open fireplace and dark wood panelling, flowers and gods painted with an Italian hand on the high, vaulted ceiling; or another, and enter an exquisite yellow and white breakfast room with dogs (spaniels) and French doors, opening onto a garden of light. Birds singing in a fig tree. Roses and pomegranates.

In a terrible dream kitchen, I will pull away cracked Formica from the countertop and discover something that looks like – might *be* – the murals of Pompeii. More beauties begin to reveal themselves. Often there will be a courtyard with a fountain. A closet, when I have struggled through the old bicycle parts and other rubbish, proves to have a second door at the back. I open it, and there is the sea. Sparkling. Somewhere, on some floor, earlier or later in my tour, I will meet my grandmother's black-and-white tiles. It is always like this. The marvels – gifts that are being bestowed on me – differ. But it always begins, my viewing of this place I will be allowed to live in, as quite ordinary, exceptionally shabby, or unpromising.

For this reason, the realtors' warnings about the proximity of the road, and how "It doesn't look like much from the curb," did not dissuade me. Neither was I alarmed when what I saw first, inside the house, taking up most of the floor space in the kitchen, were several racks of dresses. (One of the men was a dress designer, that's why.) Now, for the first time, I think of the racks Maria and I had hidden behind, before my sundress was destroyed; then, I saw the racks as part of the debris I knew from my real-estate dreams as a prelude to better things.

It was a surreal beginning anyhow, and should have told me that these people were not completely sold on the idea of selling their house. (In real real-estate life, I was more accustomed to *inducements*: fresh flowers, a fire lit, cinnamon sticks, or vanilla beans simmering on the stove.)

I moved to the window, thinking *I will want this. And they will let me have it.* Yes. And so I wanted, instantly, to live with this small river. Eramosa, Eden Mills – these were very good names, I thought. I thought, here one *inhales*; in Victoria, with the great sea and the mountains beyond, my breath had gone the other way. But I liked this too, equally, this other phase of breathing; this closeness to another kind of water – moving, intimate water, which I could hear. This water and the prospect of an enclosed, a *secret* garden undid me once again.

I wanted the house too. Saw us in it, with ease. There were bookshelves in the kitchen, or the dining area – always auspicious – and the wall behind them was painted my particular shade of dark green; all the living rooms of my childhood had been this colour. It was not a baronial library, you understand; it wasn't even a proper dining room. And there were no black-and-white tiles, not anywhere. But there was a stone fireplace in the living room that would take big logs; there were old beams and old pine floors and deep-set windows. The main floor of the house had been wonderfully, I thought perfectly, restored. I'd been told this, and it was so; I'd been told that the floor above and the one below would take a lot of work, and that was also true.

It was the one below that worried me, containing (I had been informed) a large L-shaped "rec room" with roughed-in bath, laundry, and furnace room. A basement, in short. And this seemed depressing, since we would have to live partly in these rooms; the house was not large enough for us otherwise. The floor, when I encountered it in the flesh, was a shocker: orange shag carpeting that had been peed on for decades by cooped-up cats. But even as I was reeling from that, I knew – this was the clincher – it would be okay, it would be wonderful, because there was the VIEW again, closer, a wall of glass looking out, actually looking DOWN, onto the back garden and the river. Since the house was on a steep incline, we were still well above ground; if I'd opened the glass doors and stepped outside I might have broken a leg, for the deck we would build wasn't there yet. It may not sound like much, but this elevation felt like a high-grade miracle to me.

So they sold us the house, after much persuading, and that's where we live now. The L-shaped rec room was really our bedroom and Leon's study, once doors had been added to the short leg of the L. Cat pee, we found, comes up quite well with ammonia and deep sanding. (Just occasionally, I catch a ghostly whiff which might be ammonia, or possibly one of our own cats.) We fixed the upstairs too, a study for me and a bedroom for Jonathan. We added a sunroom off the kitchen, to get more light.

My mother died last summer. Now, in Eden Mills, I have with me some of the things that came from my grandmother's apartment in New York: a seventeenth-century French desk in my study, two small marble tables, an oil painting of horses with a great tear in it and a disintegrating gold-leaf frame. We have looked up the painter, a nineteenth-century Englishman who drove a stagecoach before he turned to painting. This hangs now in our living room, where the stagecoach drivers used to drink.

Who knows what we have done to the sensibilities of former owners of this stagecoach hotel? The nuns I'm told lived here once? The butcher? The brothel owner? For now that we have decided that we never want to sell this house, we want to keep it, I am wary. Already there are rumours, concerning the old bow-string bridge we have fought to keep in Eden Mills.

If that comes down, the road will be widened, and if the road is widened – well, they say, there's a good chance the front of the Rookes' house will have to go.

So that's where we are now. Inside one of my real-estate dreams, or almost. Safe as houses, as usual.

LEON ROOKE

Bury Him at Home

~

My neighbour Joe, not the name you know him by, tells me that as a boy he hated home. He hated each of the various houses in which he from time to time lived, each of the gravel streets those houses sat upon – hated the whole of the vile town. If this was home, he wanted no part of home.

He remembers most clearly, he says, the two upstairs rooms he lived in during most of the years of World War II.

He remembers a bell.

The bell's reason for being was neither ornamental nor aesthetic. It was not there to summon servants.

The bell was suspended by a cord from a window in the rear room. It was there to summon help, in the event Joe's father returned.

His father did not live any longer in this town. He lived in Norfolk, two hours away. It was not known what he did there.

The one rule, or law, that existed in Joe's home was that the father not be allowed in the house.

If the man did somehow gain entrance and Joe's mother said no to him, no on any account, he would be enraged, especially if he were drunk, which he would be; he would break down the door and beat them all to death.

The *them* included Joe, his older brother and sister, and their mother.

Several times already he had come close.

Each of them knew with certainty that one day he would return.

It was crucial, therefore, that a means be devised whereby they might summon the law.

Hence, the bell.

They had no phone themselves, and were never likely to, but the woman next door did, and a promise was secured from this person that she would get the police running at the first ringing of this bell, whatever the hour.

She did not accept this assignment readily. She had seen the man in action and knew that she could easily become one of his victims.

In that town at this time people locked their doors and put out their lights early. A knock on anyone's door after eight o'clock was all but unheard of.

Their father would come at night when he could not be seen. He would come after the town's two taverns had closed, provided, Joe's mother said, that none of the tarts who hung out there let him take them home.

So long as he had his tarts everyone except the tarts would be safe.

Their two upstairs rooms had but a single entry and exit. If he got in, they would not get out.

Entry was gained by a door off the front porch.

The children, little Joe among them, were trained to race for the bell at the first sound of footsteps on the porch. If creeping was heard on the stairs, it already was too late.

"Practise," Joe's mother said. "We must practise."

She was speaking of the bell.

Joe was about four at the beginning of this period. His brother was six. His sister was eight.

His brother and sister had suffered under their father's hands a good deal more than Joe had. They had the quicker memory.

All four of them remembered the most recent incident. They were all tied to a bed. He was beating them with his belt.

Joe says that he remembers he very much wanted to be the person giving the alarm. But the others could run faster than he could; when rehearsing, he always was last to reach the bell.

It terrified him to see his mother running, his brother and sister running, and Joe chasing at their heels, because he would be the party his father first snatched up, and the one first to die under his knife or belt or fists.

Joe and his brother slept together on a narrow cot in the rear room, the kitchen. The sister slept with their mother in the other room, on the double bed where not long ago they had been tied.

How many times, drifting off to sleep, did they hear him? How often did Joe wake to see his brother, trembling in his pyjamas, standing by the window in the dark, ready to yank the cord?

Or the four of them, crowded together, silent and listening, trying to decide what sound it was they had heard, or if they had heard a sound – a creak on the stairs; stealthy footsteps on the porch – and whether they should not this instant be ringing the bell.

This, Joe says, was home.

"You'll forgive me," he says, "for not having romantic attachment to this idea of home."

In those days the older children and their mother willingly discussed the man's propensity for violence. Later on, this would not be the case. Later on, which in this instance means these days, Joe's sister cannot bear to hear her father's name mentioned. She collapses on the spot, or races away in tears.

He did return home from time to time; rumours would reach their mother: how he had got into this or that fight, a scrape with this or that woman – some nastiness at one of the taverns.

Once, Joe saw his father's picture in the paper. It was not the picture of anyone he recognized, though the caption contained his name. The headline said this:

AREA MAN CHARGED WITH ASSAULT.

What most surprised Joe was how normal he looked.

In the spring of 1944 Joe's mother took up briefly with a man named Tracy Bibb. That is to say, she went for an occasional walk with him. Once in a while, she sat with him in her kitchen. Once, she went with him to a dance. She came home from that dance with a bloody mouth and blood in her hair; she had to be helped up the stairs. Afterwards, she and her daughter locked themselves away in the bathroom, and remained there a long time whispering to each other.

Joe remembers his brother standing in his pyjamas on their side of the locked door, endlessly asking, "What happened? What's going on?"

– Who did that to you? Was it Tracy Bibb?

The sister kept telling them to shut up and go to bed.

Sooner or later, Joe guesses, they all did.

But it was not an easy sleep. Either Tracy Bibb, or their father, meant to break down the door, climb the stairs, and kill them while they slept. So Joe's brother lengthened the cord running from the window to the bell, and slept that night with the cord tied to his arm.

The news came at daylight, with someone pounding on the downstairs door.

Tracy Bibb was trussed up on the front steps, with rags stuffed in his mouth. A note was pinned to his clothes. The note said THIS IS WHAT HAPPENS TO YOUR BOYFRIENDS. It said I CAN HAVE YOU ANYTIME I WANT.

A ladder leaned against the side of the house. Their father had climbed the ladder during the night and removed the clapper from the bell.

So that, Joe says, was home.

When his father died, years ago, a pauper and a drunk in Norfolk, Joe's brother drove there, claimed the body, and brought it home.

This is not a deed either his mother or sister, he says, is ever to know.

"He was the meanest man who ever lived," the brother said, "and ruined all our lives. But it still seemed important to me that he be buried at home."

JANE RULE

Choosing Home

∼

I was still a child when I gave up trying to make myself at home. Someone always then put me in my place instead. To be born is to invade other people's territory, and by the time a child is ambulatory, it is alien to domestic order, cribbed and playpenned, sometimes even tied out of harm's way. To earn even marginal freedom is to learn to hear the hiss of danger everywhere from the butts in the ashtray to the cord on the lamp, from the potatoes in the bin to the wishbones drying on the chandelier. There is nothing cosy or comfy or safe no matter how many grown-up laps, cups of cocoa, and lullabies try to offer that illusion.

I first lived in a mock Norman castle built by my grandfather to advertise a housing development. The room I shared with my older brother had a balcony which overlooked the living room from which we could spy on the adult world. When I was three, we moved to an ordinary house where I had a room of my own, which meant no more to me than that I had to stay out of my brother's unless invited in. Mine was a place where I was sent until I could behave. At school I ended up in the hockey-stick closet for the same reason. I was slow to learn the rules, then puzzled by them or forgetful of them.

"Your child will be run over by a car while you're *explaining* why she should get out of the street," my grandmother complained.

We were only under grandparental scrutiny intermittently. We moved again and again, outrunning the depression, then at the edge of war. Sometimes we lived in other people's furnished houses while we waited for our own belongings to arrive, held up by a dock strike, a lost shipment. We learned to move as lightly as ghosts in places where other people's clothes hung in the closets, other children's toys out of bounds on the screen porch. Released into a house in which we were expected to settle, we were less enthusiastic than our parents about stocking shelves with familiar objects, hanging pictures, unrolling rugs. If there was a room away, in the attic or basement or out over the garage, my brother was given it. I envied him that independence, but I wonder now if he didn't each time have some sense of banishment. My room was usually larger than my younger sister's because I had to have twin beds and share with any guest, usually a grandmother who draped underpants over the bedside lamp and ate sticky candied fruit into the night.

My transient suburban childhood was not an unusual experience at that time when depression and then war dislodged a great many people, but it was not yet an accepted or expected way of life. Our grandparents lived in houses in which their children had grown up, even in houses where they had grown up themselves, attics and basements full of the accumulation of generations, the sorts of things we sold at yard sales every time we moved. When we went "home," it was to another generation's childhood where we were expected to have the manners and skills of country children. Of a summer we nearly learned to milk a cow, pluck a chicken, shoot a rabbit, quilt, embroider, preserve, but those lessons atrophied over the long suburban winters, during which we needed to learn how high to wear our socks, how to comb our hair, what sort of lunch-box to carry. What was visible was relatively easy. Attitudes were harder to come by, whom to admire, whom to ignore. A form of respect in one community ("Yes, sir," "No, ma'm") was not acceptable in another ("Yes, Mrs. Bolton," "No, Mr. Dively"). Most of the kids we met had had only one telephone number and one address through their whole lives. What they thought and how they behaved was what everyone thought and how everyone behaved. They were at home. We were not. In New Jersey, California, Illinois, Missouri, and Kentucky we were never at home.

I would not have said I had a geographic identity until I took my first trip to Europe. It was soon after the war. I was nineteen. For the first time in my life I was not simply an outsider. I was an American about whom there were all sorts of negative expectations, a number of which I inadvertently fulfilled: jumping queues, speaking aloud in train compartments, being unnecessarily generous with cigarettes, expecting friendliness. But gradually my hard-earned adaptive skills brought me that grand compliment, "You don't seem like an American at all." At the end of that summer I phoned my parents from New York to tell them I'd had a safe crossing. "Gosh," I said to my mother, "you sound American." "I am American!" came the indignant reply.

I had pledged allegiance to the flag of the United States of America in dozens of classrooms all across the country, but the "justice and liberty for all" part of it had translated years ago into "bias and custom," "bigotry and conformity." And now I watched those distortions being acted out on the national stage with Joe McCarthy and his hearings, the new loyalty oath demanded of people in government and universities.

In 1956 I joined the migration north, a latter-day Empire loyalist, a precursor of Vietnam draft dodgers, and found in Vancouver a population of foreigners, immigrants from all over the world in a city whose downtown was still mainly parking lots. The sea and the abrupt mountains on the north shore provided the setting for a city yet to be built.

I moved into furnished digs, chosen for a fine, old roll-top desk and a grand view of the mountains, in which I intended to continue my apprenticeship as a writer. Like everywhere else I had lived, it was more a stage set than a home, with no more than a few familiar belongings. If I hadn't then begun to share my life with a woman with experience and need of home, I might never have graduated into an apartment we had to furnish ourselves. Among her other household goods, Helen brought with her a family dining-room table, marked at the edges by a teething sister. The chairs included two with arms, my first experience of the comfort and power of heading our own table. But the apartment itself was confining without view or garden, and Helen was soon walking the neighbourhood in search of a house to buy.

All my life I'd bought things with a mind to how well they would pack or store. I checked a shirt to be wrinkle-free before I tried it on, bought books but never paintings which would have to be crated for a move. I had borrowed furniture or made do with what could be left behind. Owning a house was a fantasy of stability beyond my imagining, and it frightened me. Only the reluctance of the mortgage broker to grant a mortgage to two women without the signature of a man restored my courage. What I discovered about owning a house was that it was a place where things could be left behind in their own places and returned to again and again. A trip to Europe no longer meant an uprooting. Home was a place you could leave behind intact, and it would be there for you when you got back.

I was in my early thirties before I really learned to make myself at home. We had found only a few blocks from where we lived a large, old house with a big garden and marvellous views of the sea, city, and mountains. It had been lived in by a family with five children, the upstairs a rabbit warren of small bedrooms which we transformed into one grand bedroom and bath and Helen's study. The master bedroom on the ground floor became my study. In the high basement we put in rooms for students in winter, for guests in summer, a workshop for an old printing press and wine-making equipment. There I learned the names of trees, shrubs, and flowers in the old garden and helped to redesign it as our own.

In the twenty years we lived in one neighbourhood, I learned not only the names but the needs of our neighbours. I knew whose dog barked, whose kid practised the trumpet. I knew the names of the clerks in the local stores, a baker who could make us an emergency wedding cake for a friend, a butcher who could help us impress guests with a crown roast.

Being at home expanded from the neighbourhood into the city, where we helped to establish the Arts Club, meeting many of the writers, painters, actors, musicians, and architects, all of whom were involved in shaping the cultural life of Vancouver, building its much-needed theatres, galleries, and museums. We wrote letters of protest against the design of the new post office, forced the *Vancouver Sun* to keep and then expand its book page to include reviews of Canadian books, aired our views on local radio stations, went to each other's performances and openings, and imported artists from elsewhere.

Then I was asked to attend the founding meeting of the Writers' Union of Canada. Over those years I had become not only a writer but a Canadian writer with national responsibilities to my tribe and my culture, even eventually a representative of Canada abroad.

The first time I travelled with a Canadian passport, I had some sense of guilt in accepting kindness and welcome at every hand. Surely I hadn't changed so much as to be unrecognizable as the ugly American traveller I had once been. Gradually I learned simply to be grateful that the citizenship I'd chosen packs and travels so well.

Writing for me has always been a means of making sense of experience. The rootless richness of my childhood gave me lots of options and few assumptions, and perhaps it took me longer to discover what has been mine to say and how to welcome my readers into the worlds I make, but the compensation has been that I was free to choose what home is, what I have needed it to be.

JOHN RALSTON SAUL

Rivers

∾

Home. What is home? Where? That comfortable illusion of a house somewhere, a piece of land, a swinging gate, linear memories tied to physical objects, has always escaped me. I say illusion, not delusion. There are illusions worth having. We all need a bit of emotional comfort.

The children of soldiers find theirs in a different form. I could list off my homes – mostly army quarters in various parts of Canada. Some of them are still there. Some have been ripped down. There was the little wartime construction outside of Calgary in Currie barracks, surrounded by mud my mother remembers. There wasn't much time for grass in an army trying to shrink itself from one of the world's largest fighting forces to a peacetime outfit. Or there was the row house on the edge of a small camp in the middle of the prairies. Rivers Camp. Or the house overlooking Fort Henry outside of Kingston.

Various homes in four provinces; over a dozen schools. A country childhood because most of these places were either lost in the country or outside of a town. In many ways a perfect childhood, because our home, our neighbourhood, was at the same time the army and the country as a whole. Mine is a peculiar generation. We are the children of the men who fought the World War, who landed on D-Day, who won.

Of course, many men did that and then returned to civilian life. But our fathers remained in the army, and there everyone had been part of those landings and battles. Some were heroes, some just good soldiers, others time servers. But there was a general atmosphere of public service as a normal state of being. Everyone was relatively poor. Officers, like my father, were badly paid, and the other ranks were paid even less. Money was never discussed, certainly never discussed as something to be sought. The schools had a special atmosphere because they included all the children, from those of the commandant to those of the privates. There was a sense in one way of ranks and structure, but in another of an integration which is unusual except in a small town. There were people from all over the country. English and French Canadians. All the classes and backgrounds. Among the officers, there were those who had fought their way up from the ranks (literally, given the war); others who had come the middle-class route of RMC.

These people all knew the country, at least as a geographical reality and, through their own experience, as a reality capable of fighting for a great cause. I never heard as a child the endless self-indulgent discussions about what it was to be a Canadian. They simply knew themselves to be Canadian. That was enough. No doubt that included multiple contradictions, prejudices, and weaknesses. That's not my point. And those contradictions were often discussed. What I am referring to is a basic self-confidence as to who they were and what they served.

The strange thing about an army family was that it took geography for granted. Every three years we would move, more often than not a few thousand miles. Some of my friends were lost sight of – sometimes forever, sometimes for a few years – then we would find each other again for another three years at the other end of the country.

You might imagine that this would destabilize a child. But let me go back to the rare atmosphere of self-confidence which reigned around us. We knew what we were. We knew that our fathers served the larger interest. We knew they had risked their lives for it. We sensed relationships among them which, of course, had elements of careerism and ambition, success and failure, but also of having been involved together in putting their lives on the line. Each of them knew the details of the others' specific glory and/or failure. A kind of existential memory hung over them like an aura.

It wasn't discussed. I have never heard a real soldier fall into war stories. It simply hung over us, as a part of that peculiar stability which counted for far more than the absence of mere geographical sedentarism.

Once every few weeks, the officers would squeeze into their mess kits – ever harder to do as the years went by – and go off to mess dinners with our mothers. And then the anonymous ribbons of the daily uniform would be transmogrified into that mystical thing, a row of medals – stars, circles, silver, bronze, hanging down on striped ribbons of different colours, stripes of red and green and blue, each detail of width and hue signifying something. They would hang there on the breasts of their astonishing dress uniforms. I say astonishing because most men when they dress up put on dark suits or vague black dinner jackets. But my childhood was filled with men who, although professionally tough, wore skin-tight trousers and bright red jackets and bits and pieces of pink or sky blue or mauve with elaborate trims.

As for the medals, these men knew, of course, the real meaning of baubles – that George didn't really deserve his DSO, that Henry should have got an MC for what he did, but. . . .

Father, William Saul, landing in midwinter
on the prairies outside Rivers Camp

But above all, it was a world in which the force of headquarters bureaucracy was still held more or less at bay by the simple presence of so many experienced field soldiers. The imbalance of the 1980s and '90s – a time when press officers and information control would seem to be of greater importance to some generals than public service – was still far away.

One of those homes in which I lived was on the edge of a little camp two hundred-odd miles west of Winnipeg, almost in Saskatchewan. In fact, the country and the culture were those of the great rolling wheat plains of Saskatchewan.

Rivers Camp no longer exists. It was a training centre for flyers and parachutists – one of the most romantic types of the modern soldier. A few thousand men, women and children lived in this tiny artificial world surrounded by prairie and wheat fields. It was a place where, more than most, the men were engaged in being men. There wasn't anything else to do. My father – then forty – commanded the jump school and jumped out of an airplane once a week, winter and summer. This is not the equivalent of a squash game between taking meetings in an office tower.

Winter reached Rivers in early autumn. Piles of snow were often still melting away in June. The snow and cold were so heavy that we were often picked up for school by one of those lumbering tank-size snowmobiles painted in white camouflage. We – the children – loved this place. Our mothers, almost without exception, hated it. Isolation, little to do, almost no books or anything else as diversion. No possibility of work. Just bringing up children and surviving the cold and the heat and once in a while escaping to Brandon or Winnipeg or farther. And for some two months every year the men went off all together on northern exercises – what in the nineteenth century had been called manoeuvres – or training courses, leaving the women to their own devices. If you will forgive a cliché, the wives were the real heroes of the place.

But for children, it was another matter. If I came out of my house and walked down a short sidewalk, I came immediately to a low fence. That was the end of the world as officially defined. Beyond that we could disappear and roam in valleys and little woods. We could have roamed for a thousand miles if dinner and school hadn't interfered. We walked away from reality at every opportunity. Explored what for children had never been explored. Imagined a wild world which we seemed to be on the edge of. Started fires on the prairie, sometimes with disastrous results.

The sense of size and movement and clarity which dominated there marked my view of what life and even ideas could be. Canada was never a quiet protected village by a stream or a city living on its own belly button.

When the annual waves of insects arrived, we could see them as a blackness across the horizons, hundreds of miles away. Weather moved in and out like a Wagnerian opera on a gigantic stage. Yes, the ice melted in June, but in July we baked and in August the wind blew so hard and dry that sand always found its way into our wooden houses. This was a place described again and again by Tolstoy and Lermontov. Somewhere on the steppes, where the earth and the sky rolled out from nowhere and on into eternity. We were camped, like Métis on the annual buffalo hunt, somewhere in the midst of this great flow.

And so it was a sort of home, I see now, quite outside of the norm. Shooed outdoors at recess in January into that dry, deep, deep cold of the West, we would look up beyond the drifts of snow to see flying boxcars on the horizon. These almost square transport planes with a double tail joined by a cross wing would take off with the end removed from the big cargo hold – like a truck with the back open. Our fathers, bundled in white arctic gear, would have clambered up inside to wait in the plane's belly in minus-thirty- or -forty-degree air as the boxcar lumbered off the ground and flew slowly about until the agreed moment came. Then they threw themselves out into the void.

And we would look up from our playground to see our fathers not returning from an invisible office or factory or even from a known tractor or fishing boat, but throwing themselves like crazy acrobats out of what looked like a prehistoric monster into a frigid sky, only to float down onto a land of heaving snow. Such a strange reality or irreality.

They tell me the camp has been shut down and the houses given or sold to natives who have trucked them away. I love this idea. Not just my childhood, but the homes themselves float away from one place to another. What remains is the land. And the land, that most animist idea of place itself, has always been at the heart of my idea of home.

CAROL SHIELDS

Living at Home

~

Children know how to live at home. Their world is microscopi-
cally comprehended and precisely knowable. Their sensory
equipment takes in the contours of the crack on their bedroom
ceiling, the exact pattern of the linoleum in the kitchen, the
shortcut to the garage through the prickly bushes, the mole on
their mother's neck, the frayed end of clothesline hanging on its
basement hook, the cup of bent nails on their father's workbench. In all probability very young children feel that their
homes and their bodies are continuous.

But a few years pass, and the map of home is never again as
accurately possessed, for the larger world intrudes, blurring dis-
tinctions and demanding reduction. It's as though we suffer a
diminution of our eyesight as we grow older. The clutter of home
becomes generalized, without scent or inscribed touch, without
particularity, and without the kind of worn and subtly lit spaces
that constitute the essence of the familiar for most of us.

And without the same comfort. My second-grade teacher,
Miss Sellers, must have known this. She established a reading
corner in our classroom, and furnished it with two small rugs she
brought from home. On the scratched bookcase she set a tiny

shaded lamp, and if we finished our work quickly we were given the reward of turning on this lamp, bathing the dark corner with yellow light, then settling down on the floor with a book. Our refuge from homesickness.

Some of us really do suffer from this disease more than others, and I certainly was one of those children who longed for home even in the benign atmosphere of the neighbourhood school. The teachers were, somehow, too attentive, the surfaces too carefully maintained and assigned. At home there were beguiling liberties. I could stretch out, kittenlike, on top of the living-room radiator and listen to the radio serials in the late afternoon. Warmth, familiarity. Jack Armstrong. Tom Mix. Here was my space. I had found it and claimed it as my own, and all this was allowed.

At five I became homesick while visiting a favourite cousin in Wisconsin and had to be brought home several days early, to everyone's inconvenience, but to my grateful relief. Later, I was homesick at Girl Guide Camp, and ended up in Healthy House with a strep throat, caused partly, I'm convinced, by away-from-home misery. At university, three hundred miles from home, I remember curious weepy episodes which would arrive in the midst of even the happiest occasion. My room in the women's residence with its matching curtains and bedspread was only a pathetic imitation of home. It had the wrong noise, the wrong dimensions. And certainly it was not a place where one could burrow. (Was it Auden who said that life is mainly a question of burrows?)

The day comes, of course, when the need to stay home is at odds with the need to flee, and I can only suppose there is something Darwinian about this phenomenon. The cover of one of my books, *Various Miracles*, illustrates this curious state beautifully. Jane Zednick, the cover artist, has titled her piece *Trying to Fly*, and in it we see a small creature (an angel in training, perhaps) lifting her frail wings and looking skyward, a look of perplexed hopefulness on her face. But she is securely tied to earth by a snake which is wrapped tightly around her ankle. This tension between rootedness and its opposite has, I think, characterized much of my adult life. At home I yearn to travel; travelling I hunger for home.

I have, of course, learned to make my own homes – permanent and temporary – in such places as Toronto, Manchester, Ottawa, Brittany, Paris, Vancouver, and now Winnipeg, and to these homes I've brought the small attentions that Miss Sellers lavished on our second-grade classroom: softly lit corners, the comfort of textured surfaces, permissions granted and accepted. These habitations, lovingly constructed, beckon to me whenever I'm away.

Some years ago my husband and two younger daughters and I spent ten days in the Scottish town of Kerkudbright, venturing out each day in search of ancient monuments. Our accommodation, a modest bed-and-breakfast, was comfortable enough, despite the fact that our landlady had plastered the house with small notices: Careful not to let door slam, Please leave bathroom tidy, Kindly place empty teacups on hall table. We ate rather ordinary suppers at this woman's table, and felt compelled for some reason to offer her extravagant compliments on her cooking. Our rooms were freezing; Scotland was experiencing a chilly August. Our daily sightseeing trips, though, were full of marvellous adventures, and we remarked on how fortunate we were to have given ourselves such a leisurely block of time.

On our last evening in Kerkudbright my husband and I went to the local pub for a farewell drink, and later found our way home down a dark, rainy street lined with narrow houses. The curtains to one of these modest houses had been left open, and I saw, seated on a deep red sofa, a young woman reading a book. A coal fire burned in the grate, and the light from this fire sent a warm glow across the room's surfaces, falling on the woman's hands and face, transforming the whole into a kind of golden stage setting. She never looked up from her book, but turned the pages with a sense of absorption, almost of devotion.

It seemed to me that I had never seen a creature so rootedly "at home," nor had I ever before completely understood what that phrase – at home – meant. What I felt, watching her, was a pang of profound envy. The woman with her book was at home, and I was not at home. But tomorrow – a mere twenty-four hours away – that's where I would be.

Sometimes, returning home by air, I look down at the immense width of prairie space, its fields and rivers and geological folds, and then I catch a glimpse, finally, of that strange, improbable disc of population at its centre. Why of all places is it there and who is it that lives in this random spot?

And then the thought comes to me: I do. This is my *home*, the place I come from.

MERILYN SIMONDS

The Chalk Boy

~

Come, walk with me through the village. It isn't very large: two
streets draped down the hillside to the river, a few connecting
roads that cross. It will take less than an hour. And really, I'd
rather not go alone.

This is where I grew up, the years until I was well into school,
then again through adolescence. That charmed hiatus of middle
childhood I spent elsewhere. I have claimed other places longer,
it's true, but whatever my address, this is always home. Not
because family still lives here: because here are my dead.

There's not much to it, is there? Hardly more than can be
taken in at a glance. If this were Europe or South America, it
might seem exotic, a few hundred souls clustered together by the
river's bend. But this village was never poor enough or pretty
enough or sufficiently remote for the prophets of progress to pass
it by. It has suburbs now. And a quickie mart. And a video rental
store. All the conveniences, and only twenty minutes to the mall.

Oh, it's been here quite a while. Two hundred years, they
claim: a surprising boast from the offspring of the Scots and
Pennsylvania Dutch settlers who held verity so dear. In fact, the
land was virgin forest then, the village but a gleam in the eye of

an enterprising miller, if that. But it did thrive once, about a century ago: there were stores and half a dozen churches and even hotels where the stagecoach to London stopped.

When my mother's mother's people settled out on the 10th, this was Town. When the boys grew up and left the farm, this was where they headed. Where they built the planing mill that left them deaf. And where they finally took jobs in the carriage factory, painting gold and silver filigree, thin as half a dozen ermine hairs, on the sides of piano-box buggies, delivery wagons, and democrats. The carriage factory, which became Wallbanks' Spring Factory, and then The Buggy Works, a weekend antique market, where I found a wooden cheese box filled with inlaid ebony dominoes like the ones my grandfather played. Though I wanted them more than anything, I left them there, for they cost as much as two weeks' groceries for my young family, and that night the building burned to the ground: the hand-rubbed maple crokinole board, the ruby glass kerosene lamps, the cruets and rattan fern stands, all the frayed quilts and overpriced china figurines that schoolboys, now grandfathers, had won for their mothers at the fall fair, all of it turned to ashes, not even worth sifting through, though I tried, there on the corner, where those used cars are parked in rows.

Sometimes I try to see it, this village of mine, through the eyes of a stranger, a young man, perhaps, thinking to buy one of those bungalows lined up like Monopoly pieces in Scott's horse pasture, back behind where the brickyard used to be. Or maybe a middle-aged woman like myself, just passing through on a sunny afternoon drive, looking for quaint corners of Canadiana to frame in watercolour for living-room walls. There's one: Doctor Stephens's place, the stately red brick with the white pillars and the waving pines. Though the matching pair of houses planted on the front lawn ruins the effect, don't you think?

Alice Simonds

First day of school, age six

So much has been converted, made useful in that sensible Scots way. Like that apartment building kitty-corner from the doctor's. That's where I started school, P.S. 24. The row of windows on the right, that was Miss Goetz's class, Grades 1 and 2. I still see the splatter-painted maple leaves taped to the glass, someone's kitchen now.

Every fall I collected leaves at that corner, first for my mother, then my teachers, my sister after she left, mementoes for myself. I wonder why they cut that tree down. It bore the biggest darkest leaves you ever saw. Leaves the colour of carpet in a fine hotel; leaves the colour of dried blood.

I brought Karl here when I first started looking after him, all those after-school afternoons. We'd pick the most immense, magnificent leaves, and all the way home we'd play peek-a-boo, hiding behind those scarlet fans to squish our faces into goofy glares and grins, then whisking them aside, surprise! We never stopped the game, even when he was too old and I only babysat after dark, we still played it everywhere, the last night, too, as he held up his arms, his sweater caught around his ears, and I pulled it off, and there he was, cross-eyed, tongue lolling, and we fell to the floor laughing so hard I thought I'd.

Well.

You wouldn't believe it, how fragrant the village was then. That dry-leaf smell, with a faint whiff of stewing crab-apples and chili sauce drifting out from back kitchens, the air sharp with woodsmoke, an acid tinge of pig manure if the wind was blowing from the east, and, every so often, the stink from the sandpaper factory heating up glue. The closest farms have since been surveyed and paved, the wood furnaces converted to gas. Leaf-burning is banned, but the factory survives. A particular kind of industry gives the place its smell now.

I wish I could show you the village I first knew: English's General Store with barrels of apples on the verandah and inside, glass jars filled with cookies, a certain flat type with a crinkled top crusted in pale orange crystal sugar, a gingery chewy confection, the taste of which I've never again found. There were two general stores, a bank, post office, two hardware stores, an appliance shop, butcher shop, fire hall, lumberyard, feed mill, restaurants, hairdressers, even, I remember, a woman of easy virtue, it was said, who lived above one of the stores.

I still see it. The way it was, the way it is, all the stages I witnessed between and some I only imagine: a perpetual becoming. The buildings shape-shift as I pass, writhing through their metamorphoses, porches falling away, decks emerging, sheds collapsing, garages rising in their place, clapboard in succession a dozen different hues, the iron V-frame of the swings where I swung and then pushed Karl convoluting to this playground of arsenic-green wood.

Could we stop a moment? Please. The flickering forms, a trick of the light no doubt, it makes me feel quite unwell. I'll just close my eyes, if you don't mind, or maybe squint a little. I find it helps at such times to concentrate my attention on one particular thing.

That's better.

Do you see that house, the buff-coloured brick? My great-aunt and -uncle lived there. Every Saturday my mother, my sisters, and I, when I was old enough, would clean their house, and the houses of my grandparents and the other great-aunts and -uncles in the village. Alice and her girls, that's what they called us. The houses all smelled the same, of overheated stale breath and damp flour in rusting tins. My older sisters and my mother did the kitchens and the baths. I beat the rugs, mopped the floors under the beds, and dusted, my favourite job, raising the glass fronts of the Wernicke Elastic Bookcase (I read the label a thousand times), running the cloth over the olive green and burgundy spines: *Helen of the Old House*, *Pride and Prejudice*, *Mother's Remedies*. I did my work well, polishing the frets under the strings of my great-uncle's mandolin, wiping fingerprints from the piano keys, taking care not to bend the hands of the adamantine mantel clock. I lingered longest at my great-aunts' dressers, where I lifted one by one the French Ivory puff box, the nail polisher, hand mirror, and clothes whisk off the cutwork cloth, the narrow silver tray of amber and tortoise-shell side combs, the blown glass ball with the rose trapped inside, its slender stem hung with garnet and cameo rings. I rubbed Hawes' Lemon Oil into the dark wood, spread a freshly ironed cloth embroidered with ballerinas or baskets of pansies, then returned each cherished object, rubbed spotless, to its memorized place.

No one can renovate those houses. I fixed them in my memory with each brush of the dusting cloth. The Charge of the Light Brigade is etched in copper on my own cells; the painted metal woodpecker eternally tips toothpicks from its cast-log trough. The great-aunts and -uncles' houses, and newer ones, too: Karl's house up on the hill, past where the sidewalks stop, too modern to have changed much on the outside, but inside, the red cowboy bedspread snugged forever under his eight-year-old chin.

You don't see any of this. I apologize. I go on like an old crone, although my own children have barely come of age. I am not a very good guide, I'm afraid: I see what was and look past what's here. Though we walk side by side, we walk through different streets.

And how crowded they are! I try not to stare at the people who pass, but I always steal a glance, certain the features will be familiar. Was she the one Miss Goetz forced to clean up her own vomit from the floor? Was she that little friend of Karl's?

Or is she flesh and blood at all? For I see apparitions everywhere. There, on that lawn. A young woman, black hair sleek as mink and a long lovely body inside a simple shift, startlingly stylish, not from English's, certainly, nor made on a mother's sewing machine. He comes to her, the young man who lives in that house, the one who taught me to read, not words but the souls of books he brought to me as I babysat Karl in the house up the hill, and he slips his arm around her waist as if it were his own, and leads her up the stairs to his front door, his back to me, unseeing, but she turns at the last moment, watches me hurry past.

These phantoms triple, quintuple the population figure painted on the highway sign. They push through the wrought-iron gates into the park where the factory now stands, the men waiting with grain sacks, fragrant and freshly emptied for the race, children riding bicycles streaming gold and red crêpe. They stroll into town from the cemetery that overlooks the river, those great-aunts and -uncles and their friends who take up positions in other people's parlours, my own dear mother a spectre at the piano beside an old man with a violin. And I am everywhere among them, a toddler, a child, too, a teenager skating round and round the arena to all the old songs, "Now and Then There's a Fool"; "Walk on By." I wander down the main street watching two-tone Fairlanes cruise by, eating vinegar-soaked chips from bags split down the side; I wait outside the church door, by the row of black cars, pulling at the buttons on my short tight gloves. And I sit at the kitchen table in my own house there, watching my father walk briskly up the hill instead of turning down our street, though he does this too eventually, stamps his feet on the mat and stands in the doorway, explaining the keening of car brakes I'd heard.

I don't know how they bear it, the ones who never left. How they walk through streets so obstacled, past landscape that won't stay still. But perhaps they learn to make allowances, to ignore the shifting architecture, find ways to keep the ghosts at bay. Perhaps it is only those of us who try to leave and then come home who suffer.

This street? Yes, it continues up the hill. But really, I'd rather not. The walk through the village always wears me out. I don't do it every time I visit. Only once a year. And I never go up there, past where the sidewalk ends, where the chalk boy lies, Karl's silhouette in white on the grass.

ESTA SPALDING

Laka's Chant

~

Sister's Cry

1996. Picking salt on this island, *Moloka'i*. I have been fourteen years, half my life, away. Returned to my father. To my
brother.

We three – crouched on the rocks, ass on ankles – sweep palms
through sharp water, and scoop upwards, our hands massed
with salt shards, the slur and crash of waves, annealed into
diamond.

The towel is piled with salt – everything that can and cannot be
said. Everything the body is, titrated – those billions of years of
evolution – from the sea.

What my father is, how my father made us from the chorus of his
genetic chains – exchanged with the wailing, angular gestures of
the *hula* – is in our bent figures, the stinging skin scratched by
rock salt, and the lift upwards when the salt glints like a prayer
chanted to the sun.

What hard work walking the red dirt road to the shore, balancing, rock-by-rock, making our way to the tide pools. The lines of dried sweat like lace on my skin.

~

1982. An immigrant in Toronto. I pronounce Yonge Street *Yongee*. No interpretation for the laughter.

Frozen in June, I wear a hooded parka. Both invisible and garishly *out of place*. My voice softens. My sister and I are sent to dance lessons. Our customs declared, *Shy*.

~

1976. We camp at *Kamaka'ipo*. My father, descendant of missionaries, translates *Kamaka'ipo*, *Night Guardian*. So I know no matter how close my feet are to the high breaking wave, no matter which ghosts dance here, my sleep is safe.

~

Kamaka'ipo, cove where the road widens between the *kiawes*, the coral juts into sky. Where waves, trapped in the reef neck, swell the beach. *'Opihi* and *pipi'i* hooded in their hard shells nurse on volcanic rock. Overhead, vigilant stars.

~

The lesson: places are fixed through a name – to dig into the sand at *Kamaka'ipo* is to dig into its vocabulary. How else can I say this?

Who doesn't desire to string her own letters? As if the word place were a *lei* of brief *pikake* flowers and she could open the garland for a moment, thread new blossoms on the string, knot herself to that history. However tenuous.

∼

Each wave has a name. And yet each wave is no thing. Just a possible outcome of the tide, wind, geology.

When I ask my brother for the names of the waves he surfs around Oahu he says,

Brother's Cry

Wave Names

Rock Piles, Canoes, Queens, Uluwatus, No Place, Old Mans, Rice Bowls, Tongs, Winch, Radicals, Graveyards, Sleepy Hollows, Lighthouse, Halemanus, Cow Piss Corner, Hunakais, Bones, Tosh Kanes, Oki Choo Choo, Secrets, Toes, Snips, Blue Hole, Turtles, Kevorkians, Mental Oafs, Makapu'u, Cockroach Bay, Magnums, No Can Tells, Black Outs, Way the Fucks, Pyramid Rock, Sugar Mills, Crouching Lion, Pounders, Bong Water Reef, Revelations, Velzyland, Sunset Point, Pupukea, Pipeline, Rubber Duckies, Waimea, The Pouch, Alligator Rock, Himalayas, Icons, Speed Reef, Silver Channel, Yokohamas, Pray for Sex, Makuas, Free Hawai'i, Makaha, Green Lantern, Sewers, Maile Point, Point Panic, Bomburros

∼

Sister's Cry

Are there apostrophes?

The names speak of possession. His and another's: sometimes a bone or a mountain, sometimes a song, a drug, or the old Japanese man called Tosh Kane.

So I always say *Yon-gee* because I can now. I am half my life in Canada. Half my life away from my brother and father. I belong to two places. Once torn or twice blessed?

~

1996. I ask John Kaimikaua, a *kumu hula*, what *Kamaka'ipo* means. *Sweet Place*, he says.

The names mean what I need them to mean.

~

Ka'ana, ka hula piko.
Ka'ana, birthplace of *hula*.

The word for birth place, *piko*, navel –
a child's *piko* is buried under a stone,
every birth digs a fresh hole.

~

1300s. At *Ka'ana*, Laka learned the *hula* from her sister. A dance for life. Laka's brother mastered the *lua*, death dance.

∽

He moved below *Ka'ana* to a plateau between that mountain and the sea. Students arrived on the waves, then climbed towards *Ka'ana* carrying gifts: *taro*, coconut, baskets of *'opihi*, dried fish.

No matter how fierce the wind, her brother called to Laka telling of the visitors. The hill conducted his voice to her ear.

Chanting born between sister and brother. Life and Death. Carved by the island's slope that smells of crushed grass.

∽

John can chant the human path that knowledge took arriving from Laka's mouth to his lips. A thousand-line song.

∽

Chants arrive from deep in the earth, erupting out of wounds between continental plates. Volcanic, they pour new rock onto old. Widening each island's edge, as a blossom opens in heat. Giving birth to new islands as if stringing these stone blossoms in *leis*.

One chant sings of the *lehua* flower, a form the goddess *Pele* takes. Red tassels burst from branches of the tree first to grow on charred earth of lava fields.

The names of Gods, humans, animals, and plants are woven into a net fine enough to strain the Pacific.

Salt chants, blood swept through the heart.

∼

As children we changed the chants so we could hear our own names in them. We called back and forth, swinging higher, pumping our legs in and out. Brother and sisters holding hands between the steel chains, urging our swings into harmony.

∼

We said the words as we heard them.

Now when I ask John what *ahina ikawehiwehi* means he says, *Nothing. That's not Hawaiian.*

∼

1982. Most confident at the cemetery, Mount Pleasant, I hear it as a command. Typically Canadian. Where is the mountain it speaks of? A gradual rise from the harbour up the slope of the absent lake, *Iroquois*. A rise from Queen to St. Clair.

The cemetery speaks the names of ancestors with such authority. None of these names is mine, but their consonants are more familiar than Hawai'i's staccato vowels. It's true, then: in Hawai'i I am foreign.

When I discover her ravines, her rivers, Toronto begins to sing. Here are the signals, transactions of original stories. Buried history erupts from them. And complicity.

~

1976. My father taps stones together and chants the names. He will walk a ridge, returning the story to the land.

My father finds things. The gods lead him there. He has no compass but his voice, the songs that have been taught to him. These earned belongings.

(What he has tried to shed of his colonialness always drags its tail in the grass.)

He finds *heiaus*, home sites, sacred stones. He finds sources for the names in the chants. And burials – pulling back the rock to reveal a paper body, its stones, calabash. A body named in his song?

At night, by lantern eye, he maps these sites and those things we have found with *our* songs: deer antlers, gun casings, adze heads, *ulumaika*, once a case of dynamite.

~

Submerged altars shaped like weirs lace *Moloka'i's* edge. They praise the sea while trapping fish. I don't trust the mapmaker because the altars are missing from his map. Because he says which edge is North and which South instead of which is *mauka*, towards the mountains, and which *makai*, towards the sea.

Are my father's X's a swarm of insects, a snowflake blizzard on a tropical map? Or are they an X-ray showing secrets the mapmaker couldn't hear, *Moloka'i's* bones?

∿

1996. Three A.M. My brother and I drive the long artery to *Ka'ana, piko.*

Wearing coats thick as parkas, passing a thermos of sweet coffee back and forth, we hike the last miles. With the dawn, the wind comes too, stinging our eyes – so we walk with our backs to the wind, our faces pointed at the night.

If we uncover Laka's grave, crawl inside, will we be home?

∿

Perhaps Laka didn't die at *Ka'ana.*

She emigrated. Danced on other island chains. Taught the chant as far as St. Clair Avenue, found another hill that might carry her voice to her brother.

Beside an absent sea, under night's salt eyes, no strange wind mocked her cry.

for Sage Cooke Spalding

Providence. And Independence.

~

When you drown, they say, your life passes through you in moments. But what about fire? What about air? My brother and I had the same source; I always thought we were two pieces of one thing. His solidity, my flightiness. His yang, my yin. I, of the two of us, was prodigal, although who would have predicted this, looking at the taciturn young girl and the handsome, wild man?

I begin with Providence because that is the last place we were together, and being there together was a return to an earlier journey we made with our parents. I went to Brown to teach for a semester and my brother came to see me there and later our mother came and my brother's children and we all went to the outer reaches of Providence to see the house where we had lived for a short time during the war, when our father was training to be an Air Combat Intelligence Officer at Quonset Point. The house was not at the Navy base, because our parents had wanted privacy. Even now, as we drove by it, Mother gestured at the base with disdain. "Imagine," she said, "living there!"

Instead, our father rode for an hour on a train each way, although it isn't far by our standards now. The train ran along the rocky shore, everyone looking out, perhaps even leaning out to look for ships and planes, the shore and its outlines taking on a new intensity. Our father, in particular, had to know the shapes of airplanes at a great distance. This was his assignment. A brief glimpse, a flash in the eye. Enemy or ally. Type, size, purpose, capacity. Earlier, when he'd arrived alone for his duties, he had described this to Skip in a letter, saying nothing to his son that the military could find irregular. He was going to plan missions over Indochina. He was going to be stationed in the Philippines, although he didn't know that yet.

Mother drove from Kansas to Providence with my brother and me because our father was already there. All the paraphernalia, all the worry about gasoline and ice on the roads. Her hat box taking up too much room in the car but essential. The ten-year-old boy and the dog and the baby. An attendant at a service station looking at me in my car crib and shaking his head. He was sorry about my condition, he said, and my mother asked him what he meant by that. Heart condition, he reported sadly, pointing to the dark moons under my eyes. The first evidence that I should not have survived my brother.

But there was a house waiting for us in Providence and Mother put her worries aside and drove on boldly across the weather-beaten continent. She was a beautiful woman. She was on a mission. She loved our father and Roosevelt in that order and she had no doubts about taking two children across the country in wartime in order to serve both of them.

Our father was thirty-three years old. I don't know whether his reactions to the war and his own enlistment were complicated or straightforward. Mother says it would not have occurred to him to stay put. The men who did that were not men you would want to know, she says. And I was a "war baby," she contends. "We had you for the reason a lot of people had babies around then – something to look forward to, something to show faith."

I was born when my brother's character was already formed; his habits of thought were already in place. He and my mother and father were already a family with a history and customs and private jokes. They were a unit that was impregnable, into which I never fit. They had had two dogs and four different dwelling places by then, settling at last in a bungalow in Highland Park, in Shawnee County, in Kansas. The dog of that time was named Powder. She'd landed in our father's lap when he was surveying an artillery range for the Army in an open jeep. He drove back home with the terrified creature in his arms and my mother, who had longed for a real collie, could never entirely forgive this mongrel for its wild, gun-shy, upstart ways. A year later or a little less, I arrived as well. Skip told me, the last time I saw him, that he never bore me any grudge. "You took a load off me," he said, although parental attention wavered back and forth between us over the years. I got the strongest beam of it when I was around, but I was the wanderer, the prodigal, wild and gun-shy. I don't know if it ever evened out. What I know is that I misunderstood everything up until Providence.

My mother's mother said things like that. *Up until.* I like to say I come from peasants, but there are no peasants in America. Where I come from you get educated or you don't, and that's the only difference that counts. Mother worried when she met Father because he wore his hat in the middle of his head. He wasn't sophisticated. She was a Kansas City girl and he was a country boy. He'd grown up on a patch of land with three brothers and each of them had dug a lake instead of planting corn or wheat. It was the water, in that dry corner of the midwest, that supported the family, since people paid good money to come out to the property and camp and fish. But our father was going to be a lawyer like his father before him. While the boys cut ice from the lakes every winter to store in icehouses and sell in the hot summertime, Granddaddy Dickinson took a bus all the way into Kansas City every day to practise law. He charged money for the privilege of fishing in the lakes and he grew a good crop of hemp and milked his own cows every dawn before he got on the bus, but defending the rights of people who needed help was the occupation of his heart.

Father called Mother Dythe, not Edith. She was a beautiful, willowy girl when he met her at Kansas City Junior College, her hair in waves along the sides of her face and pulled into a chignon. Her mother made all her clothes on a treadle sewing machine and they were stylish, vampish. It was 1930. Mother wanted to be a dancer but Katie wouldn't hear of such a thing. The theatre, she called it. Instead Mother got skinny dresses and plenty of beaus.

This grandmother was called Katie by everyone, as if she had no right to a title. I remember how surprised my friends were when I called her this, or when Mother did, but it wasn't a name, it was a significance. Grandmother seemed too general, as if it applied to every old woman around. Katie was a widow, but I never thought of her that way. She was alone. Another significance. In all my born days, until I went away to college, I knew only four grown-up single women. There was something unique about each of them; with Katie it was physical. She was deaf.

My brother was called Skip because, in a moment of prophecy, a nurse placing him in Mother's arms for the first time said, "Here's your little skipper." As a child, he was devoted to Mother's brother Bill, who wore a leather jacket and a cap with flaps and managed, against the usual odds, to become an Air Force pilot right at the start of the Second World War. But who knows which of them inspired the other? Skip had always wanted to fly. When he was three or four years old, Mother looked out the window in time to see him propel himself off the porch rail in a noose. It wasn't suicide. It was his first flight.

Uncle Bill tested airplanes in California and taught other boys to fly them and one day he turned the controls over to a student who made the kind of mistake that is fatal in airplanes. Both of them were killed. Katie received several medals from the government. Skip was nine years old at the time. (How do children react to such loss?) And Mother was shattered. She hadn't decided how much her brother mattered to her and he was already dead. She sat by the pool at the modest country club my parents had joined so that Skip could learn to swim. She watched her son dive off the high board and thought about her brother and retreated into a private part of herself that none of us has any access to. Her father had died suddenly and now her brother's plane had gone down. I wasn't yet born, but it was all going to be repeated exactly in my own life.

When I look back on my childhood, there is a lot of Katie in it and not much of Skip. But that can't be right. Katie lived in another town altogether. She lived in Kansas City, clear across the state line. We didn't even talk to her on the phone. My mother wrote letters, typed, and Katie wrote back, longhand – a terrible scrawl. She put quotation marks and parentheses around everything. I can see it still. And that scrawl, as if she were writing in haste, actually betrayed a very hurried education. Her own parents had divorced and she'd been sent to a convent school and then married at sixteen.

Katie was my mother's mother. My father's mother was Grandmother Dickinson and that was different. There was the education, the upbringing, the settled, respectable past. I never knew her; she died during the war. But Skip spent a big part of his childhood at the lakes with Grandmother and Grand-daddy Dickinson. Summers. The house spartan, Grandmother Dickinson using a woodstove, our grandfather in his white beard looking like God.

The Lakes. It should be capitalized: a place experienced by every-one but me. I was too late. It is part of the "unfitness" of my life that I missed the central location of family life along with most of the stories of the four wild brothers, whose escapades kept dinners at the grandparental table lively for thirty years. Grandmother died when Skip was twelve and Granddaddy lin-gered on but it didn't matter; it was over. I remember a house-keeper named Mrs. Munroe who was opposed to wine. My grandparents were good Baptists, but Mrs. Munroe was something else. She spoke in tongues and disapproved of everything – even the spartan joys of Granddaddy's last years. She must have worn a housedress and a tiny bun. That's how I see her. And black, tie shoes. She was no replacement for the diminutive grandmother whose erudition and quick wit and temper were her legacies. The mother of four sons who died while one of them was being picked up at the train station on his way home from the war.

Each of these people deserves remembering, but who am I to remember the dead? They surround me. They precede me. The Dead. The last time Skip visited us here, in Toronto, we rented the John Huston movie and made him sit through it, which he did politely while I slept on the couch beside him, hating it even in my dreams. He'd wanted to watch the one about wolves, assuring me that it wasn't sad. But he was too sleepy, after watching our choice, to stay up for his. He had to get up early to get his plane off the ground. So I watched the one about wolves and it wasn't sad but I missed having him next to me and I wished we had let him have it his way. I think of these small, stupid cruelties, these little competitions in taste, and I want to give him everything. The things I have done and left undone, the gifts ignored, unused, unremarked, the attention that strayed off course.

When Katie was dying in her own slow fashion, none of us could follow her. It was only a matter of going part of the way . . . along the track of her mind, which wandered in and out of our reality. I was living in Hawaii then, although I came home at least once and was taken out to the nursing home to visit her – an experience that resulted in one of my first, short, unfinished stories. I was captivated by the fact that, even though senile, she had tried to escape. In fact she'd succeeded. She'd climbed over the locked half-door of her room and glided out into the orchard that surrounded the nursing home. So much do we hate, in my family, being bound to anything!

And Skip went with her. He sat by her bed in that place and listened to her describe the river she was not yet ready to cross.

He *listened*. He was already familiar with death. He'd already invented The Good News Bad News Church of Everlasting Life, which was a new-age version of the old food chain. He gave the chicken human incorporation by swallowing it. He swallowed everything. He went into the ocean and into the air. He loved motorcycles, boats, skis, planes. He was out there on the river with our dying grandmother riding rapids, the way, as a small boy, he had tried to fly away.

In high school, Skip bought a Model T. One day he told me to climb in while he went around to the front to crank it up. When it took off, suddenly hurtling down the street, he chased it down, while I sat quietly in the passenger seat, waiting to be saved. I see him running along beside me, the street visible between the floor-boards, the car swaying and tipping, rounding corners precari-ously. Or maybe I only wanted to be inside. I watched him with such passion. When he was away from home, I used to go down to the laundry room in the basement and try on his clothes. I walked around in his jeans. His shirts and sailor caps. I put them on like a better, male skin.

Later, he had a motor scooter hidden in a neighbour's garage and drove it around secretly, hoping that our parents, who had forbidden its use on the grounds of danger and unrespectability, wouldn't catch him. (When they insisted that he wear a wool suit to church, he kept his pyjamas on underneath.) In college he bought an enormous sailboat, a C scow that had to be transported up and down the continent. A boat with wings.

When he got married the first time, at the age of twenty, he travelled west to the wedding by river, in an inner tube. Later, with Mary, it was a Harley. Sea kayaks. Canoes. Scuba dives. And the first plane.

He was a pacifist. He joined the Coast Guard so he wouldn't have to take up arms. He became a Quaker, too. But it was his ship that was sent out to arrest the Quaker captain of the *Golden Rule* who had sailed into the atomic testing range to protest the use of atomic weapons. Torn between two lovers Skip must have been, for we are a legal family and we play, always, by the rules. I suppose towing the Quaker ship back to land was all part of the Good News Bad News Church of Everlasting Life, things operating as they were meant to operate. I suppose that's what he must have felt. I remember asking him, but I can't remember what he said. The heart is often pitted against itself.

When the salmon travels upstream, its face changes. The jawline juts forward. The nose sharpens. The eyes and cheeks realign themselves so that the fish, on reaching its source, is transformed.

I only wanted the male life, the male body.

I only wanted him.

To keep up, I spent my summers in a Quaker camp in Iowa. While my friends went to Wisconsin or the Ozarks and learned to paddle canoes, I watched movies about atomic bombs and held hands with a boy or two while everyone sang "The Ash Grove" after dinner. When the Coast Guard sent Skip and Ruth to Honolulu, I went on an airplane to spend the summer with them. I was fifteen and Hawaii was not yet a state. We lived only two blocks away from my future mother-in-law's apartment but there were no highrises in 1958. There was only our squalid apartment block with its giant cockroaches and a Chinese graveyard at the end of the street. Skip and Ruth had a baby by then, but that didn't interest me. I was interested in the sailors with their buttoned pants, in the local boys without socks, and in my brother, who told me boys never mean what they tell you.

I was interested in Patrick Ko, Irish-Hawaiian, who gave me a ring decorated with the sacred heart of Jesus. And told me it had been his mother's.

And I kept it. In spite of Skip's warning. In spite of the fact that it turned my third finger green.

Skip and Ruth moved to Oklahoma, where he studied architecture with Bruce Goff. I went back to Kansas. But I didn't stay. Not after Patrick Ko, who'd led me into the waves at Waikiki. I took train rides down to visit my brother and once kissed a sailor in the dome car. Before long, I married a boy from Hawaii. Then I spent fourteen years on those islands where I had once lived with Skip.

When the plane crashed, all of us changed shape. We didn't know how to speak to the new faces around us. Son, daughters, mother, sister, former wife. Skip had lived in Kansas, going up and down, up and down the river of air over our continent while the rest of us fanned out. When he and Ruth divorced, he found his high-school sweetheart. She'd grown up two doors away from the house where Mother lives now, which is not such a big coincidence in a small town. Her parents are buried a few feet from my father, although they weren't friends. And now they'll all lie there together as if there's anything resolved in soil. They'll lie there. If what we put in the ground were the ashes of Skip and Mary.

Who can believe in such a death?

Three months after they disappeared, I was in Kansas with Mother, and my daughter flew out to visit us. We drove to the airport in Kansas City to meet her. It was September already, the fall of the year, and we took her to lunch somewhere and then talked about what to do with the rest of the afternoon. Mother and I usually go to outlet stores when we're in Kansas City, but for some reason I suddenly suggested something I'd been wanting to do for years. Something I had wanted to do with Skip. And I knew it might be too late, that I might have waited too long to press my claim, but I pressed it anyway. I said, "Let's drive out to the Lakes."

Mother looked stunned.

I said, "We could go home by the old road. I haven't been out there since I was a baby. I'd really like to see what it looked like." I knew it was a dangerous idea. I knew I shouldn't force Mother, so soon after Skip's death, to confront a site where so much had been vouchsafed the three of them, my mother, my father, and my brother. But I persisted. "You should show the place to us."

"Take Independence Road," she said quietly, looking not at me but straight ahead. "The house is gone. You know that, don't you?"

"Sure I know."

The heat that covered us as we drove was predictable. What else could rise from that river of stories that had connected three generations of Dickinsons? Waves of it rose off the asphalt around us as we passed the evidence of American industry – Burger Kings and Dairy Queens and insurance companies – an endless chain of buildings meant to stand twenty years, no more, some of them already having served that purpose. The air-conditioning in the car matched the unreality around us, a mirage of modernity that covered something older, more basic, something as hard and unhurried as the weather. We drove for half an hour or so, full of our lunch and our various purposes. Mine was simply to win back the dead. I can't speak for my mother and daughter. The two-lane highway and the metallic and glass surfaces surrounding it reflected all of us in a vaporous haze. My mother shut her eyes. "This is Independence," she said after a while.

"Truman lived across the road from Granddaddy," I said.

Mother's eyes snapped open. "Where'd you get that idea?"

"That's what you always said. You and Daddy. I've told people that a million times." I had a clear picture of my grandfather waving to Harry and Bess as he walked by their front porch on his way to catch the bus into town.

"Nonsense. They weren't out there and the Dickinsons didn't know them."

"But. . . ." I felt I could no longer trust my mother. She was changing the stories. "He was Granddaddy's friend."

"They never met."

"We must be getting there; here's Dickinson Road."

"There won't be anything to see."

"The Lakes. We can see the Lakes. I remember right where they were, not too far from the porch." Skip had told me that when he was sick in the hospital several years ago, unable to speak or move as the result of Guillain-Barré, he'd kept himself alive by moving through the rooms of the old house inch by inch. He'd made himself remember the minutest details. Doorknobs. Window shades. Ornaments. But the house was gone, the property long ago converted to a park. Swimming pool, closed for the season, bounded in a chain-link fence and connected to a barracks-like changing room whose musty interior I could imagine from as far away as the parking lot.

So my daughter and I climb out of the car, promising to be back within minutes. "I just want to show her one of the lakes," I said, although my purposes, as I've said, were stranger than that and harder to explain. All summer, after the crash, I'd heard the thrumming of a small plane overhead. I knew Skip and Mary were present, but they were unavailable even so. We hadn't even put their ashes in the ground because we had not received them. There was no explanation for the crash and no evidence that it

316

had occurred. We had been shown certificates. But there is more to death than that. Who knows what the source of a child's amazement is at the end of a noose?

We cast long shadows on the ground, but unbelievably, unbearably, the ground threw everything back at us. We were assaulted by heat so intense that our bodies sagged and our lungs hurt. There were bushes ahead crackling and humming in the dense, muggy air. "This way!" I shouted. "Over here!" We were taken in. Incorporated in a vegetation that belonged to our ancestors. There was a chimney ahead. Grey stone covered with weeds. I pushed further, deeper, brushing wings and sounds off my arms and neck and face, wet now and dizzy and blind in the green. I couldn't see but I had to keep moving if I wanted to find the water. Poor Mother couldn't stand this kind of heat. She hated it. Air-conditioning was a necessity to her but she was back there in the open car, surrounded by the old past and her new grief. Dying to be gone. . . . "Mother!" I turned around, pushed against leaves. She shouldn't be up there alone. What was I thinking of? I wasn't used to looking after her. Skip always did that, staying close to her over the years like a good son and guardian. I'd never been the one to live nearby or deal with her. I had my own life. I lived in Canada, for Christ's sake. I couldn't even find my way back to her. I didn't know the lay of this land. I didn't know what the door-knobs had looked like or what the salt shakers had looked like or where the root cellar had been.

I climbed back to a place where the light was hotter and brighter. I got out of the bushes and back on the dusty grass. I found the parking lot and saw the car, both of its front doors open and a pickup truck parked next to it. "Mother!" I shouted again, to let her know I was back, looking after her. I'd given up my quest. I couldn't find the lakes alone and there was no one to guide me. What I had instead was a mother who should be sitting in a mall drinking iced tea. The truck worried me. I had left my mother sitting alone in a parking lot in what was clearly a backwater. A time warp. The truck had not been there when we arrived. And it was empty.

So was Mother's car.

Someone had dragged her down to the woods. It was impossible not to imagine this new horror and the new, shocked disbelief of the family. First Skip and Mary disappear in thin air and now this! "You took her out there and left her alone?"

I must have been yelling.

"Mother! Mother!"

Then I realized it was my child. Yelling at me. It seemed odd. That I should be a mother when I was so unready. That I should be anything but a girl looking for her big brother in the woods.

"Where's Grandmother?"

"I don't know!"

"Criminy! You go look over there, past the pool. I'll go back down to the woods!"

We wandered back and forth. There was a set of swings, motionless, empty. A walnut tree, my father's favourite kind. Motionless. Empty. The changing room. Locked. The swimming pool. Bare. And the great buzzing swallowing vegetation that had eaten up our past.

We were drenched, too. Although we hadn't found a drop of water, we had manufactured plenty of it. We searched the park around the swings and pool and the edge of the bush, stabbing at branches blindly, calling out in sharp, frightened voices: Mother! Grandmother!

Then suddenly she stood in front of us. "I think it was right here," she said. "The kitchen door. They didn't put the bathroom in until Granddaddy got sick, but it was over there. Your grandmother used an outside pump her whole life. And she never got around to hanging drapes. She gave up on things. Carpets. Nice furnishings. They didn't have to have bare floors but she never liked this place. That's my theory. Granddaddy's parents built it to be close to the Latter-day Saints. Because they'd lost a child and they thought they could get in contact with him again. With his spirit, at least. Did you find a lake?"

"No. Nothing."

"They dried up then. Or got drained."

"I found a chimney."

"Those were for campers. So they could cook their fish."

"Not for the house?"

"They had no fireplace!"

"Shall we go on back? Get some iced tea someplace?"

"Whenever you're ready. It's too bad there's nothing left to see."

So we began in Providence and ended in the same place. As a family. The last time I saw my brother he taught me how to cut flowers diagonally, holding the stems under cold running water. We had driven out to Walden Pond, where we sat in the car and argued about the merits of tomato sauce and talked about my life in Canada and whether it was working out. We'd gone to a fruit market and bought bags full of good things to eat and I had thought: This is something my people do. We buy food and carry it around with us wherever we are. But I was surprised by the flowers. They were for his daughter and they were as beautiful and impractical as the fruit was edible and ripe. After he washed the peaches and apricots and plums, he unwrapped the flowers very carefully and turned the cold water on full force. Then, gently, deftly, he sliced through the green stems as if they held blood and he was unwilling to spill any of it. As if they were slender green fish and he was carrying them from a pond to a better, cleaner place. As if air is the danger. Maybe the flowers were not part of the good news or the bad news but outside all that. The flowers were beautiful and they had been cut for us. Only the good die young, our mother used to say. But it's easier to be good before things happen to you. Change. There is no life without that. The trouble with death is its innocence. It goes on forever, forever changeless. The hard part of life is to keep moving. And Independence. Even in borrowed clothes. To find how empty it is.

JOHN STEFFLER

Explosion

~

German Mills, Ontario

I have two homes: one – otherwise vanished – which I carry in my imagination like a much-folded, taped-together map, and another which surrounds me as I write, which I'm in the process of inhabiting, which is still foreign, still rich with mysteries after twenty-two years moving in.

My first home was a broken-down farm that my parents bought in 1948, a couple of years after my father got back from serving with the Canadian Army in Europe. It was at the southern end of

Markham Township north of Toronto. We had horses and chickens and a large vegetable garden, but for a living we relied on my father's job at a factory in Scarborough.

The farm had been a large, prosperous concern in the nineteenth century, with three barns, a cookhouse, and various outbuildings in addition to the main house, but it had long been in decline when my parents bought it. For the last few years before we moved in, the house had been vacant; squirrels and raccoons were living in its walls. My father tore down the collapsing barns and sheds, salvaging only half of one of the dairy barns and the concrete milk-house.

Like most people, I developed a strong attachment to my first home. The attachment, in my case, was very much to the physical place. This was partly because the farm was fairly isolated and fairly primitive. Our lane out to the highway, where the nearest neighbour lived, was half a mile long. In the winter, when the lane was full of snow, we left the car at the highway and pulled our groceries back to the house on a sled. We got our drinking water from a hand-pumped well and used rain water from a cistern for washing. Because of our plumbing arrangements I usually chose to piss outside under the Manitoba maple tree. In this way I got to know the stars and moon very well. We had crickets chirping in the heating ducts during the winter, toads in the earth-floored cellar; and every year noisy chimney swifts would make their nest in a disused chimney in the wall of my bedroom.

But it wasn't just the removal from urban life and the exposure to nature that drove this first home so deep into my psyche. It was also my own isolation as a child. My sister was already going to school before I was a year old. There were no other children to play with. My father was away at work; my mother was busy with

Bones, machine parts,
broken plates, summer 1949

housework and sewing. I wandered around outdoors with a dog and adopted a dog-like point of view. Plants, trees, rocks, and the weather became my companions.

The objects which attracted my interest the most were the ones that carried some of the farm's past, that revealed bits of the lives which had already been lived there, which I somehow felt were all around me embedded in the place. Foundation beams and grassy mounds showed the outlines of vanished barns. Old ploughs, old buggies and sleighs lay in pieces, entangled in weeds. In the driest weeks of the summer, the grass would yellow over the outline of the cookhouse's huge hearth. Brittle black leather harness was apt to turn up anywhere: under rotted grain on the barn floor, under the woodpile, under a flower bed my mother was making. The garden constantly yielded brass harness fittings, horseshoes, old coins, once a brass trigger-guard, a flint spear point, a stone scraper, an arrowhead. The place's human past clearly went back beyond the farm.

I took an interest in digging. I collected fragments of china-ware and tarnished glass, machine parts, buckles, Indian flints. I tried to imagine the pasts these remnants belonged to. The life of the farm – which of course was the most recent, most accessible layer of the past – seemed to me fraught with contrasts. It was vig-orous, like the natural world it was situated in, loud with red-winged blackbirds and sunlight, full of the satisfactions of physical work and big meals. But it also seemed to me to have been dark and brutal. The rusted scythes, forks, hay-knives, the rings and hooks on the barn's timbers, the black harness, the broken black buggies and horsehair chairs – so much was black – seemed either funereal or designed to torture and dominate living things. This impression was reinforced by the nineteenth-century farming manuals that were left in the house. Their black steel engravings of grotesquely diseased horses and stiff-looking people wielding lancets or whips helped to convince me that we were emerging from an era of torment and dread.

And this is where my account of home gets complex and inter-esting, because on the one hand I thought of this vigorous black past as my own past; its secrecies and oppressions and horrors seemed to be part of my own family's legacy – in digging and uncovering things on the farm I was discovering myself, learning my family's character – but at the same time I was always aware, subliminally at least, that where I grew up did not really belong to my family and that my future there was limited.

For one thing, I absorbed my parents' sense of being newcom-ers. The farm was in an area that had been occupied by the same

families for generations. My parents did not feel completely
accepted by these families and continued to think of Elmira,
where they'd grown up and where many of our relatives lived, as
home. The things I dug up, I think, spoke to them only of the
lives of strangers. This would have been different, I suspect, if the
farm had been in Waterloo County, if it had once been a
Mennonite farm or Pennsylvania Dutch. As it was, the first layer
beneath us, that of the Feeneys, seemed to them too Irish, too
profligate: this was the layer of the final degeneracy, the era of the
shotgun holes in the stairwell, the moonshine equipment. Below
that layer, the layers of the Cherrys and Johnsons may have
seemed too Anglo Upper Canadian. To my parents the farm did
not smell of family the way it did to me. I wanted to stay there
forever, getting to know its past, aging along with my surround-
ings in an ideal slow-changing world. But as I got older it became
obvious that this wouldn't be possible.

The main obstacle was the looming presence of Toronto,
which in the 1950s and '60s had begun sprawling in all directions.
Markham Township, eager to welcome the expansion, rezoned its
southwestern region from agricultural to industrial. To attract
businesses, the township's planners published a brochure that fea-
tured an aerial photograph of the area – our house and barn were
clearly recognizable in the centre of it – with a network of super-
highways, overpasses, and rail lines artistically superimposed on
the plain rural landscape.

Obscure superior powers had decided our future. Water and
sewer lines were laid along the highway, new roads cut through
the fields. Taxes shot up, all the neighbours were selling out.
Apartment and office towers had been marching north from
Don Mills for several years. I had watched their distant advance,
sun glinting on their walls, as I waited for the school bus each

morning on a hilltop on German Mills Road. Suddenly bulldozers and earth-moving machines were all around us, levelling hills, changing the course of the brook that flowed under our lane. My parents sold out and moved to a place not far from where they'd grown up. Factories replaced the farm; the old landscape was gone. I worked and travelled, went to university and got married, and, when my wife and I finally settled down, the place we chose was Newfoundland.

This was partly a reactive choice. Newfoundland had a distinct culture and history of its own; it felt like the farthest you could get from Toronto within Canada. It was poor instead of prosperous, rocky rather than fertile, woodsy and thinly populated instead of suburban, dominated by weather not commerce. It seemed old-fashioned and slow-changing. Maybe it reminded me of the way the world had seemed when I was very young.

But in spite of my fundamental affinity for the place, Newfoundland still feels in some ways like a foreign country. Strangers here continue to ask me where my home is, meaning where I'm from. My voice marks me as an outsider. But even more than the society, it's the landscape, the climate, the physical character of the place I struggle to understand and come to terms with. In Ontario it was possible to believe that the human spirit might find fulfilment within the order of the natural world. In Newfoundland that idea seems like a delusion: so much is cold, hard, prickly, wet. I find the island beautiful but alien – sometimes dangerous, frightening.

The force of the urban explosion that threw me out of southern Ontario is not spent. I'm still in motion. At times I've felt like an exile in my own country, regretting the loss of roots. At times I've thought the ideal thing would be to embrace homelessness as a cultural position. But I go on looking for home. For me the very act of writing is a making of home, a familiarization, a location of self. Home is a blending of self and place I constantly need to recreate. It's an ongoing effort to solve a mystery, to understand the strangeness I live in.

~

30 June 1996: In the Blomidon Mountains, Newfoundland

I was sitting on my pack in the shade of a small aspen near the derelict Scout camp at the foot of the Blomidons. Farther down to the north the water of Humber Arm was invitingly wind-ruffled and blue. I had taken my boots off to let my feet cool and was eating a melted chocolate bar with one hand, defending myself against blackflies with the other. It was just after five in the afternoon and hotter here at the base of the mountain than it had been on top, and the flies were worse. Russell's dog, Lennox, a huge thick-furred malamute, lay beside me looking exhausted and unhappy, drops of blood from fly bites on his nose. Russell's pack and Ellen's pack lay nearby in the dust at the edge of the parking lot.

What could have gone wrong?

Six of us had hiked up into the Blomidons early the day before by way of the Copper Mine trail about ten kilometres to the west. We had made our camp by Blomidon Brook in the tablelands and had gone on to explore Simms Gorge in the afternoon. On the morning of the second day, half the group – Ellen's father, Harold, her husband, Ken, and their thirteen-year-old son, Mark – had decided to head back early by the same way we'd come in. This was a difficult unmarked route from the top of the Copper Mine trail, among nondescript hills, through steep valleys and matted black spruce thickets. But Harold knew the area and had topographical maps with him.

Ellen, Russell, and I had chosen to stay in the high boulder-strewn tablelands for the rest of that day, hiking to Round Hill, watching caribou. We had decided to make our return trip by a more open route, past Mad Dog Lake and down the cliffs and scree to the old Scout camp. On their way back into town, Harold or Ken was supposed to have driven Russell's car from the base of the Copper Mine trail to the Scout camp and left it for us to pick up. But when we'd reached the Scout camp, Russell's car wasn't there.

Maybe they'd lost the keys. Maybe the battery was dead. They had set out at 8:00 in the morning; they should have got down to the cars by 1:00 P.M. at the latest.

A pickup truck pulled off the road into the gravel lot in front of me. A stocky, rugged-looking man in rubber boots, jogging pants, and T-shirt got out and came toward me. He said he'd come to pick me up and that Ellen was waiting at his neighbour's cabin. I asked if both cars were still at the Copper Mine trail. He said they were. So Harold, Ken, and Mark were still in the woods. Someone must have got hurt. Maybe Harold's heart; he was seventy-two years old. Unlikely they'd be lost.

I threw the packs in the back of the truck and tried to get Lennox to jump in. He wouldn't. I wrapped my arms around him, a heavy, smelly, barrel-chested dog, and hoisted him onto the tailgate, but he jumped back down. "Do you mind if he rides in the cab with us?" I asked. "Not at all." I opened the door and Lennox jumped up and sat on the seat, nervous but willing. The man and I now introduced ourselves. "Frank," he said. We leaned forward and shook hands across Lennox's chest, and I thanked him for his help. "Anything we can do," he said.

When Russell and Ellen had found the cars were still where we'd left them, they had gone to the closest cabins to phone the RCMP. This is how they'd met Frank and Grace and their neighbours, Henry and Lorraine. None of the cabins along the coast had phones; so Henry had taken Russell to York Harbour to call from the store, and Frank had come to get me. Ellen was waiting at Lorraine's.

Lorraine opened the door when Lennox and I arrived. "Come in, come in," she said. "Don't take off your boots, it's only a cabin." She saw that Lennox was thirsty and set a china bowl of water on the deck by the door. Would I like ginger ale or beer? she asked. I wanted beer but thought I'd probably need to stay sober and active, with the police on their way and everything. "Ginger ale," I said. She gave me a tall glass of it with ice. One sip told me she'd also added a generous shot of rye.

"I knows what you're goin through," she said, lighting a cigarette, sipping her drink. "My own son was lost in the woods three nights last October, and it was the worst time of my life I can tell you, and the police were no use, kept askin me questions like did he have friends in Toronto, did he have any reason to run off. I said he hasn't run off, he's in the *woods!* But instead of goin and findin him, all they wanted to do was ask me questions."

She described what her son had gone through. He'd been hunting, and he didn't have a sleeping bag or matches. "Now, if he smoked, see, he would of had a lighter." But he didn't smoke. He survived by covering himself with garbage bags to stay dry, sleeping during the day when it was warmest and walking at night to keep from freezing. Lorraine gave Ellen another drink and patted her hand. "You go and lie on the bed in there, dear. Son, husband, and father all in the woods! What you must be goin through!"

Ellen kept to her chair. She was clearly upset but staying calm and enjoying Lorraine's company. Lorraine made me another drink. Grace set a plate of tea biscuits on the table. We discussed things that might have gone wrong up in the bush – a sprained ankle, a broken leg – and talked about helicopters and search parties. Frank straddled his chair, his face full of sympathy. I was in love with these people. I wanted nothing more than a cabin alongside theirs, casual visits, chats about anything at all.

"I think I will take my boots off," I said. My feet were cooking. "You take off whatever you like," Lorraine offered, "whatever makes you comfortable." As I set my boots on the deck, Lennox came into the cabin. I tried to make him go back out, but Lorraine intervened. "He's lonely out there," she said. "Let him be." He had sprawled in the middle of the small floor, his belly fur matted with bog silt and twigs from our two-day walk. Grace and Lorraine made much of his good behaviour. "I don't like dogs as a rule," Lorraine said, "but he's right quiet, he is, he could sleep on my bed and I wouldn't mind."

There was the sound of a car on the shoulder of the highway above us. We dashed out of the cabin. A police cruiser had pulled up with Russell in it and also a man with a battered face. The officer got out carrying a clipboard and wanted to speak with Ellen.

Russell and I talked. "I'm trying to get him to call out a helicopter and organize a ground search, but he won't commit himself to anything," Russell said.

"There's only a couple of hours of daylight left. We have to do something soon."

"I know."

"Who's the other guy in the cruiser?"

"He was sucker-punched in the club in York Harbour last night," Russell said. "He's pressing charges. That's why the cop's here."

The man with the battered face got out of the car and came around to us. "Look, forget about the cops," he told us. "I'll get some of my buddies along the road here and we'll go and find your friends." I said we'd take him up on it, if the police didn't come up with something soon.

The officer was back in his cruiser. I went to his window. "These people are not silly day-trippers," I said. "Harold's an experienced woodsman. Something's gone wrong. We should call out a helicopter while there's still daylight." He looked noncommittal or sceptical or at a loss for how to proceed; I couldn't tell which. "I'll see about it," he said. He drove a short distance away, and I could see him using his car phone.

Russell and Ellen had decided not to wait any longer; they were going to walk back up the Copper Mine trail. "I'm coming with you," I said. I changed into long pants and got the flashlight out of my pack.

We were just crossing the road toward the trail to begin our climb when, a couple of hundred yards away, Harold, Ken, and Mark came clambering up out of the gully of the Copper Mine brook onto the edge of the road. We ran to embrace them. They were staggering under their packs, white-faced, covered in cuts and scratches. Mark's shoelaces, I noticed, were in shreds. The foam sleeping pad he had tied to the top of his pack had been chewed away on both ends till there was hardly anything left.

"We weren't lost," Harold said. "We've been getting glimpses of Governor's Island since one o'clock, but we got into this bloody valley and couldn't get out. We'd get down so far and come to a waterfall we couldn't get over; so we'd have to go up and around it, but the banks are all straight cliffs or half-dead branches you've got to climb through. Most of the time our feet weren't even touching the ground."

As I listened I was thinking about how we wait for ideal weather and try to find beauty in these rough hills. Lorraine, I noticed, had taken Mark by the hand and was leading him down to her cabin to feed and comfort him after his day's ordeal.

Roughness and beauty. Roughness and beauty were what I was thinking about.

The Trail That Led to Me

~

For years, I thought I knew what home was, but I've since discovered it is not a place at all, not even a landscape. It's the strangers I carry in my blood.

I learned this from my Aunt Mary, a one-room-school teacher from Picton, Ontario, who, one day in her seventies, with arthritic hands, decided to write the family history. Though she had been there all along, I really only discovered Mary at the end of her life. In the early days of my childhood at the end of the 1950s, the nostalgic days of family values, we rarely visited our family.

My father owned a car, always a second-hand car with a radiator that blew on long-distance journeys. Every year during his two-week vacations, we'd set out for Smiths Falls to visit my mother's mother, who had by then given up her farm. The trip to Grandma's was a full day's journey on a narrow two-lane highway with a stop for a picnic lunch. Fast-food restaurants hadn't yet been invented. They were scary to me, those relatives we visited. My grandmother was a matriarch; she seemed to me as tough as the barbed wire she had once strung around the homestead she'd somehow managed to save after her husband died at the age of forty-five leaving her with eleven children. My mother was the baby. There were strict rules to be kept at my grandmother's, and my mother was always struggling to hold her wild daughters in check. Great-Uncle Willie lived with Grandma, and we had to be quiet since he seemed always to be asleep in the front room in the leather armchair, his silver watch chain rising and falling over his paunch, his black vest stained with snuff. The best times were when we went to visit the home of Aunt Lizzy Bluett – how we loved that name – and she would spread a feast of fresh vegetables and pies over the huge harvest table. But to us children these people all seemed old and frail and like phantoms, surfacing in our lives for only two weeks every summer.

In my memory, we went to visit my mother's sister Mary just once in all those early years. She and her husband, Nellis, had a farm in Napanee. There would have been only three of us children then; two were not yet born. In a photo I have we're standing in bathing suits and caps in front of the farmhouse facing the lake, me with one arm stretched protectively around the shoulders of my older sister Patricia, the other hand on my baby sister Sharon's head. I had already assumed the protective stance since I was the one who knew the world was dangerous, but I was still confident I could beat it up if it came too close. We'd never seen a farm before, and we went wild, jumping from the high rafters into the hayloft and pestering the horses. Mary called us hoodlums and said we had scared the cows from their milk. My mother was highly insulted and we never went back again.

I thought it was because nobody in the family approved of Nellis. He was eight years younger than Mary, and they said he'd never worked at a proper job. He kept the farm haphazardly, occasionally drove taxi, played the fiddle, and hunted bears. Everyone felt sorry for Mary, who had to teach school and earn all the money. But all along Nellis had been haunting local auction sales and had filled his barn with what the family referred to as "Nellis's junk." When he died suddenly of a heart attack, he left more than a hundred thousand dollars he'd squirrelled away from selling that junk. Two days before he died he sold the old violins he'd collected, some dating back fifty years. We went to the funeral for Mary's sake, but the man in the coffin with the grey hair that still sat up like a cowlick was a stranger to the rest of us.

Every Christmas, there were Mary's letters and Grandma Guthrie's frozen turkey with the molasses cookies sent by express rail, but we so seldom saw those members of my family that my idea of family never stretched beyond my mother and father and, by now, the five of us children. Then gradually the world changed and people travelled in fast cars on six-lane highways with restaurants, but by that time all these strangers were either dead or in old folks' homes.

I found Aunt Mary in Hay Bay Rest Home in 1985. When I asked my mother's advice about a present, she suggested I buy Mary a pair of soft-soled shoes. When I gave them to her, Mary said she hoped I hadn't paid a lot for them because she wouldn't have time to wear them out. Then she gave me the family history she'd written out in longhand in her perfect schoolmarm script, eighty pages illustrated with daguerreotypes and photos dating back to 1847 when the Irish Morrisons had fled the potato famine. And there they were, all the phantoms I had been afraid of in my childhood.

When I was in my early twenties, searching out literary shrines – were those dead writers a kind of family? – I'd been to Sligo to visit Yeats's grave, not knowing at the time that my great-great-grandmother Mary Morrison had buried two children in the same cemetery before despair sent her in quest of a new and more just world. In her book, Mary imagined her great-grandfather Darby Morrison speaking to his wife: "They're saying in Sligo Bay we can go to Canada, Mary. The Flahertys, the O'Gradys, the MacNamaras are leaving. The government pays the passage. They owe us. Two's enough to bury." Mary Morrison was forty-five and pregnant with Bridget when she crossed the ocean. You can be that tough, I guess, with nothing to lose. They used to say in the family that Bridget crossed the ocean and never saw the water. The British government gave the Morrisons two hundred acres, a cow, a pig, a plough, an axe, and a shovel when they arrived, and they started to carve out a life among the rocks of Smiths Falls which laid a faint trail through the bush that eventually led to me.

It is curious to read a story and know it is your story. Not just written for you, but maybe even explaining you. As I read it, it is Mary who surfaces from its pages. She had gathered the family history from her father's mother, Catherine Guthrie. When Mary was a child, they would come to her farm and sit with her in the evenings. Mary especially remembered the look of contentment on her father's face as he turned the wagon onto the side road that led to her house. She said: "His heart was always at the old homestead." Trussed up in her kitchen rocker in front of the open stove, Great-Grandma Guthrie would get out her basket of pictures and tell the stories of the people in them, and sometimes she would recount some of the old Irish tales. I can almost see them all sitting there before the open wood fire. Much later, when I finally went to Ireland and traced down lost cousins, we sat before a similar kitchen stove with our Irish whiskey, and the neighbours came from miles around bringing gifts of white heather and more family stories.

Mary said she kept the stories for the edification of the younger generation. "Perhaps some of the stories may help some members of the family to make a right decision which will bring happiness and contentment," she wrote in her Preface. For her, it seems life was a matter of right decisions.

Every life was a story to Mary. Her great-great-grandmother Mary Morrison and her husband, Darby, had had ten children, including Annie, Saul, Bridget, Jeremiah, Sara, and Catherine; the youngest was born in 1855 when Mary Morrison was fifty-three. My aunt tells each of their stories, and I discover her great-uncles, the ones who went off to the American lumber camps or became volunteers in the Boer War. She tells about great-uncle Saul's soldier's uniform that was kept for years up on a kitchen shelf at the old farm until one day her mother cut it up to make a pair of red boots for my Aunt Kay who was then a toddler, and everyone superstitiously expected the sky to fall down because it seemed a sacrilege to turn a soldier's uniform into baby boots. It was Saul who bequeathed his two hundred acres on Georgian Bay to my grandfather, who traded it to the Massey-Harris dealers for a grain binder and ever after said his binder cost a farm.

Aunt Mary was too honest to leave out the black sheep. There was the story of her great-aunt Annie whose husband, William Blake, drank too much. On a drunken binge he came home and killed Annie and her daughter, and hanged himself the next morning. The son, Willie, somehow managed to escape the slaughter. He made a life as a cook on the boats that went up the Rideau River, often living at the Guthrie farm to help out when he was not on the river. He was a good cook and a fastidious housekeeper. Mary and her siblings didn't like him because he was always making them "put things up," and once they snuck into his room and cut up his fancy ties. Her father hid Willie's whisky in the potato bin next to the hive of bees in the cellar where he knew Willie, afraid of all insects, would never look for it; but he would produce the bottle when Willie got "restless." There was Annie's brother Jeremiah, who, in his teens, got the hiccups and couldn't stop and died within the week. Annie's sister Sara began to "fail" in her early teens and "faded away and died." It must have

337

been TB, but the stoic tenderness of that ghostly fading lingered in my Aunt Mary's mind.

My favourite is Mary Morrison's daughter Bridget, the pretty one, who always worked in the field in her bare feet. (She's in my blood somewhere; I too can't stand shoes.) When she was twenty-one she went with her mother to a vaudeville show in Smiths Falls. One of the "showmen" fell in love with her, and, though she gave him no "encouragement," he stuck like glue. Her father said no showman was going to call on his daughter, but the man persuaded Brid to go with him to the fair in Perth. In the tea room of the local hotel he proposed. When she refused, he spiked her tea with poison, vowing if she didn't marry him, she would never marry anyone. With Brid unconscious on the floor, he saw "his work was accomplished." He was never heard of again. Mary said the showman had used too much poison and Brid had vomited it up. This saved her life. The family eventually tracked her down and brought her home, but she was always referred to as simple Aunt Brid after that and she would spend days at a time sitting and staring into space. Of course I wonder if my Aunt Mary couldn't resist a good story, and if so, what moral she intended for me. At least I've never been seduced by a circus man.

Catherine, Mary and Darby Morrison's last daughter, is the one I find most fascinating. Beautiful in the Irish way, with straight black hair that reached below her waist and "flashing" black eyes, she was her father's favourite. She hated domestic work and could be found out in the fields ploughing with the men. According to Mary she was high-spirited, outspoken, and vain. Men she regarded as a sort of "legal prey," and when Douglas Guthrie came along he didn't stand a chance. Her sister Brid would tease her: "Watch at the window for Gentleman Guthrie to come a-calling with his prancing black horses and fine carriage and his silk top-hat and gold-headed cane." Douglas,

Great-grandmother
Catherine Morrison, c. 1870

then forty-five and widowed, was a stone mason. The marriage wasn't a happy one. Catherine used to say she couldn't walk, talk, dress, or do anything to suit her husband, nor the many stepchildren who were her own age. After two years and the birth of her son, my grandfather, she headed back to the farm. When she decided to return to town, she found the stone mason's house was locked up; he'd gone out west. He'd bought her a smaller house and, through a lawyer, had left her a small annuity. She never saw him again. Her child, Jeremiah, became her project. She would educate him – education provided "the wings to get away." She worked as a cook at the Arlington Hotel in Smiths Falls and, later, on the tourist boats travelling through the Thousand Islands and plotted her son's escape from that narrow life. She bought him a bicycle – in his late teens my grandfather become National Cycling Champion for Canada. But in his twenties, Jeremiah thwarted her desires – he upped and married a Protestant wife. Despite her independence, Catherine remained a staunch Irish Catholic and never accepted her daughter-in-law nor ever quite forgave her son.

I find Catherine's stubbornness amusing. In 1905 her wealthy cousin Daniel Grady invited her to join him in Providence. Having made his money in cement, he was by then widowed and looking for another wife. Renting herself some fine jewellery on a six-month trial – why buy when the future was uncertain? – Catherine headed south. But she soon found the rich life smothering. She couldn't stand how the day was laid out in dresses: in the morning she was expected to have a bath, then to put on a special gown to comb her hair, then a breakfast gown, a street dress to go to market, an afternoon shopping dress, and then a fancy dress for dinner. Every day was planned for her! Catherine headed home.

I can find Catherine's equal in fiction. She is Hagar Shipley, a woman whose independence, finding no outlet, turned sour. Catherine disinherited her son for marrying the Protestant and willed the small property she had left to his child, her grandson.

The more I read the family stories, the more real my ancestors become. And even though I have only met them through Mary's eyes, I am now very fond of them. This poem was written for Mary in 1987. It's rather gothic, but that was my mood then. I guess I was talking about the mystery of identity. How much of who we are is the product of our own choices? How much is determined by genetic make-up? How much am I the creation of all those strangers in Mary's story, whose lives wove the complex web in which my own life began? I once asked Mary if she would consider publishing her book, but she said she wrote it for the family. Strangers might misread it. But I admire my ancestors' toughness, their humour, and their sheer will for survival. And

I am less fearful of them now. In fact, I hope to spend more time
unearthing those phantoms I hear calling in my own blood.

Words

Aunt Mary used to warn me about words.
They never stay where you put them.
They're loose.
Any no-good can use them.
Like a woman, she tried
to keep them safe in the family.

Family was her story that added down to me
– always fenced with a lesson:
words break loose if you let them.

She stored the family photos in a basket.
Trussed up in her rocker, warty as any gourd,
each night her hands plunged the corridors of blood.
I knew she was hooked on danger.

She could go all the way back to wind,
how it falls and picks itself up in a field.
Or fog empties a valley till all you see
is your hands where the world was.

From her I learned there were others
pacing inside me.
She said they had made me up.
I was meant to love them.

But it terrified me to think I was lived in
by strangers I had never met
or knew only by name.
They made me alien fiction.

In my bones
an old woman dies over and over,
I dare not look
in the room with the blooded axe
nor speak to the men who walked out.
Their tracks in my blood. Their lust
for edges.

I could spend
a lifetime digging graves
in my head.

JUDITH THOMPSON

Winter Camping

∼

I once went winter camping at Gould Lake outside of Kingston, Ontario. It was January 1969, about thirty-eight below zero. I was fourteen years old, and I didn't know anybody else in the Outward Bound club. I was assured by Brian, the tall and kind leader with the black wavy hair and the wire-rimmed glasses, that the hot stew in my stomach plus the thermal sleeping bag would keep me snug and warm. My parents reluctantly went to the local Sears and bought me all the gear, which I carried in a backpack that was brutally heavy, something like carrying our dining-room table on my back.

On a starry Friday evening, we were driven out to the lake in a van, and as soon as we got out of the nice warm car we set up camp. There was no one even to make small talk to, except the two girls in shag haircuts and blue mascara from what was disdainfully called the "occ squad," or the occupational stream at the high school, who had each brought about twelve choco- late bars because they were under the impression that frozen chocolate would keep them warm. They talked a lot about the chocolate, and this theory. They complained a lot. I liked that.

I was alone in my tent, and I froze all night. I have never felt such cold and discomfort ever. I began panicking around four in the morning, but I didn't want to wake anyone up. When the morning came Brian announced in cheerful tones that we would now hike around the lake. I did not understand that the weight of my pack would warm me up; I thought I would rather die than walk the four or five miles around that lake. There was only one thing in the world I wanted. I wanted to go home.

As that was not an option, I waited in the barn with the chocolate-bar girls, and we did some more complaining, and eating of chocolate bars. But I was an alien in their eyes, so I was still anxious, uneasy, and lonely, and I would have given anything to just be home.

That story came back to me recently when I heard an acquaintance tearfully describe the last few months of his dear friend's life; he was suffering mild dementia and he believed that he was on an extended camping trip, against his will. His friends would be at his beside, holding his hand, and, half blind, emaciated beyond recognition, he would grin at them and say, "Guys, this is great, but don't you think it's time we went home?" Baffled, they'd ask him what he meant, and he would explain that, "Camping is great, it's all very well, but we can't stay in the bush forever." "Surely to God," he would exclaim, "it's time to go home. Guys? Are we gonna camp forever? Don't we have, like, lives to get back to? I don't want to be camping any more. Okay? I want to go home!" As the months wore on, he became weaker and weaker and more belligerent. "DON'T YOU UNDERSTAND ME, YOU BASTARDS? I SAID I WANT TO GO HOME!! DO YOU HAVE EARS? I SAID I . . . WANT . . . TO . . . GO . . . HOME!!!"

When I was a student at Queen's, in the final year of my three-year B.A., I shared a one-bedroom apartment with an older, throaty-voiced roommate. I arrived home late from a rehearsal for *Hamlet*, in which I had just worked Ophelia's mad scene, badly, stupidly. I was tired and demoralized. My room-mate, who was involved in a torrid lesbian triangle, had pinned a note on our door declaring: "I have my lover overnight and we would appreciate some privacy." Feeling sorry for myself, I turned around and walked the few blocks to my sort-of boyfriend (who was actually in love with the red-haired guy who worked nights at the front desk at the Holiday Inn on the water). When he came to the door he gave me an "Oh no, it's you" look, and I challenged him on that and he told me to get out of his apartment, he just wanted to be alone. So I left and walked around the wet streets for a while and crouched on the corner of University and Brock near the corner store, not knowing where to go. Or what to do.

I wanted to be a child again. I wanted my mother and father to take me in their arms and bring me home.

Obviously, leaving when I did had been a bad mistake.

When I see or hear the word home, I think of my home as a child. I think of . . .

Footsteps: a rough, red bedspread, and footsteps, coming up the stairs, I always knew whose footsteps they were, I could feel the vibration in my body, and I knew, that's Daddy, or that's Mummy, or my younger brother Bill, or that's the strange footstep of the babysitter. I think of voices, downstairs, the voices of my parents. Warm, and light, and laughing, and twisted, and intertwined, and tense and raised, and low and whispered, the voices through the walls, their friends, explosions of laughter, cocktail voices singing through the house. The voices through the floor.

Stories: the bunkbed, with my beloved brother lying above me, my mother, in her soft rich theatre voice, telling me bedtime stories of a "skeetamo" named Judy. The stories shouted at the cocktail parties, followed by explosions of charged laughter as I passed the plates of canned asparagus rolled in buttered white bread and smoked oysters on toothpicks.

School: My first grand mal seizure, in the heat of June at the grade school assembly, my pink linen dress ruined. I was carried home to lie on the bed with the red bedspread, zaps and commas and arrows darting, pointing in my exhausted brain, for hours, the embarrassment, the staring. At home they do not stare. And you do not see them whisper.

The smells: of lilacs, and green grass in the spring, buttercups and violets, which grew wild all over the back yard, the bark of the Easy tree, the beer my mother used to condition her hair, the Oil of Olay she creamed on her face (it worked), the smell of my father's face and the dandruff on his lapels and the way he would pat and pat and pat my back, breaking my sobs.

That home is buried in memory, now. The new home is here. It is Ariane, Elias, Grace, and Felicity climbing all over me and my husband, on the red couch, with toys and books and pizza and important bills and scripts and student papers all over the red wool Oriental carpet, and Etta James is on the stereo, and the paintings and the green wall and the TV is blaring and sometimes the radio too, and the phone ringing and the bath running. For me it is a kind of a freedom, my own home, clear breathing; a Sunday morning and the lessons are cancelled and there is time, lots of time. Early, I go downstairs in my cold bare feet and my ripped flannel nightgown and open the living-room curtains and let the winter light pour in, the light of white snow. Filling my dark Toronto living room, my home.

My neighbourhood, Seaton Village, in Toronto, Ontario, Canada. The light, the liquidy pale light of Ontario, a November sunset through the bare trees, rich grey mid-afternoon in December with thick snow falling, hot wet summer nights, on the porch, oh glory, the rain, the unspeakable colours in autumn, the walking, my home.

This city. I have walked every sidewalk and street, at all times of day and night. I fell in love with my husband in front of Grossman's Tavern near Spadina and College. We walked and we walked back to Albany and over to Brunswick and stole into a bread truck in front of the Loretto College for Girls, had our first kiss on the piles of soft white bread. This is my city. This city is my home.

To have a seizure is to be cast away from the world, from your home. When I had the worst seizure, the one where my face turned black, I was not home; I was at school, Regiopolis High School, living a kind of hell. It was intolerable so it was natural that I would have a seizure, a form of escape because I couldn't just go home, so I had this attack, this seizure: I fell down the bottomless sick yellow hole in the ground, down and down upside down and gagged and spinning and the world was more and more muffled and distant faces, all the faces I knew so far, fading, and there was me, disappearing. Farther and farther away from home. Down into the middle of the earth. Until I screamed my way back home. I screamed, I screamed myself back into my parents' arms and onto my then-white chenille bedspread, lying on my back listening to the zigzag zaps in my brain. My name was spoken softly, their voices thick with love. This was not school. This was home.

I have a feeling that when the day comes that this is no longer my children's home it will not be my home either. I will have a house, but not a home. Everything will feel temporary, as it did after I left home and before I was married, so I won't really care about it any more, I won't care about the peeling paint, the weeping tiles, the garden, because I will be camping again. Always a little uncomfortable, a little cold. And always with a sense of waiting. Waiting, I think, to go home.

JANE URQUHART

The Frozen Lake

Bush plane landing at Lake Kenogamisis, c. 1940

There are numerous rumours and legends concerning how they found the gold in the first place. In my favourite one of these tales, Tony Oklend, the future mine owner and millionaire, fell out of a canoe, sank to the bottom of the lake, then swam to the surface with a gold nugget sparkling in his teeth. There are other, more prosaic, versions of the "find"; versions which refer to technical operations, intrusive rocks full of hard green veins, and diamond drills placed out on the ice by "Hardrock" Bill Smith. Whatever the case, gold was discovered near Lake Kenogamisis – a wilderness area a hundred miles north of the top of Lake Superior – in the early 1930s, at about the same time that my father was graduating from the University of Toronto Mining Engineering School, on the one hand, and eloping with my mother on the other.

My parents had to elope for several reasons – there are rumours and legends associated with this as well – but the main issue affecting the case was the fact that the Toronto General Hospital School of Nursing, where my mother was about to enter her final year, refused to allow their "girls" to marry while they were in training. My father had accepted a job with Little Lac Gold Mines, the result of the above-mentioned gold strike, and was about to disappear into "the bush" for what looked to the young couple like forever. They wanted to spend some time together before he departed, my mother would want to visit him there for a week or two sometime during the intervening year, and they were both unworldly enough to believe that they ought to be married in order to accomplish these rendezvous.

As seems to be the case with most of my family's history, ancient or otherwise, there are various stories about my father's arrival at the spot that would come to be known as Little Long Lac Townsite. For example, a group of Slavic miners swore that they had poled my father along the edge of Lake Superior, up Helen River, across Helen Lake, through a complicated series of smaller lakes and rivers, and into Lake Kenogamisis on a raft they constructed entirely for this purpose, and that, as a direct consequence of this, they were all given jobs when they arrived at the "site." This was the same group of miners who gathered together at the bottom of the pit to break my father's fall when, some years later, he "clumsily" (my mother's term) stepped off the elevator and into the open shaft while he was marking drill core. I am grateful to this group of miners because, without them, my father might not have survived his "clumsiness" and, as I was a very late child, I might never have been born. I am grateful to them, want to believe their story – and, as it turns out, their version is at least partly true.

In fact, my father disembarked from the northern spur of the Canadian National Railway in the middle of a dense forest at Number 39 – better known as Hardrock Station because of the unusually large granite boulder in the immediate vicinity – in July of 1934 and tried to check into Maude Gascon's log bunkhouse for the night. He did not succeed. News of the gold strike had travelled far and wide (this was, after all, the Depression), and the place was full of would-be speculators, would-be prospectors, and would-be promoters. Eventually, my father was able to rent a rocker on the front porch of Maude's establishment for twenty-five cents. In this he was more fortunate than the hundreds of would-be miners who were bedding down on either side of the tracks, men who were hoping to find employment at the mine. He had two things that they hadn't: a rocking chair for the night and the certainty of a job.

The next morning, since he had not been lying down in the first place, he was up almost before anyone else. I say "almost" because, after he had tramped the two-mile trail that led through the bush to Lake Kenogamisis, he came upon the Slavic miners, who had just finished building their craft and who offered him a ride on board. So my father and his future saviours sailed towards the several acres in the bush which were to be his home for the next twenty-odd years.

Most of the truly great adventures took place long before I was born, even before my older brothers were born, before "the roads were in," as my parents would say. My mother's first visit to the spot was one of them. According to her, she was met by my father, a dog team and sled, a full moon, and a temperature which had plummeted to thirty below zero. She had optimistically brought along an extensive wardrobe, which was a problem, since every available inch of space on the dog sled was filled with cases of whisky, ordered by the boys back at the mine and delivered by the same train on which she rode. My father was living in the bunkhouse at the mine, but, fortunately, a frame hotel had just been opened in the service town of Geraldton which was beginning to grow across the lake from the mine, so the young couple was able to stay there during my mother's visit. In the mornings my mother watched from the window as my father walked to work across the ice on the lake. At night she was often wakened by the sounds of noisy brawls or amicable singing on the part of miners who were christening the new beer parlour below.

The hotel was the first thin evidence of encroaching civilization. By the time my mother joined my father for good the following summer, however, there were four or five log houses at the townsite of Little Long Lac Goldmine, a two-room hospital with a red cross on its roof for the benefit of bush planes, a hangar at the end of the lake, also for the benefit of bush planes, and a bridge across the lake to Geraldton, which itself now sported a dance hall called The Goldfield (later it was renamed Dreamland and had a band called The Highstrutters), an Anglican and a Catholic church, and a Royal Bank. It was also home to two splendid brothels, one of which was called Coffee Annie's because the proprietress did not approve of drinking. My highly entertaining future godfather had arrived by this time, as a member of a lively team of Irish shaft and development miners who, after emigrating from the old country and before heading north, had spent the past few years building Maple Leaf Gardens

Father, Walter Carter (seated, left), with mining camp cook and
prospectors in front of log cookhouse, c. 1934

and then working on the tunnels which led from the depths of
Lake Ontario to the new waterworks in Toronto.

The summer of the magnificent and terrifying fires happened
before I was born as well, but the stories about them were surely
almost as impressive as the fires themselves. I was told about how
the soles of my father's shoes became burned when he and all the
other men of the community went out to fight the blaze, and
how barges of logs were hastily constructed so the women could
fill them with household goods and set them adrift in Lake
Kenogamisis. It was reported that the doctor's wife needed an
entire canoe for her sterling silver and bone china, and that my
own mother insisted that her books and her collection of *New
Yorker* magazines be removed from harm's way. Every house on the
water's edge was eventually empty – except for ours. My father
and godfather left the refrigerator in place in the kitchen and
regularly restocked it with beer. Everyone slept outside at the

water's edge so that they could join the furniture if necessary. Occasionally, after hearing these stories, I would imagine my mother and father's large spool bed, the dining-room table, all the familiar furniture of my home, floating on the night lake, a murderous orange sky in the distance.

More than a decade passed between the summer of the great fires and my birth in the two-room hospital at Little Long Lac. By then there were roads and schools, stores, and a movie theatre called The Grand in Geraldton. Most of the men working at the mine had married, and the "ladies of the night" had returned to Montreal. Still, the house we lived in was made of logs and was situated on a point of land which, from the air, resembled a huge bird's wing floating on the water or resting on the ice. When I looked out our windows I saw ice and snow and the dark pines of the opposite shore. The house was near enough to the hangar that many of my first memories are of the appearance of small bush planes emerging from the clouds or glinting in the sky, then touching down on skis on a smooth white surface. It seemed always to be winter. Even now a glimpse of snow on the branches of fir trees or the open white expanse of a frozen lake can make me believe that I am five years old. As soon as I could walk I was given a tiny set of snowshoes for outdoor mobility. The cook at the mine made me a doll carriage, which, under the circum- stances, had to be equipped with sleigh runners. Each day, when I went outside to play, I believed, as all children do, that everyone lived the way we did: with clean white snow, fierce cold sun, the warmth of shellacked log walls and stone fireplaces. The pastoral landscapes in my picture books seemed to me as fanciful and "other" as the princesses and elves who inhabited them.

I remember that one cold, clear, winter day, my mother told me that she would take me outside after dinner so that I could see a star. I must have been about four at the time and interested in

| Summer bath with father presiding | In front of the log house, age four |

poems such as "Winken, Blinken and Nod," which in my books were accompanied by illustrations of five-pointed yellow shapes with cute smiling faces. We bundled up in padded clothing, scarves, and mittens. Perhaps we strapped snowshoes on our feet as well, before we stepped out into the dark. Except that it wasn't dark. There must have been a partial moon illuminating the snow as we walked on the frozen lake, for my memory is of blue, navy and royal and powder blue, rather than grey and black; of that and of the ochre, liquid light which spilled from the windows of our log house and made long rectangles on the snow.

I was disappointed by the star, a speck of white dust in the sky. It was my introduction to what would become a sustained belief for me – that books and their illustrations are able to outshine the reality that inspires them. But my mother pointed out that there were millions of such specks throughout the whole sky, that they were farther away than we could imagine, and that some of them might be complete worlds. For the first time the understanding of distance, its limitlessness, entered my child's mind, the understanding of space. We were facing north, I remember, and I was suddenly able to comprehend that, although the roads had been in for some time and we could drive a thousand miles from here all the way to my grandparents' southern Ontario farm, we nevertheless lived in a territory where the roads stopped. After us came unending space, unimaginable distance, the unsurveyed rest of the world.

It is no longer fashionable to define our country in terms of "the north," no longer fashionable to make reference to the idea of a wilderness region that may or may not be present in our collective psyche. But although the gold mine closed when I was five years old and my mother and father, after twenty years in the north, went to Toronto, I still feel a genuine ache of homesickness when I think of the clear, frigid days and nights, the snow, blindingly white under a winter sun, the hugeness of the winter night sky, the frozen ground under it which stretches all the way to the Arctic. When we moved to Toronto for a while, I would experience moments of panic when I realized I wasn't able to identify the house where we lived on a street lined with similar-looking dwellings. And at the large brick school a few similar blocks away, when we were asked to make a drawing of our home, I remember colouring in the night sky, bright blue with a sprinkling of stars, the dark pines of the far shore, a log house with lit windows shining above the drifts of snow.

GUY VANDERHAEGHE

Finding Home in Heule

~

A number of years ago when one of my books was translated and published in Holland I received a telephone call from the producer of a literary program on Belgian television. He had recognized the Flemish origin of my surname and wanted to know from what part of Belgium my family had originated. I had no idea but, after rooting around in the few documents which had survived my grandfather's death, I discovered his mother's funeral announcement with an address scrawled on it. I sent the address to the producer, and a few weeks later he phoned to inform me that the house where my grandfather had been born was still standing in what had once been the village of Heule, but was now a suburb of Kortrijk, and the owner was a first cousin of my father's. Moreover, my grandfather's youngest brother lived about a kilometre distant. The news that my great-uncle Valere was still alive came as a shock. No one in my family but my grandfather wrote or spoke Flemish, so the last strand of communication with Valere had been severed when my grandfather died. Twenty years of silence had ensued and everyone simply assumed that my grandfather's brother was long dead and buried.

The television producer wanted to arrange for me to pay a call on these relatives and film the meeting. He had already sounded out the Belgian Vanderhaeghes and they were enthusiastic. Was I interested?

I was and I wasn't. A family reunion conducted before television cameras struck me as artificial, absurd. However, if I visited on my own, there would be the language problem to overcome. The producer was ready to ease difficulties by providing both a translator and a driver to ferry my wife and me from Amsterdam to Kortrijk.

Although I had been to the Netherlands several times before, I had never made the effort to take the short trip into Belgium; now a stranger was volunteering to put me in touch with my family. Suddenly, I was eager to learn something of the history of a grandparent whom I had passionately loved, intrigued by the prospect of seeing the house in which he had lived as a boy. Several friends and acquaintances had gone on similar pilgrimages and returned with glowing, emotional reports about their experiences. One had journeyed to Scotland to crisscross the land of his ancestors. Another had visited Jerusalem and prayed at the Wailing Wall. Other people I knew were learning their grandparents' languages, then trekking off to Germany, to Ukraine, to Sweden. They had been rewarded, I was assured, with epiphanies of self-discovery, revelations of identity. Everybody seemed to be beset with nostalgia for the first home, the roots of the family adrift in the diaspora.

Banking on a similar payoff, I agreed to cooperate with the television producer. On a grey day in which the clouds were bunched overhead so near I felt I could reach up and touch them, my wife, Margaret, and I set off from Amsterdam in a white Opel, accompanied by our driver, Frank, and translator, Ernst.

The journey, however, was not commenced without some apprehension. Ernst struck me as a fine man, but the fact he was wearing face makeup and eyeliner caused me some uneasiness about his reception by the Kortrijk clan. One of the few things I had learned about my grandfather's people was that they were staunch, even fervent Catholics. He, however, had abandoned the Church the moment he set foot in Canada. This had caused strains with his family overseas; year after year, until she died, his mother had written him, begging the lost sheep to return to the fold, but he had always stood his ground and refused.

This wasn't all. Before leaving Amsterdam I had met with several staff members from Belgian television, and over drinks they had prepped me about where I was headed. I learned that at the turn of the century this region had been poverty-stricken, a place fled by emigrants determined to make their fortunes in the Congo or North America. It was the heartland of Flemish nationalism, an area which clung to a rich peasant dialect and assiduously nursed long-held grievances against the French-speaking Walloons. Someone laughingly confided there was even a famous folk song about my grandfather's village, "Tineke of Heule," which eulogized the perfect Flemish woman: prodigious cow-milker and scyther of flax, sweet-natured, fertile, and contented as the cows she milked. He confessed he sometimes sang this ditty to his wife, an art historian at the University of Antwerp, whenever he felt she was putting on airs. I had my fingers crossed that nobody would sing this salute to the ideal woman in Margaret's presence, or, if they did, bother to translate it.

"Yes," this man had mused aloud, "West Flanders is the Texas of Belgium." Recalling his words as the Opel hurtled across the flat Belgian plain, I couldn't help wondering how Margaret and the cosmetically enhanced Ernst were going to hit it off with the Texans of Belgium.

I didn't have a lot of time to worry, distances in the Low Countries being so short. In Ghent we rendezvoused with the television crew and ate lunch in a restaurant. Through its windows the house of the writer Hugo Claus was pointed out to me. In this part of Belgium, opinions were deeply divided about Claus. For some, he was a culture hero who had overcome the disadvantages of a little-known, obscure language to become a European literary celebrity. For others, he was an embarrassment because his novel, *The Sorrow of Belgium*, anatomized the collaboration of Flemish nationalists with Nazi occupiers during the Second World War.

In Heule, our convoy came to a halt in a narrow street of brick row houses. The producer wanted the first meeting between Valere and me to occur in front of the sheds where Valere and my grandfather, Georges, had worked side by side curing flax for the linen trade. A carefully choreographed, theatrical touch. We all trooped out back and stood in a small courtyard to await the arrival of the car the producer had dispatched to deliver my great-uncle.

Within minutes, a vehicle pulled up and an old man and woman struggled out of it. At eighty-four, Valere was a dead ringer for my grandfather in the years just before his death. The same nut-brown skin; the same square, powerful body and big round head settled solidly on a stump of neck. I couldn't take my eyes off him as we shook hands, nodding and smiling. He said something to me in Flemish. The television producer said Valere remembered me as a baby. This was wrong. I hadn't been born when he made his one visit to Saskatchewan; he was recollecting my Uncle Dan's son. I am Clarence's son, I repeated over and over. Clarence. Finally, he understood. Clarence the cowboy, he said. Everybody laughed. At last, I was placed.

The old man wanted me to show him my feet. A little puzzled, I did. The feet aren't right, he declared scornfully. Vanderhaeghes have big feet. Proudly, he displayed his own, shod in black high-topped workman's boots polished to an anthracite sheen. Everybody crowded around to admire his tremendous feet.

We moved off to the house, where we were greeted by Joseph and his wife. More smiles and nods, nods and smiles as we crushed our way into a narrow, cramped dwelling, dark as a Rembrandt painting. I was trying hard to imagine my grandfather and his six siblings, survivors of his mother's fifteen pregnancies, inhabiting these sombre rooms. But try as I might, I couldn't situate my grandfather here. The attempt to thrust the man I had known back into this place gave me a strange feeling. Somehow, he wouldn't fit.

A table spread with lace was loaded with pastries and bottles of genever. There weren't enough chairs for the crowd. The producer shooed all of the Vanderhaeghes along with Ernst and Frank into seats while the crew propped themselves against the walls. In the confusion of the first meeting, Margaret hadn't been introduced as my wife. Consternation was general; they hadn't known she was coming. "*Vrouw? Vrouw?*" Joseph's wife asked, pointing at her, voice rising in amazement. After her identity was confirmed for the second and third time, the woman went and stood by Margaret's chair, patting her tenderly on the head as if she were a baby.

The producer started to introduce the rest of the strangers. Abruptly, the old man interrupted him. He wanted to know who the Dutchmen were. We all shared a moment of uneasiness, wondering who was going to finger Ernst and Frank, but they owned up themselves. The old man spoke again. "He says he remembers the Dutchmen from the days when they came to buy the linen," the producer translated. "They always ate too much and paid too little for it."

With this happy observation we all attacked the food and drink. Valere unbent, grew jollier, more and more expansive. I had the strong impression this had more to do with the genever and the presence of television cameras than it had to do with me. Given the circumstances this was perfectly understandable.

To be truthful, the family reunion was a labour for all concerned. I kept prodding Valere for anecdotes about my grandfather's boyhood, but the lack of a common language made for difficulties. At one point, in his Oxbridge-accented English, Ernst whispered to me, "The old man is speaking some abominable dialect. I've never heard anything like it. I can hardly make out what he is saying."

Meanwhile I was behaving with false animation, talking too loudly, asking too many questions. The more I strove to unearth some bond between us, the more discouraged I became. My outward exuberance was a sham, masking an inner detachment that regarded my play-acting for the cameras, for the relatives, with a cold and clinical eye. The epiphany I'd come seeking was drifting out of reach. These were lovely, welcoming, kind people; there was no denying that. And I liked them. But my naïveté had deluded me into expecting more.

So we continued drinking and gossiping, playing our roles until the producer discreetly signalled for the party to break up; the crew had a schedule to keep. Awkwardly formal, I presented the gifts I had brought from Amsterdam, and one stage of the homecoming was concluded.

The crew escorted me out to be interviewed, with the sheds where Valere, Georges, and, in his time, Joseph had prepared the flax as a backdrop. The interviewer questioned me about the old man's "earthiness." In my writing he believed he could detect traces of the Flemish peasant's love of vulgarity, a similar deep attachment to the soil. Was this the case? Was there a link? I was supposed to say yes, but in all honesty I couldn't see this as the truth. I was so ignorant of Flemish culture that such a link could only have resulted from some mysterious transmission accomplished by blood, a notion I found bogus and distasteful. A successful TV program depended on my declaring my "Flemishness," but that I couldn't bring myself to do. As I squirmed my way evasively through question after question, the interviewer became more and more downcast. The interview concluded on a note of perfunctory failure.

There was one last journey to be made. The old man and his wife wanted us to see their home. When we parked outside it, I knew why. It resembled a suburban Canadian bungalow and was, by the standards of the village, a lavish house. Valere conducted us on the grand tour, with particular emphasis placed on the fact it had two bathrooms. He led us to a hallway where framed photographs of John and Bobby Kennedy were hung. By some photographic trick the two brothers wore shimmering haloes of light. As we were admiring these, as we had earlier admired the old man's feet, Valere bustled off with the air of a man with an important errand to perform. My great-aunt seized this opportunity to spring the question: Was I a Christian? The last of my resolve had evaporated during the interminable fencing with the interviewer. I said yes. Catholic? she asked, daring to hope. I shook my head. Ah well, she said without conviction, it's all the same, isn't it?

For a long moment of silence we stared at the Kennedys. Valere is a great Christian, she confided at last. He spends hour after hour in the basement, on his knees, praying.

Just then we heard Valere clumping up the stairs from the basement, breathing heavily. Had he slipped below decks for a quick spiritual pick-me-up? Apparently not, because in his big, broad hand he clutched a brown envelope. This he thrust at me, growling something. The producer said, "He has no children. He says he's going to die soon. You must have this."

The manila envelope was stuffed with photographs. Quickly, I began to sort through them. They were pictures my grandfather had mailed back to Belgium, forty years of them. In the majority, he was posed beside a new piece of farm machinery: a binder, a hay rake, a threshing machine, a tractor. To his family back in Belgium the machinery established his credentials as a success. In the others, children and grandchildren were gathered in his arms or at his knees. The children established his credentials as a patriarch.

In all these black-and-white snapshots, people squint into the stunning prairie sun; ebony shadows are stencilled on the earth; the prairie sky looms like a great grey slate, cloudless, empty. Occasionally, a clump of poplars hovers on the edges of the photographs, the camera registering leaves molten in the glare of the sun.

Looking at those photographs, I had the small epiphany I'd waited for, recognizing home, recognizing my grandfather. The landscape and his attitude in it, cocky, a little defiant, defined him for me, would always define him. It was in this immense space he belonged, not the dark, brown, claustrophobic rooms I had just departed.

I turned over one of the photographs and saw writing on the back. But I couldn't read the words; they were Flemish. I might as well have been examining a rune. Passing the picture to the television producer I asked him what my grandfather had written. He studied it for a moment and said, "I don't know exactly. It's Flemish, but it's all wrong. A kind of English-Flemish."

Well, this was my grandfather too. The things he had forgotten, or only half-remembered. Perhaps the writing on the photograph was a metaphor for him, a bizarre mix of Flemish and Canadian, a record of loss and gain. I had often wondered how it was possible for him to forsake everything he had known, his country, language, religion. But the fact remained, he had *chosen* what to lose and what to gain. If he had any regrets, he kept them to himself.

Nearly twenty years before, thinking about this loss and gain, I had written a short story about a Belgian immigrant overwhelmed by Canada, broken, because he had surrendered too much. But now I saw the source of that story was my own speculation: what would happen to me if I were ever forced to renounce everything I saw in the photograph, my grandfather's bequest to me?

My grandfather chose a home. And I have spent all of my life in the place he picked, everything familiar, easy, second nature. But one portrait of my grandfather given to me in Heule lets me see it fresh, anew. The one in which he stands, face to face with the sun, grinning.

JAN ZWICKY

Poppies

~

Some days, the wall that separates us from the future
is too thin. Standing in my mother's garden
by the bed of poppies on the northwest slope, wind
in the trees and the five-mile sky billowing over us,
I am caught again by their colour: water-colour,
sheer, like ice or silk, or, we imagine,
freedom. Their petals on the ground
collect in drifts, explosions
of arterial light.
                    Or perhaps it's that we are
that membrane, an instant thick, days
shine right through us as we charge around,
looking for some explanation in what hasn't happened yet
or what will never happen again. Like last night at dinner:
glancing up at the picture, the one that's always hung there,
the sudden clear presentiment that I would live
to walk into that dining room someday, after
the last death, and find it
waiting for me, the entire past
dangling from a finishing nail.

Poppies, what can they teach us?
The windshot light fills them
and they are blind.

About the Contributors

Andrew MacNaughton

MARGARET ATWOOD was born in Ottawa in 1939, and grew up in northern Quebec and Ontario, and later in Toronto. She is the author of more than twenty-five books – novels, short stories, poetry, literary criticism, social history, and books for children. Atwood's work is acclaimed internationally, and she has won many awards and honours, including the Governor General's Award, the Trillium Book Award, and the prestigious Le Chevalier dans l'Ordre des Arts et des Lettres in France. Her most recent books are *Alias Grace* (a novel) and *Morning in the Burned House* (poetry). She lives in Toronto.

Don Hall

SANDRA BIRDSELL was born in Manitoba. She is the author of three short-story collections and two novels. Her most recent collection of short fiction is called *The Two-Headed Calf*. A children's book, *The Town That Floated Away*, will be published in the fall of 1997. She is currently living in Regina, Saskatchewan.

ANNE CARSON teaches ancient Greek for a living and is the author of *Eros The Bittersweet*, *Plainwater*, and *Glass, Irony and God*.

Gary Gellert

WAYSON CHOY was born in Vancouver, has taught English for twenty-five years at Humber College in Toronto, and is past president of Cahoots Multicultural Theatre Company. His first novel, *The Jade Peony*, was co-winner of the 1995 Trillium Book Award as well as winner of the Vancouver Book Award, and was on the *Globe and Mail*'s bestseller list for twenty-six weeks. He is currently at work on a sequel.

Beverley Rockett

ADRIENNE CLARKSON is the television producer and writer whose current program, "Adrienne Clarkson Presents," now in its eighth season on the CBC, is the only prime-time series devoted to Canadian culture. The show has won numerous awards nationally and internationally. Formerly Ontario's agent-general in France, she is an Officer of the Order of Canada and chairwoman of the Canadian Museum of Civilization.

JACK DIAMOND, born in South Africa, came to Toronto in 1964. He is a principal of A. J. Diamond, Donald Schmitt and Company, a noted architectural firm whose practice extends across Canada, the United States, Europe, the Middle East, and the Far East. He has taught architecture at many distinguished universities, founding the Master of Architecture program at the University of Toronto, and has held the rank of professor at York University and the University of Texas. In 1996 he held the Graham Chair in Architecture at the University of Pennylvania. In 1989 he was recipient of the Toronto Arts Award for Design and Architecture, and in 1996 was appointed an Officer of the Order of Canada. He is the co-author of *Works: The Architecture of A. J. Diamond, Donald Schmitt and Company 1968-1995*.

John Frederick Ecklington

DAVID DONNELL's previous books include *Settlements* (winner of the 1983 Governor General's Award for Poetry), *Water Street Days*, and *China Blues* (winner of the City of Toronto Book Award). His poetry has been widely anthologized in Canada and the United States. He has also written songs which have been performed in Toronto bars and at the Music Gallery. His most recent book, *Dancing in the Dark*, is a collection of poems and short stories about under-thirties youth culture in the 1990s.

371

David Homel

TREVOR FERGUSON is the author of six novels, most recently *The Timekeeper* and *The Fire Line*. His early work is being reissued in Canada and the United States beginning with *High Water Chants* and *Onyx John* in 1997. He lives in Hudson, Quebec.

TIMOTHY FINDLEY, born in Toronto, now splits each year between Ontario and France. After an international career as an actor, he left the theatre in 1962 and has since become an award-winning writer of novels and short fiction, of plays, and of dramas and documentaries for radio, television, and film. His most recent fiction is a novella, *You Went Away*, and his most recent play is *The Stillborn Lover*. In 1996 he was named Author of the Year by the Canadian Booksellers Association, and in France was made a Chevalier dans l'Ordre des Arts et des Lettres.

MARIAN BOTSFORD FRASER is a writer, journalist, and broadcaster, and was president of PEN Canada in 1994-95. She was born in Kirkland Lake, Ontario, and has lived in England and

New Zealand, Vancouver and Ottawa, and now lives in Toronto with her grown-up daughter Katherine and two cats.

Henry Fiks

ALISON GORDON is the author of *The Dead Pull Hitter, Safe at Home, Night Game, Striking Out* (shortlisted for the Arthur Ellis Award), and *Prairie Hardball*. Past president of the Crime Writers of Canada, she is currently the North American vice-president of the International Association of Crime Writers.

Bernard Clark

WAYNE GRADY is a writer, editor, and translator living in Kingston, Ontario. His essays and articles have appeared in many Canadian magazines, and he has written six books, the most recent being *Toronto the Wild: Field Notes of an Urban Naturalist*. He has also edited several anthologies, including *The Penguin Book of Canadian Short Stories, Treasures of the Place: Three Centuries of Nature Writing in Canada*, and (with Matt Cohen) *The Quebec Anthology 1830-1990*. In 1989 he won the Governor General's Award for his translation of Antonine Maillet's *On the Eighth Day*.

RON GRAHAM is a freelance journalist and writer. He has written two books on Canadian politics, a book on religion in Canada, and a personal history of Quebec, as well as numerous magazine articles. He is currently the president of PEN Canada (1996-97).

Henry Fiks

TERRY GRIGGS was born in Little Current, Manitoulin Island, in 1951, and currently lives in London, Ontario. She has published a collection of short stories entitled *Quickening*, and a novel, *The Lusty Man*.

KRISTJANA GUNNARS is the author of six books of poetry, two short-story collections, two novels, and two non-fiction books. She teaches English and creative writing at the University of Alberta in Edmonton. Her latest book is *The Rose Garden: Reading Marcel Proust*.

374

Don Hall

LOUISE BERNICE HALFE, also known as Sky Dancer, was born in Two Hills, Alberta. She was raised on the Saddle Lake Indian Reserve with a six-year stay at Blue Quills Residential School. Her first book of poetry, *Bear Bones & Feathers*, was short-listed for the Spirit of Saskatchewan Award, the First Book Award, the Gerald Lampert Award, and, in 1996, the Milton Acorn Award. Her second book of poetry, *Blue Marrow*, a mixture of prose, poetry, and journal writing concerning the lives of native women during the fur-trade era, will be published in the fall of 1997.

Weitzel Studios/ Mark Brennan

DIANA HARTOG has lived in Canada for more than twenty years, arriving from San Francisco to settle in British Columbia in the 1970s. She has published three books of poetry. Her poems and stories have been published in literary magazines and anthologies in Canada, the United States, and England. Her first novel, *The Photographer's Sweethearts*, was published in 1996.

Mary Huggard

STEVEN HEIGHTON has published three books of poetry, including the 1995 Governor General's Award finalist *The*

Ecstasy of Skeptics; two short-story collections, *Flight Paths of the Emperor* and *On earth as it is*; and, most recently, a collection of essays, *The Admen Move on Lhasa: Writing & Culture in a Virtual World*. He has received the Gerald Lampert Award for Poetry and a Gold Medal for Fiction at the National Magazine Awards, while his story collections have appeared in French translation and are published in Britain. Heighton lives with his family in Kingston, Ontario, where he is working on new poems and a novel.

GREG HOLLINGSHEAD grew up in Woodbridge, Ontario, and now teaches at the University of Alberta in Edmonton. He has published a novel, *Spin Dry*, and three collections of stories: *Famous Players*, *White Buick*, and *The Roaring Girl*. His work has been shortlisted for the Commonwealth Writers Prize (Caribbean and Canada Region) and the SmithBooks/Books in Canada First Novel Award. In 1993 he won the Georges Bugnet Award for the Novel, and in 1993 and 1996 the Howard O'Hagan Award for Short Fiction. In 1995 *The Roaring Girl* won the Governor General's Award for Fiction. He is currently working on a novel.

JANICE KULYK KEEFER was born in Toronto, and has worked at universities in Canada, England, and France. Her most recent books are *Travelling Ladies*, *Rest Harrow*, and *The Green*

Library, which was nominated for the Governor General's Award for Fiction. She teaches at the University of Guelph and lives in Eden Mills, Ontario.

YANN MARTEL is the author of *The Facts behind the Helsinki Roccamatios*, a collection of short stories, and *Self*, a novel. He lives in Montreal.

DON McKAY's eight books of poetry include *Birding, or desire*, which won the Canadian Authors Association Award for Poetry in 1983, *Night Field*, which won the Governor General's Award for Poetry in 1991, and his most recent collection, *Apparatus*. He has taught English at the University of Western Ontario and acted as Director of Creative Writing at the University of New Brunswick, where he served as editor of *The Fiddlehead*. He now lives in British Columbia.

ROHINTON MISTRY is the author of a collection of short stories, *Tales from Firozsha Baag*, and two novels, *Such a Long Journey* and *A Fine Balance*. Both novels won the Commonwealth

Writers Prize for Best Book and both were shortlisted for the Booker Prize. *Such a Long Journey* won the Governor General's Award and the SmithBooks/Books in Canada First Novel Award. *A Fine Balance* won The Giller Prize and the Los Angeles Times Book Prize for Fiction, and has been shortlisted for the International IMPAC Dublin Literary Award, to be announced in May 1997. Born in Bombay in 1952, Mistry came to Canada in 1975 and has lived since then near Toronto.

Kristen Ross

ALICE MUNRO was born and grew up in Wingham, Ontario. She won the Governor General's Award three times, for *Dance of the Happy Shades*, *Who Do You Think You Are?*, and *The Progress of Love*, which was also selected as one of the best books of the year by the *New York Times*. Her work has been translated into thirteen languages, and her last book, *Open Secrets*, won the W. H. Smith Award for the best book published in the U.K. in 1995. Her other works are *Lives of Girls and Women*, *Something I've Been Meaning to Tell You*, *The Moons of Jupiter*, *Friend of My Youth*, and *Selected Stories*.

Isolde Ohlbaum

MICHAEL ONDAATJE was born in Sri Lanka and came to Canada in 1962. A novelist, poet, anthologist, and filmmaker, Ondaatje has won numerous awards for his work. His books include *Running in the Family* (a memoir), *The Cinnamon*

Peeler: Selected Poems, and the novels *In the Skin of a Lion* and *The English Patient*, which co-won the Booker Prize, won the Governor General's Award and the Trillium Book Award, and was made into a multi-award-winning film. He lives in Toronto.

P. K. PAGE is a poet, prose writer, and painter who has travelled widely and has received numerous awards for her work. Her books include *Evening Dance of the Grey Flies*, *The Glass Air*, and *Brazilian Journal*, a memoir. Her most recent book is *Hologram*, a book of poetry. She lives in Victoria.

PAUL QUARRINGTON is a novelist, screenwriter, and playwright. He has been nominated three times for the Stephen Leacock Medal for Humour, which he won in 1987 for his novel *King Leary*. In 1986 Quarrington was included on the Canadian Book Information Centre's list of ten best writers under the age of forty-five, "45 Below." In 1990 he received the Governor General's Award for *Whale Music*. Other novels include *Home Game*, *The Life of Hope*, *Logan In Overtime*, and, most recently, *Civilization*, about the early days of filmmaking in Hollywood. Quarrington has sat for four terms on the board of directors of PEN Canada, and is currently chair of the Writers' Union of Canada.

Rafy

NINO RICCI was born in Leamington, Ontario. He is the author of the novels *Lives of the Saints*, which won the Governor General's Award and the SmithBooks/Books in Canada First Novel Award, and *In A Glass House*. In 1995-96 he served as president of PEN Canada. *Where She Has Gone*, the third novel in the trilogy, will be published in the fall of 1997.

SHARON RIIS is a novelist and screenwriter living in Saskatoon, Saskatchewan. She is the author of *The True Story of Ida Johnson* and has recently come out of the closet as a poet.

SHELAGH ROGERS has spent the best years of her life in the service of CBC Radio. Her voice has been heard on almost every program. At the time of writing she is host of "On Stage" and deputy host for "Morningside." She shares her home in the country with two miniature schnauzers and her betrothed.

CONSTANCE ROOKE, critic, academic, editor, and short-story writer, is Associate Vice-President (Academic) of the University of Guelph. For ten years, she edited *The Malahat Review*. Her books include *Fear of the Open Heart: Essays on Contemporary Canadian Writing*. She is the editor of both *Writing Away* and *Writing Home*, and served for several years on the board of PEN Canada.

LEON ROOKE is the author of numerous short-story collections, including *A Bolt of White Cloth*, and novels, including *Fat Woman*, *Shakespeare's Dog*, and *A Good Baby*. Rooke is also a playwright, an editor, and a recipient of the Canada-Australia Literary Award and the Governor General's Award for Fiction. He was born in North Carolina and lives in Eden Mills, Ontario.

JANE RULE was born in 1931, and is the author of a dozen books, including *Desert of the Heart*, *Lesbian Images*, and *Memory Board*. She lives on Galiano Island in British Columbia. Retired.

Beverley Rockett

JOHN RALSTON SAUL is a writer and essayist. He is the author of five novels and a philosophical trilogy: *Voltaire's Bastards: The Dictatorship of Reason in the West*, *The Doubter's Companion: A Dictionary of Common Sense*, and *The Unconscious Civilization*, which collected the 1995 Massey Lectures and won the 1996 Governor General's Award. He was president of PEN Canada from 1990-92.

CAROL SHIELDS likes to stay home in Winnipeg where she writes novels (*Swann, The Republic of Love, The Stone Diaries*). She won the Marian Engel Award and *The Stone Diaries* won the Governor General's Award, the National Book Critics' Circle Award, the Pulitzer Prize, the Prix de lire, and was shortlisted for the Booker Prize. Her new novel, *Larry's Party*, will be published in 1997. She is Chancellor of the University of Winnipeg.

Wayne Grady

MERILYN SIMONDS is the author of ten non-fiction books, on subjects ranging from gardening and games to architecture and war. Her most recent is *The Convict Lover*, a work of creative non-fiction shortlisted for the 1996 Governor General's Award.

She lives in Kingston, where she is working on a collection of travel memoirs called *Stubborn Particulars of Place.*

ESTA SPALDING is the author of two books of poetry, *Carrying Place* and *Anchoress.* Her work has been anthologized in *Blues & True Concussions: Six New Toronto Poets.*

LINDA SPALDING is the author of *Daughters of Captain Cook* and *The Paper Wife* and a forthcoming memoir of her travels in Borneo, *The Follow.* She edits and publishes *Brick, A Literary Journal* in Toronto.

JOHN STEFFLER lives in Corner Brook, Newfoundland. His books of poems include *The Wreckage of Play* and *The Grey Islands.* His novel, *The Afterlife of George Cartwright,* was short-listed for the Governor General's Award and won the 1992 SmithBooks/Books in Canada First Novel Award and the Thomas Raddall Atlantic Fiction Award. A new collection of his poems will be published in 1998.

ROSEMARY SULLIVAN was born in Montreal. Her books include a biography, *By Heart: Elizabeth Smart/A Life*, and two books of poetry, *Blue Panic* and *The Space a Name Makes*. Her most recent book, *Shadowmaker: The Life of Gwendolyn MacEwen*, won the 1995 Governor General's Award for Non-Fiction.

JUDITH THOMPSON is a playwright, radio dramatist, screenwriter, and director, as well as a professor of drama at the University of Guelph. She is the recipient of numerous awards, including two Governor General's Awards for Drama. Her plays include *The Crackwalker*, *White Biting Dog*, and *Lion in the Streets*. Her television films include *Life with Billy* and *Turning to Stone*. She was born in Montreal and now lives with her husband and four children in Toronto.

JANE URQUHART is the author of three books of poetry, a collection of short fiction, *Storm Glass*, and three internationally acclaimed novels: *The Whirlpool*, *Changing Heaven*, and *Away*. Her fiction has won awards and honours, including the Trillium Book Award, the Marian Engel Award, Le prix du meilleur livre étranger (Best Foreign Book Award) in France, and, for her long-time national bestseller *Away*, a place on the shortlist for the prestigious International IMPAC Dublin Literary Award. Her new novel, *The Underpainter*, will be published in the fall of 1997. She has been named a Chevalier dans l'Ordre des Arts et des Lettres in France, and has recently served a term as writer-in-residence at the University of Toronto. She lives in southwestern Ontario with her husband, artist Tony Urquhart.

GUY VANDERHAEGHE was born in Esterhazy, Saskatchewan, in 1951. He won the Governor General's Award twice, for his first book of stories, *Man Descending*, and for his most recent novel, *The Englishman's Boy*. His other books include the novels *My Present Age* and *Homesick*, which was co-winner of the City of Toronto Book Award, and a second collection of stories, *Things As They Are?* He has also written two plays, *I Had a Job I Liked. Once.*, which won the Canadian Authors Association Award for Drama, and *Dancock's Dance*. Vanderhaeghe lives in Saskatoon, where he is a Visiting Professor of English at S.T.M. College.

JAN ZWICKY's home is in west-central Alberta. She is the author of five books, including *Lyric Philosophy*, *Wittgenstein Elegies*, and her most recent collection, *Songs for Relinquishing the Earth*. She now lives in Victoria, British Columbia.

The Pen Is Mightier

by

The Board of PEN Canada

PEN Canada stands for freedom of expression – at home and around the world.

We are the Canadian branch of International PEN, a London-based organization made up of 12,000 members of the writing community – broadly defined to include playwrights, publishers, editors, screenwriters, translators, and journalists, as well as the Poets, Essayists, and Novelists of its acronym – in 124 autonomous centres. Founded in 1921, International PEN quickly developed into one of the world's first human rights organizations, a force against censorship, and an advocate for fellow writers in prison.

It has enjoyed many successes over the years. During the Spanish civil war of the 1930s, when the Hungarian-born writer Arthur Koestler was imprisoned and condemned to death, PEN's efforts were instrumental in his release. During the Cold War, its campaigns on behalf of Boris Pasternak and Alexander Solzhenitsyn, later on behalf of the Russian poet Irina Ratushinskaya and the Czech playwright Vaclav Havel, brought the plight of dissidents to world attention.

But not all of PEN's stories have happy endings. The post-Cold War era has produced a new geography of oppression. Since 1989, British author Salman Rushdie has lived under a *fatwa*, or sentence of death. In November 1995, intense and prolonged efforts by International PEN, in particular PEN Canada, were not enough to save the Nigerian novelist and activist Ken Saro-Wiwa from a brutal execution. Nevertheless, we have ample evidence of our usefulness in countering the ruthlessness of oppressive regimes, whatever their political ideology, if only by letting them know that we are always watching – while letting the imprisoned writers know that someone out there is working for their release.

"I wish to thank PEN Canada for the wonderful things you have done for me," Saro-Wiwa wrote in a poignant letter from prison six months before his execution. And the Kenyan writer Koigi wa Wamwere wrote, after his release on bail from jail in December 1996, "So to PEN I say, Thank you, and to PEN I say, Don't put your pens down – not yet."

First established in Montreal in 1926, then reconstituted in Toronto in 1983, PEN Canada has emerged as one of the most active branches of International PEN. Drawing from a well-researched list of some nine hundred cases, we are currently working on behalf of thirty writers in prison or under threat in seventeen countries, including Nobel Peace Prize winner Aung San Suu Kyi in Burma, journalist Gao Yu in China, novelist Yasar Kemal in Turkey, publisher Christine Anyanwu in Nigeria, and poet/scholar Doan Viet Hoat in Vietnam.

Each of these "honorary members," as we call them, is assigned a "minder," a PEN member or group in any part of Canada who tracks the case closely, sends letters and parcels to prisoners, and serves as a two-way conduit for information. Simultaneously, the three staff members at PEN's efficient Toronto office provide organizational support through research and lobbying. We petition foreign heads of state and ambassadors through letters, faxes, postcard campaigns, and direct meetings. We enlist the support of Canadian cabinet ministers, MPs, and officials in the Foreign Affairs Department through annual briefs and regular communications. We bring the story of our writers in prison to the general public through media releases, special events, educational material, and our Internet site (www.pencanada.ca). And sometimes, as with the Ethiopian writer Martha Kumsa and the Sarajevo poet Goran Simic, we welcome into Canada those who have been forced from their homelands.

At the same time, within Canada, PEN is active whenever there are violations of freedom of expression involving state censorship, from the seizure of books by Canada Customs to libel chill to Internet censorship.

PEN Canada does all this investigating, lobbying, networking, campaigning, and organizing on an operating budget of around $200,000 a year, with no government funding of any kind. Our administrative expenses are pared to the bone; every one of our fifteen directors is expected to volunteer a great deal of time and effort; our staff is overworked and extremely dedicated. About half our revenue comes from our annual gala benefit in Toronto. The rest comes from memberships, donations, and the sales of various items, including *Writing Home* and its companion volume, the travel anthology *Writing Away*, which to date has earned over $100,000 for PEN Canada since its publication in 1994.

That's why we are so grateful to Constance Rooke, herself a writer and former board member, for again taking time from her onerous responsibilities as associate vice-president (academic) at the University of Guelph to approach so many busy writers, collect so much good writing, and edit this collection so skilfully.

We are also extraordinarily grateful to have the generosity and friendship of McClelland & Stewart chairman Avie Bennett. Beyond his many other contributions to PEN Canada over the years, he is once again giving us all proceeds of the sale of this book above the bare cost of manufacturing and paper. His example was matched by the generosity of the authors who donated their time and talent so selflessly, and by all those at

McClelland & Stewart involved in publishing, marketing, and distributing the book. Heartfelt gratitude goes as well to Best Book Manufacturers and Lasersharp Inc., who contributed to the production costs of the book. And to Canadian booksellers: each copy of *Writing Home* sold to a reader makes a contribution to PEN Canada.

Our ultimate thanks goes to you, the buyer, for helping too. And we urge you to contact us at PEN Canada, 24 Ryerson Avenue, Suite 309, Toronto, Ontario, M5T 2P3 to find out how you can join us in our valuable work, whether as a member or an associate member, a volunteer or a patron, a minder or a benefit supporter. We need you – because there are so many who need us.